Text copyright © 2015 A.K. Celer
First Print Edition Paperback - Perfect Bound 2016
Kwill Books ISBN-13: 978-84-945020-2-6

Kwill Books,
Plaza De La Marina 1,
Málaga 29015 Spain

Kwill
PUBLISHING HOUSE

www.kwillbooks.com/akceler

Back Cover Image: World Telecom Network © Freepik

MOSCOW VENTURE

A. K. Celer

Chapter 1

Chesterbrook, Pennsylvania. Monday, July 22, 1991

John Baran fought to curb his emotions on the way to the hospital. He needed to stay calm. On Friday, his closest friend and coworker David Chernov had been in Moscow managing their company's business venture, and now he was in a Philadelphia hospital intensive care unit.

What had happened? John didn't know what to think, and he didn't know exactly what he felt. The early morning call from the CEO's secretary instructed him to get the details of Dave's medical condition from the hospital staff, but had otherwise explained little. An emergency medical service had apparently flown David back to the States for treatment for sudden paralysis. No one knew what happened, and venture personnel in Moscow could not be reached for an explanation.

It didn't add up. David had always been in top physical shape. They'd met during their training in Fort Benning as members of the Army's Special Operations Command. They'd jumped out of the same airplanes, drank in the same bars, and even went out on double dates together. After their army service, they'd both gone to work at Cellcomm, an international cellular communications services firm, and remained close friends.

David, paralyzed? John couldn't believe it. Still, he braced himself for the horrid possibility.

Ninety minutes later in the hospital's ICU, he asked to see David Chernov.

A tired-looking nurse behind the counter with a drooping tag that read 'Nancy' looked puzzled by his request. "May I ask who you are, sir?"

John told her.

The nurse's eyes saddened. "I'm sorry sir; Mr. Chernov—I mean Mr. Chernov's body—is in the hospital morgue. He died—" She glanced at her watch. "Three hours ago."

1

He stood frozen with disbelief.

She observed him for a moment. "Are you all right, sir?"

He raised his hand, his movement jerky, and lied. "I'm okay."

Nancy gave him a hesitant nod, and slowly said, as if to make sure he understood, "Mr. Chernov's parents were here earlier, and Mr. Chernov's father said you'd probably be calling. He instructed the hospital to release any information you ask for."

John nodded in slow motion, his jumbled thoughts latching on to the first thing he needed to do, for his boss and his own peace of mind. "I need to see the attending physician."

The nurse walked John into a nearby windowless consultation room, her shoes emitting soft squeaks in the otherwise quiet area. "Please wait here. The doctor will be in shortly."

Fifteen minutes later, a short man in his mid-forties with long hair drawn back into a ponytail walked into the room. He looked as tired as the nurse, but thrust his hand forward with a focused, assertive manner. "Mr. Baran?"

John nodded, not trusting his voice.

"I'm Dr. Chu." His name matched his Asian features. "I'm the neurologist familiar with Mr. Chernov's case."

Chu's handshake was strong and confident, but his expression was one of concern. John cleared his throat. "What's the cause of Mr. Chernov's death?"

"He died from a massive hemorrhagic stroke."

John's chest tightened. "No. No way. He was my age and was in perfect health."

The neurologist nodded. "I don't understand it either; it's a mystery to me."

"*Mystery?*" John couldn't help the incredulity and anger behind his words. "What do you mean, *mystery?*"

Dr. Chu took a step back. "The CT images—I've never seen anything like it. It's as if millions of microscopic firecrackers went off in his brain."

John glared. *Firecrackers? Is this guy a wacko?*

"How did he die?" John pressed for details.

"That's just it. During the CT scan."

"The *X-rays* killed him?"

The neurologist looked worried now. "The CT scan couldn't have caused the death, if that's what you're asking."

"No, just trying to understand," John reassured Dr. Chu.

"While Mr. Chernov was undergoing his scan, it appears he had a traumatic episode. It's as if multiple mini-strokes happened all at once. Like I said, I've never seen anything like it."

John tried to understand the physiology of such an incident, but couldn't conceive it. "What caused the episode?"

"We don't know. And we won't know, since there'll be no autopsy."

"Why the hell not?"

"The deceased's parents wouldn't allow it."

"Why not?" John asked, but he already knew the answer.

The neurologist lowered his voice. "Their religious beliefs prohibit cutting into or dissecting the body."

"What about the medical examiner? Doesn't he have something to say about this?"

Dr. Chu shook his head in disappointment. "Mr. Chernov's family doctor said that the parents would fight any attempt to declare their son's autopsy a compelling public necessity. They already have an attorney, as some government agency had already tried to order an autopsy."

"That's it? We can't find out what killed him?"

"We need an autopsy. If you can get Chernov's parents to agree, we'll be glad to perform it." The neurologist turned and started for the door.

John sat down on a plastic stool and gazed at the floor. When he looked up, Dr. Chu was gone. He continued to sit for a few moments, thinking about David and his parents. The black emptiness within him grew. He rose to his feet stiffly and moving like a robot, he walked out of the consultation room and out of the hospital.

On the way to the parking garage, he envisioned his imminent meeting with his boss, the company's CEO, Wulf Ober. He dreaded it. The news he had to bring was sure to set the chief off like a missile.

The loss of David's unique and possibly irreplaceable management talent now threatened the future of the entire Moscow project. Then there was David's bizarre stroke.

Regardless of what the chief decided to do about that, John resolved to get to the bottom of his friend's unexplained death, no matter what it'd take.

Chapter 2

Philadelphia, Pennsylvania

In the hospital parking garage, John put the key in his car door. Before he could open it, he heard an authoritative male voice behind him. "Lieutenant Baran?" He tensed and quickly turned to face the speaker—he hadn't been addressed by his army rank in seven years.

A man in a dark business suit stood six feet away, gazing at John with an impassive expression. He possessed a military presence. John met the stranger's gaze and tried to recall him from his army service days, but the man's indistinctive features supplied no clue.

"You don't know me, Lieutenant Baran," the stranger said, as if he read John's thoughts.

"It's *Mister* Baran to you, whoever you are." John peered at the man. "How do you know my name?"

The stranger produced ID. The badge looked authentic, and John shifted his shoulders to ease their tension. "Well, Agent Parker, what does the CIA want now?"

The agent scanned the parking garage discreetly, as if to make sure no one was nearby. "Can we talk?"

"We've talked. I gave you my answer back in Langley."

When John was discharged from the Army's Special Operations unit seven years ago, the CIA had tried to recruit him for what they claimed were important operations in the East Bloc countries. His Army unit was trained for missions inside the Soviet Union in times of conflict, and the CIA saw his training, his fluency in Russian, and his Slavic background as assets they wanted. After four full days of aptitude and psychological testing sessions, interviews with the psychiatrist and other specialists and staff, including a medical exam, John found out that the CIA was looking for an analyst to "interpret" the content and innuendos of Central

Committee and Politburo members' public statements. It was nothing like what James Bond did in the movies or what Cold War spy novels had described and glorified.

He turned the agency down. He wasn't ready to be chained to a desk. He wanted to get back to civilian life and use his college training in the business world where the action promised to be more exciting than producing internal CIA memoranda.

Then two years ago, the agency had contacted him again to see if he'd changed his mind. He hadn't. If this were another attempt to recruit him, he'd talk to them as a courtesy, but not now. "I have to report to my boss right away. Give me your contact information, and I'll get back to you."

"It'll only take a few minutes." The agent pointed to John's car. "We can talk in there."

John waited, and when the agent made no move to produce any information, he decided that if Parker could find him in a Philadelphia hospital parking garage, then he could find him anywhere if it was important enough. "Sorry, I've got to get going." He opened his car door, climbed in, and put the key in the ignition.

"It's about David Chernov," Parker called out before John could close the door.

John stopped. What did the CIA know about David? He wanted to hear it whatever it was. He could afford a few moments, but only a few—his CEO was waiting. He motioned for the agent to get into the front passenger seat. The other man climbed in and closed the door.

John peered at Parker. "What about David Chernov?"

The agent eyed the garage surroundings again as if to make sure no one was looking and turned to face John. "We've updated your security clearance and decided to approach you again in the hope that this time you would agree to help us as a civilian. We're not recruiting for the Agency."

John shot Parker a sharp look. *"You what?* What are you talking about?"

"We ran another background investigation on you a few weeks ago, preparing for any eventuality. We hoped it wouldn't come to this."

John glared at the man sitting next to him. He didn't like what he was hearing. "It wouldn't come to *what*?"

"Before I go any further, I need to remind you that you're still bound by the agreement you signed in Langley."

"It wouldn't come to *what*, Parker?" John's patience thinned.

"Asking you to cooperate with us, and continue the work that your friend Chernov had been doing for us."

"What? David was a CIA collaborator? I don't believe it. He never told me anything about—" Then John saw the connection. David was of Ukrainian background, had the same training as John, and was fluent in Russian. The CIA must've convinced him to at least collaborate with them, if not join them. *Is that what got him killed?*

Parker continued, his tone grave. "We've gotten reports of unusual activity at the highest levels of the Soviet government, especially at the KGB and the defense ministry. The hardliners are up to something— something not good. If they follow through with what we think they're planning, U.S. security could be threatened. Your friend was in a unique position to help us find out their plans."

"What unique position? David was in Moscow to build a cellular network, and not in any *unique* position to do your work. Are you serious?" But he knew that the CIA didn't joke around. Then what exactly had David been doing for the agency? Was Cellcomm involved? Was the company's Moscow venture a front for the CIA? No, that didn't make any sense.

"David Chernov considered his work for us his patriotic duty," Parker said and paused, seeming to wait for John to grasp the import of the statement.

John looked without focusing at the cars around them, thinking. After the silence dragged on a moment too long, he turned to the agent. "So what now?"

"We'd like you to continue Chernov's work for us."

"Hold it, Agent Parker. First, I'm not in Moscow. Second, my friend's death could be the result of his collaboration with you. The KGB deals swiftly with foreign spies who don't have diplomatic cover."

"David Chernov's collaboration with us had nothing to do with his paralysis or his death."

"And how do you know?"

"We know."

"Are you suggesting he died of 'natural causes'?" John snapped.

"I'm suggesting nothing."

"Then what are you talking about?"

Parker fell silent.

"What do you know about David's death?" John yelled, jarring the agent.

The agent looked at John with a blank expression. "Money. Money was probably involved. It always is with the Russians."

"How?"

"We don't know exactly, but we're certain it wasn't connected to us."

Now John wondered if his CEO knew about David's involvement with the CIA. If he did, it would cast the Sovcell venture in a different light. "What exactly did David do for you?"

"Our agent in Moscow will brief you."

"I'm not in Moscow, so I'm not in any 'unique' position to help you." John started the car. "I've got to go."

Parker took a deep breath. "We're asking you to go to Moscow and continue your friend's work. We need the cooperation of the American manager of Cellcomm's Moscow venture. You'll see why. We believe that, at a minimum, Soviet hardliners will reignite the Cold War when they execute their plan. If things go badly for them, there's no telling what they might do. We need to know what they're up to. You can help us find that out."

"*I'm not in Moscow*, Agent Parker. What you're asking me to do is not under my control. Even if I wanted to go to Moscow and continue Chernov's work, I can't just *do* that. My company makes the decision."

"Ask your company to send you to Moscow as the replacement for Chernov."

John shook his head in exasperation. "Why don't *you,* the CIA, ask my company to do *its* patriotic duty and send me to Moscow?"

Parker instantly shook his head. "Your company mustn't know anything about this."

The agent's response did not bode well. "Did my company know about David's collaboration?"

Parker again shook his head. "We're confident that you can convince your CEO that you're the best and the only replacement for your friend right now."

"Confident, are you?" John frowned. "I'm a planner, a good planner, but I've never run an operation. My CEO wouldn't take the chance."

Parker went on as if he didn't hear John. "All we're asking is that you meet with our agent in Moscow and listen to what he has to say. I can't go into any more details now." He glanced at the dashboard clock. "I'm afraid I've taken up my few minutes. What do you say, Lieutenant?"

"I've already said it. If you didn't get it, then you don't understand the position I'm in." He took hold of the gearshift and waited for the CIA agent to get out.

Parker gave John a look as if he wasn't concerned about what he heard and didn't press any further. He opened his door and put his right foot on the garage floor. "As they say in the movies, Lieutenant, this conversation never happened." He climbed out, closed the door, and disappeared among the cars.

John sat in the car, replaying the conversation. He had questions about the CIA's involvement in the venture, but with David's death, only the CIA had the answers to those questions. He reran Parker's statements. *Money. Money was probably involved.* What money? How?

Or had Parker lied? Had the KGB discovered David's connection to the CIA and taken action? The suspicious stroke? John didn't know. All he knew was that he wouldn't find those answers by looking for them in Cellcomm's offices in Norristown, Pennsylvania.

He put the car in gear and headed for the garage exit, wondering how the hell he'd get those answers.

Chapter 3

Earlier that same day, General Vladimir Kryuchkov, chairman of the KGB, sat behind his mahogany desk and gazed in contemplation at the Turkmen Tekke carpets on the floor of his ornately decorated office. Serious and dangerous contemplation: Disintegration threatened his beloved Soviet Union, and he had to take action to stop it.

Shivering, he pulled on his unbuttoned jacket to cover more of his portly body. At 67, he easily chilled in the damp air produced by an impossible-to-control air conditioner. Several times he'd wanted to call in the Germans to install a system that worked properly, but he feared his Politburo colleagues would misread his actions.

Today, he wore a gray V-neck sweater over his white shirt, with his tie loosened for comfort. Adjusting his large, amber colored horn-rimmed glasses, he stared disgustedly at the file on his desk. It contained the New Union Treaty negotiated by Mikhail Gorbachev, the President of the Soviet Union, Boris Yeltsin, the President of the Russian Federation, and the heads of nine other republics. The treaty, ironically, was Gorbachev's attempt to preserve the Soviet Union as it crumbled under his own reforms. Five of the Soviet republics had refused to have anything to do with the New Union, or any union the Kremlin wanted to preserve. The liberalization and democratization promoted by Gorbachev's *Perestroika* and *Glasnost* reforms had emboldened the maverick republics to seek independence from Kremlin rule.

Glasnost, the new policy permitting open discussions of political and social issues and freer dissemination of news and information, had transformed the country from an isolated society to a more cosmopolitan one; one that was open to Western ideas and Western products. Kryuchkov himself had no intention of supporting American imperialism by smoking

Marlboro cigarettes, consuming Snickers bars, or listening to American rock music. He hated everything American.

Perestroika, the restructuring of the Soviet political and economic system, allowed more independent action from various ministries and introduced some market-like reforms. The KGB chief saw mortal danger to Communism in these sweeping changes. Could private individuals, and not the State, begin to control the means of production and commerce? Not in his lifetime. He would see to it.

He did not forget that Gorbachev had promoted him to his current post over two senior officials, but friendship went only so far when the survival of his Soviet Union was at stake. The old, powerful Soviet Union of Andropov and Brezhnev was at stake. Gorbachev's treaty would emasculate and fracture that Union. If Gorbachev succeeded, Kryuchkov and other true patriots in the Center, the apex of Soviet government, would become irrelevant.

When survival is at stake, friendship is irrelevant.

Hearing a light knock on his open door, Kryuchkov looked up. The two visitors he had summoned stood in the doorway. He gestured to the two chairs in front of his desk, and they took their seats.

The visitor taking the chair on the left, the shorter, scholarly-looking one was Colonel Aleksandr Sposobnik, a brilliant Second Chief Directorate analyst with a doctoral degree from Moscow State University in Sociology and Politology. With a fair complexion and a baby face, he looked young for forty-nine. A pragmatic communist ideologue, Sposobnik had become the resident expert on political control of Soviet citizens. He gazed at the KGB chief expectantly.

Kryuchkov liked the young colonel—admired him. Highly intelligent, honest and forthcoming, Sposobnik, when asked, told it like he saw it, unembellished by fawning or political or intellectual servitude. He feared Sposobnik's fresh and often cutting opinions would not last, as Sposobnik himself would not. He was a baby sea lion among the *nomenklatura's* great whites. So far, Kryuchkov had been able to shield him from their jaws.

The other visitor, one of Kryuchkov's deputies, was Lieutenant General Victor Petrov, head of the Third Chief Directorate, which controlled military counterintelligence and political surveillance of the armed forces. A bureaucratic survivor that looked old for fifty-eight, Petrov wore his full uniform. Kryuchkov suspected that the general used his uniform to inflate his importance. He was an obedient soldier, and Kryuchkov could depend on him to carry out an order, but not for any initiative to produce an original, bold thought.

The KGB chief picked up the New Union Treaty, shook it like a dishrag, and threw it onto his desk in the direction of his visitors. Pointing an accusatory finger at it, he said, "This is a prescription for the disintegration of our Union. It gives far too much self-governing power to the republics. Comrades, the breakdown of the Soviet Union and its institutions is the very thing we in state security are entrusted to prevent. We *must not* allow the collapse of our beloved Union. That is our responsibility and our sworn duty."

He frowned. "Six years of Mikhail Sergeyevich's reforms have resulted in breakdown of order and clamor by our citizens and by our republics for independence and democratic rule. The Baltic States and Georgia have already dared to try and declare their independence. Months ago I warned our country that destructive elements with extreme radical political tendencies, very well funded and morally supported from abroad, would shatter our society and destroy Soviet rule. This is the work of the Americans. CIA agents of influence are successfully operating in our country, instigating *democracy*. I've had as much *democracy* as I can stomach." He stopped and gazed at Petrov and then at Sposobnik. He waited for a response to his opening volley.

Sposobnik slowly shook his head, his expression showing apparent disagreement with what the KGB Chief had said.

Kryuchkov stared at Sposobnik. "Colonel?"

Sposobnik appeared to hesitate.

Kryuchkov raised his voice. *"Colonel?"*

"Our people," Sposobnik said in a quiet voice, "have had the taste of freedom and democracy because of the policies of *Glasnost*. Having tasted it, they want more. The Americans encourage it, but they cannot take credit for it."

The chairman shot Sposobnik a stern look, but said nothing for fear of stifling the young colonel. Kryuchkov waited, he knew the colonel had more to say.

Sposobnik continued. "The term of the treaty ceding power to the republics is Yeltsin's idea. He wants to rule Russia with no interference from the Center. He forced those conditions on Gorbachev, so you can blame him for precipitating the crisis."

Kryuchkov considered what the colonel had said and had to agree. Yeltsin was as much to blame as Gorbachev for the New Union Treaty, but Yeltsin did not start the disastrous reforms. "Mikhail Sergeyevich has gone too far with his reforms and must be stopped. He is flying as a blind man and doesn't know where he will land. It's time to act." He looked at the analyst and waited. He expected the Colonel had still more to say.

After a moment Sposobnik spoke. "I fear, Comrade Chairman, it may be too late."

"What do you mean, 'too late'?" Kryuchkov said in a loud voice. "Too late for what?"

"It may be too late to reverse or even to stop the reforms," Sposobnik said in barely audible voice.

"The reforms are out of control!" Kryuchkov shouted. "They must be stopped."

Sposobnik nodded. "I believe that President Gorbachev himself is also of the opinion that the reforms have spiraled out of control, but he's helpless to stop it. The new treaty is his attempt to hold our Union together. It's his attempt to save the Union."

The KBG chief spat. "He cannot save our Union by pursuing his disastrous reforms. Enough of this."

"Comrade Chairman is precisely correct." The colonel eagerly nodded his agreement. "Our President has embarked on an impossible goal. He wants to institute reforms and preserve our communist system, but freedom, democracy, and market economy are deadly to our ideology. If his reforms continue, they will destroy Communism."

Kryuchkov peered at Sposobnik thoughtfully. "Do you think, Colonel, he's now come to realize that?"

"I believe he has, Comrade Chairman," Sposobnik said. "He's a good communist; at least he claims to be. And I believe that he's beginning to realize that democratic reforms will do to Communism what consumption of sugar will do to a diabetic."

"So why is he eating the confection of democracy?" Kryuchkov said.

Sposobnik shrugged. "Maybe he likes the taste of it."

The KGB chief gave a penetrating glare. "Are you being funny, Colonel?"

"No, Comrade Chairman, our president may already be addicted to it."

Kryuchkov didn't want to believe that, but he feared the colonel could be right. He filed that thought in the back of his mind: Mikhail Sergeyevich might be past redemption. He turned to his military chief and nodded.

General Petrov took his boss's cue and offered his observation: "Colonel Sposobnik is correct. Our president will be receptive and, I believe, will welcome whatever action we take to stop our Union's deterioration."

"I hope you are correct," Kryuchkov said. "We will need to enlist his cooperation." *His cooperation?* Kryuchkov wondered how one convinces a communist democracy addict to quit the habit because it's killing him. If democracy addiction was as strong as drug addiction, he knew that the chances of rehabilitation were nil, as the dismal results of Soviet drug laws and treatment camps confirmed.

He turned to Sposobnik. "Colonel, prepare a report on the probable reaction of our citizens if a state of emergency were to be declared, activities of political parties and movement were to be suspended, and the censorship of the press were to be implemented."

Shocked by the KGB chief's statement, Sposobnik sprang to his feet like a jack-in-a-box and vigorously shook his head. "That is no longer possible...that is no longer possible to achieve."

Kryuchkov calmly raised and lowered his hand. "Sit down, Colonel," he instructed. "I will decide what is and isn't possible. Just prepare the report."

Sposobnik sat down but continued to shake his head. Then, as if he had a sudden revelation, he abruptly stopped and began to nod. "Yes, Comrade Chairman."

Kryuchkov turned to his military chief. "Viktor Petrov, prepare a report on what military measures will be needed to seize and control all government functions and neutralize opposition."

The general nodded. "Yes, Comrade Chairman. Perhaps we should approach Mikhail Sergeyevich and ask him to officially declare a state of emergency. That will be within the Constitution, and therefore legal."

The Chairman shook his head. "Not yet, we're not ready. What if he refuses, discloses our intentions, and takes action against us? No. If we ask, we will ask when we are ready to carry out our plan, with or without him. Whether he agrees or not, it would not matter then." He looked at the calendar on his desk. "Mikhail Sergeyevich will be going on his vacation on Sunday, August 4, three weeks from now. We will meet again on Tuesday, July 30, to discuss the findings in your reports. He plans to return from his vacation on Monday, August 19, for the signing of the treaty on Tuesday, August 20, in the Kremlin. The signing must *not* take place."

Kryuchkov considered the time remaining. "We don't have much time to develop and implement a detailed plan of action. I don't want any delays. Have your reports ready when we meet." He stopped for a moment and waited. When the colonel and the general remained silent, he said, "Any questions?"

Sposobnik and Petrov shook their heads.

The Chairman turned to the general. "Viktor Petrov, is the instrument you received from our Communications Minister operational?"

Petrov shook his head. "They call it cellular telephone, and it doesn't work yet. The network is built by the Minister's American partner in a joint venture called Sovcell. The minister promised that the cellular network would be turned on soon." His expression turned puzzled. "Didn't he offer *you* one of those instruments, Comrade Chairman?"

"I told the minister that I'd accept the instrument if and when communications over the cellular network are made secure. Until then, these mobile telephones must not be used for official business by anyone in the government."

Petrov nodded that he agreed with his boss. "The minister said that he had a plan to secure the network."

"Perhaps he does," the chairman said. "But I don't trust his American venture partner even if the network is pronounced to be 'secure'. Our minister would have to take complete control of the network to make it absolutely safe. As long as the Americans are involved in the venture, the network will never be one hundred percent secure." He paused. "I'll have to pay more attention to the reports I'm receiving on this Sovcell. I don't want this cellular network to become a problem for us. I don't trust the Americans."

"The minister said he had a plan," Petrov repeated.

Kryuchkov shot Petrov a skeptical look. "The only way the minister could fully secure the network is to take it over." He shook his head in disgust. "Current laws protecting foreign investors make that almost impossible." He rose. His visitors stood, preparing to leave. He pointed his index finger at them. "You are not to discuss your assignments with anyone." The visitors froze momentarily, nodded, and then departed, their expression a mixture of puzzlement and fear.

Kryuchkov saw their expressions and realized he had just involved them in a conspiracy bordering on treason. He deemed it a necessary step in preserving the Union. When they closed the door behind them, he walked over to the window of his Lubyanka third-floor office and looked down at the square. He focused on the statue of Feliks Dzerzhinsky, the secret police founder. In an almost inaudible voice, he said, "I hope we're not too late, Comrade, to save our Union." He became worried. *Would* his plan save the Union? Or would it trigger a peoples' revolt and result in a bloody civil war that'd tear apart the Soviet system and destroy Communism and him with it?

Chapter 4

South Philadelphia

John exited the hospital parking garage and headed to Cellcomm's headquarters in Norristown. It was nearly noon, and the sun was already baking the city. By the Veteran's Stadium, where he saw the Army beat the Navy last December in the traditional rivalry with pomp and brouhaha, he maneuvered onto the Schuylkill expressway, heading west toward Norristown. He placed a call to Wulf Ober. Klaudia, the CEO's secretary, answered.

"Is the chief available?" he asked.

So much had happened already that morning it was hard to believe it was only a few hours since his world had imploded. He hadn't yet developed a plan of action to find answers to what really happened to David in Moscow, but he'd find a way. First, he'd see what Ober had decided about the venture.

"He's out of the office right now," Klaudia answered. "What did you find out about David?"

He told her, stressing the suspicious nature of the stroke.

"I'm really sorry, John. The whole paralysis thing sounds horrifying."

"Thank you for your sympathy." He waited to hear if there were any new developments in the CEO's office—she'd always give him a heads-up.

"The chief had called a headhunter he'd used before," she said after a moment. "He wants a replacement for David right away, and he's waiting for your report."

"I'm on my way. Be there in an hour, if Schuylkill traffic doesn't choke me." John hung up. He didn't look forward to making his report. Ober had often gone to extremes in his reactions to problems affecting the company. He acted as if it was his family business. While seldom wrong in his evaluation, he communicated his convictions with a verbal delivery that would sting a porcupine.

John's thirty-mile drive to Norristown turned out to be thirty miles of rubbernecking. The Schuylkill Expressway, a bumper-to-bumper snake, slithered with fits and starts along the Susquehanna River. He tried to control his impatience, breathing deeply and exhaling slowly. He began to wonder about the JV's future, about Agent Parker, and about David's collaboration with the CIA. If there was foul play involving money, as Parker suggested, what provoked it? What did David do? And what would Ober do now?

Just before the Conshohocken exit the traffic slowed to a snail's pace. Horns blared. When John reached the trouble spot, he saw a stopped car on the shoulder that hadn't completely cleared the traffic lane. Drivers steered around a protruding left rear fender of a Rolls Royce Silver Spur. The trunk of the Rolls was open. An elderly woman, dressed in what looked like her churchgoing clothes, stood by the trunk and looked at the rear left tire. It was flat. She had an expression of helplessness and confusion.

He considered stopping and helping. He checked the time and knew that Ober was anxious and waiting to hear his report, which already would be delayed into mid-afternoon. Still, looking at the distressed woman, he decided that an additional fifteen-minute delay was a risk he was willing to take. He pulled off the road, stopped behind the disabled vehicle, and climbed out. Heat and exhaust fumes hit him, and he coughed in reaction to the assault on his lungs. A glance at his Oldsmobile Regency's dashboard revealed the outside temperature: 97 degrees. He took off his suit jacket, threw it in his car, and walked up to the distressed woman. "Can I help?"

"I'm so confused. And this terrible noise, I don't know what to do next." She looked visibly shaken.

He tried to place her Eastern European accent. Ukrainian, he decided. "Can I help?" he asked again, this time slower, to calm her down.

"I'm so upset." Her hands fluttered in the air as she rapidly glanced with fearful eyes between the flat tire and John. "I tried to call for help, but my car telephone is dead. My husband told me to use our driver, but I wanted to give him the afternoon off and drove myself. Now look what happened."

"I'll change the tire, ma'am."

"Oh, would you? I'd be so grateful." She lowered her hands to her side, the creases of anguish on her face slowly receded, and her eyes calmed.

He loosened his tie, stuffed it inside his shirt, and rolled up his sleeves. He retrieved an emergency reflector out of his car and placed it inside the road pavement three feet from the flat tire. Traffic shifted to clear the reflector, and the horn volume kicked up. John worked fast. He didn't know how much time he had before an irate driver abandoned his courtesy and ran over the reflector, and maybe over him. In ten minutes he had the tire changed.

The women looked at John, at the changed tire, and managed a small smile. "I'm so grateful to you, young man; how can I repay your kindness?"

"It was no problem." He tried to brush dirt off his hands.

She looked at his palms and his white shirt. "Oh, my goodness," she said. "Look at that, you're all smudged. At least let me pay for the cleaning of your shirt and pants."

"That's all right ma'am, glad I could help," He picked up the reflector and looked at the angry traffic. "You'd better move your vehicle, ma'am."

She thanked him several times, reached in her purse, pulled out a business card, and handed it to him. "If you ever need anything, and I mean anything at all, please call the private number on the card. My husband never lets a good deed go unrewarded. Do you have a business card, young man?"

John gave her his card.

She examined it. "Thank you, Mr. Baran. God bless you. I'll give this card to my husband and explain everything." She got into her Silver Spur and eased back into traffic.

John checked the card in his hand. A red emblem of crossed swords appeared at the top. WORLDWIDE PRIVATE SECURITY appeared below the emblem, and below that, the name Maximilian Gromylov. A 215 Philadelphia area number was printed at the bottom.

He put the card in his pocket and examined his hands and clothes. He needed to stop to wash up. He'd do that in a Norristown Café he frequented for lunch; it wasn't more than ten minutes away from the Cellcomm building and next to a flower shop he also needed to visit. He wiped the sweat off his forehead with his sleeve, climbed into his car and cranked up the air conditioning to full blast.

As he eased back into Schuylkill traffic, he thought about Worldwide Private Security. Were the crossed swords symbolic of what Maximilian Gromylov did? Maybe John could call Gromylov about a job, if Cellcomm shut down the Moscow venture, cut back on international business development, and furloughed him. Security muscle he could do without any additional training.

Before he reached the Norristown exit, his phone rang. David's father.

"How are you, Mr. Chernov?" John said, thinking about the elderly man on the phone. "I'm very sorry about David. I can imagine what a shock it must be to you and Mrs. Chernov." John knew David's parents well enough to know that David's mother would be devastated by the loss of their only son.

"Thank you John, but I would think you're doing your share of grieving. You two were like brothers." Chernov was right. John choked up when he thought about David.

"How is Mrs. Chernov?"

"Not well. Our family doctor gave her some sedatives to calm her down. He said it might take a long time for her to fully recover, but I don't think she'll ever *fully* recover."

"I'm sorry to hear that."

"John, the reason I called is to ask if you can help us find out what happened to David in Moscow. We don't believe his stroke was due to natural causes. I've talked to the State Department about this, but they said there's nothing they can do about investigating the cause of death. They said that the local authorities in Moscow were responsible for doing the investigation. But since David died here in the U.S. and his death was ruled natural, they thought the Russians wouldn't even consider launching any kind of investigation."

"Forget about the Russians, Mr. Chernov. They wouldn't investigate anything that might implicate them."

"You're right, John. In my desperation, I did call the Russian Embassy in Washington. Frankly it was a dumb thing to do—I didn't get to the first base with them. That's why I'm asking you to help us find out what really happened in Moscow."

John wanted to say something encouraging, supportive, but he didn't know what. He thought about Dr. Chu. "Mr. Chernov, David's neurologist also doubted the stroke was naturally caused, and he wanted to have an autopsy performed, but said that you wouldn't agree to it."

"It wasn't me, John. Mrs. Chernov couldn't bear to have our son's body cut or dissected. As much as I'd like to go ahead with the autopsy, I don't think I should go against her wishes. Not now. Not in her condition."

"I understand."

"Is there anything you can do about finding out what really happened?"

Sympathy for David's parents welled up in John. "I'll contact Chris Ashley, our man in Moscow, and see what I can find out."

"Thank you, John. We're grateful for you doing this."

A sudden resolve gripped him. "If I have to, Mr. Chernov, I'll go to Moscow myself to get to the bottom of this."

"Thank you again and God bless you." Chernov ended the call.

John didn't know how he'd get to the bottom of it, but he was determined to help David's parents find the answer. Since the answer was in Moscow, he had to first figure out how he'd get there.

Chapter 5

Norristown, Pennsylvania

After cleaning up from changing the tire and stopping at the flower shop, John entered the Cellcomm CEO's office suite. It was almost three in the afternoon. He was late. Klaudia, an epitome of accuracy and precision, looked at her desk clock, sighed, and muttered about his lateness. He ignored her censure. "Have you told the chief?"

"He asked, and I couldn't lie." She cocked her head toward the CEO's office door. "You can go in, he's waiting. Just so you know, John, he's fuming."

"Before I inhale those fumes, happy birthday, Klaudia." He pulled a dozen red roses from behind his back, unwrapped them, and presented the flowers to her.

Her face flashed surprise, delight, and then a big smile. "They're lovely." She took the roses and examined them slowly. Her eyes savored every brilliant petal. She looked up at him. "I'm not going to say that you shouldn't have done this, because, if I may use the expression, you made my day." She gave him a strange look. "You know, John, you look a lot like Harrison Ford, my screen flame. If I were twenty years younger—"

"If you were twenty years younger, Klaudia, I'd be in seventh grade."

She sat up erect in her chair and assumed a businesslike presence. Slim, tall, and dignified in her navy suit, Klaudia was all business now, but he was sure she'd turned plenty of heads back when he was struggling with algebra. She looked at his shirt and pointed to the smudges. "Car trouble?"

"Flat tire." He buttoned his jacket and gestured toward Ober's office. "You wouldn't have any protection I can use against those fumes? I don't have my Indiana Jones bullwhip with me."

"A serene mind, John."

He tipped his imaginary hat to acknowledge her counsel and strode off toward the CEO's office.

He knocked on the door and walked in. Ober stood behind his titanic desk, looking like an NFL lineman, set to tackle whatever was in front of him. He wore no helmet, and John didn't think they made them large enough to contain the man's head. Behind him was a large window extended all the way to the ceiling. The glare of the afternoon sun obscured a clear vision of Ober, who motioned to a chair facing his desk and glanced at the cuckoo clock on the wall behind John. He contorted his face into an expression of disapproval, but said nothing.

John sat down. His boss remained standing. John heard the little door in the clock fly open and the 3:00 P.M. cuckooing began. The CEO raised a remote control, pressed a button, and the birdie shut up.

"Sorry about your friend, John." Ober spoke in his rarely-heard soft tone. Then, leading with his steam-shovel chin, he leaned across his desk and bored his cold blue eyes into John. "What did you find out?"

John shielded his eyes and delivered a concise, but complete report. Then he squinted to see the reaction.

Ober's neck muscles tightened and his face flushed.

John cringed. *Uh oh, the fuse is lit.* He wondered what collateral damage was going to follow the explosion.

Ober stayed silent for a moment. Then parting his lips and flashing clenched teeth, he raised and slammed his Goliath hand on a four-inch file on his desk. The receiver on his telephone rattled, the picture frame on his desk marched toward the edge, and the walls seemed to vibrate. "My predecessor's dive into the Russian snake pit is the result of this overblown, naïve business plan. It produced a river of red ink, and now, in addition, loss of life." He fired his words like round-bursts from a Schmeisser.

John looked at the file labeled SOVCELL, SOVIET-AMERICAN JOINT VENTURE. *Oh, shit. Where is he going with this?* He shot Ober a sharp stare. "The business plan is *not* naïve, chief. The market for Sovcell's services has been demonstrated, and the business model is sound."

The lineman paused, seemingly considering John's defense of the business plan, but then waved a dismissive hand and continued his tirade. "When I took over this company, I discovered that my predecessor had in addition to setting up the venture, agreed to have a Russian general director run it. Hell," he said as if he'd been there, "that's like agreeing to have an alcoholic run the liquor store."

In spite of himself, John liked the analogy. He didn't agree with the previous CEO's decision allowing the Russians to name the general director.

"I tried to kill this project," Ober went on. "But *nooo*, the board wouldn't let me pull the plug. The sapheads in the Commerce Department convinced our chairman that investing in the 'new' and 'improved' Soviet Union was in our country's interest. An act of patriotism, they said. The Don Quixotes claimed that capitalism would conquer Communism. The Washington boneheads fell for the *perestroika* sideshow."

He paced behind his desk, stopped, pulled a cigar out of his desk, took off the wrapper, clipped one end, lit it, and puffed to get it going. Blue smoke rose through the sun's rays and exposed a kaleidoscope of whirls and swirls. A whiff of the smoke reached John. He leaned back and blew the smoke back to his boss.

Ober swiped the whirligig with his mammoth hand, like a grizzly would an annoying fly, and pointed to the Sovcell file. "*You* are the architect of this disaster, *you* wrote the business plan," he bellowed. "I should send *you* to manage it. If, as you say, the plan isn't naïve and the business model is sound, then this would be the perfect opportunity for you to prove your claim by implementing it yourself. Heh, heh, you could show us how it's done, Mr. Baran." He forced his laugh with disdain.

"I accept the challenge," John shot back, seizing the opportunity.

Ober froze in place. *"What?"*

"I accept the challenge. I'll go to Moscow and manage the venture."

"You?" Ober had an incredulous look on his face. He shook his head as if to make sure he'd heard John correctly. "Don't make me laugh.

You're no replacement for David Chernov. You produce paper, not operating results."

"I don't produce operating results because I haven't had the opportunity. Besides, you have no one else."

"I'll find someone else. I'm already looking."

"And when will that be, chief: a week, a month, six months? You'll have a hard time finding someone who knows Russia. And when you finally do, the venture could have gone kaput by then."

Ober sat down and appeared to consider John's challenge. John pushed for closure. "I'm first-generation Belarusian-American. I know how the communists think and how they operate, and I'm fluent in Russian. You need someone there right now until you find David's permanent replacement. We must try to salvage the millions we've invested."

Ober looked off into the distance, deep in thought. After a few moments he nodded. "You're right. I need someone in Moscow right now trying like hell to save the venture from complete collapse. The schedule has slipped too many times." He paused and with a determined expression on his face, added, "I've decided that if we don't begin providing service by the end of August, I'm going to cut losses and shut it down. I'll have enough ammunition to do it this time." He flashed a derisive grin. "It's been a black hole, or should I say a *red hole,* for Cellcomm's cash since last fall."

"I'll leave right away."

"Whoa." Ober raised his hand like a traffic cop. "You're bright, and you could probably pick up operations quickly. But do you have the balls to deal with the commies?"

"The U.S. Army thought I had plenty of balls to deal with them."

"What?"

"I trained in Special Forces for missions inside the Soviet Union." Ober raised his eyebrows. "I would've been dropped behind their lines if hostilities had broken out."

Surprise flashed on Ober's face. "That *would* take balls. But this isn't about blasting your way in and blasting your way out. This is about working with them every day."

"Trust me, Chief, I can handle them," John said and believed in his ability to do that—figure it out, if he needed to.

Ober shook his head, as if he didn't like what he was about to say. "Okay, okay, let's try you in operations. As you say, I don't have anyone else right now. We'll talk about objectives and results before you leave. In the meantime, I'll still be looking for Chernov's permanent replacement."

"Thank you, Chief. I'll get going right away."

Ober assumed a grave demeanor. "You must know that this assignment could be dangerous. Chernov's death may have been ruled natural, but when the Russians are involved, I'm always suspicious. I wouldn't dismiss the possibility that they…" He sat and stared at his desk.

John waited, and when his boss said nothing more, he picked up the file and stood up. "I'll be on my way, Chief."

"John, if you can pull this one out, you can name your next assignment. But if you fail and the venture continues to bleed us, I'm shutting it down; and your services, or anyone else's connected with the venture, will no longer be required. I'll tell you from personal experience that the odds are slim. We're on the commies' turf, and they make the rules of the game, if you can figure out what the rules are at any one time. The best Western lawyers over there can't give you a straight answer." His face flashed a hint of resignation—a condition, Klaudia boasted, Ober rarely displayed. He pointed at the Sovcell file. "Read the last email in there from David that Klaudia didn't share with you yet. See what you make of it. I think it may contain a clue to what happened there."

John nodded. "One last thing before I go. I'd like a straight answer to a question."

Ober eyes widened. "What?"

"Is Cellcomm in any way working with the CIA?"

The CEO's mouth dropped open. He looked like he didn't know what to say. When he regained composure, he regained it with anger. "What the hell are you talking about? The mere suggestion of it is outrageous and offensive."

"Is the Moscow venture a front for the CIA's covert operations?"

"*Hell no!* You should know better than that."

"Sorry, Chief, I had to ask."

"And why did you have to ask?"

"Personal reason."

"Goddamn it, John. Get out of here."

"Yes, sir." John did an about face and marched out. He'd gotten what he asked for. And more. His boss had raised the stakes, but John wasn't as concerned about losing his job as much as he was concerned about keeping the venture afloat long enough to find out what happened to David. He was determined to deliver on his promise to David's father. He had crossed the first hurdle: he'd be in Moscow soon. He'd just have to figure out his next step when he got there.

Chapter 6

Back in his own office, John closed the door, put down the file on his desk, and opened it to David's last e-mail, dated Thursday July 18, just four days prior. He began to read through the routine reporting of progress made in implementing the network, but tensed up when he reached the last paragraph. Apprehensive, he read it slowly.

> *After our last manager left and before I got here, Burian Trush, Sovcell's General Director, convinced our previous CEO to approve a $800,000 remodeling contract of the venture's offices and equipment rooms. I examined the remodeling work, and it doesn't seem to add up to the sum the contractor charged. I plan to ask Trush tomorrow for the contract's details. I want to see where and how the $800,000 was spent.*

John reread the paragraph and kept staring at the email. Was this the clue Ober referred to? Was there something David was about to find out, but they, whoever they were, shut him up before he uncovered it?

Then again, John thought, maybe his collaboration with the CIA got him killed. But Parker said there was no connection between David's CIA work and his death. Parker was sure of it. Money, he said, would be behind any Russian foul play. Was there enough money to kill for? And who did it, if it wasn't KGB's reprisal for David's CIA connection?

According to the emergency repatriation information, David had been flown to New York on Sunday July 21, transferred to a hospital on a medical helicopter, and was checked into the emergency room that same evening.

More questions arose. What happened between the times David sent the e-mail on Thursday and his repatriation on Sunday? And what happened during his meeting with the Russian director on Friday?

John checked the time and added eight hours: 11 P.M. in Moscow. He placed a call to Sovcell's finance director, Chris Ashley, at his Moscow apartment, but of course he couldn't get through. He then dialed the San Francisco/Moscow Teleport, a number in the U.S., and was connected to the e-mail service. The satellite link to Moscow was up. He sent an email to Chris with his questions and waited. He knew that the teleport service in Moscow had a local access number, and if Chris's phone worked locally, he could check his email. He just hoped that Chris had his Compaq notebook computer with him, that he wasn't asleep yet, and that he would check his email before going to bed.

Twenty minutes later he received Chris's response:

Hi, John, how are you all doing back there?

To answer your questions, here's what happened:

David asked Trush for the contract details first thing Friday morning. After his meeting, he told me that Trush became angry that David even questioned the job. Trush said he was insulted. David said that they had a heated exchange and he left without getting satisfactory answers to his questions about the remodeling costs.

On Saturday morning I called David, and when he didn't answer I became concerned (We made our weekly shopping trips to Sadko, Stockmann, and Izmailov market on Saturdays). I went to his apartment and knocked on the door. He didn't answer. I let myself in (I have a key to his apartment, and he had a key to mine for safety reasons). He wasn't in the living room or the kitchen.

I went into his bedroom and found him lying in bed, but when I spoke to him, he didn't respond. I shook him but he just lay there staring at the ceiling as if he was dead. But he wasn't dead: he had a pulse. I became frightened and called an ambulance.

The doctor at the local hospital (Botkin Hospital) examined David and said that he was completely paralyzed and unable to move or speak. He wanted hard currency to proceed with more testing, but I said no. There's no way in hell I would allow this third-world medical facility to treat David.

I called World Medical Service and they arranged for David's repatriation.

I hope this is helpful, and if you have additional questions, shoot me an email. International phone communication here is hopeless.

Now I have some questions for you. What's going to happen with the venture? I heard nothing from Ober. If he wants to keep the venture going, he better send a replacement and quickly. We need someone from Cellcomm to take a stand, circle the wagons. I can't do it alone.

If Ober doesn't act, here's what going to happen: The Russians' voracious appetite for hard currency will drain Cellcomm's investment down to its last dollar. Cellcomm will abandon the project and write off the losses. Russians will get another Western sucker, and the process begins all over again. I've seen it happen more than once.

I want to hear from you guys. What is Cellcomm going to do?

Best regards, Chris.

John picked up the phone and dialed the CEO's office. When Klaudia answered, he said, "I need a visa to travel to Moscow as soon as possible."

"As soon as possible will be no sooner than this Saturday, July 27," Klaudia said.

"Get the visa please, and get me a flight for Sunday, July 28, departure from JFK."

Chapter 7

John arrived at New York's Kennedy Airport, boarded Pan Am Flight 30, and settled in his window seat. At 7:25 P.M., two hours later than scheduled, the airplane doors closed. He felt the Boeing 747 taxi, lift off, and shake and rattle as it roared through patchy fog toward its cruising altitude. As it turned northeast, he looked through the window back at New York City. A hint of twilight kindled the city lights. Suddenly a strange feeling of impending regret tried to take hold of him.

He had no idea how he was going to pull the venture out of the hole. He didn't know if that was even possible. Then he thought about David and Mr. Chernov's request. The possibility that David was murdered was becoming more real to him. Whether he was murdered for money or for his CIA connection didn't matter. David was dead, and John suspected that if he wasn't careful, he'd wind up in a hospital morgue. He forced these thoughts out of his mind, turned to the man in the seat next to him and introduced himself. He hoped a chat with a fellow passenger would take his mind off these troubling questions.

"I'm Harry Morton," the man said. He looked to be forty-something, had neatly cut desert-sand hair and a sharp-featured stone face. He looked like he might have been a prizefighter at one time.

"Been to Moscow before?" John asked, seeking to strike up a common interest and maybe learn something.

"Too many times, mate," Morton said.

"You sound like you're from Down Under. How'd you get up here?"

"Called up from Sydney by our New York office."

"Going to Moscow on business?"

Morton gave John a puzzled look. "No other good reason. Sometimes I do see an organized tour group on the flight, but no individual vacationers or tourists." He swept his arm around the cabin, as if confirming his statement.

John looked around the plane. Including Morton and himself, there were about thirty passengers in the business-class section. None looked like tourists to him. He looked into the cabin behind them. About a dozen passengers were scattered throughout the economy section of the 747, less than five percent of its capacity. He turned back to Morton. "What do these groups see on their tours?"

"Whatever the Soviet government wants them to see. Churches they haven't destroyed, monasteries, imperial palaces—all attractions built by the czars before 1917. Since then, the communists haven't built anything worth seeing."

John steered the subject back to business. "What kind of venture do you have in Moscow?" he asked and wondered if he was getting too nosy. He resolved to continue the conversation until Morton told him to mind his own business. He sat next to maybe an arsenal of knowledge about conducting business in Moscow and he wanted to arm himself with as much of it as he could.

"We're remodeling a Soviet-style hotel to Western standards."

"How's it going?"

The Aussie shook his head.

"Problems?"

"It's a long story," Morton said in a way that seemed to say it was a painful subject and changed the conversation. "What about you, what brings you to Moscow?"

"We're building a mobile telephone network with international access."

"Excellent, I want a phone as soon as you get it working." He looked at John with a sad face. "Maybe I should say *if* you get it working. But if you somehow do get it up and running, you'll make heaps of money. Hell, when I'm lucky enough to get through on the Russian network, I'm paying eleven dollars per minute to call the States. And the Russian operators make you wait before they connect you, hours. And when you get the connection, the quality isn't worth a pinch of shit. Every Western businessman in Moscow will gladly pay top dollar for a prompt and clear connection to his home office."

John was pleased to hear confirmation of his business plan's assumptions. "That's precisely the market we intend to address."

"What's the name of your venture?" Morton asked.

"It's called Sovcell."

"And who's the American partner?"

"Cellcomm."

Morton grinned. "Well, well, isn't this a shrinking globe."

"You know the company?"

"No, but I know your new CEO: a no-shit exec that cuts to the bone every time. Sometimes through the bone."

"You know Wulf Ober?"

"He was our CEO, and he was against this hotel venture. Seems he had first-hand knowledge of what happens to Western companies trying to do business in the Soviet Russia. In the end, he clashed with board members, and the chairman let him go. Result? Our loss, your gain."

"Well, he didn't change any of his views about doing business in Russia."

"So when do I get my mobile phone?"

"As soon as Sovcell's operational, I'll deliver the phone to you personally."

Morton produced a business card and offered it to John. "When do you expect to be operational?"

"We'd better cut it into service by the end of next month, or the no-shit exec will shut the venture down."

"Heaps of luck, mate," the Aussie said, reclined his seat, and leaned back.

John pulled out his venture file and a copy of Tom Clancy's *Cardinal of the Kremlin* and was deciding which one to read.

Morton saw the book and pointed to it. "There is one rule in Russia you can depend on: *The canon of money*. You can buy anything for enough greenbacks, including spies in the Kremlin. If you simply remember that, you can succeed in Russia, if you don't run out of money first." He stretched and yawned. "We better try to get some sleep; it'll be a trying day tomorrow. By the way, where are you staying?"

"Hotel Kosmos."

"Then you better get some sleep, mate." Morton leaned back again, and this time he closed his eyes.

John reclined his seat and closed *his* eyes, but he didn't fall off into sleep. He wondered about Morton's Hotel Kosmos comment and the "trying day" he would face tomorrow. Could it get any more trying than it had already been?

Chapter 8

Cellcomm's Venture Partner Facility, Moscow. Monday, July 29

Burian Trush, the Russian Director General of Sovcell, began the morning with his usual routine. He opened the left bottom drawer of his desk and took out a liter of Stolichnaya and a beaker. He then opened the right bottom drawer and took out two sealed packages of smoked sturgeon. As if he was performing a chemistry experiment, he held the beaker up to the window light and poured into it exactly fifty milliliters of the vodka. He checked the amount again as if it was a medical prescription and then quaffed it. He followed it with one pack of the sturgeon *zakooska*. He repeated the procedure and put away the bottle and the beaker.

It doesn't get any better than this. The privileges of the communist's elite gave him access to special restaurants, exclusive food shops, a car with a driver, and a superior apartment. He even put an addition on his dacha. Hard currency and a foreign bank account—thanks to Cellcomm, his American venture partner—gave him access to Western quality goods: apparel and cosmetics for his wife, jeans and sneakers for his children, and appliances that worked. He took his family to exotic places for rest and relaxation. The ruble was worthless outside Comecon countries, countries that offered nothing that he wanted to see. He dreamed of returning to Bali, his wife and his two boys' favorite place. His only concern was that nothing should stop him from plucking dollars from his latest American goose.

He reviewed last Thursday's communiqué from Cellcomm, which contained the announcement of John Baran as the new American deputy director. Following Chernov's death, Trush expected that his relation with his new deputy would be uncertain, and prepared himself for a potential adversary. He wanted to know everything there was to know about Baran, and had asked Colonel Arseny Lisov, his local KGB watchdog, and Alla

Markova, Sovcell's marketing manager, for background information on the new American.

Markova, a major in the Ministry of Defense GRU, the Soviet Union's foreign intelligence agency, had been seconded to Trush for the Sovcell venture. She had close ties with her GRU colleagues and had access to information that the KGB didn't always have. He considered Lisov, his KGB watchdog, a necessary nuisance at best. Lisov's constant surveillance of his affairs irritated him, but he accepted his Party's mandate with silent resentment. He was ready for their reports.

Lisov and Markova arrived and took seats at the conference table. He joined them.

His eyes fell on Markova. She looked radiant, as usual. Her conservative dress could not hide her feminine assets. He thought of her as a Russian Marlene Dietrich: dark hair, fair skin, but with voluptuous physical endowments. A waste for her to simply be a soldier, even a GRU soldier, but he was happy to have her. Their relationship had grown close. Very close. He had availed himself of amatory services his wife could not equal. He felt a stirring and commanded himself to stick to business.

He shifted his eyes to Lisov. A letdown. An ordinary bureaucrat, Lisov was average everything: average height, average weight, average brown eyes, average balding dome, and that eternal average brown suit. Trush sighed and opened the meeting.

"Mr. John Baran, the new American First Deputy Director General of our Sovcell joint venture, is arriving today," he said, displaying neither delight nor disappointment. "He will replace Chernov. What reports do you have on our new American?"

He stared into Markova's lovely, stoic face and nodded for her to speak.

Markova glanced hesitantly at Colonel Lisov as if she was deeply suspicious of him before shifting her gaze back to Trush. "Baran was born in the United States, but his parents were born in our Belarus. They left BSSR and moved to Germany in 1944 during the Great Patriotic War when the fascist cowards were on the run. We believe that they left voluntarily, and were running away from our advancing Red Army that liberated Belarus from the Nazi oppressors. They did not return to the BSSR after our victory in 1945, but immigrated to America in 1950 from a refugee camp in Germany. At the time, they would have been considered as Nazi collaborators, enemies of the State for deserting the Motherland."

"And what would they be considered now?" Trush said, trying to humor her. He wanted to tell her that she was reciting irrelevant, ancient history.

"Since the Stalinist era is gone, they would be considered neutral, unless of course Baran brings with him a hostile agenda."

"And do we know if he does?" Trush asked.

Markova shook her head, turned her dark, penetrating eyes to the colonel, and waited with pursed lips.

Trush followed her gaze. "Colonel Lisov, what does the KGB know about this Baran?"

Lisov shifted in his seat. "The First Chief Directorate is preparing a full report on the American, and I should receive it shortly."

"Have you any information now?" Trush asked, hiding his impatience.

Lisov cleared his throat, furled his brows, and directed his remarks to Markova.

"We know that his knowledge of the Russian language and culture is excellent. He is not your typical American businessman. We *also* know that he served in the American Army Special Forces from 1980 to 1984. We further know that his unit was designated for internal USSR missions."

Lisov stopped talking but kept looking at Markova as if to see how she would react. The expression on his face appeared to say, *'you and your military GRU friends, Comrade Major, are amateurs in the intelligence business and you should stay out of it.'*

Trush leaned slightly toward Markova. "Why does the Army intelligence not know about Baran's service in American Special Forces?" His voice carried noticeable annoyance. "And what else do we not know about this American?" He shook his head in disbelief that the GRU would have missed such a basic fact about Baran.

Markova cast a venomous glance at Lisov. "First Directorate agents have large budgets to buy information."

Lisov stood up. "The GRU is a superfluous agency and should be—"

"Enough." Trush raised his hand and silenced the argument. He looked at Markova. "Tell me about the nature of these special forces."

"They are highly trained insurgents," she said. "At deployment, they would be parachuted inside our Union when the American aggressors attack us. Their objective is to locate and destroy critical military assets. They are also trained to organize partisan action against our government, especially in the republics. They would have been at least as effective as our partisans were against the fascist occupiers of our land in the Great Patriotic War. Baran would probably have been dropped in Belarus. American Special Forces members with Ukrainian background would have been dropped in Ukraine, and so on, possibly covering most of our western republics." She looked up at a large portrait of Lenin hanging behind Trush's desk. "With Baran's knowledge of our language and our country, he would have been most effective in carrying out these objectives."

Trush sighed. "I do not doubt that it would have been so, but this is 1991, and the Americans are here as investors in our country, not insurgents."

"Yes," Markova said with fervent urgency. "And instead of our military assets, these investors are destroying our culture and corrupting our socialist ideology with their capitalism." Her dark eyes firing up, she glanced back at Lenin's portrait and nodded as if affirming his teachings.

Trush waved a dismissal. "I do not worry much about that." He wished she would amend her tunnel ideology with more practical aspects of contemporary life. "I do worry, however, about Baran being an agent. He has the knowledge of our country, he is fluent in our language, and he would be a most effective American spy."

"Comrade Trush raises a good point," Lisov said. "The full report on Baran will reveal his true intentions. But personally, I do not think that he is an agent."

"And why not?" Trush asked.

"Because," the colonel glanced at his nails, "it would be stupid of the Americans to plant an agent without diplomatic cover. That would be dangerous for the agent: a quick way to lose him. If, on the other hand, Baran was one of the hundred and twenty first-secretaries, second-secretaries, counselors, or attachés at the American Embassy, then I would not be surprised if he worked for the CIA. In fact, I would expect it."

Trush nodded to show he understood Lisov's point. "Did you ever suspect Chernov, our previous American Deputy Director?"

"We suspect every foreigner, especially the Americans, but we never discovered any connection between Chernov and the CIA."

"Still, I expect that you will order full surveillance of the new American," Trush said.

"I already have," Lisov said. "It will start with his arrival at Sheremetyevo today."

"Good." Trush was pleased. Whatever else the colonel was, at least he was efficient. "I shall expect to see the First Directorate's report as soon as it is ready. In addition, I want periodic reports on your surveillance of Baran."

Lisov nodded. "Yes, Comrade Trush."

"That is all I need from you right now," Trush told Lisov and waited a moment, allowing the colonel to leave. When the Lisov didn't get up, Thrush said, "Thank you, Comrade Lisov." Then, turning to the GRU major, he said, "Alla, please remain for discussion on another matter."

Lisov hesitated for a moment, cast a cynical glance in Markova's direction, and then he rose to take his leave. On the way out, he shot Trush a look of surprise, as if he didn't expect to be excluded from the "another matter" discussion.

Chapter 9

When Lisov closed the door behind him, Trush turned to Markova. He was concerned. "The KGB surveillance of Baran may be useful to us, but we have a special interest in the American, an interest about which the KGB must not have any knowledge. You must be prepared for Baran. *You know what to do.*" Without waiting for her to respond, he stood to indicate that their "discussion" had ended.

"Yes, Comrade Trush," Markova smirked. "I know what to do." She rose and started for the door. Trush resumed his seat and turned his attention to the papers on his desk.

Before opening the door to exit, she turned. "Tonight?"

He looked up, grinning with anticipation. "Of course," he said, his tone suggesting that her question was unnecessary.

She smiled and withdrew.

After Markova left, Trush reviewed his situation. He considered his next move. As far as Baran was concerned, he decided that no immediate action was necessary apart from surveillance by the KGB. As far as his superior, the Communications Minister, was concerned, Trush knew he had to make his report. His superior was also his patron, and he had the power to advance or to withhold Trush's name within the *nomenklatura* authority. He did not want to jeopardize his privileged status, or be withheld from advancing in the Party.

Deferential compliance, even fawning to superiors, was a requirement for not only advancement within the Party, but for basic survival as well. Vigilance and ruthlessness toward subordinates was a mark of a rising star in the Party. He secretly admired Comrade Stalin's style, though he would never admit it to anyone. The old Soviet glory days were gone with Stalin, and he feared they would never return.

These guiding principles had served him well. He was the youngest Party member to have advanced to the level of his position. He also knew that it was necessary to keep his superior constantly informed not only on all matters that related to his responsibility, but anything else that might affect him or his superior. He picked up a secure red phone with a direct connection to the minister and heard the distant phone click on. He identified himself and waited.

A booming bass came on the line. "Comrade Trush, how are affairs?"

"They are good, Comrade Minister. I would like to report that Cellcomm, our American venture partner, has named a new deputy director general." He followed with the details.

"I hope he is a healthy one. I do not want any more delays in the project."

"And I hope he is experienced, as well as healthy. Network implementation is behind schedule."

"You are to do everything to help this frontier capitalist to complete the installation of the network." The minister's imperative voice was palpable. "I do not want anything or anybody, including your greed for the American dollar, to interfere with my objective of taking control of the venture as soon as the network is operational."

"Yes, Comrade Minister." Trush let the greed comment slide and wondered how much the minister knew about his dealings. He concluded that the minister knew nothing. That knowledge was tightly controlled— only two other Russians were privy to his scheme. Still, being in the position that he was, he had to be careful. He had to subordinate his greed to the minister's greater greed: The takeover of the Sovcell network. But he wondered how the minister would take control of the venture, as recently passed laws protected foreign investments. He felt he should remind the minister of the legal hurdles, but decided against it. It was not his place to question his superior.

"When the Americans complete the installation," the minister continued his directive, "then you will do whatever is necessary to convince our venture partner to abandon their capitalist adventure in our Union. I'll let you decide what method to use. I will then be able to take full control of Sovcell. Our military will benefit greatly from American high-technology equipment and computers. You are to keep me fully informed of your progress toward that goal. Do you understand?"

"Yes, Comrade Minister."

"Any questions?"

"No, Comrade Minister."

"One last thing, I want the network operational in two weeks."

"In two weeks?" Trush was surprised by the sudden deadline; his superior hadn't displayed any urgency in the past.

"No later than August 12th," the minister said and terminated the conversation.

Trush heard the phone click off on the distant end. He held the receiver in front of his face and spoke into the dead phone. "And what is so special about August 12, Comrade Minister?" He received no reply. He thought about the deadline and panic swept over him. He didn't see how the network could be completed by August 12, as critical equipment hadn't even cleared Customs yet. He realized that the minister's directive required modification to Markova's instructions, and he called her back into his office.

Later, Trush watched as Markova came in and took a chair in front of his desk. She crossed her legs. He gazed at her exposed thighs. *Not now*, he commanded himself and looked up. He explained the minister's directive and the deadline, and said, "So you see, Alla, we must forgo our original plan for now. You must be friendly, helpful, and cooperative with the new American, this Baran. We must all assist him in completing the network installation in the next two weeks."

Markova nodded and smiled, as if she was pleased with the change in her instructions. "I shall be *especially* friendly and cooperative with Mr. Baran until the project is complete. In fact, I look forward to it. He looks handsome on his visa application photograph. He looks like Jack Ryan."

"Who?"

"Well, I mean the American actor who played Jack Ryan, Indiana Jones, and Han Solo."

Trush frowned and raised his hands to the ceiling in a what-are-you-talking-about gesture.

"I'm sorry, Comrade Trush, it's just that I'm a student of American film."

"With the State's sanction, I presume?"

"Of course, it was part of my training, and Jack Ryan novels and movies were required reading and viewing."

Trush shook his head in disbelief. "The GRU training contains some incredible things these days. Now, back to Baran. I don't presume to tell you how, but it would serve us well if you could hook your feminine assets deep enough into Baran, your 'Jack Ryan,' to gain his complete trust. I assume that technique was part of your training also?"

Markova grinned and nodded. "It is a proven technique, and it has worked on the most disciplined Americans."

Trush raised his eyebrows.

"The United States Marines in the American Embassy."

"Yes, of course, I remember. Were these the 'swallows' setting honey traps?" He wanted to show he was on top of the subject.

"That is a crude KGB technique that uses sex to entrap. GRU operatives are trained to be more subtle, use intellectual approaches. GRU's entrapment is ideological, emotional, and when it succeeds, it succeeds completely. The target subject is in the bag, as the Americans would say."

"Does that technique succeed often?"

Markova frowned. "Sometimes." Then she smiled. "Sex is more reliable."

Trush shook his head in wonder and stood up, his usual signal that the meeting was over.

Markova took her cue and started for the door. Trush thought of the minister's deadline and called after her. "Alla?" She stopped, turned to face him. "Find out from your GRU contacts if the date August 12 means anything special."

A puzzled expression spread on Markova's face. "August 12?"

"Yes, August 12." He was upset to hear the annoyance in his own voice. He felt he should have known why the minister set an explicit deadline. "Something the Politburo or the army may be planning." He was guessing.

Markova's puzzled expression didn't leave her. She seemed to wrestle with the question of the sudden, specific deadline. Finally, she appeared to give up and said, "I shall attend to the matter immediately." She turned and strutted off, her derriere oscillating in rhythm with her steps.

Trush watched until Markova closed the door and then turned his thoughts to the business at hand. In view of the minister's instructions, he considered the balance he had to maintain with Baran. He reasoned that if Baran became inquisitive about the remodeling contract, he would have to "discourage" the American from pursuing that course, but in a way that didn't disable him from finishing the network installation.

But...if Baran's prying should somehow get dangerously close...well, one Cellcomm executive was already dead.

Chapter 10

John was roused by the announcement of his flight's approach to Moscow's Sheremetyevo Airport. After simulating sleep for six hours, he felt tired. He checked the local time: 1:35 P.M. He pulled up the window shade and looked out. Farm fields carved up green, wooded areas into a multicolored jigsaw puzzle, with the airport coming into view. From the air, it looked just like the satellite reconnaissance photos he'd seen during his training: a long rectangle, bisected lengthwise by two runways. Sort of like the deck of a Midway class aircraft carrier.

Morton leaned over from his aisle seat and looked through the window. "That gray building area on this side," he attempted to point to a structure on one side of the runways, "is Sheremetyevo 2, the international terminal."

"The *island*," John said.

"The what?"

"The bridge of the carrier."

Harry looked puzzled for a few seconds, then caught on. "Except this bucket isn't going anywhere. It's marooned, just like the Soviet Union."

"What's on the other side of the runways?" John pointed to what looked like another terminal.

"That's Sheremetyevo 1, the domestic terminal. If you travel by air within Russia, or any of the other fourteen republics, you'll use the Sheremetyevo 1 terminal. You'll fly Aeroflot, the Soviet Union's glorious achievement in civil aviation."

John glanced at Morton, saw a derisive smirk, and prepared himself for sarcasm.

"But before you board an Aeroflot flight and soar through the Ruskies' friendly skies, mate, you need to know the answer to a riddle that can save your life." He looked at John and waited.

"Okay, Harry, what's the riddle?"

Morton grinned as if he'd gotten himself a chump. "What's the difference between Aeroflot and Scud missiles?"

"You mean the Scuds that Iraq fired into Israel during Desert Storm?"

"Those are the ones."

John thought about the Scud missiles' dismal performance, but he didn't know exactly how to connect it to Aeroflot. "I give up."

"The answer is: Aeroflot kills more people." Morton held a straight face for a few moments, and then broke out in laughter.

"It's a joke, right, Harry?"

Morton stopped laughing. "It may sound like a joke, but there's enough truth in it to convince me to take the train when I travel inside the Soviet Union."

"Back to Desert Storm." John began to gather his personal items. "You were here working during the conflict, weren't you?"

"Of course, it officially ended in April."

"Did you get flak from the Russians when Schwarzkopf routed Hussein's army?"

"Personally, I didn't, but there were organized demonstrations against the U.S. and its allies. The Russian people don't give a shit about the Iraq war. The country is still licking their wounds from Afghanistan, their Vietnam. The average Russian is now concerned about his survival: his next drink and his next meal. In that order."

John heard a bell and saw the no smoking and the fasten seatbelt signs light up. The flight attendant discharged instructions to stow away trays and return seats into upright positions. The 747 made its final approach, landed, and taxied into parking position. John retrieved his carry-on luggage, stepped out of the plane onto the jetway, and hit a wall of hot, humid air that reeked of used lubricating oil and exhaust fumes. He stopped for a moment to slow his breathing and reduce his intake of the polluted air.

As he stepped off the jetway, a strange feeling came over him. He never thought he'd see the day when he would be stepping out of a commercial airliner onto Soviet soil to build a business, rather than jumping out of a military aircraft to destroy designated targets. He waited for Morton to catch up, and when Morton did, they made their way toward passport control.

John surveyed the surroundings. Officials, standing like honor guards, lined the passageway, their eyes darting from passenger to passenger, as if searching for someone.

"Is this our welcoming party?" John tilted his head in the direction of the honor guard.

"Don't expect any hugs or a handshake, that's KGB. The ones with green piping on their uniform are KGB Border Troops, and the plainclothesmen are the KGB's Second Chief Directorate counterintelligence agents. I've had the 'pleasure' of their acquaintance, but you, mate, will be a new pigeon for them."

"Why are they standing there?"

"They're looking for spies."

John looked at the sullen faces of the "welcoming party" and felt like he was attending a funeral. He almost expected to view a coffin at the end of the honor-guard line.

"Look at these miserable bastards," Morton said, shaking his head. "The fuckwits were told that all foreign visitors to the Soviet Union are spies. And you, John, take top honors. You're American, their main enemy."

"But we're not here as enemies," John protested.

"Somebody forgot to tell them. The poor bastards are years behind."

They passed the spy-searchers and descended into a cavernous passport control area. Cool, musty, dead air hit them. More officials lined the perimeter of the cavern. Low-wattage, bare light bulbs dangled from the ceiling wiring in a vain attempt to illuminate the cavern. John and

Morton joined over a hundred other just-arrived passengers corralled in front of four staffed passport control booths. John learned from a German in front of them that an earlier Lufthansa flight had not yet even cleared immigration. The herd jostled forward with imperceptible progress.

An hour later, John stood in front of a passport control official. He handed his passport and visa to a blond kid in the booth. The kid took the documents without saying a word, laid the passport's picture-page down flat on a glass plate, and stared at John with a dead expression. If he believed that John was his main enemy, he didn't show it. John waited. The teenager kept staring. No words were exchanged, and John wondered if the kid was mute. Five minutes elapsed. A light appeared next to the glass plate, and the teenager stamped the passport and the visa, tore off the entry portion, handed the documents to John, and waved him on.

The kid offered no "Welcome to our country," no "Enjoy your stay," and definitely no "Have a nice day." John looked at the passport-clearing setup and wondered what mechanism or who sat at the other end of what seemed like a periscopic contraption, and why it took five minutes to clear his entry. When he looked up, the kid gave him a stern look and pointed toward Customs in a get-going gesture. John followed the kid's instruction and moved on.

He was inside the Soviet Union. And although he hadn't crossed the Rubicon, he nevertheless felt that a die, uncertain and precarious, had been cast.

Chapter 11

John left Passport Control, made his way to the baggage claim area and started to look for his suitcase in the baggage trough. Other bags from the same flight were jammed into the narrow trench, but he didn't see his. He had begun a second search when Morton walked up.

John frowned. "How long does it take to transfer luggage from the plane? We've been here over an hour."

"Lower your expectations, mate. This is a socialist country; people have zero motivation. Everyone has a job, but few actually work. My experience with their brand of socialism is that you wait until *they're* ready to provide service to you. But, if their self-interest is involved, then they have heaps of motivation. Like right now, for instance, they are probably going through your bag, looking for valuables."

"You mean—"

"Yes, they're probably ransacking your baggage now, but I see they're done with mine," Morton said, pointing to a bag sliding down into the trough from behind a rubber curtain. "They're not going to find anything valuable in my luggage that they can sell on the street."

John saw his bag drop after Morton's. He examined the small lock on the bag: broken. He checked an inside compartment where he'd packed a video camera and a compact tape recorder. Empty. "Son of a bitch," he muttered.

Morton nodded as if this was all completely normal. "Well," he said, "it looks like some baggage-handling dill will smoke Marlboros and get drunk tonight."

"How do I report the theft?"

"Don't waste your time." Morton moved toward Customs. He grabbed two forms from a box on a counter nearby and handed one to John. "Fill this out. List all currency, jewelry, and electronic equipment that you still have." He snickered. "List all other items of value and don't lose the form; you'll need it when you leave," he added and cringed.

"What for?"

"To clear Customs on the way out of this paradise." Morton looked up at the ceiling and shook his head. "The Soviets want to make sure you don't take out something you didn't bring in, or take out more currency than you brought in. If you make a purchase, have a receipt for it if you want to take it out. And make sure you are 'permitted' to take the item out of the country. If you want to take that Notebook back home with you when you leave," Morton pointed to John's computer bag, "you must declare it when you go through Customs."

"Why do they go to all this trouble, when you *leave* their country?"

"The official reason? The Soviet government doesn't want you to take out any of the country's 'national treasures.'" Morton let out a laugh.

"And what are these Russian 'national treasures?' I thought they didn't have anything of value we could buy?"

"Old icons, antique samovars, certain period paintings, rugs, and any other items the Customs official feels like confiscating from you when you leave." Morton started filling out his Customs form. John did the same.

Forms in hand, they joined another herd in front of four Customs stations. After jostling for another hour, John had his baggage cart in front of the Customs official. A red-faced, red-eyed hulk manning the station stuck out his paw. John gave him his declaration form and waited. The hulk glanced over the items on the front of the form. John declared no weapons, no narcotics, no antiques or objects of art, and, of course, no USSR rubles. The hulk opened the form and looked inside. His eyes widened when he saw the amount of U.S. dollars John declared. His gaze shifted from the form to John and back to the form several times, as if he didn't believe what he saw. John felt his stomach tighten.

Have I done something wrong? He recalled his foreign duty orientation session for his Moscow assignment. He was told to bring sufficient cash for a three-month stay, as credit cards were not in widespread use in the USSR. And he was told to bring new one-hundred-dollar bills, as hard currency establishments preferred the larger denomination and would not take a worn, dirty, or in any way marked up note. He was following instructions, so why the surprise on the hulk's face?

The hulk stopped switching his gaze and stared at John. "You have thirty thousand American dollars?" he asked in Russian.

John stared back and shrugged his shoulders. He decided to act dumb. The hulk waited for a few moments and then called an interpreter. The interpreter came up next to the hulk and repeated the question in English.

"Yes," John said in English.

"Show me the money," the Customs hulk demanded in Russian. The interpreter repeated the demand in English.

John unbuckled his belt and pulled it out of his pants. The hulk, the interpreter, other passengers, and a Customs pit boss watched with interest. Some passengers snickered. He unzipped a long compartment on the inside of the belt and started to pull out one-hundred-dollar bills. The new, crisp notes crackled and popped as he unfolded, flattened, and stacked them in front of the hulk. When he was finished the hulk picked up the money and handed it to the pit boss behind him. The pit boss looked at John, looked at the wad in his hand, turned, and disappeared into a back office.

John waited. Everyone behind him waited and watched. The Customs station was down. After five minutes, he began to worry. What were they doing with the money? Did they suspect the notes were counterfeit? Were they copying the serial numbers so they could track his spending? It wouldn't take long: most of the numbers were sequential.

He looked at the passengers around him. Some had an expression of anxiety, some of frustration. A few looked shocked. Some, looking wary, were cagily counting their money. He looked at Morton in the line behind him and saw a smile on his face. Morton made an okay sign, as if everything was proceeding normally.

John didn't think the situation was in any way amusing—he Customs officials had his thirty thousand.

Five minutes later, the pit boss came back with the bills, said something to the hulk and handed him the money. The hulk handed the bills to John and waved him through without examining his luggage. John thought that was strange. The passenger in front of him had his suitcase turned upside down in search of only the hulk knew what. But then, he thought, the hulk probably knew that his luggage had already been examined. Ransacked. John counted the money, holding up the passengers behind him, ignoring the hulk's glare. It was all there.

He shoved the cash into his pockets, put on his belt, and started to push his way into the arrival area. He turned to look at Morton at the Customs station, waved goodbye, and said, "I'll give you a call." Morton smiled, snapped a salute, and gave John another okay sign. John would ponder what the hell just happened later, but he needed to move on and look for his ride.

Greeters, drivers, and, no doubt, state security agents, crowded the arrival area. A front-line offense of impudent taxi drivers assaulted the arriving passengers. Dressed in garb the Salvation Army would reject with indignation, unshaven, hair uncut, they thrust themselves on the passengers, yelling, "*Tuxee, tuxee.*" Aggressive and obnoxious, they made used-car salesmen look docile. John pushed through the taxi drivers and kept scanning the crowd until he saw a hand-printed sign held up by a Russian-looking man in the back of the crowd. It read MR. BARAN. He began to muscle through the assaulting mob toward the sign.

Whatever he'd gotten himself into had begun.

Chapter 12

When John reached the sign-holding Russian, he saw an American standing next to the man. That had to be Chris Ashley, John thought. He hadn't personally met Chris, but had "spoken" with him via e-mail so many times that he felt he knew him well.

Chris looked thirty-something years old, medium height. He had a mop of reddish hair, wore a dark suit that fitted him well, and had the face of the Marlboro man, minus cigarette and cowboy hat. John remembered David hiring Chris for the finance director's position when Chris' employer, an American cosmetics firm, abandoned their venture in Moscow. Chris was a seasoned expat, who had extensive experience in business dealings in Russia. That experience, David had then said, was invaluable to Sovcell, or to any other Western venture in the Soviet Union.

"Welcome to Moscow, John," Chris said in his cheerful Southern lilt and thrust his hand forward for a firm handshake. "It's good to finally meet you in person." He gestured to the man standing next to him, holding the sign. "This is Fyodor, our driver." The Russian nodded in a subordinate manner. They quickly moved away from the arrival hall herd, and walked outside the terminal.

"I hope you don't mind me giving you some basic tips right off the bat," Chris said.

"I need all the tips I can get, I'm a greenhorn here. Don't ever hesitate to set me straight if I begin to stray."

"Well," Chris pointed to the barking crew behind them, "don't use those taxis if you can help it. Arrange for your own contact to pick you up. The taxi drivers can be real ugly, and you never know which one of them will set you up for assault and robbery."

"What happened to law and order in the Soviet Union? The communists touted Moscow as the safest city in Europe, didn't they?"

"That was before Gorbachev reforms. Things are different now."

As they stopped outside the terminal and waited while Fyodor got the car, John looked around the airport grounds. The terminal building looked sinister, a block of steel and concrete that begged for a good steam cleaning.

He studied the people around him. There was a clear dichotomy in appearance between foreigners and locals. The foreign visitors were dressed either in business attire, or wore casual clothes that didn't look dirty or shabby. They moved as if they had a purpose in mind. The shabbily dressed locals stood around watching the foreigners. Did they have a purpose?

Chris checked the time. "It'll be after five by the time we get to our building. Do you want to go directly to the hotel, rest, and try to shake off your jetlag? Trush wants to meet with us first thing in the morning."

John shook his head. "No, I want to see the Sovcell facility first. I don't think I'll be able to sleep right now."

Fyodor pulled up in a beat-up 1987 Volvo 740, parked, and began loading John's bags. The Volvo looked like it'd been through a demolition derby. John pointed to the dents and scratches. "Russian driving?"

"Some, but most of it is the result of swinging a sledgehammer."

He stared at Chris.

"Theft prevention," Chris said. "Russians like new-looking things, whether it's money or cars. It's as if their senses have been deprived of color and freshness for so long, they'll steal anything that shines and sparkles. They won't steal this junky-looking Swedish tank. It looks too Russian for them." Chris then added as a second thought. "If they do steal it, it'll be for parts."

The driver finished loading the bags, took a pair of windshield wipers out of the trunk, and installed them on the Volvo. John looked at Chris with raised eyebrows.

"Have to do it every time you park, or the wipers, and anything not secured, will be stolen." Chris motioned for them to get in the back seat. Inside the vehicle, John immediately opened his window; the car was a sauna on wheels. He looked at the dashboard.

Chris followed the direction of John's gaze. "Sorry, the air conditioning doesn't work, and you can expect that of most things in Russia."

As the Volvo pulled away from the airport, Chris turned to John. "Welcome to the Wild East."

"The *Wild East?*"

"That's what we call it. The desperados here may not wear six-shooters and ride horses, but they're just as lawless and reckless as any outlaw in the old Wild West."

"You know, Chris, I've yet to hear anything positive about Moscow."

"And you won't."

"Then why are you here?"

"Because in the midst of chaos there are opportunities."

"Have you found these opportunities of yours?"

"Well, yes and no," Chris cracked a faint smile. "You'll see for yourself."

They left the terminal and joined the exit traffic on the airport access road. Within minutes the driver eased into a six-lane, divided highway heading southeast toward Moscow.

"If you ever drive to Leningrad," Chris said, "and God knows why you'd ever want to do that, you'd take this road in the opposite direction, heading northwest. It's called Leningrad Highway."

"Isn't Leningrad now St. Petersburg?"

"Technically, you're correct. The citizens of Leningrad voted to change the name back to St. Petersburg in last month's elections."

"If I don't drive to St. Petersburg, how'd I get there if I had to? Would I fly?" John wanted to get Chris's take on Aeroflot.

"Hell no. You'd take the overnight train, but make sure you lock the doors of your compartment. And since most of the compartment locks are broken, take some strong wire with you to secure the door."

John gave him a questioning look.

"You'll be knocked out and robbed if you don't."

Chris pointed to a hedgehog structure on the side of the highway. Three eighteen-foot-high erections stood on a concrete platform. Each consisted of three beams at right angles to each other, resembling leaning crosses. The framework looked like the anti-tank obstacles used during World War II.

"That's a monument to the defenders of Moscow," Chris said, pointing to the structure. "The Red Army stopped the Germans—or as they say, Hitler's fascism—at that point in December of 1941. The Germans were less than twenty miles from the Kremlin."

"I remember that part, but now that you mentioned fascism, where did they stop Napoleon's imperialism?"

"That egocentric frog got all the way into Moscow, froze his ass, gave up and left in October of 1812. He lost more than three-quarters of his six hundred thousand troops. During his retreat, the Russian winter killed another ninety percent of what was left." Chris looked puzzled. "And for some reason, Hitler learned nothing from Napoleon. Every despot, it seems, thinks he's unique and invincible, thinks he's immune to the laws of history. The lust for power blinds the dictator to historical events. Did you know, John, that Hitler marched on Russia on June 22nd, the exact same day Napoleon invaded Russia in 1812?"

"I didn't know you were a student of history."

"I brushed up on this shit before I got here. It's interesting." His smile winked on again as the car sped through the highway's thin traffic. "Not only the French and the Germans froze their asses trying to conquer Russia and then turned back, but a century before Napoleon, the Swedes, and twenty-four centuries before the Swedes, the Persian Empire met the enemy against which they were powerless: The Russian winter." He threw up his hands. "Does anyone study history anymore?"

"And now that *we're* here," John said, wondering not for the first time what the hell he had gotten himself into, "Where do you think they'll stop American capitalism? Do Napoleon, Hitler, and the others have a lesson for us here?"

"Hedgehog, weather, they won't stop an ideology. If it's stopped, it'll be inside the Kremlin through laws and decrees. What we have now is creeping capitalism, and if it's not stopped, it'll begin to displace their bankrupt socialism. I'm optimistic about our chances; we have a strong ally."

"What ally?"

"Greed. The craving for all things capitalism can offer."

"Are these bankrupt socialists willing to exert the effort required to create the things capitalism offers?"

Chris shook his head with conviction. "Unfortunately, that concept is foreign to them right now. But I'm optimistic that they'll discover the connection. For now, we have to deal with an abhorrence of honest work, corruption, sharp practices, and, surprisingly, a popular disregard for the law. It's as if Gorbachev's liberal reforms spawned *criminal* capitalism: individual initiative channeled in the wrong direction. Call it criminal entrepreneurship."

"That's quite an indictment."

"I've been here over two years, and I speak from *personal* experience."

They came up on what looked like a cloverleaf interchange, but wasn't.

"We're crossing the Moscow 'beltway,'" Chris said, gesturing to the ten-lane, divided highway below the overpass they were on. Five or six miles later, the driver made a shallow left onto an eight-lane divided major thoroughfare. "We're on Leningratskyi Prospekt," he explained. "Our facility is off this street, about six miles down. Actually, we're off Gorky Street. Leningratskyi Prospekt turns into Gorky Street in the Moscow Center. We're located close to Mayakovskaya Metro."

As they entered the more densely populated area, gasoline and diesel exhaust fumes filled the car. John coughed and rolled up the window. He began to overheat and reluctantly rolled the window back down. Buildings crowded both sides of the road—multi-story, dreary, gray monoliths, stained by pollution. The buildings' ground floors were dotted with state stores. John read the pallid signs above the storefronts: FOOD PRODUCTS, CLOTHES, MEAT. Long lines formed outside the food and clothing stores, but he saw no lines in front of the meat stores. He sent a questioning look to Chris for an explanation.

"No meat." Chris nodded toward the stores. "It looks like some foodstuff and clothes might be coming in." Doubt spread across his face. "It's more likely, though, that somebody started a rumor about the food and clothes." Chris's face saddened. "Poor people, they're powerless. What the communist regime has done to this country is criminal."

John shook his head in dismay. "I read about the shortages without much thought, but seeing them with my own eyes..." He couldn't find the right words. "A superpower that has a space program and maintains a nuclear arsenal, but can't feed its own people? How long can that continue?" He pointed to the lines. "How do you explain that? Russia has vast natural resources, and an educated population."

"It's simple," Chris said. "The communist system lacks the engine of private initiative that drives a country's economic progress. That engine is fueled by free enterprise. The state is incapable of doing that. Now add to it a bureaucracy that is riddled with humongous incompetence and blazing corruption and you get what you're seeing out there." He waved his hand in the direction of the lines outside the stores.

"I didn't know you were also an economist, Chris," John remarked.

"I can make a pie out of an apple."

"But bureaucratic incompetence and corruption exist, in various degrees, in all socialist and totalitarian systems. I've been in many of those countries, and I didn't see anything like this—excepting the third world, which has its own special problems."

"True, but those countries didn't compete with America. What drove the final nail into the bankrupt Soviet coffin is Brezhnev's quest to keep up with the U.S.A. in military buildup at the cost of everything else. That policy ruined their country. They're broke. Gorbachev has been trying to reverse Brezhnev's policies, but I think it may be too late."

"So what's going to happen?"

Chris shrugged. "Not sure. Without Western aid, nothing good is going to happen."

They drove in silence for a few miles. Chris pointed to a clean-looking building set off the street on the right. "That's the Aerostar, a Western-style, newly opened hotel. We use it for American visitors, mostly technicians and installers."

After another few minutes the driver made a turn into a side street. They went a short distance and turned into a fenced-in parking area. Four Russian-made cars, a small truck, and three vans took up half of the parking lot. A two-story, cement building stood on the left. A uniformed guard, armed with a Kalashnikov sub-machine gun, stood at the entrance to the building.

"What's with the assault trooper?" John nodded at the guard.

"Compliments of our partner," Chris said. "Since we keep hard currency in the building, Trush insisted on protection against Russian mafia. He ought to know."

"What did you mean?"

"Nothing," Chris said. John looked at him with a quizzical expression. "I'll tell you later," Chris said and nudged a shoulder toward the driver.

John nodded; he got the message. "Speaking of hard currency, I have some cash I need to put in a safe place."

"I'll put it in my safe. We'll talk about Trush inside."

Chapter 13

They entered the Sovcell building's second floor, and Chris led John through a wide hallway that lead directly to David Chernov's old office. An oak desk stood at the far end with a conference table in front of it. Behind the desk, a hazy window, absent of any shade or curtain, looked out onto the parking lot. The walls looked freshly painted, but were otherwise bare. A lone calendar with July's picture of Philadelphia's Independence Hall hung on the wall. Chris motioned to the conference table, and they sat down.

John smoothed the table with his palm. "Nice furniture. I thought there wasn't anything worth buying in Moscow."

"There isn't. Everything you see here, from furniture to equipment, to hammer and nails, is imported. Soviet economy offers nothing for the consumer. Whatever their broken down central planning can scrape up goes to the military and propaganda programs to glorify Communism." He rapped the table with his knuckles. "Solid oak, Denmark's finest."

John slowly scanned the walls, the ceiling, and the floor. "Before we discuss any sensitive issues, is this office 'clean?'"

"David swept the entire complex when he got here and made sure this office stayed clean."

"What about right now? The office was unoccupied for over a week, right?"

Chris stood up. "I'll be right back."

He returned in a minute with an RF Sweep Detecting Unit and went around the room pointing the probe. When he was finished, he made an okay sign. "If you're not sure, you should always do this before discussing any sensitive stuff."

"Now, what did you mean by that remark in the car about Trush and the mafia?"

Chris winced. "That's just it. In Russia you don't know who the *real* mafia is. In a sense, everyone in Russia is mafia of one type or another. Only some operate inside the law, and others operate outside the law. Mother Russia has become Mother Mafia."

"Corruption?"

"Criminal *and* absolute."

John nodded and got to the more urgent question. "What can you tell me about David's onset of paralysis?"

"Not much more than what I said in my email, except that I have my own view of what happened, but I don't have any proof."

"Go on."

"David's stroke had to be induced. Something he unknowingly ate or drank."

"How and why?"

Chris narrowed his eyes. He seemed to ponder the question. Finally, he said, "I don't know how. What I do know is that the Soviets have been active in bioweapons research for decades. They've probably developed agents that induce stroke, heart attack, cancer, or organ-of-your-choice failure. And in spite of what treaties they have signed, these agents are still stockpiled in the bowels of their research labs and secret military installations."

"How do you know all that? Are you an intel agent, in addition to being a historian and an economist?"

"Sources."

"What sources?"

"I don't want to talk about them unless it's absolutely necessary. Let me just say that you can buy information about the stuff I'm talking about; and you can buy the stuff itself for enough hard currency. Hell, everything in Russia is for sale, especially the government bureaucrats."

"You're saying some of that 'stuff' was used on David?"

"My conclusion."

"By whom?

Chris shook his head. "Don't know."

"All right, assuming the stroke was caused by some drug, what do you think was the reason for it?"

"I don't know that either, but David was pushing Trush hard to get the remodeling contract details and all the invoices for work done. He told Trush he needed proof that there actually *was* $800,000 worth of work performed. He said that he didn't see more than $500,000 worth of construction and asked Trush to explain where the remaining $300,000 had gone. David told me that Trush hit the ceiling, got very mad, and said he was insulted. On that Friday, the July 19th meeting, he told Trush that if he didn't produce the documentation on Monday, David would go to a higher authority with evidence of fraud."

"What evidence and what higher authority?"

"I asked David that question, and he said he didn't know yet what higher authority. I asked what evidence he had, and he said he didn't have it, yet."

"Are you saying David's bluff cost him his life?"

Chris shrugged and shook his head in an I-don't-know manner.

"If David believed he could get the evidence," John said, remembering his promise to David's father, "Then we should be able to get it, too."

"How?"

"I don't know for sure, but I'd say it has to be in the remodeling contract details. Let's see the invoices."

"*The* invoice is in my office, down the hall." Chris stood and left.

John pulled out a copy of Chris's email and was re-reading it when Chris returned and put a single piece of paper on the conference table. John stared at it: Corrotto Construction invoiced Sovcell for $800,000 with two line entries: Labor—$400,000 and Material—$400,000.

"That's it?" John looked to Chris for more.

"That's it. David was trying to get the details behind the invoice: cost of specific materials used, man hours for various labor categories. The remodeling work was done *before* David or I got here. It seems Trush was able to convince the former CEO of Cellcomm to authorize the capital expenditure."

"I didn't see any capital expenditure authorization in the Sovcell file."

"Trush could've gotten verbal approval."

John shook his head. "For eight-hundred thousand there needs to be a piece of paper, a justification for the expenditures. That's in the bylaws of the venture. Get the details on Corrotto Construction. We may have to pay them a visit." Exploring another angle, John asked, "Did David have any close relationships with any of the Russians?"

"Well," Chris mused for a moment, "There is Markova, our marketing and sales manager. She's one of the Russians that were originally selected by Trush. She's good at her job. Hell, her English is better than mine." Chris seemed to drift off. He looked like he was trying to decide if he should say what's on his mind.

John waited. Then, "What?"

"David had a relationship with her," Chris finally said. "He spent time at her place. Nights."

"What kind of relationship?"

"He never talked about it, but it doesn't take a propulsion engineer to figure it out."

"Did Markova 'belong' to someone?" John asked, looking for a possible murder motive that could be related to jealousy.

"She's been Trush's lay before David started his visits to her apartment. Trush's wife is uglier than a mud fence. She's also fat. If she were an inch taller she'd be round. Story is that he married her to get ahead in the Party; she's the daughter of a Central Committee member. As a result, they say that Trush is being groomed for a higher position, a ministerial spot."

"Could David's cutting in on Trush's lay be a possible murder motive?"

"Maybe, but I don't think so. Russians don't give a shit about that, but money is another matter. They'll go to any lengths for hard currency."

"Back to the $300,000 David suspected Trush had pocketed in a kickback scheme with the contractor. I want to apply pressure to Trush on the contract issue just as David had done and see if we can flush him out into an action that could give us a clue. We'll have to be ready, of course, for whatever he does. We'll turn up the screws on him in tomorrow's meeting, and we'll use the same screwdriver as David had used: the remodeling contract."

Chris gave him a weird stare. "Just remember what happened to David when he turned that screwdriver."

Chapter 14

John ambled around the office, shaking his legs to work out the cramps. "You have a copy of the org chart?"

Chris produced the chart and placed it on the conference table. "Everyone here is Russian and handpicked by Trush. I'll have to say that when it comes to technical matters, these Russians are sharp as tacks. You'll note that, not counting the temporary tech reps that come to install and service the equipment, you and I are the only permanent Americans in the venture."

John sauntered over and looked down on the chart. "Is this imbalance in personnel unusual?"

"No, most ventures are similar in structure. It's costly to staff the organization with expats. Cost of living, foreign assignment, hazardous duty, and various R&R allowances can more than double the base salary of an expat. Russians are paid nominal wages, and they're thrilled to have a job in a foreign venture. They're thrilled to be able to work with the latest technology which they've seen only on paper in the classroom."

John counted twenty-four Russian nationals, two of which were at the manager's level. "What can you tell me about these two managers?"

"You should meet these two as soon as you can. They are Nikolai Orlov, the operations manager and, of course, Alla Markova, the marketing and sales manager."

John took his seat. "Tell me more."

Chris nodded. "Right. Nikolai Orlov is well connected and knowledgeable in the workings of the government bureaucracy. He's somewhat unusual, compared to our average Russian employee. He spent time in the West and acts sympathetic to Westerners. He wants to be like an American, and he tries to act like one. You can have a reasonable and frank discussion with him about their system without being stonewalled by communist ideology."

"Then I intend to have that reasonable and frank discussion with him," John said. "I always wondered how they'd rationally explain one of the most bizarre economic theories in all of history. But it sounds like Nikolai is a 'white-hat' Russian."

"Well, I don't know. He's been spending a lot of time with Trush."

"Reporting on the operations?"

Chris shook his head and frowned. "I'm not sure what he was reporting on; there hasn't been much to report on lately that has to do with operations."

John furrowed his brow. "What, then?"

"Not sure. You ask me, he's one of Trush's informants. Maybe his chief informant."

John asked, "Did Nikolai manage the Corrotto contract?"

"I already talked to him about that. He managed the operations side only, the day-to-day construction. He said all paperwork related to terms and payments was handled personally by Trush."

"Then Trush holds the answers we'll want to get." John pointed to the block on the chart labeled MARKETING AND SALES. "What can you tell me about her?"

"Alla Markova is a loyalist, a gung-ho communist, and she's the complete opposite of Nikolai when it comes to her attitude toward Westerners. She hides those feelings well, though, so don't be fooled. She seems to be even better connected within the government than Nikolai. She's especially successful in marketing our services to the Russians. She's also quite a woman. She's slicker than owl shit, we'd say back home."

"Was that a compliment?"

Chris rolled his eyes. "Like *wow*. And she's a master at using her female assets to accomplish her goals. You'd better stir some saltpeter in your morning coffee before you meet her." Chris tried to keep a straight face, but failed and broke out in laughter.

"No problem," John chuckled. "The stuff the Army put into my scrambled eggs is still working."

"Don't say I didn't warn you."

"Back to the organization. Are there any KGB agents inside Sovcell?"

"I'm not sure about agents, but we have heaps of informants. On any one day, somebody is always visiting with Trush. But there is one man you should know about, and he's not in our organization. He's Arseny Lisov, a KGB colonel. He has an office in Trush's building, on the same floor, in fact."

"What's a KGB colonel doing there?"

"He's the resident political officer. A watchdog. He makes sure Trush toes the Party line ideologically and operationally. Trush is responsible for the ministry's long-distance network, and most of his time is spent managing it. He's the general director of Sovcell in absentia, to use a fancy term. Since the Party keeps a close watch on *all* communications facilities, Lisov, I'm sure, is watching us as well."

"Should we be concerned about the colonel?"

"I don't know. He's been a puzzle so far. As far as the venture is concerned, he hasn't been involved directly, though, as I've said, I'm sure he knows exactly what's going on here."

John stood and stretched again. He felt the jetlag's disruption of his body's rhythms. "Let's take that tour of the facility before my mind sinks into a fog. I want to see what Cellcomm's gotten itself into."

Chapter 15

As they walked out into the hallway, Chris explained that the entire building had been remodeled with offices on the second floor and equipment rooms on the first. They took a fast walk through the office area. John noted the substandard material used in the remodeling. The quality of work was passable, barely passable in some places. They walked downstairs, and Chris led John into the switchroom. Racks of equipment filled the room.

"It's ready and waiting." Chris swept his hand inside the doorway, inviting John to step in.

"Waiting for what?" John asked.

"Waiting for the most important part. The processor racks, the brain."

"They were shipped weeks ago."

"Yes, I know. They're sitting in Customs."

"And?"

"And we have a problem. The Customs crooks want hard currency to clear its entry into the country. They want a goddamn bribe."

"Hard currency? I thought nominal gifts greased the bureaucrats."

"Customs is different. The crooks know the value of the equipment and they want to get their slice."

"How much?"

"They're asking for three thousand dollars, and I'm not going to do any of that creative accounting shit to pull cash out of operations."

"Isn't our partner supposed to attend to this?"

Disgust spread on Chris's face. "Trush won't lean on Customs. There's honor among crooks, a kind of professional courtesy."

"How so?"

"One bribe extorter won't interfere with another bribe extorter when the other one is extorting his bribe, if you know what I mean. But you can raise that question in tomorrow's meeting with Trush. See how far you'll get."

"I'll do that." John pushed on the equipment room door to open it fully and felt the heavy metal door's resistance. "What's with the bank-vault door?"

Chris stepped inside and rapped on the wall with his knuckles. The sheet metal vibrated, and the sound reverberated throughout the room.

John looked at him with a what-gives expression.

"Trush's design. He insisted the room be enclosed in metal."

"What the hell for?"

"He said it was to prevent our equipment from 'eavesdropping' on Soviet secrets. Said our equipment could otherwise pick up their RF signals, and it could also emit potentially harmful radiation to 'jam' their communications. Even the AC power had to be fed through low-pass filters."

John shook his head. "They're more paranoid than I thought."

They left the equipment vault and walked down the hall to a locked door. Chris unlocked it, and they stepped into a twelve-by-twelve room. Cases of vodka stacked to the ceiling, boxes of chocolate were piled three feet high, and hundreds of cartons of cigarettes filled the room.

"Holy shit!" John yelled. "What's this?"

"These are the 'gifts' to grease the bureaucratic palms. Stolichnaya vodka and Marlboro cigarettes for the Russian male, and Lindt chocolate for the Russian female."

John tried to count the cases of vodka and then gave up. "You can get the whole of Moscow drunk on that stash. And look at the mountain of cigarette cartons; that's enough to give all those drunks lung cancer."

"You're looking at the next best thing to hard currency. You can get a cab ride for a couple of packs of Marlboro, a permit for a bottle of Stolichnaya, and for a box of Lindt you get favorable treatment from a female bureaucrat in battling red tape. If you ask me, I think the Soviets invented red tape and raised it to an art form. It's also safer than dollars, marks, or pounds, since it's illegal for Russian nationals to hold hard currency. But they'll accept gifts openly; hell, they expect it."

"Well, perhaps I should stash a couple of Marlboro packs in my pockets, just in case."

"Remember this, John, when you do business with Russians, official or not, you better have something in hand, or you'll accomplish nothing. After seventy years of socialism, the attitudes of give-me and what-can-I-get-out-of-it are ingrained in their culture. You won't hear a Russian ask how he can earn it."

"Doesn't all this grease add up?"

"Sure it adds up. And this grease is just for the low-level officials, the peons. The bigger fish get special merchandise and trips to the U.S. and Western European countries."

"How do you account for that?"

"Trips go under 'training' and special merchandise is treated as business supplies."

They walked to the end of the hallway where John saw what looked like a kitchen and an eating area with tables and chairs. "What's this?" he asked.

"Trush hired a cook to prepare breakfast and lunch for the workers."

"Who's paying for this socialist welfare?"

"We are, of course. Trush wants to provide meals to the workers since they have a hard time finding food in the stores. They'd be standing in those lines we saw driving in. To do that we have a full-time driver dedicated to the cook who scours Moscow for bread, potatoes, vegetables and milk. Sometimes he finds fresh eggs, and that's a real treat for the Russians. And as you might guess, we haven't seen meat in a long while."

"What's it costing us?"

"Not very much for the food. But the socialism had gone further than food. Trush used to give out bonuses to his favorite employees for no reason that he could explain; five hundred or a thousand given out per bonus. And that added up."

"What kind of bonuses?"

"Rewards for his favorite informants, obviously."

"Shit, did you confront him about it?"

"David did, and Trush hasn't done that since."

"Back to the remodeling contract. Now that I've seen the work Corrotto Construction did here, I agree with David. There isn't eight-hundred thousand dollars' worth of construction here." John rubbed his neck and stretched.

Chris noted John's action and said, "You should be checking into your hotel. Get some rest before tomorrow's meeting with your boss, the 'honorable' director general of Sovcell."

John gave Chris a stare, but said nothing. He was too tired to argue with Chris about who John's real boss was.

Chapter 16

As they walked out of the kitchen, a middle-aged Russian, dressed in a grayish suit, white shirt, and a red tie, ran down the hall toward them. "Mr. Ashley, Mr. Ashley, we have problem," the Russian yelled in English. When he saw John, he stopped. "I am sorry for interrupting, Mr. Ashley, but our American microwave technician was picked up by militia," he said, scrutinizing John.

"Calm down, Nikolai," Chris said. "First I want you to meet John Baran, our new First Deputy Director General. He's David Chernov's replacement." Chris turned to John. "John, this is Nikolai Orlov, our manager of operations."

John extended his hand. "I'm pleased to meet you, Nikolai."

"It is pleasure, Mr. Baran." Nikolai shook John's hand and smiled, as if he was really happy to meet another American.

"Now what's this about the technician?" Chris said.

Nikolai looked at John and waited a moment. When John said nothing, he turned to Chris. "Technician was driving Sovcell car and crossed solid line on Gorky Street. GAI stopped technician and asked for papers, but technician did not have papers. No passport and no international driver permit. GAI called militia, and militia arrested technician."

Chris groaned. "Nikolai, he wasn't supposed to drive a car in Moscow, why didn't you provide a driver for him?"

"Technician took keys from driver, said, 'Go have smoke Ivan,' and took off." Nikolai raised his hands in a gesture of helplessness.

"Goddamn it, here we go again," Chris said. "We should let the tech rot in the Russian jail for a few days, just to teach him a lesson."

"No, Mr. Ashley." Nikolai vehemently shook his head. "Technician is needed to work on microwave installation. We need to finish."

Chris looked to John in an obvious deferral of the decision.

"Get him out," John said.

"Okay, Nicolai," Chris said, "Find out how much that's going to cost us."

"Yes, Mr. Ashley." Nikolai threw John what looked like a salute. "It was pleasure to meet, Mr. Baran." He turned and left.

Chris screwed up his face into an expression of weariness and fatigue. "Welcome to Moscow."

"Arrested for traffic violation? This happen often?"

"Often enough. Every time a Russian in any authority looks at a Westerner, he sees an opportunity to enrich himself, be it by a liter of vodka, a carton of American cigarettes, or even hard currency."

"What'll happen with the technician?"

"We'll try to get him out with booze and smokes, but if they demand hard currency, we'll have to "negotiate." We'll see how this thing goes."

John rubbed his eyes. "I think I'll call it a day. We'll have to let other problems keep till tomorrow. Now, where's this Hotel Kosmos?"

"It's north of here by the Ostankino Tower, close to Trush's building. Your boss booked you there; it's the pride of Soviet hospitality, all 1,700 rooms of it."

"Stop calling him my boss; my boss is in Norristown, Pennsylvania. What do you know about Kosmos? An American passenger next to me on the flight didn't seem to think much of the place."

"Your fellow passenger must know Moscow. The hotel was built in 1980 for the Moscow Olympics. It's a Soviet-style hotel, but it's better than most of their dumps. The fact that a lot of foreigners stay there—partly because of its availability and partly because of its relatively low cost—makes Kosmos a kind of Soviet version of the Grand Hotel, where people come and go and a lot happens in between."

"Like what?"

"Like anything an adventurous traveler might want. They even have a bowling alley in the hotel."

"Why did Trush book me into in a Russian-style hotel?"

"He thinks Western-style hotels are bourgeois. In one sense, he's right. You'll pay over three hundred and fifty dollars a night at Penta or Savoy.

Besides, I think everyone should experience Soviet hospitality at least once," Chris tried, but failed to put a serious expression on his face.

"One last question," John said. "Anything I need to know before I meet with Trush that you haven't already told me? Any warnings?"

"As you know, Burian Trush is in charge of long distance network for the communications ministry. He got where he is by ruthless elimination of his competition. He's smart, and he's young to hold a post like that, so bear that in mind. He's no slow leak, as we'd say back home." Chris anxiously glanced at his watch. "I have a previous engagement for tonight. I'll have the driver take you to your hotel. I'll pick you up at eight tomorrow morning for our meeting with Trush. You ready?"

John picked up his computer bag. "On to the 'Grand Hotel' for some Soviet-style hospitality," he said with faux enthusiasm, wondering just what he was getting into.

Chapter 17

As they left the Sovcell building and walked out to the parking lot, John bid goodbye to Chris, climbed into the Volvo, and before he could close the car door, Nikolai popped out of the building and rushed over to him urgently waving a slip of paper.

"I did not want to forget," Nikolai said, now standing next to the Volvo's open door. "As you Americans say, all work and no play, Mr. Baran, make you dull." He handed the slip to John. "Ticket for Soviet National Ballet on Wednesday night."

John eyed the ticket and hesitated. He didn't want to disappoint Nikolai, but ballet was not presently on his mind. "Thank you, Nikolai, but I'm not sure I'll be able to make it Wednesday."

Nikolai's expression registered disappointment, maybe disapproval. "In Moscow and not see ballet is cultural crime. Wednesday evening is special. Juliana Kovar is Odette."

"Who's what?"

"You Americans, big technology, small culture. Kovar is our prima ballerina. She dances Odette in *Swan Lake*."

"The doomed princess?"

"But very beautiful one. She is most beautiful Odette to dance on Moscow stage." John turned to Chris for guidance.

"You'll enjoy it," Chris said. "Russian ballet is extraordinary; you'll be a pleasant evening."

"Well, then," John said, "I don't want to commit a crime, even if it's just a cultural crime." He checked the price of the ticket: fifteen rubles, or fifty-five cents. The seat was probably on the fifth balcony, or however high it gets, and in the standing only section to boot. But when he looked closer, it was for Orchestra level, Row 4. "Is this price correct, Nikolai?"

"It is correct, Mr. Baran. The state provides culture to citizens. You have good seat in center very close to stage."

"Then I don't want to anger the state by rejecting its culture." John pocketed the ticket. "Thank you, Nikolai."

Appearing pleased, Nikolai smiled and marched off toward the building.

Chris tapped on the Volvo's roof. "Fyodor, take Mr. Baran to Hotel Kosmos." He turned back to John. "Don't forget to change some dollars into rubles for incidental expenses, or if you want to eat at a restaurant in Kosmos." He rolled his eyes. "The hotel has a money exchange station on the mezzanine in the lobby. You'll get 27.6 rubles to the dollar. Another Soviet rip-off. With state stores empty the ruble is worthless. It should be called rubble, not ruble."

Fyodor pulled out of the parking lot, made several turns and ended up going north on Prospekt Mira. Forty-five minutes later, John saw in the distance a building of unusual shape: half of a vertically-cut cylindrical shell. When they got closer, Fyodor pointed to the building. "Hotel Kosmos." A few minutes later, he pulled up to the entrance.

The area swarmed with burly characters buzzing around the entry door. Were street thugs holding a convention? John got out, took his bags and started for the door. The thugs stopped their conversations and looked at him with cigarettes hanging out of their mouths. He kept moving without displaying any curiosity until the hotel door closed behind him. He looked back and made a mental note to ask Chris about the entry-door welcoming committee.

Inside, he scanned the surroundings to see what a Soviet-style hotel looked like. The train-station-sized lobby was a beehive of activity. Young women milled around, dressed in polyester stretch pants and tank tops that stuck to their bodies like the skin sticks to a grape. The women's garb disclosed the most minute curves in their fleshy bodies, some...a dab too fleshy. They eyed new arrivals. Some conducted what looked like 'business' negotiations with guests waiting to check in. Men dressed in poorly-fitting suits stood like statues in corners and nooks of the lobby and gazed at the foreign guests. They reminded John of the 'honor guard' at the airport. He headed for the reception desk and joined the line to check in.

It wasn't a minute before flesh-in-polyester came up close to him and made her pitch in broken English. He ignored her. The woman persisted for a few minutes, lowering her price. When he continued to ignore her, she left muttering something. John didn't catch exactly what she said, but it didn't sound like a welcoming phrase.

When he reached the front desk, the receptionist took his passport and gave him a form to fill out. Then she filed the completed form, gave him a stamped piece of paper with his room number on it, and pointed to the elevators. She kept his passport.

"My passport," John said and stuck his hand out.

The receptionist looked at his hand and shook her head. "Come back later."

"The key to the room," John said, keeping his hand out.

"Go to your floor," the receptionist said.

"I need the key to get into my room."

The receptionist became visibly irritated, stood up and, like a Lenin statue, extended her right arm in the direction of the elevators. "Go."

John didn't move, waiting for the key. The Lenin statue stared at him for a moment and then barked a commissar-like command. "Go to your floor!" Surprised by the receptionist's aggressive demeanor, John took a step back and bumped into the person in line behind him.

"You will get your room key from an attendant on the floor," a British-accented voice said behind him.

John turned around. A middle-aged, graying gentleman dressed in a business suit shrugged. "When in Rome…and all that rubbish." He thanked the Brit and headed for the elevators.

On the 14th floor, he found a sullen, heavy woman sitting at a small desk by the glass entry-door to the hallway. The sight of the woman jarred his memory. She was the *dezhurnaya,* the floor lady. Institutionalized by Stalin's NKVD, KGB's predecessor, the surveillance scheme assigned older women to hotels, dormitories, and other buildings to keep watch. The floor lady sat there all day, allegedly to assist guests and to keep their room key for them. That way she knew everybody's business as she watched everyone come and go. In addition to having links to the KGB, she often involved herself in activities of ill repute to supplement her income. A Big Sister with elicit interests? Would his personal items be safe from her scrutiny? He'd have to make sure he didn't leave any sensitive information or valuables in the room.

The floor lady took his stamped paper and gave him his room key with a baseball-sized wooden sphere attached. She pointed to the hallway on the left. He tried to put the key in his pants, but couldn't shove it in without tearing the pocket. He walked down the dark, narrow hallway checking the difficult to see room numbers, stopped in front of 1435, and fiddled with the lock until he got it open. He stepped inside and surveyed the Soviet-style accommodation.

The room, about ten-by-twelve feet, had a large window opposite the entry door. Pale blue walls and reddish-yellow laminated imitation-wood furniture oozed a redolence of smoke and mildew. Two twin beds, of height suitable for midgets, butted against one wall and two single-drawer end tables hung from a low wainscot on the sides of the beds. A pygmy desk and dresser drawers butted against the opposite wall. The edges on the tops of the laminated imitation-wood desk, dresser, and especially the end tables, were marred with cigarette burns. The end tables, suspended from the wall, had their perimeters outlined with cigarette burns on the faded blue carpet beneath. He looked inside the bathroom. Cream-colored, sheet metal walls enclosed a small space, barely allowing the door to fully open. A small tub stood in one corner. No shower. He shook his head in amazement. *All this Soviet hospitality for a mere one hundred and eighty dollars a night?*

He took in the view outside his window. Located on the inside of the cylinder shell, his room faced Prospekt Mira and the hotel entry. Across the street on the left stood a shining obelisk the height of a 30-story building. Straight ahead was a large area, nearly half a mile in width along Prospekt Mira, and running out maybe two miles. The area looked like exhibition grounds, with fountains and pavilion-like buildings. He consulted his guidebook. The obelisk, a streamlined shaft of titanium-plated steel, represented the blast-off of a spaceship. The Soviets, his guidebook trumpeted, were the first to launch a man into space: Yuri Gagarin, Columbus of the Cosmos. The guidebook called the complex *Exhibition of Achievements of National Economy (of the Soviet Union)*. John considered the name. *What economic achievements are they talking about, and what could they possibly have to exhibit, besides propaganda?*

It was now after seven. Though he didn't feel hungry, he decided to have some dinner before he turned in; he hadn't eaten in over eight hours. He called information and was told he could have dinner in the Kalinka Restaurant. On the way to the elevators he had to pass the floor lady. Before he could exit the hallway into the elevator area, she stopped him, stuck her hand out and demanded that he hand over his room key. He obliged. When in Moscow…

Chapter 18

Hotel Kosmos, North Moscow

Kalinka Restaurant, John guessed, could seat three hundred, but he saw only three occupied tables with a total of seven customers. He stopped in front of the maître d'. The beefy woman looked him over with suspicion, said nothing, checked some papers on her podium, and then led him to a table in the middle of the practically empty restaurant. She pointed to a chair that faced her podium, and he obediently sat down.

Murky plastic covered the table, but it didn't hide the soiled tablecloth underneath. A waitress, who looked like she might've been a weightlifting contender in the men's division, brought the menu and stood waiting. The fifteen-page booklet-menu had three sections: chicken, fish, and beef. Each section had at least twenty entries. He studied the fish section and, though skeptical about its availability, decided to order broiled salmon. He held up the menu for the waitress to see and pointed to it.

The waitress snickered and shook her head.

He moved down the page and stopped on baked sturgeon.

"No fish," the waitress said, annoyance in her voice was palpable.

He flipped the pages and stopped in the chicken section. He held up the menu again and pointed to roast chicken.

She folded her arms over her chest and looked down on him with what's-the-matter-with-you expression. *"No chicken."*

He stopped reading the menu and asked her what was available.

The waitress pointed to number 16 in the beef section.

He looked and pointed to number 17.

Her expression irritable, the waitress shook her head with excessive zip.

Oh, what the hell. He pointed to number 16.

When number 16 arrived, it looked and smelled like it came out of an Alpo can. Chopped pieces of uncertain quality of beef were mixed in brown gravy with ingredients a culinary institute graduate couldn't identify. Was this a gastronomical achievement of the national economy of the Soviet Union? It couldn't be Alpo because Purina had not yet come to the Soviet dog. He looked at the amalgam on his plate and wondered how dog food tasted, but decided against trying it. He remembered the snacks in his carry-on bag and asked for the check.

The weightlifter brought the bill.

As he tried to figure out how much the Soviet culinary delight had cost him, a non-descript man dressed in a Western business suit appeared out of nowhere and sat down at his table.

"Do you have a few minutes?" the stranger said, surveying the restaurant surroundings. He sounded American with no particular accent. He looked like he might be from the Midwest: State University graduate, football player, strong-featured poker face. John gave him a puzzled look.

"My name is Roger Moore," the man said, and extended his hand.

John scrutinized the stranger. "Of course you are. *The Man with the Golden Gun.*"

"What?" Moore said.

"Nothing, just a memory flash." John shook Moore's strong hand. "Not a 007 fan, are you? What can I do for you?"

Moore ignored the 007 remark. "I believe we have a common objective, Mr. Baran, and would benefit from mutual cooperation."

"First of all, Mr. Moore, if that's who you really are, how did you know my name? And second, what objective do you suppose we have in common?"

"Your name and other information came from my colleague, Agent Parker, whom you met in Philadelphia. He said that you would be receptive to working with us. Our common objective is the security of the United States."

John leaned back in his chair to get a wider view of the stranger. He studied the man's face, but couldn't read anything in it. Dark hair, dark eyes, stocky, Moore looked maybe forty-five. "Agent Parker stretched the truth."

"He said that you would be tough to convince, but he was optimistic I could enlist your help. At least give me the courtesy and hear me out. Your country needs your help."

John rolled his eyes at the call to patriotism. "I'll need positive identification before we go any further." Yes, he would hear the agent out; he wanted to find out just how deep David was in with the CIA.

Moore produced no identification. He looked at the dog food on John's plate. "I'll buy you a steak dinner at the American Embassy, and we can continue our conversation there."

"Not tonight, Mr. Moore, I'm tired." John looked at his plate. "And I've lost my appetite."

"Then I'll meet you tomorrow evening at six in the embassy cafeteria."

"I accept your invitation. It might be the only steak dinner I'll have in Moscow."

"You can enter the embassy compound through the gate on Bolshoi Devyatinskyi Pereulok. Bring your passport." Moore stood and disappeared as quickly as he had appeared.

John paid the eighty-three-ruble dog-food bill and left the restaurant. The Soviet delight had cost him three dollars.

Back in his room, he retrieved a package of Planters out of his bag and popped a few peanuts in his mouth. He picked up a bottle of complementary hotel water on the pygmy desk and opened it; he wanted to wash down the salty taste. Warm, carbonated liquid fizzed and spilled all over his hand. He took a sip and immediately spit it out. It tasted like bubbly seawater, saltier than the peanuts.

The impact of the jet lag and lack of sleep finally hammered him. He called an end to the first day of his adventure in the Soviet Union's capital, hit the "sack," and almost crashed through it. He writhed in the tiny bunk trying to find a comfortable spot on the paper-thin mattress, gave up the effort, and closed his eyes. A blanket of mildewed, dead, hot air covered him. *Soviet hospitality.*

At 10 o'clock, his phone rang. Groggy and annoyed, he picked up the receiver.

"You have American cigarettes?" a mellifluous female voice asked.

"I don't smoke," he said and wondered if he heard correctly.

"You have American whiskey?"

"I don't have any whiskey," he yelled into the phone.

"You like company?"

"What the hell…" He realized what was going on and slammed the phone down.

Twenty minutes later the phone rang again.

"You like company from pretty Russian girl?" another sultry female voice asked.

That does it. He disconnected the phone from the wall jack and collapsed back into his bed.

Forty minutes later, a knock on the door woke him up. Tired, sleepy, and angry, he got up and walked over to the door. "Who is it?"

"Hotel security," a man's voice said.

"What do you want?"

"Your telephone not working."

"I don't want it to work, I want to get some *sleep*," he screamed. "Call off your prostitutes. I'll make the phone work in the morning."

The "security" man grumbled something about Americans that didn't sound complimentary. John waited, and when he heard the Russian's footsteps trail off, he staggered back into bed. He hoped the interruptions were finally over. He wanted the first day of his Soviet Union adventure to end—he needed rest to face the second day.

Chapter 19

At 7:30 the next morning, John reached over and walloped his shrieking alarm clock. He had slept little and was exhausted. He didn't feel like going to a meeting this morning, and he definitely didn't feel like going to a meeting with his new "boss."

He went into the bathroom to wash up and met a zombie staring at him from behind the mirror. *Holy shit. The day is just starting.* He made a hasty effort to de-zombie himself and left the room at eight. He found Chris waiting for him in the lobby. Chris eyed him for a moment and shook his head. "Didn't you get any sleep?"

"Prostitutes kept me up."

"*What?*"

"It's not what you're thinking. They kept me up marketing their services—telemarketing, to be precise. Capitalism is doing just fine in that sector of the Soviet economy. Prostitution must be their growth industry—a national achievement."

"You've now experienced Soviet hospitality, my friend. Before we go, have you had breakfast?"

"I'm not hungry. Besides, they won't have any eggs since they don't have any chickens."

"Huh?"

"Never mind, let's get going."

As they walked out, John pointed to the street thugs' convention outside the entry. "Who are they?"

"A type of Russian bear called security guards." Chris sneered. "Their job is to collect a fee from the prostitutes who seek access to hotel customers."

"Gatekeeping pimps?"

"Sort of, except these prostitutes do their own marketing, and pay an additional fee for every successful sale."

Just then Fyodor pulled up in the Volvo and they climbed into the back seat.

"I'm worried about my passport," John said. The battleaxe at the front desk kept it."

"That's normal. Every foreigner entering the Soviet Union must register with the local Department for Visas and Registration, or with the militia, who are responsible for supervising the foreigner's movement within Russia. The hotel needs your passport to register your arrival with the authorities. You'll get it back."

"So, Big Brother is watching me already."

"Every pair of eyes and ears you see could be those of Big Brother."

John rubbed his eyes to fully wake up. "I need to get out of Kosmos. I've had enough of Soviet hospitality, and I especially have had enough of their culinary art and their aggressive hookers."

"Well," Chris said, thinking. "I know that David's old apartment is already rented; we'll have to find a new one for you. In the meantime, we'll get you a room at the Aerostar for tonight. But we need to find an apartment fairly quickly. Staying in a Western-style hotel runs up the tab quickly. You'll be paying at least three hundred a night. I'll ask around." Chris lowered his voice. "These Russians will sleep in the streets to get hard currency from their rentals. And what's more amazing, it's against the law for them to possess hard currency. Caught with it, they can wind up in jail."

The driver pulled out of the hotel and headed south on Prospekt Mira. John recognized the route and said, "I thought Trush wanted to see us first thing today. Shouldn't we be going west here? You mentioned that his building was in the Ostankino Tower area." He pointed to a freestanding needle-like structure on the right. "Isn't that the tower over there?"

"I got a call at my apartment early this morning. Trush moved the meeting to ten o'clock. I don't know why. Just as well, you'll have a chance to grab some breakfast in our kitchen before we take off to meet with him. I suggest you don't go into the meeting with Trush on an empty stomach."

"Maybe I should go on an empty stomach. That way I won't have anything to throw up."

Chapter 20

At 9:55, John and Chris stood in front of Trush's office building, a twenty-story concrete structure located on Akademika Koroleva Street, half a mile west of the Ostankino Tower. The building's entrance bustled with urgent activity. Russians hurried in and out of the building as if a general alarm had sounded, threatening imminent danger. John and Chris threaded their way through the commotion and entered the building.

A fleshy blonde, wearing a pink suit and matching lipstick, already waited for them just inside the door. She made a slight nod of recognition to Chris, but didn't introduce herself to John. She led them to a security guard station that controlled access to the elevators and signed them in. Chris leaned over to John and whispered, "Trush's interpreter."

Six elevators, all apparently working, surrounded a waiting area that was crowded with buzzing worker bees. Trush's interpreter made a follow-me gesture and walked into an open elevator that seemed to be waiting just for her. She flipped a switch and pushed the button for the top floor of the building. In good English, she mentioned that Trush was very busy this morning because of a serious trouble with the long-distance network, but she didn't explain the problem. She said nothing else.

The elevator button popped out and the cage stopped. They stepped out on the twentieth floor and entered Trush's reception area. Seeing them arrive, a woman seated behind a typewriter picked up a phone and announced their presence.

A man of average build, brown hair, brown eyes, balding dome, wearing a brown suit and carrying a red folder, walked out of Trush's office and left the doors open; both of them. John examined the double-door entry that hung on two separate walls six inches apart. The outside door was made of steel and the inside door was wooden with a three-inch padding of what looked like soundproofing material. If the walls were similarly constructed, then Trush's office was shielded against RF and sonic eavesdropping. Was there a reason for it, or was it simply more evidence of the universal paranoia that beset all Russians from the street sweepers to the highest Party bosses?

The interpreter entered Trush's office and motioned for John and Chris to follow. As John had never been inside a high Soviet official's office, he looked around with interest to see how it deferred from an American executive's office.

The room measured some thirty feet long and twenty feet wide. The entry door, where they stood, was on the short side of the rectangle. Trush's desk stood on the opposite side. The long wall on the right contained windows along the entire wall. Low-level bookcases lined the opposite wall. Trush's immense desk faced the entry door. In front of the desk stood a long conference table, running the length of the windows. Three chairs stood on either side of the table.

The office had no carpet. Worn, yellow linoleum lay on an uneven floor. The desk, the conference table, and bookcases along the windowless wall were covered with the same yellow veneer John had seen in the Kosmos hotel. He examined the desk and the conference table for cigarette burns but saw none. The windows overlooked a flat Moscow skyline made up of apartment buildings of nearly uniform height. The needle-shaped Ostankino TV and broadcasting tower rose above the apartment buildings like Gulliver over Lilliput.

Wooden-framed portraits of "Soviet heroes" hung on the wall above the low bookcases. A portrait of Yuri Gagarin, the first man in space, and a portrait of Lenin hung in the center of the grouping. John saw no sign of Joseph Stalin, and he didn't expect it. De-Stalinization was official and final, even though many of the aging seniors that remembered The Great Patriotic War still regarded Stalin as *the* hero of the Soviet Union.

A single, larger-than-life portrait of Lenin hung on the wall behind Trush's desk. The Socialist god appeared to be looking over Trush's shoulders at the documents on his desk, and the image had the slightest hint of a grin, as if Lenin was pleased with what he saw. On the credenza behind the desk there stood, John counted, nine telephones; three of them were bright red. Network integration had not yet arrived in the workers' paradise. An intercom unit that looked like an operator's switchboard took up a quarter of Trush's desktop at one end.

The interpreter walked over and took a seat on the window side of the conference table. Another woman already sat on the same side. Behind his desk, Trush was conducting an intense phone conversation. His outstretched hand held a phone in space, and he was barking orders into the receiver and punching intercom keys. He did not look Russian, or, rather, he was not dressed like a Russian. Apart from the setting he was in, he could have been a CEO of a Fortune 500 company or a Wall Street investment banker. He wore a white shirt with a paisley-print maroon tie, with a perfectly centered Windsor knot: not crooked, loose, or sagging. The navy blue suit fitted him well, and it looked clean and pressed. Residue of a severe case of acne gouged his florid face. A smartly trimmed full head of dark hair completed a picture that was worthy of hanging in any town hall.

Noting John's and Chris's presence, Trush terminated his communications and strode over to greet his visitors, proffering his hand. "Welcome to Moscow, Mr. Baran," he said in Russian with a strong, commanding voice. When John took his hand, Trush shook it vigorously, as if greeting an old friend. Then he shook Chris' hand and gestured to the chairs by the conference table. He walked to the other side, and ceremoniously, like a magistrate about to hold court, lowered himself into the chair between the interpreter and the woman that already sat there. John and Chris took seats directly opposite the three Russians. The Americans faced the window and a rare Moscow sun that shone directly into their eyes. John looked to see if there were any shades or a curtain on the window, but he saw none.

Trush made the introductions. He indicated the presence of the woman on his right with a wave of his hand. "This is Sofya Perevodova, my interpreter," he said in Russian.

Perevodova nodded in acknowledgement and translated Trush's words.

John and Chris nodded in recognition.

Trush repeated the hand motion to his left. "This is Galina Samogonova, our social director."

Samogonova, John, and Chris performed their nodding ceremonies.

Trush eyed John curiously. "You do not like our Hotel Kosmos?" His tone suggested he was offended.

Surprised by the unexpected question, John didn't respond, uncertain whether his answer should be yes or no. He looked at Chris and wanted to ask how in the hell does Trush know, but then he immediately thought about the driver in the car. Fyodor was Big Brother. He wondered how many of these dumb-acting Russians understood or spoke English, and he wondered if Trush really needed an interpreter.

"Western hotels are bourgeois," Trush continued not waiting for John's response. He looked to the woman on his left. "Galina Samogonova here will find an apartment for you."

John gazed at the social director. She smiled, and eagerly nodded. Her bloodshot eyes looked like a New York City street map, and the color of her round face looked like a Key West sunset.

Trush's brown eyes bored into John. "Where is the processor equipment?" he said in a loud and accusatory tone. The moment his interpreter finished the toned-down translation, he continued his assault. "It is *your* responsibility to install an operational network."

The short hair on John's neck stood up. He began counting to ten. He wanted to fortify himself with that serene mind Klaudia was talking about, and protect himself against Trush's acrid, verbal fumes. Before he finished his count, Chris jumped in. "The equipment is in Customs. Your people in the ministry are supposed to expedite its clearance."

"Customs needs incentives to expedite clearance." Trush maintained an aggressive tone.

"We provided 'incentives,'" Chris said. "We gave Customs officials eight liters of Stolichnaya and ten cartons of Marlboro. Now they're demanding hard currency. That's against the law."

Trush shook a finger at Chris. "Do not quote the law to me in my country. If you do not install equipment, the venture with Americans will be terminated. Germans, French, British, even Finns are ready to build the network that you Americans are incapable of doing."

John's neck muscles tightened. The hair on the back of his neck that had stood u earlier began to curl.

Chapter 21

John was ready to call Trush's bluff, but then he remembered his father's Soviet tutorials. *The communists' first move will be to intimidate you.* Born in Belarus under Soviet rule, his father had often told stories at the dinner table about communists' barbaric deeds he had witnessed. His advice to John on how to deal with the communists didn't fall on deaf ears. Still, if Trush followed through, not only would the venture be finished with a loss of its investment, but his job with Cellcomm would be finished as well, and the opportunity to find out what happened to David could also be gone. He looked straight into Trush's eyes and slowly and distinctly, as is if he was instructing a juvenile, said, "We will get the equipment from Customs and install it."

Chris tugged at John's sleeve. John turned and saw a frown on Chris' face and a faint shaking of his head. Trush rose. "I have urgent communications problem with ministry transmission lines, but I wanted to meet you this morning. We can discuss Sovcell business another time. My secretary will set up an appointment." He stood and seemed to wait for the two Americans to get up and leave his office.

Chris started to rise, but John caught his arm and pulled him down. He looked at Trush and said, "I have Sovcell business that cannot wait."

"I do not have time," Trush said, anxiously looking at the flashing lights on his intercom terminal.

John thought about politely asking Trush to spare a few minutes of his time to discuss the remodeling contract. But then he remembered another one of his father's counsels. *The communists consider common courtesy a sign of weakness. The nicer you are to them, the more it emboldens their aggression.* He shot Trush a stern look and raised his voice. "This is important, and we *must* discuss it now."

Trush stared at John for a moment with an expression of surprise, as if he didn't believe what he'd heard. He seemed to consider what John had said, hesitated for a moment as if he didn't know what to do, but then sat down, saying nothing. Irritation and impatience laminated his face. John placed a copy of the Corrotto invoice in front of Trush. "This bill for $800,000 dollars was paid on your approval. I want to see a detailed statement of work performed showing how and where the money was spent."

Trush's face reddened. He shifted his eyes to the collection of Soviet heroes on the wall and then back to John. He leaned across the table toward John and, in a deliberately measured, even tone that reeked of cynicism said, "Do you question the building remodeling work, Mr. Baran?"

"I need the details for the auditors." John tried extra hard to sound firm, unyielding.

Trush sat up straight. "You do not trust me?" The volume of his voice rattled a loose windowpane behind him.

"The auditors want the details." John strived to stay calm. A shouting match would not help. "I looked at the remodeling work, and I couldn't see where and how the $800,000 was spent."

Trush's body swelled, and the cords of his neck stood out. He raised his fist and slammed it on the conference table with force. The card-table top bowed down under the force, and then sprang up. A sheet-metal ashtray on the table between them bounced into the air and flipped over, its content spilling out. The smell of old cigarette butts and ashes hung briefly over the table and then diffused toward those seated. As the smell reached John, he clamped his nose with his fingers to prevent himself from sneezing and blew the ashes toward Trush, the interpreter, and the social director. The Russian troika jerked back.

"I gave all the documents to your Chernov," Trush shouted.

John looked at Chris, who shook his head.

"We do not have the documents," John said.

"And *I* do not have the documents," Trush's voice volume dropped, but remained firm, and he sounded as if he had made his final statement on the subject.

John met and held Trush's gaze. "If you don't have the document, I'll get copies from the contractor you hired."

Trush's eyes bulged, and John thought that the next thing to hit the table would be Trush's shoe. But Trush recovered his composure. Maybe the shoe-banging rite was reserved exclusively for the first secretary of the Communist Party, and only to be performed at an international forum. Or, maybe John and Chris weren't worth the trouble to untie the shoelaces.

"I will have the contractor prepare another copy of the documents you seek," Trush said. "There will be no need for you to contact Corrotto Construction." He squeezed out the words between his clenched teeth and slowly rose.

John remained seated and glared at Trush. "I'm not finished."

"I have urgent problem," Trush said, turning toward his light-flashing intercom terminal.

The Americans remained seated.

Trush stopped, looked around his office, and then gazed momentarily at his interpreter and the social director. The expression on his face said he was confused, as if the meeting was not following some predetermined script. He hesitated, as if he was trying to decide if he should stay or leave, and then abruptly turned back and dropped into his chair.

John continued. "I want to see the capital expenditure authorization form for the remodeling work."

It was the wrong thing to say. Trush raised his fist as if he was going to bang the table with more force, but then he lowered it slowly and, opening the fist, gently put his hand on the table. He regained his composure again, and in a calm voice, said, "The authorization was verbal. I have no form for you to see. If you want to see some authorization form, look for it in America. Your company president said your accountants would generate the required paperwork." He sat back in his chair and peered at John. "Will there be anything else, Mr. Baran?" Sarcasm dripped from his every word.

"No, Mr. Trush," John said. "That'll be all for today." He stood, surveyed the three Russians, and took a minute bow. "It was nice meeting you all. Thank you, and have a nice day." He turned and started towards the door while the troika was still seated. Chris quickly followed.

"Mr. Baran," Trush called after them.

John turned.

"Before you leave the building, Colonel Lisov would like to see you."

John looked at Chris with what's-going-on expression. Chris rolled his eyes, looked at the ceiling, and shrugged his shoulders. John turned to Trush and said, "And what business would I have with the colonel?"

"It is not you that has business with the colonel, but it is the colonel that has business with you."

"And what business does the Colonel have with me?"

"Colonel Lisov will explain if you will allow it."

A session with a KGB Colonel? Whatever it was about, John needed to deal with it. "I will allow it," John said, uncertain what to expect.

Trush stepped over to his desk, punched an intercom button with excessive force, and barked an order. Thirty seconds later the man who left Trush's office earlier with the red folder opened the entry doors. He waved a greeting to Chris, and walked over to John. "My name is Arseny Lisov."

John introduced himself, and they shook hands.

Lisov looked at Trush, and when Trush nodded as if signaling approval of their previously agreed arrangement, he started for the door. "Please follow me, Mr. Baran."

The three of them stepped out into the reception area and Lisov closed the doors behind them. John glanced at Chris for a clue as to what the meeting with the KGB colonel might be about, but Chris repeated his eyes-rolling, shoulder-shrugging act, offering no hint.

Lisov turned to John and spoke in Russian, "Will you need an interpreter for our discussions, Mr. Baran?"

John shook his head.

"Very well, then, we shall talk in my office." Lisov motioned for John to follow him. When Chris tried to join them, Lisov turned and raised his hand in a stop-there gesture. "Mr. Baran only."

Surprise on his face, Chris waved an anemic so long. "I'll see you at the office. I'll send the driver right back."

John stared at Chris. He couldn't read his face exactly, but it looked like an *"oh, shit"* expression.

Chapter 22

John followed Lisov down the hall from Trush's office. They stopped in front of a massive door that might easily have been found in a medieval castle. Lisov began examining a wax seal affixed to a steel wire that looped through two heavy metal rings: one ring attached to the door, the other to its frame. When he looked satisfied with what he saw, he removed the seal and proceeded to inspect two different door locks. When he looked satisfied with the results of that inspection, he unlocked and opened the door and invited John in with a wave of his hand.

Inside, Lisov engaged two separate sliding bolts to secure the door. He pointed to a chair next to a yellow-veneered coffee table—or in this case it appeared to be a tea table—and took a seat on the opposite side. John carefully lowered himself into a wobbly chair, wondering if it would hold his weight. A rusting hotplate stood on the table with a teakettle on top. A small canister of cut tea stood next to it. The Russian writing on the canister simply said *Tea* with no adjectives or attributes qualifying it. Lisov plugged the hot plate into an electric outlet, walked over to a cabinet by his desk, and took out a cardboard box. He brought it over, put it on the tea table, and invited John to help himself to its content.

John examined the box. *Pastry,* the description of its content, appeared in faded lettering across the pale, gray sides and on the top of the box. Nothing else. No statement of its ingredients, no nutritional information, and no expiration date. He opened the box and peered at the bland, yellowish cookies that looked like they were ready to crumble at the slightest touch. Were these Soviet C-rations from the Great Patriotic War? Were they Ivan rations instead of Charlie rations? He didn't care. He wasn't having any. *And what's with the colonel's unexpected hospitality? What's he up to?*

Lisov walked over to a safe in the corner behind his desk and began twirling the tumbler. John took the opportunity to survey another Soviet office. Lisov's floor space was half the size of Trush's. Six telephones stood on his desk. Three were red. If the number of telephones the official had indicated his importance, Trush beat the KGB colonel nine to six. One of the walls between the window and the door, contained portraits, with Lenin's, the largest prominent among them. Charts, graphs, and maps hung on the opposite wall.

Lisov opened the safe and pulled out a red folder, closed the safe, twirled the tumbler, walked over to the tea table and sat down. "And how is your family?" he said, wringing his hands.

The question amused John. Asked in that manner, it triggered in John's mind an image of a Cold War spy movie, flickering in black and white. The enemy's agents in the movies had often begun their interrogations with such questions. Had the colonel watched too many old spook flicks? John felt like laughing, but kept a straight face. "I'm not married."

"I meant your parents," Lisov quickly added.

John nodded to indicate he appreciated Lisov's interest. "They are fine, thank you."

"Good, good." Lisov said several times. Then he held up the red file, as if its content contained some earth-shattering revelation. "I have here information on Mr. Ashley." Gravity weighed on his every word.

Ah, the information file. John's spy flick picked up speed. How many B-movies contained that line? He thought he was going to break out laughing, but then the urge faded as he began to wonder what Lisov was really up to. John gazed at the red folder and waited.

Lisov opened the file and slowly examined its inside as if it contained complex material, difficult to understand. John couldn't see its content, but he was sure the colonel put on an act. After a few moments of staring at the file's content, Lisov looked up. "I receive reports that Mr. Ashley is conducting inappropriate affair with Natasha," he said in a manner and tone that indicated a serious transgression had been committed.

"Natasha?" *Who's Natasha?*

"She is one of software analysts working for Mr. Ashley."

John translated inappropriate affair: Chris is screwing a Russian female employee. Was that worthy of a KGB colonel's attention? Was he missing something here?

"What kind of affair?" he asked, with a fake expression of grave interest.

"A very intimate affair, Mr. Baran."

The translation was correct. Was that a crime? He looked at Lisov with a puzzled expression. "Is that against the Soviet law?"

"Mr. Baran, Mr. Ashley's actions are socially offensive to other employees."

John gave Lisov a quizzical look and waited for the clarification of "socially offensive."

"Natasha is receiving special attention," Lisov said as if he was describing an act of crime against the State. "In Soviet Union everyone must be treated equally."

He studied Lisov, wondered if the colonel was serious. Lisov's face showed no expression. If he wasn't serious, he concealed it well. John was thinking of what to say in defense of Chris when the water boiled and the teakettle vibrated, producing a low rumble, shaking the tea table, threatening to collapse the entire setup. Steam shot out of the spout, emitting a whistling sound like a locomotive about to depart the station.

Lisov rose, walked to his desk, opened a drawer and pulled out two Russian tea glasses and a jar of sugar. He sat down and put the glasses and the jar on the table. He dumped six teaspoons of cut tea into the pot, and looked at it as if he was waiting for the tea to hurry up and finish brewing. Aroma rose from the teakettle. Darjeeling, John smelled. He waited for Lisov to speak, but Lisov remained silent. John began to wonder if it was some kind of a game the KGB colonel was playing with him. He didn't believe Lisov had invited him to talk about Chris' love affair. There had to be another reason. He looked at Lisov's blank expression and decided to play whatever game the colonel had set up. "Why are you telling me about Mr. Ashley's private affairs?"

Lisov picked up the pot and poured the tea. Looking down at the filled glasses, he said, "If Mr. Ashley continues preferential treatment of selected employees, I will revoke his visa." He took two cookies and nudged the box toward John.

John tensed. He couldn't afford to lose his finance director. That would be a severe setback for Sovcell. Russians knew nothing about Western accounting practices, and in any case he didn't trust Russian sticky fingers to handle the money. He assumed a serious demeanor and said, "I will speak to Mr. Ashley about the matter." He still didn't believe that that was the reason Lisov had invited him to his tea party. The whole teatime ceremony looked and felt contrived.

Lisov nodded his approval of John's proposed censure of Chris and abruptly changed the subject. He looked straight into John's eyes and said, "Has the cause of Mr. Chernov's death been determined?"

The question seemed sincere and had a tone of urgency. It surprised John. Why was the KGB interested in the cause of David's death? Was this Lisov's real interest, and Chris's "inappropriate affair" was only a smokescreen? John put a teaspoon of sugar in his glass, stirred it, and took a sip. It *was* Darjeeling. He peered at Lisov over his tea glass. "Mr. Chernov died from a stroke."

"Did autopsy determine the cause of stroke?"

"There was no autopsy."

"Was there no interest?"

"It was Mr. Chernov's parents' wish not to perform an autopsy."

"You do not have laws that mandate autopsy in unusual causes of death?"

Unusual causes of death? What did the KGB know about David's death? "Mr. Chernov's death was ruled natural, not unusual." John watched Lisov closely for any reaction.

Lisov seemed to be lost in thought. Then he suddenly stood. "I believe our discussions are concluded." He walked to his desk, picked up a phone, and called for the interpreter to escort John out of the building. Then he stood and waited for his visitor to leave.

John put down his unfinished glass of tea and started toward the door.

Lisov dashed ahead of John and began his routine of unlocking the door. When he was finished, John stepped out into the hall. With an expression of an official in authority, Lisov said, "Do not forget, Mr. Baran, I shall be receiving reports of Mr. Ashley's behavior." But his tone carried no urgency.

No doubt, Colonel Lisov, you shall also be receiving reports on Mr. Baran's behavior.

The interpreter met John outside the colonel's office, escorted him downstairs, and signed him out. The driver was waiting for him in the building's parking area.

On the way back to Sovcell, he thought about his meeting. He knew that the KGB didn't ask questions without a purpose or involve itself in idle chatter. Lisov's keen interest in David's stroke had to have a motive. *Does the colonel know or suspect something? Does he know about the nature of David's bizarre stroke? And if he does, how does he know it and why is he interested?*

Chapter 23

When John's driver pulled into Sovcell's lot, Chris came out of the building and stood at the entrance, waiting. He had an anxious look on his face. As John approached, Chris gave him a stare. "How are you going to get the equipment out of Customs without hard currency? The amount they want is in thousands."

"How much do the crooks want to clear Customs?"

Chris shook his head as if he didn't like the question. "I'll have nothing to do with fudging the books."

"I'm not asking you to fudge anything. How much?"

"Like I said before, three thousand. And that's in addition to the duties on the equipment. The value of the equipment is almost a million."

"Offer the crooks fifteen hundred."

"Yeah? Show me the money."

"Just make the offer." John moved toward the door. He stopped and gave Chris a long stare.

"What?" Chris said in a defensive tone.

John held back his grin. "So you know, according to the good colonel, you, my friend, are corrupting the classless society."

"What?"

"You're showing favoritism to one of your employees. You're offending the others by your actions."

"Did that KGB bastard bring that up?"

John smirked. "He threatened to pull your visa."

"Son of a bitch."

"In order not to be socially offensive, Mr. Ashley, you'll have to be equally intimate with all of your female subordinates. Think you can handle that, or will you need help?" John broke out laughing.

Chris shook his head in disgust. "Fricking commies, they're always spouting their ideological crap. They're not going to pull my visa. If they did *that*, most of the expats would be gone, taking with them American dollars, German marks, and English pounds." Chris headed off into the building.

John followed Chris into his office and closed the door behind him. Chris looked up from his notebook computer. "More of Lisov's bullshit?"

"I think the real reason the colonel wanted to see me is to find out what I knew about David's cause of death.

Chris perked up. "So what'd you tell him?"

"No autopsy, I told him. He seemed surprised and wanted to know why. What do you make of that?"

"That SOB knows something. His question isn't motivated by any concern or any human interest. Somehow, State interest is involved."

"You're right, of course, and now we have another mystery to crack. What *is* the Soviet State's interest in David's death?"

Chris frowned. "More questions, no answers."

"Now, about Trush," John said. "What's your take on our meeting with him?"

"No surprises. You can see what David was up against in his attempt to get to the bottom of the remodeling contract."

"Hey, you heard it yourself," John said in a mocking tone. "Trush promised he'll get us a copy of the contract."

"Yeah, if you believe that, I've got some land for you in Georgia bayou."

"Trush also said he got a verbal authorization to spend the $800,000."

"Maybe he did, or maybe he didn't. It doesn't matter. As the general director of Sovcell, he had control of the initial capital Cellcomm contributed to the venture. He could make disbursements over his signature."

"Not supposed to happen, Chris. Trush has a limit of $100,000. He can't sign for more than that without the board's approval."

"He can sign eight times."

John screwed up his face. "That's the goddamn problem. Cellcomm's previous CEO blew it when he agreed to let the Russian partner name the general director. Ober said it's like naming an alcoholic to run the liquor store."

"Our bulldog's analogy is brilliant."

"I don't know exactly what Trush's game is, but I'll find out. Right now, I'm ready to meet the Russian managers."

"Okay, I'll send in Markova first." Chris grinned and picked up the phone. "Brace yourself for big tits and long legs and call me if *you'll* need help."

John waved Chris off and left for his office. He didn't know what to expect, but he was anxious to finally meet the female that seemed to play a role in David's death. He was also curious to see what a "slicker than owl shit" Russian female looked like.

Chapter 24

Back in his office, John heard a knock on his open door. He looked up. A stunning, young female stood in the doorway, holding a folder, smiling. Her red, low-cut blouse and a short black skirt revealed her extraordinary physical endowments and confirmed Chris's forewarning.

"Alla Markova?" John asked after he had taken in the full view.

"Yes." She nodded with the enthusiasm of a young girl about to go on a shopping trip for a new dress.

He gestured to the visitor's chair, and Markova sat down. As she did, her skirt rode up her thigh, revealing long, shapely legs. She sat erect and her low-cut blouse stretched to contain her full breasts. She wore no bra, and her nipples made visible dents in her taut blouse. Her long, flowing hair was sable black and her pale skin looked as if it hadn't caught a ray of sunshine in months. A porcelain doll.

The color contrasts assailed John's senses. With an amatory look about her, she was a voluptuous sight. He caught himself gawking and made a mental note to talk to Chris about establishing a dress code. Markova's appearance would project the wrong image to the customers: they would be confused about what Sovcell was selling. He smiled and looked at her with as much disinterest as he could muster. "I'm John—"

"You're Mr. John Baran, our new American boss," she broke in with a smile that had a hint of sultriness. She gazed at him with inviting eyes. "Welcome to our country, Mr. Baran. If there is anything I can do to help your transition and lessen the shock of the drastic change between America and Russia, please let me know. Some say the change can be traumatic."

Her flawless diction startled John. She didn't sound Russian. She could easily have been from Nebraska, displaying no regional accent of any kind. Where would a Russian native learn such exceptional American English? He thought about exploring that question and what she meant by "lessening the shock of the drastic change," but decided to pass that for now and stick to business. He asked her for a review of the Sovcell marketing plan.

She stood, pulled a number of charts and graphs from her folder, and spread them on John's desk. She leaned over and began methodically explaining their meaning. His gaze shifted from the charts and graphs to her chest, as her breasts swelled and began to push free from their confinement. His eyes bulged, and he stared at her canyon cleavage. He waited for her mammae to spring out, but to his surprise they stayed intact. He caught himself gaping and quickly shifted his eyes back to the documents on his desk. He felt like whacking himself in the head to gain proper focus.

As she spoke, he kept nodding that he understood and didn't interrupt with any questions, keeping his focus on the charts. When she was finished, she summarized her presentation.

"As you can see, Mr. Baran, we have over three thousand pre-subscriptions to our service. The composition breaks down as follows: our government customers make up five percent, foreign businessmen make up seventy-five percent, and the remainder is made up of our new Russian entrepreneurs."

"Do all the customers have hard currency to pay for our service?"

"All customers have dollars to pay, especially the Russian entrepreneurs."

"Who are these Russian entrepreneurs?"

"We don't know exactly, since they are not registered with the authorities."

"We have a name for them in our country, and they're not registered with our authorities either."

Markova looked like she didn't know how to take John's comment. She made no response. She took a step back and sat down, her smile slowly faded, her face turned serious. She tugged at her skirt in an attempt to cover more of her thighs and waited for John's next question.

"Did the pre-subscribed customers purchase the mobile units in advance?"

"A small number did. Most are waiting for the network to be turned on before buying the units."

"Do we know who in the government has subscribed to our service?"

"Yes, except for a dozen high officials to whom our Communications Minister had issued the phones."

"Do we have any new marketing initiatives?"

"We are investigating the marketability of prepaid mobile services and rentals of mobile units by customers in Western-style hotels." Her smile slowly returned.

"Which hotels?"

"Savoy, Aerostar, and Metropol."

"What about the Soviet-style hotels?"

Markova reached in her pocketbook, pulled out a Soviet monetary note, and placed it on the desk. "Are you willing to take these in payment?"

He picked it up and examined it. The one-ruble note, a multi-colored piece of paper the size of an elongated business card, looked small for a bank note. It had its denomination written in large Russian letters across the face of the bill on one side. In subordinate, smaller print, the denomination was also written in fourteen other languages on the other side: nine in Cyrillic alphabet, three in Roman alphabet, and two in alphabets that looked Arabic to John. He *had* to ask. "How do you govern a Union with all these different nationalities, languages, and religions?"

Markova seemed surprised by the question; mildly offended, maybe. "The nationalities do not matter. There is one Soviet Union, and Russian is the official language. We have no religion to squabble about. Religion is a tool for the oppression of the weak by the powerful, and it has impeded progress for many nations." She delivered her axiom with conviction and pride.

He wanted to ask what excuse she would offer for the Soviet Union's dismal economy, as there was no religion to blame, but he let it go. Instead, waving the ruble note, he asked, "Can this be converted into hard currency?"

"Not easily, but rubles can be used for local expenses."

"Then let's conduct a limited trial for the ruble-paying customers to see how it works out."

Markova nodded in support of the idea. "We will run the trial at Hotel Begavaya. It is close to our facility here."

"Good, is there any other business you'd like to cover, Alla?"

Markova shook her head.

John stood up.

Markova sprang to her feet. "This is not business related, but on a social level I would like to give a special welcoming party for you on Friday night in my apartment." She shot John a sultry smile. She stood erect, pulled her shoulders back, and her breasts enlarged and thrust forward.

He stared at her bust. *Holy cow!*

She followed his gaze and, as if she knew what he was thinking, said, "They're real. You'll have an opportunity to verify that."

John's left brain screamed alarm, and he forced a cordial smile. "Thank you for the invitation, Alla, but—"

"You'll take a rain check?" She appeared eager to make sure that he didn't completely refuse.

"Yes, I'll take a rain check." His basic instinct wanted to keep the opportunity open.

"Then I'll leave these for your evening's enjoyment." She placed two tickets on his desk. "It's an all-Rachmaninov program at the Conservatory. You will enjoy it; he's my favorite composer." She waited until John picked up the tickets, and then slowly started for the door. She moved hesitantly, as if expecting him to ask another question or make a comment.

John thanked her for the tickets and said nothing else. Markova walked out and closed the door behind her. He looked at the tickets. *Two? Was that a hint?* She did say Rachmaninov was her favorite composer. *Oh, well,* it's probably best that he didn't take the hint. That way he wouldn't show any favoritism, wouldn't corrupt the classless society, and wouldn't give the informants anything to report to the Colonel. For some strange reason, though, he suspected that the Colonel would probably sanction his offense.

It was a good time, the decided, to talk to Chris about a dress code. He walked down the hall to Chris's office, found the door open, and walked in. Chris looked up. "So, how was your meeting with Markova?" he asked, trying to control his grin.

"Does she always flaunt her—?"

"Long legs and her huge melons?"

"We need a dress code. What will the customers think we're selling?"

"Oh, don't worry, she and the others dress conservatively when they conduct Sovcell's business. The shapely legs and big tits were for your eyes only."

John shook his head in disbelief and walked out. On the way to his office he wondered if Markova had put on the same siren act for David. She *must* have. Chris implied that David had availed himself of her assets. Was John supposed to fall for it too? It would have been easy, like falling off a log. Except, he suspected, falling off the log that Markova floated could get him more than wet.

Chapter 25

John prepared to meet with Nikolai Orlov, his Russian operations manager. Besides reviewing Sovcell's operations, he intended to find out just how frank and open Nikolai was about communist ideology. If capitalism was going to conquer Communism, as the Washington boneheads hoped, then communists must first recognize that their system was flawed. Nikolai was educated, exposed to Western ideas, and if John couldn't convince him of their system's fallacy, then there was little hope for the ardent believers. He decided to find out if he could get at least one convert. As that subject had nothing to do with operations, he needed to approach it with caution. He picked up the phone and called Nikolai.

Ten minutes later, they sat in John's office as they looked over several diagrams spread out on the conference table. Nikolai looked to be forty-something, with a smallish build, a head full of dark hair, and a round, cheery I-want-to-be-your-friend face. He had given a quick review of network operations in English. He described the overall system architecture, the completed and remaining installation phases, as well as the cutover and expansion plans. Although Nikolai's English was fairly good, save for the missing definite articles, John had offered to conduct their meeting in Russian. Nikolai had declined, saying he needed to practice his English. Concluding his briefing, Nikolai readily answered several operational questions.

John retrieved the PERT chart from his desk, put it on the conference table, and pointed to it. "How reliable is this cutover date?"

"Turning on network service is still scheduled for end of August," Nikolai said.

Remembering what Ober said about shutting the venture down if it didn't cut into service by the end of August, John asked, "Can we bring that date closer?" He wanted a safety margin in case additional slippage occurred. The only thing sure about getting anything done in Russia, David had said, was getting endlessly delayed.

"We can do it if processor racks come in week," Nikolai said, after examining the pert chart.

"Plan on it."

"I shall rework schedule for earlier cutover date."

"Tell me about your technical people, Nikolai. Are they good?"

"Technicians excellent. Trained in North Carolina in supplier factory. Everyone liked North Carolina. We want to go again."

"Did you get to see more than just the factory?"

Nikolai went on to describe in glowing terms their visits to the North Carolina beaches and Washington D.C. He was especially impressed with the cleanliness of Washington, saying that one could eat off its sidewalks.

A relative statement, John thought, but compared to Moscow, Washington was surgically clean. He let Nikolai finish his travelogue and then decided to ask direct questions, pushing on what Chris said about Nikolai: *Frank and open to sensitive discussions, won't hide behind an ideological stonewall.*

John started with Markova. "Our sales and marketing manager's English is exceptionally good. Where did she learn to speak without an accent?"

Nikolai narrowed his eyes and looked around the room, as if searching for something. Sensing Nikolai's caution, John tried to assuage his fears. "This office is clean," he said, sweeping his arm around the room.

The Russian looked at the walls, the window, and the floor. "Yes, Mr. Baran, your office is cleaned every night."

"I mean, there are no bugs," John said.

Nikolai looked at the floor and the corners of the room. "Yes, Mr. Baran, your office was chemically treated."

John wondered if his manager of operations was a comedian. "Nikolai, I meant there are no listening devices in this room. So whatever you say will be between you and me and no one else."

"Oh, I understand now. In Soviet Union we have bugs everywhere, and chemical treatment does not kill them." But he still looked uneasy and took a long moment before he volunteered the information on Markova.

"Alla Markova was major in *Glavnoye Rasvedyvatolnoye Upravlenie.*"

"The GRU?"

Nikolai nodded.

So, John thought, *Markova was a spy.* GRU was the foreign intelligence organ of the Ministry of Defense. That explained her flawless English, but it didn't explain her presence at Sovcell. "What is a former GRU major doing in a Soviet-American Joint Venture in Moscow?"

Nikolai remained silent.

"Can you explain that?" John pressed.

"I do not want to violate SSR."

"The SSR?"

"Survival by Silence Rule," Nikolai said. "In Soviet Republics, SSR says:

> *If you think it, do not say it*
> *If you say it, do not write it down*
> *If you write it down, do not sign it*
> *If you sign it, do not send it*
> *If you send it, get out of town.*"

"I do agree. Nothing pays off like restraint of tongue and pen."

Nikolai smiled and nodded as if they had reached a major agreement.

"Your rule is a good one," John said. "About the last step, how are you going to get out of town? And if you do, where are you going to go?"

The Russian looked thoughtful, contemplating John's question. He finally said, "That is problem in our country, cannot hide. So it is important to obey SSR rule."

John repeated his question about Markova's presence at Sovcell and waited for Nikolai to answer it, but the Russian remained silent, apparently invoking his SSR rule.

Was Markova spying for the GRU? If so, why? Was she really a *former* GRU major? Was the Soviet military interested in Sovcell technology, personnel, or customers? Obviously, he wouldn't get those answers from Nikolai. John moved on to probe Nikolai's supposed frank and open stance on communist ideology. "Are you a member of the Communist Party?" he asked and observed Nikolai closely. "You don't have to answer that if you don't want to," John quickly added.

The Russian waited for a few moments and then slowly nodded. Then he retrieved his Party card and opened the folio for John to see its content. Nikolai's picture wasn't flattering, but the opposite page showed that he had paid his 12-ruble dues for July.

"Tell me, why did you join the Party?"

Nikolai smiled, as if he had gotten an easy question. "To quote song: *Better to be hammer than nail."*

Now that, John thought, summarized in a few words the entire Communist Party's philosophy. "That's clever, but I have another quote for you: 'When you're a hammer, every problem resembles a nail.'"

"But it is better to hammer than to be hammered, you not agree, Mr. Baran?"

"I can't argue with that, but why haven't you hammered out the paradise Communism promised?"

"It is complicated," Nikolai said and waited, offering no more than that.

Chapter 26

John decided to push for more. "Explain the complexity to me."

Nikolai waited a beat, and then nodded. "I explain theory, Mr. Baran, putting theory into practice not always works like theory predicts."

"Let's have the theory."

"Paradise is for worker," Nikolai began. "Karl Marx said 'From each according to his ability, to each according to his needs.' Worker is happy because he has what he needs. That is worker paradise."

Flawed premise. "Nikolai, such a system punishes ability, stifles initiative, and rewards 'needs' until the entire society exists on minimal collective effort. The worker's perception of his needs always exceeds his ability and effort to produce what he thinks he needs. And why should he exert the effort to produce anything at all, if society satisfies his needs? Such a paradise is doomed."

The Russian looked puzzled, as if he was trying to understand the logic behind John's argument.

"The fatal flaw in your communist ideology," John continued, "is that it promises paradise in *this* life. Because the ideology promises what it can't deliver, it is condemned to failure from the start. You'd have a more durable ideology if you promised paradise in some next life."

The Russian looked incensed. "Mr. Baran, you're talking about religion. Religion constructs its own reality to regulate human behavior by invention of 'afterlife' reward and punishment. But it is all, as you say, fiction."

"Well, isn't communist ideology your state religion, and *it* regulates behavior not by ideas, but by force?"

Nikolai drew back as if he'd been wounded by a ghastly accusation. He said nothing, shifted in his seat several times, and began to collect his papers. John wondered if he'd pushed the Russian too far and tried to figure out how to ease out of the pinch.

Nikolai looked up from his papers with renewed confidence on his face. "We have central government to plan for prosperity."

"Where's the prosperity?"

"Soviet Union is superpower."

"An Upper Volta with a space program and a nuclear arsenal, a superpower that can't feed its people. Didn't the communists promise to eliminate the poor?"

"Communists took from rich and divided for poor. They spread the wealth."

"Looks to me like they spread poverty. They eliminated the rich and made everyone poor."

Now Nikolai looked offended. "You do not like our system?"

John smiled. "I think I'll invoke your SSR rule on that question."

"Ah, Mr. Baran, you see the wisdom of SSR rule." He seemed to relax.

John decided to end their frank discussion on that note before it turned acerbic. "Well, thanks for being forthcoming with your answers." He stood.

Nikolai rose immediately. "Mr. Baran, Mr. Ashley told me that you are looking for apartment."

John nodded.

"My uncle is in theater. He is conductor of Soviet National Ballet Orchestra. He has apartment in Moscow and dacha outside Moscow. He will rent apartment and live in dacha to get foreign money for travel. His name is Taras Provodnikov."

"Go on."

"He goes to Italy many times, and he needs dollars for expenses in Italy. I can arrange for you to see his apartment. It is more acceptable to Western standards than standard Moscow housing."

"Isn't it illegal for Russians to take hard currency in payment?"

"My uncle knows how to, as you say, get around law."

"Could I get in trouble by paying your uncle for the apartment in dollars?"

"Do not worry, you can trust my uncle."

"In that case, can you arrange for me to see the apartment tomorrow?"

"I call uncle now." He turned and started for the door, but before he could exit John's office, one of the people who reported to him ran up, looking troubled.

"Comrade Orlov!" the technician cried out as if he was in pain. "Our American field engineer expert is arrested."

Nikolai shook his head in exasperation. "Not another one," he said with irritable resignation in his voice. "What for this time?"

"For spying," the technician said.

"Spying?" Nikolai was taken back.

"Engineer was in Dzerzhinsky Square," the technician uttered, waving his hands as if animating the scene. "He was measuring RF power with field strength meter from our base station near Hotel Savoy. Militia picked him up and said he was listening to KGB communications."

"How would the dumb militia even know what he was doing?" Nikolai said.

"KGB called militia."

"When did it happen?"

"One hour ago. We must get expert out, our base station work is stopped."

Nikolai's face wrenched. "Cutover schedule is in trouble," he said, turning to John. "We will not put network into service by deadline."

John cringed. *More unexpected incidental expenses.* "Find out what it will take to get the expert released."

Nikolai dismissed the technician and turned to John. "It will take money, foreign money."

"Another bribe." John shook his head in disgust.

"As you say, money talks."

" It looks like another Soviet rule to me. If you want to move it, grease it."

Nikolai eagerly nodded his agreement. "The more grease, the faster it moves. I will find out how much grease it will take to get expert out." He started to leave.

"Nikolai?" John called out. It was after five o'clock, and he had to get going for his date with Roger Moore. He had no intention of missing a steak dinner.

Nikolai stopped, turned.

"Get me keys to a car for tonight."

Concern spread over the Russian's face. "You should not drive yourself in our Moscow traffic. You know what happened to microwave technician."

John produced his passport and an International Driving Permit and displayed them for the other man.

Nikolai shook his head and walked out. A minute later he was back with car keys and handed them to John. "Plate number is on tag." On the way out he said, "Do not cross solid line, Mr. Baran."

Ten minutes later, John climbed into the Zhiguli, and pulled out into city traffic. On the way to the American Embassy, he wondered about the exact nature of David's collaboration with the CIA. Would Moore ask John to continue David's work? How dangerous would it get? Would it compromise Sovcell? Worse, would it compromise Cellcomm and land John in deep trouble?

Chapter 27

KGB Chairman Kryuchkov sat behind his desk waiting for Colonel Sposobnik, his Second Chief Directorate analyst, and General Petrov, his military chief. He anticipated their reports. Kryuchkov knew the kind of report he would get from his military chief: dry, functional, devoid of the smallest subjective analysis—nothing controversial, safe for the general. He wasn't sure what the young, straight-shooting colonel would produce. He knew he wouldn't like all of what Sposobnik would have to say, but he wanted to hear it. He valued the colonel's opinion. He needed balance in the perspective he was seeking on the grave but necessary action he planned to take.

Following a knock on the door, Colonel Sposobnik and General Petrov walked into his office and took the visitors' seats. They said nothing other than a simple greeting and waited for the cue from their boss.

"I have discussed our ominous situation with our Defense Minister, Comrade Mazov," Kryuchkov said. He did that to secure full support of the military for his plan, without whose backing the plan had no chance. "General Mazov agreed that action must be taken to prevent the collapse of our Union. He also agreed that a state of emergency would be necessary to accomplish that goal." Kryuchkov paused.

Petrov jumped in. "Support of the military will be crucial if the need arises to enforce the state of emergency."

Kryuchkov peered at his military chief. *That was brilliant, General. Tell me something I don't know.*

"However," Kryuchkov said with concern in his voice, "if the state of emergency were to be implemented by force, a coup d'état, Comrade Mazov said that he couldn't guarantee complete loyalty of his commanders if it came to the use of force, even if it were necessary to save the Union. If physical resistance from our citizens were to develop, he said he was not sure his commanders would order their troops to fire on their own people."

Petrov frowned.

Sposobnik nodded confidently, as if what he heard was exactly what he expected. "There will be considerable resistance from our citizens."

Kryuchkov gave Sposobnik a sidelong glance and continued. "As a result of my discussion with Comrade Mazov, we have agreed to try and bring about the state of emergency through legal means."

"Legal means?" Petrov said as if the expression nauseated him, while Sposobnik nodded with enthusiasm.

Kryuchkov went on. "An order for the declaration of the state of emergency was put on Mikhail Sergeyevich's desk. I asked his chief of staff to explain to our president what we expected from him."

Sposobnik looked at the KGB chief with hopeful expressions. "Did he sign it?"

Kryuchkov shook his head in disappointment. "He is holding the document. He did not sign it."

The colonel's face dropped.

"Unless he changes his mind before August 20th," Kryuchkov said, "*We* would have to declare the state of emergency. I do not yet know who among us should sign such an order, but I don't think it will matter in the end." He looked at Sposobnik. "Your prepared report, Colonel."

"But that will be unconstitutional, a coup d'état," Sposobnik blurted out in a high-pitched voice.

"Yes, we know, Colonel," Kryuchkov said in a calm voice that had a hint of resignation in it. "And now, your report."

"Our president could change his mind," Sposobnik said, "if the state of emergency declaration is presented to him properly. It is to his benefit to sign it. And I believe that's what he really wants but is afraid to appear as the initiator of the emergency."

"Your observation is noted, Colonel," Kryuchkov said. "Most of us agree with you. Will you now get to your report?"

Sposobnik began with a long preamble about the need to preserve communist ideology in whatever emergency action was taken.

"Stop," Kryuchkov barked. "We know all that. Your report, Colonel. *Please.*"

Sposobnik shuffled his papers until he got to the last page of what looked like a twenty-page report. He scanned the page briefly, pushed it aside, looked up at the KGB chairman, and began summarizing his findings. "Declaration of the state of emergency that restricts our citizens' growing freedom which they have enjoyed over the past six years will result in opposition that could be significant and difficult to control and—"

"Let me worry about controlling the opposition, Colonel," Kryuchkov broke in. He felt creeping irritation. He reminded himself that he wanted to hear what the colonel had to say.

Sposobnik continued. "It will risk touching off widespread disorder throughout the country."

"Widespread disorder?" Kryuchkov said. "What disorder?"

Sposobnik inhaled audibly. "Deep division within the country." He peered at Kryuchkov.

The KGB chief said nothing, waited.

Sposobnik inhaled again. "Division within the military, the Party, the government, and the citizens between those *for* reforms and against the state of emergency and those *against* the reforms and for the state of emergency. Division even within the KGB." He stopped and waited it seemed, for Kryuchkov to react.

"Division within the *KGB?*" Kryuchkov raised his voice a notch. "Are you serious, Colonel?"

Sposobnik nodded several times. "It is even possible that the declaration of national emergency in our current situation could lead to civil war."

Kryuchkov did not like what he was hearing, but he said nothing, made no expression of disapproval.

"And finally, Comrade Chairman," Sposobnik continued, "you cannot trust that your orders would be obeyed. And you do not know for sure who in the chain of command will disobey it when the time comes to carry it out."

"Disobey my orders?" Kryuchkov raised his voice another notch. "Disobey" sounded outrageous to him, foreign, a notion that could have validity elsewhere, but not inside the KGB. How could anyone dare to disobey?

Sposobnik jerked back in his chair and waited, it appeared, for further reaction from the KGB chief. When it didn't come, he went on. "Many of the second echelon cadre support the reforms, but do not admit it openly, and they distrust the establishment, the old guard."

"Old guard?" Kryuchkov voice had risen to a controlled shout. "And am *I* old guard, Colonel?"

Sposobnik looked like he regretted what he'd said, but after a moment, he bit his lower lip and meekly nodded.

Kryuchkov felt his face flush, but he didn't reprimand the young colonel. He got up, walked over to the window and looked down on the statue in the square. Iron Feliks did not look back. Kryuchkov stood there for a minute and wondered what the founder of the secret police would do if he were here in this office right now. He returned to his desk and sat down. He knew what he would do.

In a monotone delivery, he began: "We're monitoring all communications on government lines and private lines of high officials and their family members. We will know who the traitors will be and we'll carry out mass arrests, if necessary." He grimaced and added, "We already know that Yeltsin and the president of Kazakhstan tried to convince Mikhail Sergeyevich to remove me and other patriots they call conservative from the offices and fill the position with liberals that support democratic reforms. We will have orders for their arrests as well." He shifted his gaze to General Petrov and nodded for Petrov to proceed.

The general began his summary. "To control potential insurrection, we will need the police in addition to the Army. We will need the support of Interior Minister Pugo."

"We have it," Kryuchkov said. His patience was slipping.

"The rest of my report," Petrov pointed to what looked like forty pages bound and enclosed in a red folder, "deals with which units of the Army, the police, and of our own troops, the Alpha Group, should be deployed where, when, and how."

"Good," Kryuchkov said with a resigned finality in his voice. He didn't want to hear the details of the general's report. "Anything else?"

Sposobnik shifted in his chair. Kryuchkov looked at him and waited. *What now, Colonel? Have you not said enough?*

Sposobnik said, "If our president will not agree to declare the state of emergency, we can try to legitimize our actions by having Comrade Yanayev, our Vice President, declare it." But then the colonel looked worried. "Our President must somehow be incapacitated to perform his duties in order for the vice president to take over."

Kryuchkov felt disgust flood over him. "*Yanayev?* That drunken clown declare a state of emergency?"

His visitors offered no opinion on the chairman's assessment of the vice president's temperance. The KGB chief looked up at the portrait of Lenin hanging on the far wall of his office. Lenin appeared to stare back at him, analyzing the KGB chairman. Except for the color of Lenin's mustache and goatee, it might have been a portrait of Sigmund Freud psychoanalyzing the conspirator. He inwardly sighed.

He considered what Sposobnik had said and wondered if at least an aura of legitimacy could be achieved by following the colonel's suggestion. He stood. "Thank you, Comrades."

Sposobnik and Petrov quickly rose to their feet.

Kryuchkov turned to Sposobnik. "I will consider your suggestion, Colonel." Then he turned to his military chief and said, "The instrument, the cell telephone, you received from our Communications Minister, is it functioning?"

"According to the minister, the network will be operational August 12," Petrov said.

"As you know General, I have advised all those in possession of such an instrument not to use it for official government business until the network is secure."

"Yes, Comrade Chairman," Petrov said. "I understand."

Kryuchkov fell silent. The visitors took their cue, turned, and left his office.

The KGB chief considered the date for Sovcell to begin operations. August 12 would be eight days before Gorbachev planned to sign the New Union Treaty. The network's unrestricted international access could be problematic for Kryuchkov's effort to gain control of the country. He would have a talk with the Communications Minister about silencing Sovcell's network when the takeover of Gorbachev's government began.

He glanced at the portrait of Lenin and groaned. "I hope, Vladimir Ilyich, our effort to restore communist order doesn't turn into a bloodbath."

Chapter 28

American Embassy, Moscow

John parked his car across from the entry gate to the new American Embassy complex. He walked into the security guards' building and asked for directions to the embassy cafeteria. He was ready for his steak dinner, courtesy of Roger More who, John guessed, was the CIA station chief. The receptionist took John's passport, logged it in, and pointed to the cafeteria location in the compound.

Inside the cafeteria, Roger Moore sat at a corner table, drinking coffee. "Where's my steak?" John said with anticipation, as he walked up, smacking his lips. Moore pointed to the cafeteria line.

They picked up their trays and joined the queue. Medium rare sirloin strip, baked potato, broccoli, carrots, apple pie, and coffee left no room for a toothpick on John's tray. They carried their dinner back to the table and sat down. John savored his bounty and took a whiff of the sizzling steak. "It's a meal to kill for in Moscow." He gave Moore a happy grin. "Thank you, Uncle Sam." He plowed in.

During the meal, Moore made small talk about Moscow weather, the people, and the economic condition. When they had finished, Moore said, "We'll talk in the old embassy building. This complex was supposed to be our new embassy quarters, but we stopped work on it back in 1985. We found out that the building was riddled with listening devices implanted by Soviet workers. The structure was a multistory pick-up microphone for the Soviets."

They left the cafeteria and walked over to a rear entrance to the old embassy building. Moore produced identification for the Marine guard, and signed John in. They walked to a second-floor office, stepped inside, and Moore closed the door and invited John to sit. Moore walked behind the desk, sat down, pulled a document from a drawer and placed it in front of John. John eyed the *Classified Information Nondisclosure Agreement*. No surprise. He scanned the room: no filing cabinets, no other furniture, not even a calendar on the wall. Was this an interrogation room? He peered at Moore. "What do you do at the embassy, Mr. Moore?"

"Call me Roger, Lieutenant Baran. May I call you John?"

"You can call me almost anything you like but don't call me lieutenant. What do you do at the embassy, Roger?"

Moore placed a pen on top of the nondisclosure agreement and waited. John thumbed through the document until he got to the last page. He picked up the pen and signed it. It wasn't his first time.

The CIA agent picked up the document, nodded, thought for a moment, and smiled. "I'm officially the cultural counselor, but don't ask me to explain the difference between sonata and cantata."

"One is an instrumental and one is a choral piece," John volunteered the distinction.

Moore showed no interest in which was which and assumed a serious demeanor. "Did you know that there are several underground levels beneath Moscow? Ivan the Terrible dug tunnels and chambers in the sixteenth century, but Stalin started a more extensive construction of tunnels and underground bunkers after World War II. In the sixties the Soviets built an underground railroad that linked the Kremlin with large underground bunkers, the headquarters of the Communist Party Central Committee, and Vnukovo Airport outside Moscow."

John shot the CIA agent a look. "Did I have to sign a nondisclosure agreement to hear that?"

Moore brushed the question aside. "We've located the railroad tunnels and were able, with some digging, to get close enough to the Kremlin to eavesdrop with highly sensitive listening devices. We've 'recruited' local Russians for the task."

John let out a whistle. "Your very own Operation Gold."

Moore looked puzzled for a moment, but then, apparently making the connection, said, "Man, that was in 1950 in Berlin, and that was blown from the very start. I see you know your intelligence history."

"It helps not to repeat it."

Moore nodded. "The problem we have is that our transmission devices on the listening bugs are too weak to penetrate the expanse of rock the signal has to travel through. We can't hear them." He looked at John and waited as if he expected John to solve his problem.

"And you want me to get you a bigger, better bug?"

Moore didn't laugh. "Your fiber cable runs in the Metro tunnels, and we've identified a location where we can dig from the underground railroad tunnel to reach your fibers. In fact, we've gone ahead and dug through, with your friend David Chernov's permission. It was his idea to use your fiber link to connect the Kremlin bugs with our receivers. We're waiting for your concurrence to continue."

"You want to use Sovcell's fiber cable to transmit your bugs' signal to some point where you can pick it up?"

"Your cable in the Ring Line Metro tunnel runs close to this building."

"Hold on, Roger. Placing a fiber access terminal in the middle of nowhere, without picking up enough commercial traffic to justify it, will arouse suspicion. There's no way I can explain it to my Russian technical manager. He'll know something's fishy. And what my Russian manager knows, you can bet the KGB also knows."

"We don't need an access terminal to use your cable. All we need is one fiber strand. We'll cut it at both ends and make our connection. We'll use the fiber to transmit the signal from our listening devices to our receivers here, beneath the Embassy. You won't even know we're doing it. All you have to do in your maintenance terminal is mark our fiber strand as defective and block it from use. In fact, you won't even have to do that. After we cut the fiber strand, your maintenance software will do that for you automatically."

"Well, then, Mr. Cultural Counselor, it seems to me that you don't even have to ask. You can do all that automatically, and no one will even know." John glared at Moore. "Do you realize what will happen if it's discovered?"

Moore nodded. "Yes, I do. And yes, the U.S. government realizes it, too. But if it's discovered, we'll respond in the typical Soviet fashion. We'll sever all connections and deny any knowledge of it."

"That's your plausible deniability?"

"We don't care. This isn't Washington—it's Moscow. They don't believe *us* and we don't believe *them* when they deny knowledge of the shit their KGB and GRU agents pull."

"Dandy for you, Mr. Station Chief. And how do you suggest Cellcomm, the American partner in the venture, respond to the accusations following the discovery?"

"In the usual manner. Deny, deny, deny. You had nothing to do with it. You didn't know someone was pirating your fiber."

John gave Moore an are-you-serious look.

Moore shrugged, as if he didn't see what the problem was.

Chapter 29

John considered the CIA scheme. If the KGB discovered the bugging operation, American Embassy officials would deny any involvement and barricade themselves behind diplomatic immunity. At worst, some would be expelled. The consequences for Sovcell, Cellcomm, and especially for himself, however, would be real; and they would be grim. What did the Soviets do to foreign spies operating inside their country? He didn't want to think about it. He shook his head slowly. "I can't agree to your scheme. It's too dangerous for Cellcomm, for Sovcell, and for me. I don't know why David went along with it." John stared at Moore. "Did he?"

Moore jerked back in his chair and sat up straight. "Hell yeah, he did, *Lieutenant Baran*. He agreed because United States security may be at stake."

"You mentioned that before. *How?*"

"We believe communist hardliners are planning to overthrow Gorbachev's government. We fear that if they succeed, U.S. security could be threatened."

"*What?* Another revolution?

"A coup by hard-line communists."

"When?"

"We don't know exactly, but when the upheaval comes and the hard liners gain control, at best we'll return to the Cold War, a Cold War II. That'll have an economic impact on us, if nothing else. We'll have to beef up our intelligence and military capabilities to the old levels, before the so-called détente with the Soviets started. At worst—and we must plan for the worst—a serious conflict between the new Soviet regime and the U.S. could break out, as we side with Gorbachev and his democratic reforms."

"You really believe that?"

"No, I've just made that up for your amusement. What the hell do you think?"

"Okay, okay," John said raising his hands in surrender. After thinking about Moore's scheme for a moment, he said, "Do you need to know which fiber strands are dark?"

"No, we can identify them ourselves. We just need your okay to proceed."

"On two conditions. First, I want to know the exact location of your cuts and splices."

Moore nodded his agreement.

"And second, whenever I request, I want unimpeded access to the information you obtain."

Moore frowned. "I can't give you that assurance. I have to clear that."

"Then clear it."

Moore left the room and returned in five minutes. "Okay, you got it, but only in matters that are likely to affect you or your company. Deal?"

"Deal."

"Good. We'll start digging, cutting, and splicing tonight, and in a few days we'll be in business."

"Why the rush?"

"Gorbachev is going on vacation Sunday, and the hardliners are now scurrying like rats to prepare for their move; they'll act in his absence. What we don't know is the exact timing of it. Meetings are going on in Lubyanka and in the Kremlin, and we want to know what they're planning."

"And I also want to know, in case my company needs to take action. By the way, don't you have moles inside the Soviet government who can feed you that information? You—we—are taking a huge risk by eavesdropping on the Kremlin."

"We're not certain our moles are reliable. We want independent verification. Besides, this'll give us the information instantly."

"One final thing," John said. "I'll have to clear this with my boss back in the States."

Moore's face flashed an alarm. "No one else must know."

"If Ober finds out, he'll fire me on the spot. If the KGB finds out, well...I don't need to tell you what'll happen."

"Like I said, you deny any knowledge of it."

"That's easy for you to say, you're hiding behind your diplomatic passport, and you're not reporting to Ober."

Moore made no response. A minute of silence passed.

"Yes," Moore finally said. "I'm asking you to take a risk."

John shifted in his chair and tried to weigh the consequences of his decision. Finally, he looked at Moore and said, "All right. Proceed." The CIA was in serious business, service to their country, and he wanted to do the same. Besides, Moore and company might be helpful in John's investigation of David's death. He decided he'd face any resulting consequences when they arose.

Moore rose and offered his hand. "Thank you."

They shook hands, and Moore escorted John back to the embassy's rear entry and signed him out.

"Keep me in the loop," John said, as he exited the building.

On the drive back to Sovcell, he was dogged with second thoughts. Was it wise to cooperate with the CIA? If the bugging scheme was discovered, well, at least he'd performed his patriotic duty—a consolation, he knew, would do little for him in a Soviet prison.

Chapter 30

The next morning, John received word that Nikolai's uncle, Provodnikov, was ready to show his apartment that evening. Galina Samogonova, the social director that Trush introduced to John during their meeting, also had an apartment to show anytime during the day. John decided to first look at what the Key West, sunset-faced social director had dug up. Whatever it was, it would obviously have Trush's approval. He arranged the appointment. He was curious to see what kind of an apartment Trush thought was appropriate for his America partner.

At 10 o'clock, John walked out into the parking lot and saw Samogonova waiting. She sat in the back seat of a Zhigulis with a driver behind the wheel. The driver puffed on his cigarette, and the smoke rolled out through open windows. He seemed eager to get going.

John joined Samogonova in the back seat and closed the door. A stench of alcohol and cheap Russian cigarette smoke bushwhacked him. He almost retched. He looked for an open bottle or a spill in the car, but he didn't find either. When Samogonova spoke to the driver giving him directions, though, he knew where the smell was coming from. He opened the back window to breathe in cleaner air, but Moscow offered only pollution.

Samogonova turned to John. "Very nice apartment in Taganskaya district. We take Garden Ring Road to opposite side of Center." She signaled the driver to get going and then lit a cigarette.

The smell of more Russian cigarette smoke, the Moscow pollution, and the stench of alcohol nauseated John. He moved closer to the open window, stuck his head out, and tried to breathe in the onrushing air like a dog going for a ride in the back seat.

The driver left the Sovcell compound, turned onto Gorky Street, then the Garden Ring Road, and headed south. John glanced back for no particular reason, but more out of habit than anything else. A black, shiny Volga trailed behind them in their traffic lane. It stood out among the dirty Ladas, Zhigulis, and Moskvichs. The Volga maintained a constant distance from them, traveling behind three other cars.

They rounded the Moscow Center and turned into Taganskaya Street. The Volga followed. They turned into a side street and pulled up in front of the first of four entrances to a long, six-story apartment building. The Volga passed them and pulled up to the fourth entrance, some fifty yards away. John had tried to look inside the Volga as it passed, but its windows were tinted, blocking his view. Samogonova pointed to the apartment building and stepped out of the Zhiguli. John climbed out and peered at the Volga. Neither the driver nor Samogonova seemed to notice it. An athletic-looking man with red hair—an unusual feature for Slavs—dark pants, and a leather jacket stepped out of the Volga and entered the building.

Oh, well. The Volga probably wasn't following them. The man apparently had business in the same building. John turned to examine the communist habitat in front of him.

Cracks in the outside cement wall of the apartment building outlined the individual prefab, concrete boxes that were stacked one on top of the other, six stories high. The common area in front of the building sprouted patches of summer weed in places where pedestrian traffic hadn't trampled them. Crumpled cigarette packages and loose papers lay on the grounds surrounding the entry area.

"Apartment on third floor," Samogonova said and started toward the entrance. John followed, curious to see what the inside of millions of apartments in Moscow looked like.

As they neared the building, he saw that the wooden, main entry door was gouged in numerous places as if it had been used as a target for rock throwing. The locking mechanism was torn out, and its hinges were ready to let the door drop. Inside, the entry area reeked with urine and feces. Soiled diapers covered tops of full garbage cans in the corner under the stairs. Samogonova stared for a moment at the two out-of-order elevators and then started up the stairs. John trailed behind, holding his breath. Stained and cracked, the concrete steps looked tentative, but they held together. Dirt had been pounded into the cracks and smoothed by foot traffic, making it look like a Rorschach design pattern. Here and there, parts of the rusty railing were missing.

The social director turned into a dark hallway, stopped in front of an apartment with no number on it, and knocked on the door. A middle-aged man in white shirt and a tie opened the door. "Greetings Galina," he said and invited them in.

Samogonova made the introductions. Then she said, "The apartment is available because Mr. Ivanov is going on an overseas assignment for a year. His wife, his two children, and his wife's mother will live with relatives in the village outside Moscow."

"Where are you going, Mr. Ivanov?" John asked.

"Cuba," he said. "Economic assistance in power generation. I am electrical engineer." He didn't explain any more, but looked at John with an expression that was laced with contempt. "I was forced to leave Iraq when your President declared war on that sovereign nation."

John restrained himself from inculcating the engineer with the facts surrounding Desert Storm and dutifully followed the engineer on a tour of the flat. He saw a small kitchen with a gas stove that looked ready to give up, two small bedrooms, a small living room with the omnipresent portrait of Lenin on the wall, and a tiny bathroom. Total living area: five hundred square feet. The rooms were furnished with the familiar brownish-yellow veneered furniture. He looked at the kitchen table but saw no cigarette burns on the veneer. The living room window overlooked the weeded common area. He decided he'd seen enough, and he wanted nothing to do with the apartment. Out of curiosity, he asked, "How much is the rent?"

"One thousand American dollars," Samogonova said.

"If he's in Cuba, how does he collect rent?"

"You will give the cash to me," Samogonova said.

John nodded. He got the picture. "Please thank the engineer for showing the apartment." He started for the exit door.

Samogonova exchanged a few words with the engineer and followed John out of the apartment and out of the building.

Outside, he asked her, "How much is the engineer paying for the flat?"

Samogonova looked like she didn't want to answer and didn't.

John repeated his question.

"Fifteen rubles per month," Samogonova mumbled as if she was embarrassed by her own answer. Fifty-five cents, John made the conversion. Samogonova quickly added, "The state owns the building. It owns all real property in Moscow, and engineer's housing is part of his compensation."

John looked at the habitat and its surroundings. "It doesn't look like building maintenance and garbage collection is part of the compensation." Samogonova gave John a sharp stare, but said nothing. He wondered if it was compensation for his services or his loyalty to the Party.

She saw John frown and shake his head, and she hastened to add: "Fifteen rubles does not reflect the true value of the apartment."

"What is the true value of the apartment?"

She looked puzzled, as if she had gotten a trick question. She seemed to take a moment to figure out the answer, and then said, "I do not know. The state sets all prices in the Soviet Union; we have no other mechanism to value property."

"How does the State determine the value of everything from a baby pacifier to an apartment building?"

"We do not ask those questions. They are not relevant. The price of everything is given."

"Given by whom?"

"We do not ask those questions —"

"They are not relevant. The price of everything is given," John finished her explanation stonewall. "Thank you for taking the time to show the apartment. I'm going to continue looking."

"You are not interested?"

"I'm not interested."

Hearing this, Samogonova became visibly agitated. "You will not find apartment in Moscow that will meet your bourgeois standards, Mr. Baran. This is not America."

He glanced at the apartment building again and then back at her. "You're absolutely right, Galina, this is *not* America."

"I will report your dissatisfaction to Comrade Trush." She lit a cigarette with shaking hands, started puffing, and climbed into the back seat of the Zhiguli. She sat up straight and stared thought the side window of her door. Her face scintillated with shades of orange and red.

Chapter 31

John ignored local convention and got into the front passenger seat to get away from the smoke. The driver gave him a curious look, but said nothing. They pulled out, passed the black Volga, and entered Taganskaya Street. John looked back and saw the Volga following.

When they turned onto Garden Ring Road, the Volga trailed behind. The driver turned off Gorky Street into the Sovcell side street. The Volga passed them and continued northwest on Gorky Street. Could it have been a coincidence that the Volga made an identical trip to an obscure apartment building in the Taganskaya district? He didn't think so, but he couldn't figure out who'd be following them, or why. He didn't think the State secret police would be so obvious; still, he had no other candidates. If someone else was interested in his movements, he had a feeling that he'd find out who, or why, in due time.

As they pulled into the Sovcell parking lot, John thought about Samogonova's threat to report him to Comrade Trush and dismissed it as typical communist intimidation. Then he thought about the engineer's apartment. If all Moscow apartments were of the same quality, as the classless society's dictum commanded, then his hope to find acceptable living quarters had been sunk by Samogonova's showing. But since the world had yet to see a truly classless society, he retained a glimmer of hope that Nikolai's uncle's apartment would somehow be different. Nikolai's uncle was a conductor of the Soviet National Ballet orchestra, a status that had to be viewed in higher regard by the State than that of an electrical engineer. Maybe the state valued Provodnikov's apartment at twenty, or even twenty-five rubles. Maybe it was worth a whole dollar.

When the driver stopped by Sovcell's door, John climbed out of the car, said nothing to Samogonova, and started toward the building. He saw her speak to the driver, who nodded and drove off with Samogonova in the back seat, puffing on her cigarette. He was sure she was headed straight to

Trush's office to inform him of the American's disdain for the proletariat's habitat. He didn't care. Trush couldn't force him to rent that dump. Besides, it was officially against the law for Samogonova to collect hard currency rent—A law the Russians, apparently, chose to ignore when it interfered with their personal interest.

Inside the building, John found Nikolai waiting for him. Nikolai looked worried; he shook his head and muttered something about the schedule. John asked him to come in and explain the problem. Seated at the conference table, Nikolai laid it out. "Militia wants five hundred dollars for release of microwave technician and one thousand dollars for release of field engineer. We must get them out. Microwave installation and base station radiation measurements are stopped."

"What's the money for?"

"For microwave technician it is fine for traffic violation and driving without license, and for field engineer it is fine for not obtaining permit. He is not charged with spying anymore."

"Since when did the militia start issuing fines in hard currency?"

"It is not fine, as you say, per se. It is, well, you know what it is."

"A goddamn extortion. That's what it is."

"Everything is prohibited unless it is expressly permitted."

"And you have to bribe to get the permit. So you're screwed if you do—"

"And screwed if you do not," Nikolai finished John's sentence.

"Offer the greedy bastards half of what they ask."

"The 'greedy bastards' will be pleased with offers," Nikolai said with confidence. "The experts will be released."

"They may be pleased, but I'm not pleased." John reached into his pocket and retrieved seven hundred and fifty dollars and handed the money to Nikolai. "I'll be broke before we're finished with this project."

Nikolai gave John a puzzled look. "'Broke'?"

"Yes, broke, busted, wiped out. In other words, out of money."

Nikolai shook his head. "So many expressions for not having money. But we Russians cannot imagine Americans out of money, Mr. Baran."

John gave him an are-you-kidding-me look, but it didn't seem to connect with Nikolai.

"To change subject, Mr. Baran, are you still interested to see my uncle's apartment, or have you found apartment with Samogonova?"

"No, I haven't found an apartment with Trush's social director, and if what she has shown me is typical Moscow housing, then I won't find one no matter how much I look."

"Not all state apartments are same, Mr. Baran."

"Oh, I thought everyone was equal, and everyone got equal housing."

"As you Americans say, some are more equal than others. My uncle is orchestra conductor. He is more equal than engineer, and his apartment is more equal than engineer apartment you saw. Uncle called and said he can show apartment this afternoon or evening, and I think you will like his apartment."

John smiled. The human instinct for money, power, and prestige was alive and well, unchecked by any ideology. The Soviet classless society *was* a myth. "Let's look at your uncle's apartment tonight after work."

"But, Mr. Baran, your ballet ticket is for tonight."

"Ah, yes." John looked at his watch. "Well then, let's look at the apartment, at two o'clock, fourteen hours, as you would say." He briefly wondered if there'd be some fallout from his rejecting Trush's approved accommodations, but dismissed it without another thought.

Chapter 32

At 2 P.M., John met Nikolai in the parking lot, ready to go and look at Provodnikov's apartment. Nikolai walked straight for the Zhiguli and started to open the driver's door.

"No," John said, "let's take the Volvo." He didn't like the Zhiguli. The Russian Fiat was a shoddy copy of the original. When John drove it, he had trouble synchronizing his shifting and ground the gears. That never happened to him before with an American vehicle. Nikolai was better at it, but its small size and poor construction made it a tin-can-coffin on the wide and wild-driving streets of Moscow. He looked around for the Volvo, found it parked in the corner of the lot, and started toward it.

Nikolai stopped John. "No, Mr. Baran, Mr. Ashley said he needed Volvo for heavy date early tonight." He seemed bemused. "What did he mean, big woman?"

"Mr. Ashley, I'm sure, has a rendezvous with an attractive and desirable female, and you can be sure that she's not heavy. It's just an expression denoting the desirability and importance of the woman."

Nikolai shook his head. "Your language is difficult and confusing. I must remember all these strange sayings to communicate."

John eyed the Zhiguli with misgiving, but then shrugged and got in the front passenger seat. He turned to Nikolai and said, "Okay, let's see how the privileged class lives."

Nikolai quickly corrected him. "We have no privileged class in Soviet Union. We are all equal." Then he grinned. "More or less."

"Okay, let's see how the more equal live."

Nikolai left the parking lot and turned onto Gorky Street heading northwest. He pointed to the back seat. "Put on cap and coat."

Curious about what Nikolai was up to, John reached back and retrieved the items: A Lenin's cap and an old raincoat. He broke into laughter. "What's this supposed to accomplish? Are we going undercover?"

"My uncle is cautious. He does not want people to see him with American dressed in Western business suit entering his apartment."

"Are you serious, Nikolai? This is 1991, not 1971, or even 1981. Brezhnev is dead. You have openness and democratization under Gorbachev. Doesn't your uncle read the papers?"

"Maybe my uncle does not believe what he reads. Put on cap and coat, please."

"Nikolai, it's not raining. I'll look stupid in this."

"Raincoat to cover your Western dress. Cap to give you proletarian look."

"I don't believe I'm doing this," John said, putting on the cap. "Don't you think it's a little warm for this?"

"Not unusual to wear cap any time."

They drove passed Belaruskaya train station on their left, and Gorky Street turned into Leningratskyi Prospekt. They passed Dinamo Stadium on the right and Aerostar Hotel on the left. Nikolai slowed down by the Aeroport Metro station and stopped on Leningratskyi Prospekt in front of a three-story bronze statue.

John looked up at the monument. No doubt the statue honored another Soviet hero. Moscow was full of bronze statues of Soviet heroes. This bronze hero had his fist raised in a half-hearted Black Panther salute, apparently ready to fight for socialism. The square behind the statue was populated with linden trees, surrounded by multistory apartment buildings, and crisscrossed by concrete sidewalks. People strode along the sidewalks in the park-like area.

A tall man walked toward the car; he wore a tailored suit that didn't look like it was made from a Russian fabric. John rolled down his window, and Nikolai waved to the man. "That is my uncle, Mr. Baran. If you will follow him, he will show you apartment. I stay here and wait for you."

As John climbed out of the car, Nikolai's uncle walked up and proffered his hand. "My name is Taras Provodnikov, and I am happy to meet you," he said in Russian. "I speak Italian and German, but very little English. Nikolai said your Russian is excellent." Provodnikov stood over six feet tall, had high cheekbones and a sharp nose. He had a head of gray hair that appeared inflated to the size of a basketball. The hairstyle looked trimmed and perfectly round. John wondered how Provodnikov maintained it—one strong gust would turn the coiffure into a mad scientist look.

"We can speak Russian," John said. "My German is rusty, and my Italian is touristy."

Provodnikov led John to an apartment building that stood on the opposite end of the square from the statue. A casual observer could've easily concluded that they were Russian, one elite and one proletarian. At the end of the square, Provodnikov walked into a six-story stone building with large windows. Not the typical Soviet prefab, the apartment building looked like it could have been in any Western European city, even on Lackawanna Avenue in Scranton, John's hometown. The building looked to be pre-revolution construction—the communists didn't build anything that solid since they took control. Inside the entrance, Provodnikov uttered a greeting and waved to a seated, female building security attendant and walked straight to an elevator cage. The attendant, a pleasant looking elderly woman, smiled at John and bid him a good day. He returned the smile and the greeting.

He examined the entry area and saw no soiled diapers or garbage, and he didn't smell any urine or other foul odor. The elevator shaft was one of those you could've seen in an old French movie. A steel frame, covered by coarse-wire mesh, exposed the lifting mechanism and its cables. Provodnikov opened the cage door, and they walked inside. He closed the door with a clank that reverberated through the open shaft, and then he pressed the number four button. The cage dropped three inches and stopped with a loud bang. A whining noise began and the cage started its slow rise. Half a minute later, the number-four button popped like a cap gun. The cage stopped at the fourth floor and then dropped another three inches with another loud bang. John made a mental note to take the stairs next time, if there'd be a next time.

The conductor opened the cage door, walked out, turned, and pointed to the misalignment between the bottom of the elevator and the level of the floor. John stepped up the three inches onto the fourth floor. Provodnikov walked directly to Apartment 128 fifteen feet in front of the elevator, unlocked the door, opened it, and invited his prospective tenant to come in.

Inside the apartment, John opened his eyes wide as he examined the furnishings. No yellow veneer in sight. The pieces were solid wood: oak, maple, birch. The living area looked the size of the Cuba-bound engineer's entire apartment, and the high ceiling gave it an airy feeling.

"Please look," Provodnikov said, sweeping his hand around. "Furniture is from Italy and Denmark, rugs from Azerbaijan, and appliances are German, and they work."

John took a slow walk through the dining room, kitchen, bedroom, and stepped inside the living room. His eyes focused on an antique piece. A beautifully refinished, red walnut C roll-cylinder desk stood by the window, next to a piano.

"The desk is one hundred years old," Provodnikov said without waiting for John's question.

Opposite the desk, bookcases covered the entire length and height of the wall. Classics, music, and travel books populated the shelves; many were in Italian and German, and some in English. John pointed to a guidebook on London and turned to Provodnikov. "You read English."

"With a dictionary and very slowly."

John moved from section to section of the bookcase, examining the content and nodding his appreciation of Provodnikov's selections. A treasure of literature and travel books lined the shelves.

Opposite the window, a long, black leather couch took up most of the wall. Above the couch was a grouping of portraits and paintings, mostly Impressionist. He recognized Tchaikovsky, Rimsky-Korsakov, a copy of Van Gogh's *The Starry Night*, and a copy of Degas' *Ballerina*. He saw no portraits of Soviet heroes and no portrait of Lenin. Provodnikov's apartment was definitely more equal than the electrical engineer's apartment, and the inequality was incredible. But could the absence of any sign of Lenin in the apartment raise a question about Provodnikov's loyalty? John concluded that the conductor was either above reproach, or simply didn't care. *This was it*, he decided, he had found what he wanted. He tried not to show his enthusiasm and asked, "How much?" He turned to examine the books on the shelves, trying to act as if he was disinterested.

Provodnikov tapped him on the shoulder, and when John turned, the conductor put his index finger on his lips. "We talk outside," he whispered and moved toward the door.

Chapter 33

Leaving the apartment, John noticed a red metal box mounted by the door. He pointed to it and looked to Provodnikov for an explanation.

"It is part of the apartment security system," Provodnikov said. "It is connected to central monitoring station. If you rent the apartment, I will explain its operation."

As they walked out of the apartment, John wondered why Provodnikov insisted on talking outside. Was the apartment bugged? Was there no privacy in Moscow even for the privileged, the elite? He concluded that the answer to both questions was probably yes, and that if he moved in, he would be spied upon as well. He'd have to make sure that the constant caution he'd have to practice wouldn't morph into the paranoia that seemed to have shot through the entire fabric of Soviet society.

Outside in the square, Provodnikov led John to a hidden spot among the trees. He looked around, and when he seemed satisfied that no one could hear him, he moved closer to John and whispered, "Two thousand American dollars."

John debated with himself if he should counter the offer. He didn't want to lose the apartment, but if he didn't try to bargain, he wouldn't get any reduction in rent. He decided on what seemed to be a working formula in the workers' paradise: offer no more than half of what they ask. "One thousand dollars," he said and tried to sound indifferent.

Provodnikov said nothing and started walking randomly among the trees. John kept following. After a minute, Provodnikov assumed another secret-telling position and whispered into John's ear: "One and one-half thousand. I can get more from Germans but I do not like Germans."

John thrust his hand forward in a you-got-a-deal manner, and they shook hands.

"When can I move in?"

"Any time. I shall transfer my personal things to my dacha right now."

John checked his cash. "I don't have the money now. Can I give it you tomorrow?

"Do not give me money directly. Wire the dollars into this bank account in Milan." Provodnikov gave John a piece of paper with wire transfer information. "Will you be able to do that?"

John nodded.

"If anyone asks, you are my guest in the apartment as part of cultural exchange. You are not paying any rent."

"I see…and what culture are we exchanging?"

"You are American expert in theater program planning, and we are exchanging our experiences."

"Of course we are," John said and shook his head in amazement. He looked at the wire-transfer information. "Isn't a foreign bank account illegal for Russian citizens?" He was curious about how Provodnikov would answer the question.

"Illegal is for masses."

But not for the privileged or the elite, John thought. Some classless society this was. "Okay, we have an agreement, and I'll move in later today."

They shook hands again and parted company. On the way back to the car John stopped to look at the statue. The inscription on the brown marble base of the monument read "Ernst Telman."

"He was German anti-fascist," Nikolai said when John climbed into the car. "This is Telman Square."

John looked at the statue again. "I didn't think there were any Germans deserving a statue in the Soviet capital."

"He was a great communist, and a great communist always deserves a statue."

"Nikolai, sometime you'll have to explain to me the real difference between the Nazi brand of socialism and the communist brand of socialism. At the core, I can't distinguish between them. Under different banners, Hitler and Stalin ruled their countries in the same way—with terror."

Nikolai drew back. He looked offended. "Mr. Baran, I am surprised at what you said. You cannot compare Communism to fascism. We have spilled our blood defending Mother Russia against Hitler's fascism."

John saw the Russian become agitated and said, "Yes you did, Nikolai." *Better get off the subject.* Mother Russia, Fascism, Great Patriotic War—touchy subjects. He peered at Ernst Telman. The German communist would turn in his grave if he saw what the proletariat revolution had wrought.

Nikolai started the car. "Do you want to go back to your office, Mr. Baran?"

"No, I need to go to the hotel and check out. I'm moving into your uncle's apartment."

"Congratulations. You have joined elite ranks of citizens."

John gave the Russian an uncertain look, but didn't comment on the elite ranks he was joining. He didn't know what that really meant.

On the way to the hotel, he wondered what an expert in theater program planning did, and what would happen if his expertise and credentials were challenged by some intrusive state official. He decided that he could bullshit his way through by mouthing GAANTs and PERTs, effective smokescreens if you didn't know what was going on.

Chapter 34

Later that evening in his new apartment, John prepared for his "culture" night: *Swan Lake,* 7 P.M., Soviet National Ballet.

At six o'clock he put on his culture clothes that included a jacket, shirt, and tie. Russians traditionally dressed up for theater performances, and he didn't want to appear an ugly American cultural barbarian. He left his apartment, walked across Telman Square to the Aeroport Metro station, purchased a token for the equivalent of two cents, slid through the turnstile, and walked down to the platform.

The descriptions he'd read of Moscow subway-station construction fascinated him. The stations' walls were inlaid with black and white marble that came from the deposits of the Ural Mountains, Middle Asia, and the Caucasus. Velvet-pink marble from regions of the Russian Far East covered the columns. The most ancient decorative material used, some two billion years old, was a coarse-grained pink marble from the southern shore of Lake Baikal.

Other materials used were gray, yellow, green, and brown marble, rhodonite, onyx, and corals, and fossilized shellfish one hundred and fifty million years old. The Mayakovskaya Metro station was especially striking with its vaulted ceiling inlayed with mosaic design. He had seen references to the stations as "Underground Palaces" and "Museums of Art," but he thought that if the stations didn't quite live up to those descriptions, they were at least unique museums of geology. The Metro system, with its nearly 130 stations, carried some seven million riders daily, and was the second most heavily traveled rapid transit system after Tokyo's subways.

The digital count-up clock above the track tunnel indicated that forty-five seconds had elapsed since the last train left the station. Another display showed the current time: 18:15, or 6:15 P.M. In less than fifteen seconds, a deafening screech announced the arrival of the next train. It carried with it a blast of warm air and the smell of oil. John boarded the train, sat down, and surveyed the passengers. Nine out of ten were reading. Most read books, some read newspapers. Gorbachev's openness and democratization reforms allowed them to read whatever they wanted. If all the reading broadened their knowledge of the world and exposed them to different cultures and different ideologies, he wondered if the current situation in the Soviet Union could exist for long.

Had Lao Tzu been advising the Politburo, he would have raised an alarm. He would've said the communist rulers needed to keep their subjects' stomachs full and their heads empty. Keep them from obtaining knowledge and developing desires that the rulers couldn't fulfill. The conditions now were just the opposite. The Russians were developing a strong desire for Western products and the Western way of life. Communism had failed miserably in developing consumer-oriented products and services. Russians' pursuit of hard currency was a pursuit of what the hard currency represented: access to all things Western—functioning appliances, dependable automobiles, durable and fashionable clothes, cosmetics, and, of course, Marlboro cigarettes.

The PA system announced the train's arrival at his destination: Sverdlov Square in the center of Moscow. He stepped out onto the platform and took the escalator. He spent three minutes on fast-moving stairs before reaching street level. He estimated the depth of the station to be over two hundred feet. He recalled the intelligence briefings during his training. The Metro system doubled as a fallout shelter, and at a deeper level—below the Metro station and its tracks, impenetrable to a nuclear blast—Stalin had built an elaborate communications and command system. John wondered if the system was still operational. More likely, he thought, it had fallen into disrepair and become another victim of Soviet government standard maintenance policy: neglect.

He exited the station and saw the Bolshoi Theater and the recently formed Soviet National Ballet theaters to its left. Since the Bolshoi offered no performances during the summer, Russian ballet lovers had been in withdrawal. As Gorbachev's reforms relaxed control of the arts in the late Eighties, the Soviet National ballet was formed. The theater's principal dancers came from the upper ranks of the great ballet companies and academies of Russia, and other Eastern Bloc countries. The Soviet National Ballet was exercising new artistic freedom made possible by the reforms.

An usher led John to a seat in the center of the orchestra level, four rows from the conductor's stand. At seven o'clock the lights dimmed. The conductor came out, bowed to the applauding audience, turned to face the orchestra, raised his baton, and began the overture. John liked Tchaikovsky's music for its simplicity and precision, even though it was a bit too lyrical for him. It drowned the listener in emotions of suffering of one kind or another, and it sparked a craving for a few heroic bars from Beethoven. He sat back to enjoy the overture and looked forward to seeing the most beautiful Odette to dance on the Moscow stage.

The overture ended. The curtain drew open, and lively, colorful, village dancers in the First Act set up the mood of the audience. As the Second Act began, the crowd broke out in loud cheers and applause at the appearance of the Princess Odette. John sat up in his seat and focused on the ballerina. The elegant clarity and grace of her opening movements stunned him. He hadn't seen anything like that in Scranton or New York. As she leaped through the air, he felt as if he was being lifted out of his seat. For the remainder of the performance he felt as if he was floating. He regained full awareness at the end of the third act, when the roar of the audience marked the end of the performance.

During the curtain call she was close enough for him to see her beautiful face clearly, as she moved toward the front of the stage to take bows and receive flowers. Her deep auburn hair, high cheekbones, pale face, and sparkling emerald eyes hypnotized him. He was desperately hoping to catch her glance. When he didn't, and the final curtain call ended, he sank in his seat. He sat there trying to comprehend what had just happened. He didn't know. When he finally stood to leave, he was the last one in the theater. As he boarded the train back to his apartment, he knew that he had to see the ballerina again. Offstage.

He exited at Aeroport Metro and started across Telman Square toward his apartment building. The ballerina still dancing in his head, he paid no attention to his surroundings. When he was in the middle of the square, he felt a sharp jab in his back. He stopped and quickly turned.

A dark-skinned man, who looked like a gorilla, pressed a Makarov pistol into his abdomen. John stared at the gorilla in disbelief.

"Hands up," the gorilla said in Russian.

Chapter 35

An icy chill struck the back of John's neck and crept across his shoulders. He looked at the gorilla's face, but saw no anger or menace. Strange, his assailant looked more like he was about to introduce himself. He appeared to be from the South, one of the Caucasus republics. Armenia, John guessed. Armenian gorilla. "Hands up," the man said again and took a step back.

John brought his hands up slowly. When they reached the level of the pistol, he swung his left hand toward the gun, grabbed the weapon by its barrel, and showed it to his right. Simultaneously, he swung his right hand to the left and slammed the gorilla's wrist. In a split second he had the Makarov in his left hand, holding it by its barrel jacket. Gorilla's right hand flagged empty.

For a moment, the assailant stood and stared at John wide-eyed, surprised. Then he reached inside his jacket and pulled out what looked like a junior Rambo knife. Holding it straight out, he made a thrusting jab into John's stomach. John jumped back, avoiding the blade. Leading with the Rambo blade, the gorilla advanced. John executed a scissors kick, slamming his right foot into gorilla's groin. The assailant bent over, moaned and screamed and lowered the knife, but he didn't drop it. John repeated the kick into the man's hand and the knife flew. Then John dropped the pistol, opened his palms, and, using them like cymbals, slammed them on the gorilla's ears. The assailant cried out in pain and covered his ears with his hands. John delivered a hatchet cut to the base of the gorilla's skull, and the Armenian collapsed.

He quickly looked around the square. It was nearly eleven o'clock at night, and he saw no one in the immediate area. In the dimly lit area by Leningratskyi Prospekt he noted people moving. They were running toward the gorilla's screams. They were running toward him. He picked up the Makarov, wiped it clean, dropped it on top of the Armenian, and left the scene trotting. He passed his apartment building and circled the block. Then he circled the block again in the opposite direction, and when he was sure no one followed him, he entered his building.

The security attendant looked up from her reading. "Good evening." She held out a small paper bag to him. "For you, some fresh cucumbers from our garden."

Overcome by surprise, John stood glaring at the woman.

"My name is Masha," the attendant said.

Recovering, he took the cucumbers, thanked her, and introduced himself. With the scarcity of food in Moscow, the offering was a genuine expression of the Russian peoples' deep-seated sense of hospitality, a characteristic the communists hadn't been able to eradicate entirely. He thanked her again and started for the stairs.

"Have you come through the square?" she asked before John could reach the first step. "Did you see a man lying on the ground, screaming? They say he was attacked and is badly hurt."

"I came in the back way, and I didn't see anything," he said, not wanting to talk about the screaming gorilla. He hurried to his apartment, skipping steps as he jumped the stairs.

He opened his door, ducked inside, and slammed the door shut. He stood and listened. Silence. Without turning on the lights, he walked to the living room window and looked down on the square. A dozen people surrounded the fallen man. Some helped him to get up, some issued instructions, some watched. Two militiamen were running from Leningratskyi Prospekt toward the scene. He pulled the curtains shut, went into the kitchen, and sat down.

His hands shook. He got up and rummaged through the kitchen cabinets looking for something strong and found an unopened liter of Stolichnaya. *Provodnikov won't mind*, he told himself, broke the seal, and dumped several ounces into a glass. He downed half of it and waited for the vodka to take effect. Within a minute the trembling and shaking subsided, and alcohol spread a warm, calming feeling throughout his body.

It gave him the illusion that all was well. But all was not well. He knew it, and fear crept in.

He walked into the living room, sat down on the couch, and closed his eyes. His brain kept rerunning the gorilla scene in his mind. He sat motionless, watching the reruns and wondering if serious fallout would result from his actions—could not predict or control the environment he was now in.

Banging on his apartment door jarred him. He jumped off the couch. He didn't expect anyone. He tiptoed to the door, stood, waited. The banging repeated, louder. Fearful that the Armenian had somehow managed to alert his accomplices and send them after him, he said in Russian, "Go away, or I'll call the militia."

"We are the militia," replied a loud voice behind the door.

The shaking returned in an instant. His fear intensified. Images of labor camps in Siberia flashed through his mind. He could already see it in the *International Herald Tribune*: AMERICAN ASSAULTS RUSSIAN NATIONAL, GETS HARSH SENTENCE. He quickly checked outside of his windows: no fire escape ladder, too high to jump. There was no way out. He trudged back to the door, took a deep breath, and opened it.

Two militiamen stood in the hall, their faces angry, their hands on their holsters, ready, it seemed, to use their side arms. An image of his father flashed in John's mind, and he heard his father's final admonition before John left for Moscow. *Don't ever get tangled up in the Soviet 'justice' system. If you do, you're finished.*

He stared at the militiamen. *I'm finished. What a fricking way to go.* He braced himself.

The older one spoke. "Who are you? What are you doing here?"

The younger one said, "And where is the conductor?" He eyed John with suspicion.

Relieved that the militiamen said nothing about the Armenian gorilla, John said, "Mr. Provodnikov isn't here. I'm Mr. Provodnikov's guest as part of cultural exchange with the United States." He hoped they wouldn't ask for details.

"Passport and visa," the older one said, sticking out his hand.

John retrieved and handed the documents to the militiaman.

The militiaman examined the documents and looked up. "You entered our country on Monday?"

John nodded.

"What is your role in this cultural exchange?"

Oh-oh. "I'm an expert in theater program planning." He prayed he didn't have to get into the GAANT and PERT bullshit—he hadn't yet made it up.

The militiaman entered something in a little notebook and gave back John's documents. "We have received an intruder alarm at the central monitoring station and we must examine the apartment."

John glanced at the security box: the red light was on. In his excitement he forgot to call the monitoring station with the code Provodnikov gave him to disarm the system. When he realized what had happened, he felt the tension in his body ease. He stepped aside and invited the militiamen in. They walked in and began checking the apartment. When they finished their inspection, the older one said to John, "Call the monitoring station and give them the code. We want to see the light turned off." John obeyed. The red light went out.

The younger man snorted and began to lecture John for a long minute on following the rules of the security system. When he finished his lecture, he turned to the older one and waited. The senior man cocked his head toward the door. John opened the door and let them out. Junior turned and said, "Do not forget your alarm next time. You do *not* want to see us again." He closed the door behind him with unnecessary force.

The *International Herald Tribune* article dissolved. He felt relieved, but anxiety lurked in his mind. What was the assault about? Was the Armenian gorilla attempting a robbery, or was John a target for some other reason? If it was the latter, what reason was there for the attack? And would it happen again?

Since the gorilla didn't accomplish his mission, whatever it was, John expected a second attempt to be made by whoever was behind the first.

Chapter 36

The next morning, John arrived in his office early and immediately called Nikolai, who came with documents in hand and looked ready to launch into a litany of network installation problems.

John pointed to the documents. "Before we get into that, I want to ask you for a very important favor." He gestured toward the conference table.

"I am happy to do favor, if I can. What kind of favor?" Nikolai asked.

"I want to meet Juliana Kovar, the ballerina that danced Odette in *Swan Lake* last night. You remember, you said she was the most beautiful Odette to dance on Moscow stage. Can you arrange that for me?"

Nikolai's mouth gaped open. After a moment, when he seemed to have fully grasped John's request, he shook his head. "Mr. Baran, what you ask is not possible." Then, as if to stress his statement further, he said, "As you would say, forget it."

"What do you mean by *forget it?*" John asked. Nikolai's idioms and colloquialisms were often misused.

Nikolai had a ready response. "Kovar's father is *persona non grata.*"

Another misapplied jargon, John thought. "And what do you mean by that? And what does her father have to do with this?"

"Her father was famous physics professor in Moscow State University. He was suspended from his position, and is under investigation for ideological subversion."

"For *what?*"

"In classrooms he praised Americans for their achievements in solid state physics. The KGB Directorate for Ideology and Dissidents interpreted his actions as praise for capitalism and said that it was ideological contamination of students."

"Are you serious? That sounds made up. The Cold War is over, and we're in the era of *Glasnost*. Democratization has come to the Soviet Union, and you can say anything you want now."

"Glasnost or not, I would not say anything I wanted to. But you are right, Mr. Baran, it sounds, as you say, made up, but many things KGB claims is made up. Truth is that university administration does not like Professor Kovar. He criticized administration and the state for dictating curriculum that he said was deformed by propaganda. He is too independent; he does not toe Party line."

"Maybe he doesn't toe the Party line because he isn't a blind communist, and he doesn't share your ideology."

"Ah, Mr. Baran, that is his problem."

"Nikolai, I want to meet the ballet dancer, not her father. Is she under suspicion too? Don't tell me she's spreading ideological contamination in the theater by praising American dancers?"

"No, she is not under suspicion, and she is definitely not praising any American dancers." Nikolai's tone and inflection said that the latter was not possible. "She is devoted to her father and fears that if she is seen in company of American, she could make worse his situation and be placed under suspicion herself. She would not take risk."

"Suspicion of what? I'm an American businessman trying to sell her a mobile telephone service. What's suspicious about that?"

Nikolai shrugged. "Who knows, KGB will fabricate something. They are experts in fabricating suspicions. I can help you meet anyone in theater except Kovar."

"I don't want to meet anyone in theater. I want to meet Juliana Kovar. If she can't be seen with an American, then we will meet where we won't be seen."

Nikolai shook his head. "There is no such place in Moscow."

"Then we will meet outside Moscow."

Nikolai gave John a questioning look. "How will you do that?"

"I don't know, but I'm depending on you to figure that out."

Nikolai thought for a few moments and then said, "I do not think Kovar will risk meeting with American when her father is under investigation. So, Mr. Baran, there is nothing, as you say, to figure out."

"Can you let her decide for herself?

Nikolai grimaced, fiddled with his cuffs, appeared to ponder the situation. Finally, his face lit up. "There may be way." He looked up at the ceiling as if it might have the answer. "Okay, Mr. Baran, I will see what I can do."

"Thanks, I owe you one."

"You owe me one, Mr. Baran? One of what?"

"Never mind." John pointed to the documents in his hand. "What've you got there?"

Nikolai spread a marked-up copy of a Moscow map and pointed to the southwest sector. "We need coverage in area of Kievskaya train station. Western-style hotel opened in area, and we have no site for our base station and antennas. I visited hotel twice to get agreement for site, but Russians in charge of building said no."

John looked at the location of the hotel. "Oh, I think I may be able to help. I know the American manager of that hotel and I'll speak with him about our need. I'm sure he'll lease space to us on his hotel's roof."

"We need to move quickly because many Western business people are guests in hotel."

"I'll deal with it right now," John said. He picked the phone and called Harry Morton. He explained to Harry what he needed, and Harry agreed to meet for lunch at his hotel to discuss the matter. John turned to Nikolai. "I'll need a car at about eleven to go to the hotel and take care of our antenna location problem." He picked up the map. "I'll take this with me. Anything else on your mind, Nikolai?"

"No, that was last location problem. Now we will have all sites we need for Phase One of network." Nikolai gathered his documents. "Technicians will be waiting to go over and survey hotel property as soon as you get agreement, Mr. Baran." Seemingly satisfied that his problem would be solved, Nikolai left.

John looked at the map and briefly wondered if Harry could prevail over the Russians who had twice turned down Nikolai's request.

Chapter 37

At 11 o'clock, John walked out to the parking lot and saw a driver standing next to a Zhiguli, waiting. He walked up to the driver and said, "Get me the keys to the Volvo, and I won't need you for the trip, I'll drive myself." The driver gave him a curious stare and rushed off into the building.

Two minutes later, Nikolai came out with the Volvo keys, but he didn't hand the keys to John. Instead, he said, "It is not safe to leave foreign car unattended in Moscow. You must let the driver take you. He can stay with the Volvo. If you drive yourself, Mr. Baran, then take the Zhiguli."

That Russian piece of shit? He extended his hand, palm up. "The Volvo keys, Nikolai."

The Russian groaned and dropped the Volvo keys into John's palm. He shook his head in obvious disapproval of John's disregard for the security of the vehicle, mumbled something, and stumped off toward the building.

John left the parking lot, turned onto Gorky Street heading southeast, turned right onto the Garden Ring Road and headed south toward Harry's hotel near the Kievskaya train station. He arrived at the hotel and, mindful of what Nikolai had said, parked in a fenced-in, paid lot that had an attendant. He headed for the hotel entry, passed the security guards, walked into the lobby, and took in a sight that was uncharacteristic of Moscow.

A fountain, shooting water twenty feet into the air, stood in the center of a spacious lobby. Above the fountain, a stained glass dome crowned the ceiling. Rare Moscow sunlight shining through the colorful dome made the lobby look like a small cathedral. Shops with Western merchandise and restaurants populated the lobby perimeter. The bright lights and vivid colors made him feel momentarily homesick. He looked toward the reception area and saw Morton coming out from behind the front desk. Morton waved and trotted in John's direction.

"I'm glad to finally see a friendly face today," Morton said, vigorously shaking John's hand.

John looked around. He didn't see any unfriendly faces. Western hotel guests milled around, but their faces didn't look particularly unfriendly— resigned or dejected, maybe, but not unfriendly. "Having a trying day?"

Morton pointed to a café on the perimeter of the lobby and led the way. "I've been battling with my Russian partners all day." When they sat down, ordered coffee, and made lunch selections, Morton leaned across the table, lowered his voice, and said, "The thugs, I mean my Russian venture partners, want to wrestle control of this property from my company. We put in millions of dollars into remodeling this dump and they put in zilch. Pulling out hard currency from operations isn't enough for them. The bastards want control of the hotel." Morton looked around as if to see if anyone heard him. Western guests occupied other tables, but none looked their way. Then he lowered his voice again. "If they get control of this property, their greed will strangle this hard-currency goose. They know shit about hospitality management, and this will become another Soviet dump."

"How are you battling them?"

"In court."

"Russian court?"

"Hell no. I'd have as much chance in a Russian court as a goldfish would in a tank of piranhas. My case is in the Stockholm arbitration court."

John pictured a tank of Fantails, Lionheads, and Bubble Eyes being shredded by the razor teeth of the South America carnivore. "Are we the goldfish here, and our Russian partners the piranhas?"

"You're catching on, mate." Morton eyed the café and the lobby the way an artist would admire his work. Then his face turned serious. "The only way they'll get control of this property is over my dead body."

"Don't say that. I hear murder is part of their corporate strategy."

"I'm betting they wouldn't dare. Too much visibility. But enough about my problems. How're you doing? How's your venture going?"

"So far, I don't see any visible takeover conspiracy by our partner."

"You're not looking hard enough."

"Well, except for maybe a stealth conspiracy, our investment imbalance is the same. Our Russian partner contributed zero capital. He claimed that the operating license he brought to the venture was worth more than the capital we contributed. We're not operational yet, and they've already pulled hard currency out of the venture. Much of it, I think, illegally."

"Legal, illegal, whatever works for them. Now, how can I help?"

John explained that he needed closet space for network base station equipment and space on the roof of the hotel for antennas to gain coverage for mobile services in the area.

"How will you connect to your switch?" Morton asked.

"In this case, a microwave shot to our facilities. We'll put the microwave dish on your roof together with the mobile telephone antennas. Most of our other connections use fiber optic cable laid in the Metro tunnels."

Morton responded without hesitation. "Send your engineers to pick out the spot they want."

"Our engineers have already talked to your building people about our needs, and they were turned down."

"The bastards are probably looking for hard-currency bribes. I'll take care of it."

"Thanks for your help. In appreciation, can I buy dinner at the restaurant of your choice?"

"Best offer I've had all day, and I'm going to take advantage of that one. Savoy restaurant won't break you?"

"I don't know. I've never eaten there." John picked up the check.

Harry snatched the check out of John's hand. "This is my hotel, you're my guest." Just then, a hotel employee rushed over from behind the front desk and said that Morton was needed in the office right away. Morton made a face and rolled his eyes. He got up from the table. "Sorry, I have to run. I'll call you about our dinner date."

John finished his coffee and left the café and the hotel. When he came to the spot where he had parked his car, he didn't see the Volvo; the parking space was empty. He searched the lot, but didn't find his or any other Volvo. Had the attendant moved it somewhere? But how, it was locked. John approached the parking lot attendant—a new Russian man, he noted—in the parking-lot entrance booth and asked about his car, pointing to the spot where he'd left it. The attendant shrugged and said, "What Volvo?" John got that sinking feeling one gets when he's been had. He returned to the hotel and told Morton what had happened.

"Say goodbye to your Volvo," Morton said. "Volvo, Mercedes, BMW are the cars the Russians crooks love. It gives them status. These foreign cars are in great demand in Moscow. If you have one, you almost need an armed driver to prevent theft. If you drive yourself and leave the car unattended, then drive a Russian piece of shit." Morton delivered the lore like a guide on autopilot talking to a naïve tourist.

"But the Volvo was banged up, looked like it barely survived a demolition derby." John shook his head. "What kind of status would that give anyone?

"Parts, mate, parts the crooks were after." Morton picked up the front desk phone and dialed. "I'll have a driver take you back. You might want to report the theft for insurance purposes. Don't waste your time with Moscow corrupt militia. They may be already enjoying their fringe benefits."

A minute after Morton spoke into the phone, a Russian showed up with car keys in hand. John thanked Morton for the favor and left with the driver.

On the way back, he reasoned that he had good news for Nikolai: the site for Sovcell equipment would be secured. But he also had bad news: Sovcell's motor pool was minus the Volvo. *Moscow.*

Chapter 38

In an obscure Senate building inside the Kremlin, KGB Chairman Kryuchkov faced Robert Maxwell across a small conference table. An interpreter sat next to the Chairman. Kryuchkov had asked the British publishing tycoon and Israel's super spy for the meeting.

The KGB chief knew that the West would regard the overthrow of Gorbachev's government as threat to the détente so much enjoyed by the West. The liberals within the country would regard it as brutal suppression. This was 1991 and a new era dawned on the Soviet Union after six years of democratic reforms. Return to totalitarian rule would be strongly resisted. To lessen the possibly violent fallout from the coup, Kryuchkov decided to seek Maxwell's help. He gestured to the Beluga caviar, thin slices of dark bread, and a chilled bottle of Stolichnaya on the table, inviting his guest to partake.

Maxwell poured half a glass of the vodka, but didn't touch the glass. He leaned his big leonine head back, pushed out his elephant belly, and looked down on the smaller man. He furrowed his bushy eyebrows, bore his dark eyes into the KBG chief, and waited, it seemed, for his host to get to the subject of the meeting.

"The current situation in our Union is disgraceful," Kryuchkov said.

Maxwell nodded curtly once.

"I and other Soviet patriots in the Center have resolved to stop Gorbachev from destroying our Union," the KGB chief said. "When we are done, Soviet order will be restored."

The publisher nodded again, as if he heard nothing new. He shot Kryuchkov a get-to-the-point look.

Kryuchkov did just that: "When I take control of our government, I will be in position to wipe out your debt to the Soviet Union."

Maxwell sat up. His brows rose and his eyes opened wide.

The KGB chief nodded. He had the superspy's attention. Kryuchkov knew that Maxwell's publishing empire was in economic distress and although four hundred million dollars wouldn't solve the problem completely, it would loosen the financial straightjacket Maxwell was in.

Mad Max, as the media often called him, hiked the glass in front of him and downed the vodka in one gulp. He leaned forward. "And what do I have to do for your rehabilitated Soviet State to merit its magnanimity?" His booming voice reverberated in the cavernous, stone-walled chamber.

Kryuchkov took a moment to think about how he would present his proposal. Not coming up with anything special, he simply got to the point. "Arrange a meeting for me with your Mossad chief and Israel's top politicians."

Maxwell looked puzzled. "And what do you hope to accomplish by such a meeting, Mr. Chairman."

"I want you to help me convince Israel's government to side with us patriots and recognize our new government when we take control"

Maxwell shook his head with more gusto than was necessary to get his point across. "Israel will follow what the United States does. You *cannot* influence them in this matter, and you know as well as I do what position the Americans will take on your second Bolshevik revolution."

Kryuchkov didn't want to hear that. He pushed ahead. "I want for the Israelis to go to Washington and convince the Americans that democracy will not work in Russia. It is better to let us return to a modified form of Communism."

"You *cannot* be serious, Chairman Kryuchkov." Maxwell's elevated, thunderous voice rattled the metal shade on the light fixture hanging above the table.

The KGB chief *was* serious. "In return I will guarantee to free thousands of Jews and dissidents in the Soviet Union and encourage them to return to Israel. Expel them if necessary. America and Israel should be giddy with delight just from the thought of it."

The publisher shook his head in a slow motion. "Israel will not accept your proposal. They will never jeopardize their relations with America."

Kryuchkov ignored the publisher's dismissal of his idea. "You, Mr. Maxwell, will be seen as a savior of all those Jews—a modern day Moses. You could organize the exodus for your people and, no doubt, find ways to profit from it." Kryuchkov stopped and scrutinized the publisher. Within a second he could almost hear Maxwell's adding machine chunking away in his brain.

A moment later the publisher broadly smiled. "I'll arrange such a meeting for you on my yacht *Lady Ghislaine* in Yugoslav waters within two weeks."

Kryuchkov rose, came around the conference table to publisher's side. "We have a deal. Let us seal it." He poured generous amount of vodka into the glasses and raised his in a toast. Maxwell raised his and they drained the vodka. Then they shook hands, and Kryuchkov's interpreter escorted the publisher out.

The KGB chief sat back down and reached for the caviar. As he munched on the Beluga, he hoped—he would pray, if he had believed in that nonsense—that the Jews would not disappoint.

Chapter 39

Juliana Kovar stopped washing lunch dishes and looked at her father. The great professor of physics sat at the kitchen table and read a copy of *Pravda*. She wished he were back in the classroom, doing what he loved to do. The way things were going, she feared, he would not see the inside of a university classroom again. Instead of a higher institution, she shuddered, he could find himself inside a correctional institution.

"Lies, lies, lies," her father shouted, shaking his head and pounding his fist on the table. His reading glasses slipped off his nose and dropped on top of the paper.

"Quiet, Papa, they will hear you."

He pointed to the copy of *Pravda*. "Did you see this? The chief prosecutor has determined that the Lithuanians are responsible for the deaths caused by the Red Army in the January TV station massacre in Vilnius. His 'investigation' revealed that Soviet troops were firing blanks, and that the Lithuanian nationalists killed their own people."

"I don't read *Pravda*, and you must stop reading it too, Papa, it is not good for your heart."

He lifted the paper and shook it like a dishrag. "All propaganda, all trash, and all lies. Do the editors really think that their readers are so stupid as to believe what they print?"

"You must not speak against the State, Papa, the neighbors could hear you. You know what they say?"

Her father stared at her. "Don't remind me."

"The walls in Moscow have ears."

"Bah." He waved her warning aside.

"You are already under investigation," she reminded him.

"So, what can they do to me?"

"They can detain you for a long interrogation, and you know it. I could not bear to think that you were languishing somewhere in the basement of Lubyanka, or exiled to some closed city like Gorky. Do I need to remind you of what happened to our great fighter for civil liberties and human rights, your own colleague, Andrei Sakharov?" She peeled the newspaper from her father's hand, crumpled it, and threw it into the kitchen garbage can.

Her father looked at the garbage can. "Careful, my daughter, if they see you do that, they will detain *you* for interrogation. He then seemed to reflect on her warning and said, "Gorbachev is not Brezhnev, and he does not exile those who seek democratic rule." He stood and walked out into the living room of their four-room apartment.

She finished the dishes and went to check on him. He sat on the divan and stared at the blank television screen. She worried about him. She didn't know what the authorities would do next, and her father's fate was entirely in their hands. Now she also worried about her own position at the theater, wondering how long it would be before she was discharged for her political activities. Surely the State knew about her participation in the democratic movement that sought liberalization and openness.

The meetings she had attended certainly had informers. The only explanation she had for her continued employment in the theater and freedom of movement was her relationship with an aging admirer who was a general in the KGB. How long would that continue? She didn't know. She suspected that her job and her freedom would come to an abrupt end the minute she spurned the General's interest in her. So far, she was grateful, the relationship remained platonic. How long would the general's admiration remain that way?

She went back to the kitchen, sat down at the table, and looked out of the window at the rows of gray, monolithic, apartment buildings. She thought about dispirited Moskovites who led a zombie-like existence and she wished she were back in Leningrad. She was happy performing with the Kirov ballet in the beautiful Mariinsky Theater, and she didn't want to leave. The Soviet National was impersonal, political, and she always felt like an outsider.

But her father could not turn down an appointment at the prestigious Moscow State University. The government said that his work on high-speed computation was valuable to the Soviet military, and that he could hold the university post and consult for the military. So he left the Leningrad State University for the MGU, an ugly Stalinist monstrosity. She came with him because she didn't want him to be alone after her mother died. Though he never asked her directly to come, she knew that that was his wish. He had since thanked her many times.

Telephone ringing in the living room interrupted her brooding. She heard her father answer it and then saw him come into the kitchen.

"Provodnikov, for you," he said with an expression of surprise.

Puzzled, she went into the living room and picked up the handset.

"Juliana, this is Taras Provodnikov."

"Yes?" Caution came over her. The conductor himself rarely called the dancers at home after hours. They exchanged the usual pleasantries, and she waited for him to get to the reason for his call.

"I will be grateful," Provodnikov said in a petitionary tone, "if you would agree to meet with me after the performance tonight."

Her caution rose. Provodnikov's request was unexpected and in some ways strange. She did not socialize with the theater crowd, not with other performers, and certainly not with the management. She began to wonder. Was the conductor instructed by the State organs to take some action, discharge her? But would the conductor perform an official duty that late at night and after the performance? No, she concluded. She suspected it had nothing to do with her dancing, and probably nothing to do with theater business. Still, anxiety gnawed at her. "May I ask what the purpose of our meeting is?"

"I will explain when we meet, but it is not connected with the theater."

She thought for a minute and decided it would be unwise to refuse. Provodnikov was a powerful man in the theater. "Very well, after the performance, then." She said goodbye and hung up.

Her father stood in the living room entrance. "What did he want?" His voice carried a trace of alarm.

"He wants to meet after tonight's performance."

"What for? Has the KGB told him lies about me, or you? Are they pressuring him to release you?"

"Provodnikov said it had nothing to do with the theater. Besides, he would not be the one to discharge me. He is not the principal choreographer, or the artistic director."

"It does not matter. I don't trust them."

"Shush, Papa." She pointed to the living room walls.

Her father looked at the walls, waved his hand as if he was deflecting a persistent fly, and walked out.

Chapter 40

At the conclusion of the evening's performance of *Giselle*, Juliana remained in her dressing room, waiting for Provodnikov. When he arrived, he offered to drive her home, explaining that they could talk privately in the car. She wondered what was on the conductor's mind, since "private" conversations meant that State organs would not—or should not—hear it.

As they left the theater parking lot and moved into the street traffic, Provodnikov glanced in her direction, as if to make sure she was still there, and began. "You must promise me, Juliana, that our conversation will remain private," he said in a commanding voice.

Private? She wasn't sure she should enter into a "private" conversation with the conductor. What if this was some sort of conspiracy against the State? She didn't want to be the recipient of any secrets that would put her or her father into deeper trouble than they already were. *A secret is not a secret if more than one person knows it.* Or maybe Provodnikov was acting on instructions from the State organs, testing her loyalty, or looking for information to use against her father. But if she didn't cooperate, she thought, tonight's performance may have been her last. The conductor's influence in the theater was powerful. Concerned about possible loss of her livelihood, she gave a slow nod. "Our conversation will remain private."

"Good, good." Provodnikov smiled to himself and proceeded deliberately to explain the request he received from his nephew. "An American businessman, an admirer of your dancing, wants to meet you. I would be pleased if you agreed to the meeting, but, of course, you must decide for yourself."

She said nothing. Admirer or not, what would be her purpose for such a meeting? What business would she have with an American? It didn't matter. Whatever it might be about, she wouldn't take the risk. Her father was already under investigation for praising Americans, and her meeting with an American could be viewed by the State with suspicion. That very notion seemed ridiculous to her, but when one was in disfavor with the State, strange and unexpected things happened.

"Such a meeting is unthinkable for me now. I cannot take the risk of being seen with an American."

"I can arrange a private meeting at my dacha. It is outside Moscow, and you will not be seen with him there."

"No, I cannot take the risk," she said in a tone that she hoped indicated the end of discussion about meeting the American.

Provodnikov looked disappointed. Wrinkles gathered around his eyes and his face tensed as if he was trying to figure out a difficult puzzle. Then his face lit up. "Just take a look at him to decide if you would want to meet him. There is no risk in that."

"There's always a risk." She tried to imagine how "a look" at the American could be arranged, but she couldn't conceive of a plan. Curious, she asked. "How do you propose to create such a situation?"

Provodnikov had a ready answer. "On Tuesday you dance Juliet. During the performance he'll be in the first row on the orchestra level right behind where I stand at the podium. You can look at him as many times as you like, and nobody will suspect anything." Provodnikov nodded and smiled with satisfaction, as if he had just worked out a brilliant chess move.

She peered at him with a mixture of puzzlement and amazement. Of course, that meant that she would be able to see the American at close distance, and no one would suspect anything. She was visualizing that arrangement when her ride came to an end, and Provodnikov stopped the car in front of her apartment building. He turned to face her. "You can choose to look, or not to look, at him. But if you look and smile at him during the final curtain call, you will make him very happy. He will interpret that as a sign that you will agree to meet him."

She reviewed the proposed plan in her mind and again saw no danger in it. Since she always smiled during the final curtain call, she would have to be careful on Tuesday night where she looked and when she smiled.

"Very well, I will look at the American. *And there will be no smile for the man in Row 1, no matter what pleases you, Comrade Provodnikov.*

"Thank you Juliana and good night to you," Provodnikov said and opened the door for her.

Before stepping out of the car, she turned and out of curiosity asked, "What business does the American have in Moscow?"

"He is building a mobile telephone network."

Her interest suddenly shot up. "Is that the network that provides connections for those portable gadgets that can make a call anywhere in the city?"

"That is the one."

"Interesting," she said, climbed out of the car, and stood watching the Volga drive off and disappear around the corner. She was glad she had asked the question, as it explained what her admirer General Petrov meant when he boasted about his mobile telephone. She began to see the possibilities the American new gadgets could offer.

Back in her apartment, she prepared a cup of tea, sat down at the kitchen table, and looked out of the window. Darkness veiled the ugly Moscow skyline. She wondered what the American looked like and decided that it didn't matter. She will smile at him and she will meet with him. If he is building the network for the mobile units, then he has access to the connections the gadgets use and could listen in on others' conversations. She would just have to figure out how to enlist the American's cooperation in eavesdropping on the Soviet officials. Information obtained by listening to General Petrov and other high officials' conversations could be valuable to the democratic movement. And she would do anything to stop the hard-line communists who, according to her democratic insiders, were planning to take over the government and halt the reforms.

Chapter 41

First thing Monday morning, John called Chris and asked, "Did we get anything from Trush on the Corrotto contract?"

"Hell, no," Chris said. "We'll see that godless commie cross himself and pray the Rosary before we'll see any contract details from him."

"Time to act. Get keys to a car, because we're going to see Signor Alberto Casone, the director general of Corrotto Construction. We'll ask *him* for the contract details. He should know—he did the work."

"Should I get a driver?"

"You're driving. The Russians mustn't know where we're going. I want to pay a surprise visit to the signor."

They left the parking lot in a Zhiguli and Chris turned onto Gorky Street. "You actually believe Casone will cooperate?"

"I don't believe anything right now, but I want to get to the bottom of this and Casone is a logical place to start."

Chris eased onto Garden Ring Road heading south, turned off on a side street, pulled in front of a fenced-in compound with its gates closed, and waited. "We're here, Corrotto Construction."

The security guard at the gate left his station and walked up to them. He had a large, round face with rosy cheeks, a look easily achieved on a bread-and-potatoes diet, washed down with vodka. His spare tire pushed his uniform over his belt and his side arm.

"State your business," the guard said in Russian, staring at Chris with suspicion.

John leaned toward the open window on Chris' side of the car. "Mister Baran and Mister Ashley from Sovcell to see Signor Casone."

The guard walked back to his shack, picked up the phone, and spent a minute talking and waving his hand as if describing a complicated situation. He put the phone down and walked back to their car.

"Secretary said you do not have an appointment," he said and started back toward his post as if the matter was closed.

John climbed out of the car and walked up to the guard. "Let me talk to Signor Casone," John said in a firm and commanding voice.

The guard looked at him with a blank expression, made no move, and stood silent.

John stepped closer until he was into the guard's face. The Russian stepped back, put his right hand on his holster, and unsnapped the cover of his pistol.

John stopped his advance. He looked directly into the guard's sullen eyes. "Signor Casone will not be happy if you turn away his customers." He waited for the guard's response. Did the term "customers" mean anything to the Russians? Was it even in their socialist dictionary?

The guard walked into his shack and picked up the phone. He spoke briefly, waited, and then extended the receiver to John.

"A thousand pardons, Mr. Baran," Casone sang. "My secretary didn't consult me, and the guard may be efficient but he is not very bright. Please come."

"Thank you, Signor Casone," John said.

The guard opened the gate and pointed toward an office building at the distant end of the parking lot. Chris drove through the gate and parked in front of the entrance to Corrotto Construction's two-story prefab. They climbed out of the car and started toward the entry.

A young female met them at the entrance, and John eyed her curiously. She looked like a Russian version of Venus de Milo, arms attached. Her lips were ruby red, her hair platinum blonde, her breasts noticeably enhanced. *What's with these Russian women?* Was socialized medicine providing the benefits of cosmetic surgery to those in need, those in want? If Venus de Milo saw the set of knockers her Russian copy wielded, she would've turned green. He shifted his gaze from the Russian goddess to Chris and saw his finance director gawk at the woman with his eyes popping out. *Oh-oh, Chris had better keep his hands off of that package.* This Venus, no doubt, had a sugar papa.

The goddess of sexual passion led them upstairs to a corner office and knocked on the door. At the prompt, she walked in and invited them to follow. As they entered, a rush of cool air engulfed them. Casone's office had a functioning air conditioner—a welcome respite from the Moscow August heat.

"Welcome," Casone chimed, rose from behind his polished, mahogany desk, and moved toward them. A paragon of fashion, Casone wore an expertly tailored suit (*Armani*, John thought, but he really didn't know and didn't care), white shirt, and a silk tie (*Ferregamo*, maybe). Gold rings glittered on his fingers, and a gold watch and gold band sparkled on his left wrist. Had he worn a gold chain around his neck, John thought, Casone would have mixed in smoothly in certain circles along the New Jersey shore.

Casone turned to his secretary. "*Mille grazie,* Lyubochka," he said in a tone that carried more affection than would pass for a normal boss-secretary relationship. Sugar papa had spoken.

The goddess smiled erotically, turned, swung her hips, and walked out with just enough spring in her step to bounce her breasts. John saw Chris' jaw drop, but he restrained himself from reaching over and pushing his mouth shut. He'd have a word with Chris later.

Casone motioned toward a conference table. After they were seated and introductions were made, he began his overture.

"I'm humbled by your presence," he said in English in a groveling tone with musical qualities in it. "This is indeed an honor for me. It is I who should be visiting you." He looked to his right at a closed cabinet next to the conference table. "May I offer you some wine? I have a bottle of Isonzo Pinot Grigio, 1984. *Cooled.* I keep it for special occasions. I also have some Russian vodka, but I wouldn't insult a Westerner by offering it." He smiled an artificial, polite smile.

Casone's reception was cordial, but his mannerism appeared forced. He tapped his fingers on the table in a fast rhythm and switched his gaze frequently between John and Chris.

John declined the wine offer and looked at Chris who shook his head no.

Casone brushed his mustache with his fingers and patted what few hairs he had on his head. "How can I be of service?" he said, looking at John then at Chris, as if he didn't know to whom he should put the question.

John spoke. "Your firm remodeled the Sovcell facilities, and we want to see the contract and detailed statement of work. Labor, material, costs."

Casone's eyes shifted in slow motion to the door behind John, and then to his wardrobe cabinet in the corner, then to a modern rendering of Teatro La Scala in Milan on the wall behind Chris, then to his desk, then back to the conference table as if he saw these things for the first time. He shook his head slowly, as if he was mourning a dearly departed. "This is most unfortunate," he said in a tone suggesting lamentation. "Corrotto is performing a general audit of Moscow operations. All detailed documents are at our headquarters in Milano." His speech had a tortoise-like pace. He seemed to appraise every word.

John questioned the veracity of Casone's statement. Was Corrotto conducting a general audit in August, Europe's vacation month? He didn't think so. He leaned in Casone's direction to stress his next request. "Then we would like to talk to the construction supervisor on the Sovcell contract."

Casone repeated his eye-shifting procedure around his office at a faster pace. He seemed to draw his responses from the objects around him. "This is also most unfortunate," he chanted. He shook his head as if he was deeply troubled by the situation. He leaned back in his chair, looked at the ceiling, and, accentuating each word as if to import its validity, he said, "Signor Sospettori is in Milano. He took the documents to Corrotto headquarters."

Visibly agitated by Casone's responses, Chris started to fidget. He opened his mouth to speak, but before he could complete the first word, John cut him off. "Then I will go to Milan to get the information we seek. Please arrange a meeting for me at your headquarters for next week, Signor Casone."

The color on Casone's face faded, and in spite of the cool air blowing from the window conditioner behind him, droplet of perspiration began to appear on his forehead. He stared at his visitors with wide-open eyes and said nothing for half a minute.

John waited.

Casone cleared his throat with a synthetic cough and said, "I will attempt to communicate with our home office. But communications being what they are in the Russia, it may be necessary for me to travel to Milano personally to make the arrangements. If so, I must seek an opportune time. I will contact you as soon as I have definite information."

I bet you will. "Very well, Signor Casone," John said, "I will be expecting a call from you. Thank you for your time, and we will take our leave now."

Casone jumped up, scurried to his office door, and opened it. "I will be in communication with you, Signor Baran, as soon as I make the arrangements."

They shook hands, and the two Americans left Casone's office. On the way out, Chris jogged over to Venus de Milo's desk and whispered something in her ear. The goddess blushed and said something to Chris in an endearing manner. A hard-faced Casone looked at the two cooers through the open door of his office. John walked over to the goddess' desk, grabbed Chris' elbow, and guided him toward the exit.

Outside, John stopped, gripped Chris' arm, and turned him to get his full attention. "About Casone's secretary—"

"Lyuba Bogyna is her name," Chris said, beaming. "Isn't she a doll?"

"A goddess," John said and shook his head. "The trouble with you, Chris, is that when you need blood in your brains the most, it rushes elsewhere."

Chris' jaw muscles tightened. "That's a low blow."

"If I read Casone's expression correctly, you better keep away from that doll."

They walked to the car in silence.

When they left the Corrotto compound, John said. "You interested in shopping for some groceries tonight after work?"

"Sorry, not tonight. I have something lined up for the evening."

John raised his eyebrows. "Not the doll, already?"

"Nah." Chris sounded disappointed. "But I think I'll take your advice about the doll and keep my hands off that package. You're right on the money about her—Casone would kill me if he found out. Italians are not Russians; they're serious about their *amore*. By the way, you're not going to go to Milan, are you?"

"Casone doesn't know that."

Chapter 42

When John returned to his office, he found Nikolai waiting for him outside in the hallway. The Russian looked troubled. John invited him into his office and waited for the bad news.

"Mr. Baran, we went to hotel by Kievskaya to locate place for our equipment as you instructed, but we were not allowed in hotel to look. Russian management said there is no agreement to allow it."

A dreadful feeling welled up inside John. Something had gone wrong; Morton said there'd be no problem. He picked up the phone and dialed the hotel, and when the receptionist answered, he asked for Harry Morton.

"Mr. Morton is no longer with our hotel," the receptionist said.

A chill swept over John. "What do you mean Mr. Morton is not with your hotel? I just met with him at your hotel on Thursday."

"Mr. Morton is no longer with our hotel," the receptionist repeated in a tone indicating official annoyance.

A horrid thought ran through John's mind, but he stayed calm. He tried to humor her. "If Mr. Morton is not with your hotel, then what hotel is he with? Where can I reach him?"

"You cannot reach Mr. Morton because—"

"Why the hell not?"

"Because Mr. Morton is dead," the receptionist said, as if it was an official and final proclamation, and before John could respond, the phone went dead.

He felt blood drain from his face. He had trouble dealing with deaths of his friends and the people he knew, and Harry had become a friend in the short time he had known him.

Nikolai looked at John in a strange way. "Something wrong, Mr. Baran?"

"Nikolai, do you have connections in the militia?"

"I do not, but my uncle does. He has connections everywhere."

"Find out if there is a militia report on the death of an Australian named Harry Morton. Do it immediately."

"I will call my uncle," Nikolai said and stood motionless.

John gave him a sharp look. "What're you waiting for?"

The other man seemed to hesitate, but then said, "I have answer for you about Kovar, Princess Odette, the ballerina."

It took John several seconds to make the mental switch from Harry Morton to Juliana Kovar. When he realized what Nikolai was about to say, nervous tension spread through his body. He wasn't ready for more bad news. "Well?" he asked with a faint smile.

"As you Americans say, I have good news and I have—"

"Cut it out Nikolai," John raised his voice. "Get to the point."

"She will not meet you, but she will look at you to decide if she will meet you. She—"

"Stop! I'm in no mood for your doubletalk. *What* are you saying?"

Nikolai pulled a small piece of paper out of his pocket. "Here is ticket to performance of *Romeo and Juliet* tomorrow. You must be in this exact seat," he said pointing to the ticket. "Kovar will signal her answer to you during final curtain call. She knows you will be in this seat, Row 1 on orchestra level, right behind my uncle, the conductor."

John felt embarrassed. "Sorry, how will she signal?"

"She will smile to you."

"Does the smile mean that she will meet with me?"

"Yes, Mr. Baran, smile means that she will meet with you. But I would not, as you say, bet on it."

"Thank you. I owe you another one."

"You owe me two now, Mr. Baran. But two of what?"

"Never mind, I see you don't know all the expressions."

"I will look it up." Determination spread across Nikolai's face as he started to leave, seemingly eager to research the idiom.

John called after him. "And find out about the militia report as soon as you can."

"I will attend to it immediately," the Russian said, walking out.

John slumped in his chair, his thoughts returning to Harry Morton. What did he say? *The only way they'll gain control of the property is over his dead body?*

Did the Russians use murder to carry out their corporate strategy? Was there a conspiracy to take over Sovcell? Harry said John should look for it. *Who? How? When?*

Chapter 43

Trush prepared to leave for his late morning meeting with the minister to deliver a status report of Sovcell progress. He expected the meeting to be brief as there was little progress to report. As he started for the door, his intercom buzzed with an incoming call on one of his Moscow city lines. Ignoring the blinking light, he walked out into the reception area and prepared to leave the building. His secretary stopped him. She covered the telephone transmitter with her hand and in a low voice said, "Mr. Casone, he says it is an emergency. He sounds like he is in panic."

Trush shook his head in disgust and walked back to his desk. Standing, he picked up the phone.

"Signor Trush, it is I, Alberto Casone."

"And how are you Alberto?"

"I had a visit from Baran and Ashley, the two Americans."

"Don't say anything more over the phone."

"But this is important."

"I am sure it is Alberto, otherwise you would not have called me. And because it is important, we must not talk on the telephone. I have told you this many times."

"We must meet as soon as possible." Urgency smothered his every word, like an Alfredo sauce would a plate of fettuccine.

Trush's meeting with the minister would be in the Central Telegraph building on Gorky Street, and he decided to meet Casone in the nearby Savoy hotel after he finished with the minister. He could not allow the panicked Italian to go unhinged. He feared Casone, in his hysteria, would do something stupid. He wondered if he had struck the deal with the right contractor.

"Alberto?" he said.

"Si, Signor Trush."

Trush glanced at the clock on his desk. "Savoy bar in two hours."

"Savoy bar in two hours. *Mille grazie*, Signor Trush."

…..

An hour later, Trush walked into the minister's reception area and was told that the minister was ready for him. He thought that was unusual—a thirty-minute delay was the norm. Had the minister elevated the importance of Sovcell's business? Whatever the reason, he was pleased that he didn't have to wait. He needed to move on to his real problem: Casone.

He walked into the minister's office and stopped short of his boss' immense desk. He looked at the chair in front of the desk, but the minister didn't invite him to sit. *Quick meeting. That's good.* Trush opened with a short report on the Sovcell network installation progress: not much had happened since his last report. Then he said, "Everything is ready. We are waiting for the processors to arrive so that we can complete the network installation."

The minister listened without interrupting. Then, with noticeable annoyance in his voice, he said, "Are you telling me, Burian Trush, that the network is not operational because you are *waiting* for equipment? You do not remember our conversation about the deadline?"

"August 12," Trush immediately affirmed the date. He didn't like the meeting's direction.

The minister peered at Trush with an expression Trush had seen many times before. *Trouble.* "Do you think, Comrade Trush, that you can complete the network in the short time that remains? You do not even have all the necessary equipment. Have you checked the calendar?"

"It is Monday, August 5, Comrade Minister, and the network is almost operational."

"*Almost?* What does it mean to be *almost* operational, Comrade Trush?" Frost covered the minister's every word. The room felt like a

Siberian tundra. "We *almost* won the war in Afghanistan. You do not remember what happened?"

"Only two racks of equipment remain to be installed—the processor racks." Trush did not want to touch the painful subject of Afghanistan.

"And where are these processor racks?"

"In Customs."

"What?" The minister sprang to his feet and glowered at Trush. "Why are they in Customs and not in Sovcell's equipment room, *installed?"*

"Customs officials have not cleared them for entry."

The minister glared at Trush with icicles in his eyes. "Are you waiting for *me* to clear the equipment, Comrade Trush? Are you not capable of taking care of this routine matter?"

Trush snapped to attention. Only one response was appropriate. "I will attend to it immediately, Comrade Minister."

"Get it done! I do not want to hear about the processor racks again. Anything *else?*" The minister's volume rose.

"No, Comrade Minister." Trush got the message.

"I do not want to have another meeting on the *absence* of your progress in completing the network." The minister sat down and turned his attention to the documents on his desk. The meeting was over.

Trush marched out of the minister's office and quietly shut the door behind him.

Outside, he stomped to his car, climbed into the back seat and slammed the door. "Hotel Savoy," he barked. He still didn't know the significance of the deadline, but he had no doubt that it was important to the minister. That much was clear. He'd attend to the Customs clearance immediately after his meeting with Casone. He didn't want to have another session with the minister to explain his failure to put the network into service by August 12.

Thirty minutes later Trush entered the Savoy bar and found Casone sitting at a side table, away from the other customers. It looked like the Italian had moved the table to secure privacy. A bottle of beer on the table in front of him, Casone kept looking around the bar in a jerky head motion, tapping his fingers on the table. When he saw Trush come in, he leaped to his feet.

Trush greeted Casone casually, as if the two of them had always met in this bar at this time. He pulled up a chair, sat down, and scrutinized the other man. The helpless Italian unnerved him. "Your Americans visitors left empty-handed, right?"

"Right, but—"

A waiter materialized at their table. "Welcome Comrade Trush," he said. "It is a pleasure to see you again." He gave Casone a curious stare, as if he wondered who the expensively dressed, bejeweled foreigner was.

Trush waved his hand to the waiter in acknowledgement of the greeting. "Stolichnaya, Dmitry." The waiter nodded and left.

Trush turned to Casone and, with notable displeasure in his voice, said, "But *what?*"

"Baran plans to go to Corrotto in Milano."

Trush saw disaster brewing. "Why does Baran want to go to your company headquarters in Italy?"

"I told him that all our records were in Milano because Corrotto was doing a general audit."

"And are they?"

"No, the records are in my office."

"Then what's the problem, Alberto?"

"Baran persisted. He wanted to talk to the construction supervisor on the remodeling project."

"And did he?"

"No, I told him the construction supervisor was in Milano with the records."

"And is he?"

"No, he's here, in Moscow."

The waiter brought Trush's Stolichnaya. Trush picked it up and knocked it back. Right now, he could use more than one drink. He peered at Casone with a stern expression. "Here is what you will do Alberto. First, you will get rid of your construction supervisor."

Casone jerked back. He looked at Trush with terror in his eyes.

"Send him back to Milan," Trush said. "Then you will 'lose' all records related to the Sovcell remodeling contract."

Casone's eyes went wild: "I cannot destroy my company's records," he said in a tone filled with fear.

"Then you must stop Baran." After Trush said it, he realized he wasted his breath. Casone couldn't stop Baran from going to Milan any more than he could stop the August heat from roasting Moscow.

The Italian shook his head with lurching motion. "I may be able to delay him, but I cannot stop him. "If he gets to Corrotto headquarters, then—"

"Do not say it. I know what will happen." Trush looked at the statues holding up the ceiling on either side of the bar entry. He felt as if the ceiling's weight had suddenly been transferred to his shoulders. He ordered another vodka and lapsed into thought. Casone picked up his beer and drank it. He tapped his fingers on the bottle as if it was a flute and he was playing a fast tune. When Trush had finished considering the problem, he turned to Casone. "I think I know what to do about Baran," he said and abruptly stood up. Casone sprang to his feet.

Trush assumed a commissarial stance and poked his finger into Casone's chest. "You delay Baran's trip to Milan for as long as possible, drag it out, find excuses. I shall take immediate and convincing action to discourage our American from pursuing his reckless quest." Not waiting for Casone to respond, he stormed out of the bar, leaving the Italian to pay the bill.

Chapter 44

Chris charged into John's office and heralded: "We're in business. Processor racks are here." He grinned with satisfaction. "Nikolai picked up the equipment from Customs late yesterday while you were out, and the technicians are installing them this morning. The manufacturing rep says we can run initial tests as early as Thursday morning. Hot damn! Next week we'll be raking in the dough."

"That's great!" John joined in the enthusiasm. Then he remembered. How much did we have to pay the Customs crooks to clear the racks? Correction, how much did I have to pay?"

Chris made zero sign with his thumb and index finger. "Zilch, zip, zot. And that's the damnedest thing. Customs official calls Nikolai and tells him to pick up the equipment and get it out of Customs *immediately.*"

"That's it? No extortion? No demand for hard currency?"

Chris spread and raised his arms as if he was expressing gratitude to the heavens for a miracle. "Haven't seen anything like it in all the time I've been here."

"Maybe it's an indication that the business climate for Westerners is improving in Russia. A business-friendly Customs?"

"Not in our lifetime. It's an indication that someone gave them a direct order to release the equipment."

John nodded. "It looks like someone in power wants our network to cut into service. So let's do just that. Worry about who, or why, later."

A rapid knock on John's door interrupted their jubilation. Chris opened it and found Nikolai standing outside, mumbling to himself in Russian. His eyes darted about as if he didn't know where he was. John waved him in, and Nikolai shuffled inside. "Mr. Baran, you said militia report on Mr. Morton was important."

John tensed and prepared himself for what he sensed would be dreadful news. "What did you find out?"

Nikolai took a deep breath. "Militia report says Mr. Harry Morton was shot dead on Sunday, outside Kievskaya Metro. It says gunman fired eleven bullets from Kalashnikov submachine gun."

"Jesus!" Chris's face turned pale.

Nikolai sat down in a chair as if he needed to rest from exhaustion. "Report says it was contract hit because weapon was left in plastic bag near murder spot. Militia has no suspect."

"And the goddamned militia *won't* have any suspects," Chris blurted out.

"Bastards!" John called out. He stared silently into a space on the wall. As if talking to himself, he said, "The thugs solved their corporate power struggle with murder." He lapsed into silence.

Chris and Nikolai gazed at John with concerned expressions. They seemed to be waiting for him to say something, take some action.

"*John?*" Chris said with apprehension in his voice.

Snapping back to the business before him, John pointed to the project status chart on his wall. "We can make that cut in a few days if we buckle down, starting right now. All the equipment is here, Nikolai. You have everything you need to complete the network. Install it and turn the system on." He eyed the mobile unit on his credenza. The size of a brick, the phone stood vertically with an antenna rising from its top. He picked it up and said in a loud, angry voice, "Let's make this damned thing work by the end of the week."

Energized by John's directive, Nikolai snapped to attention. "Yes, Mr. Baran, I'll alert staff and mobilize troops, as you say. And I also have good news about Kievskaya area. We have found good roof space close to hotel. It will give us network coverage we need."

"Well then, Nikolai, get cracking," John commanded.

Nikolai smiled and threw a salute. He understood the "get cracking" order. He made a military about face and was ready to march out of the office. Then he turned and placed a piece of paper on John's desk. "Red Army Choir on Saturday at the Kremlin Palace of Congresses."

John picked up the ticket and gave it a weary glance. "More cultivation for the low-cultured?"

"Red Army Choir is for entertainment, Mr. Baran," Nikolai said and marched out.

When Nikolai closed the door behind him, John looked at Chris anxiously. "You and I better be careful. These Russian thugs won't stop at anything to gain control."

An unsettled expression spread across Chris's face. "You think it's wise to push Trush on the remodeling contract?"

"Probably not. But I *must* find out what happened to David, and the remodeling contract is the only tangible lead we have."

"I hate to think—"

"Don't think," John quickly cut Chris off.

…..

At 6:40 P.M., that evening, John sat in Row 1 on the orchestra level of the Soviet National Ballet Theater. He was early. For the twenty minutes before the performance, he created in his mind scenarios. He would only consider positive scenarios, those that began with Juliana smiling at him at the end of the performance.

At 7 P.M. the lights dimmed, and a spotlight lit up the podium in front of him. Provodnikov walked up from the pit and bowed to the applauding audience. He smiled briefly at John, faced the orchestra, picked up the baton, and tapped the music stand. He raised his baton and thrust it downward. Scene 1, Act 1, of *Romeo and Juliet* had begun.

In minutes the "Hatfields" and "McCoys" of Verona were feuding. Before the scene ended, John counted six bodies amassed in a heap in the middle of the stage. Trouble in Verona.

Scene 2 began and the crowd broke out into wild applause, as Juliet appeared in her room. John tensed, his eyes widened, and he followed Juliet's every move. He hoped she'd glance in his direction, but she didn't.

She didn't look at him throughout Act 2, or the first three scenes of Act 3. He felt a cloud of despondency descending on him.

The final scene began. Juliet lay in the crypt. Romeo, believing her to be dead, took the poison and died. Juliet awoke, found Romeo dead, anguished over her lover's death, stabbed herself with Romeo's dagger and died. She died without giving John even a glance to acknowledge his presence. The curtain closed.

The audience stood, roared, applauded, and yelled *Bravo*. The curtain opened. Hatfields and McCoys took their bows, and then Romeo and Juliet came out. The crowd screamed, yelled, and whistled. Ushers delivered red roses to Juliet, and the crowd threw flowers on the stage. Juliet stepped forward, eyed the admiring audience and took several deep bows, but made no eye contact with John. Didn't she know where he was sitting? His heart raced, he waited, hoped.

She took a final bow and slowly raised her head. Then she looked straight into John's eyes, and a bright smile glowed on her face. Light twinkled in the depth of her eyes.

John's face lit up with a smile the size of Montana. His heart swelled and was ready to spring out of his chest. The curtain closed, and the house lights came on. His mood buoyant, he floated out of the theater, humming a tune, visualizing blissful scenarios for tomorrow, the next week, the next month…

Chapter 45

On Wednesday morning, John called Nikolai into his office. He told him what had happened during the final curtain call and asked him to set up an introduction meeting with Juliana Kovar. Nikolai looked puzzled. "I am surprised, Mr. Baran."

John didn't care whether Nikolai was surprised or not—the ballerina decided. "The meeting, Nikolai, can you set up the meeting for me?"

"You must now call my uncle, Mr. Baran. He will handle your meeting with Kovar. He, as you say, took charge of this matter."

John gave Nikolai a questioning look. "Explain."

"Nothing to explain. When uncle says he is in charge, well, he is in charge."

"Okay, I'll call the man in charge. Thank you."

After Nikolai left, John called Provodnikov and asked him to arrange a meeting with Kovar. He described the curtain call and the smile. He began to stress the importance of the meeting, but before he could fully explain its urgency, the conductor stopped him. "Do not talk over telephone. We must meet face to face to discuss such matters. Can you meet me in the apartment in one hour?"

"Of course."

"I will see you then," Provodnikov said and hung up.

John considered what the conductor had said. *Do not talk over the telephone?* He'd made a simple request to meet a ballet performer, and the conductor sounded as if it was some sort of conspiracy. John didn't know what to expect.

......

An hour later in his apartment, he started to explain his request to Provodnikov. The conductor promptly raised his hand in a stop-talking gesture, put his index finger on his lips, and pointed to the door.

"Telman Square?" John said.

The conductor nodded. *I don't believe this.* But John quietly walked out.

In the square, among the trees, John tried again. "Kovar smiled at me during the final curtain call last night. Nikolai said that that means she's willing to meet with me, does it not?"

"Well, yes, but it's not that simple. She cannot be seen with you. It will be difficult to arrange such a meeting." Provodnikov's face took on a grave expression as if he was facing an impossible task.

"Difficult? Why?"

"Juliana Kovar cannot be seen with an American."

"I don't believe this."

"She has a delicate situation with her father. My nephew should have explained it to you."

"I didn't believe your nephew, either."

Provodnikov shrugged and said, "What you believe or don't believe does not change her situation."

"Okay, okay. Difficult, but not impossible for you, I trust?"

Provodnikov flashed a self-satisfied smile and his face lit up. "I will arrange for you to meet Kovar in my dacha on Sunday. We will have lunch and then you can spend time with her in the afternoon."

John began expressing his appreciation, but the conductor kept on talking as if he didn't hear him. "I will have to drive you to get past the checkpoints. I will require one hundred American dollars to pay bribes and three hundred American dollars for taking risk myself."

John instantly understood why Provodnikov took charge of the matter. The service fee for the favor was steep, but it didn't surprise him. Nothing, it appeared, got done in Moscow without hard currency greasing the way. He considered haggling over the conductor's fee, but dismissed it, lest the deal would be put in jeopardy. "Agreed," he said.

"I will talk to Kovar tomorrow about your rendezvous," Provodnikov said with an expression of prideful accomplishment. "I will telephone you and inform you of her decision. If she does not change her mind, and I believe she will not, you must be in front of Ernst Telman statue at noon on Sunday. I will pick you up and we go to my dacha. She will already be there. I will have a collaborator in this operation and he will expect to receive an incentive for his part, but I will take care of that."

John reached in his pocket for the money.

Provodnikov stopped him. "Do not pay me now, but after our plan is executed," he said, putting his hand on John's arm. "Any questions?"

John shook his head.

.....

When he returned to his office, Chris was waiting for him. "Has Casone gotten back to you about your 'trip' to Corrotto's headquarters in Milan?"

"No, and I have a feeling that'll happen when Italy runs out of olive oil."

"So how are we going to get to the truth behind the remodeling contract? We're not going to let the whole thing die, are we?"

"Hell, no. It's time to turn the screw on Signor Casone, flush him out." John picked up the phone and dialed Corrotto Construction.

"I am listening," a mellifluous voice said. The goddess was at her desk. John identified himself and asked for Casone.

"One little minute," she said. The phone went silent.

A minute later, Casone came on the line. "An infinite pleasure to hear from you, Mr. Baran."

"Signore Casone, have you been able to set up a trip to Corrotto headquarters for me?"

A long delay.

"A thousand pardons, Signor Baran. Scheduling now is impossible. Europe, as you know, is on holiday in August."

"Then I'll schedule the trip myself," John said. And for another turn of the screw, he added, "I'll be in Milan on Friday. Please arrange to have Signor Sospettori, the contract manager, and the contract details available to me during my visit to Corrotto headquarters." John waited for Casone's response. Silence. Half a minute passed.

Chris made a face. "Are you serious?" he mouthed.

John shook his head. "Signor Casone?" he called out into the receiver.

"A thousand pardons, Mr. Baran," Casone chimed. "I am just finishing giving instructions to my secretary."

"I'm sure you are, Signor Casone, take your time." John covered the telephone with his hand and grinned at Chris. "Signore Casone is giving instructions to his secretary."

Chris rolled his eyes. "I'll bet he's *giving* it to her."

Another half a minute passed.

"Ah, yes, yes," Casone came back on the line. "It is most unfortunate, but I have not been able to reach Milano. Rest assured, Mr. Baran, I will get back to you as soon as I make contact. Of course, I would like to join you, but unfortunately I have an engagement of utmost importance on Friday. Please accept my deepest apology, Mr. Baran."

"It's quite all right, Signor Casone, I will go myself." John ended the call and turned to Chris. "That's strange, Casone didn't voice any objections to my going to Milan. Are we wrong in suspecting that Trush extracted a kickback from him?"

"Nah," Chris said. "Casone, or more likely Trush, already have a plan to stop you from getting the incriminating evidence."

"I wonder how they'd do that. Break my legs?" John let out a nervous laugh, thinking about Harry Morton.

"About Milan, you really going?"

"I'll have my secretary make the reservations, and I'll make sure all the Russians here know that I'm off to Milan. I want the news to get back to Trush. I'll cancel the reservations later."

Chris laughed. "There'll be a traffic jam of informers outside Trush's door."

"If that's the worst of it, then there's no problem. But I expect Casone or Trush to take swift action to stop me from getting near Corrotto headquarters. I just don't know what they're going to do."

Chapter 46

Trush held his regular midweek meeting with his reports when the secretary buzzed his intercom. *This better be important.* He gave instructions not to be disturbed. He left the conference table, stomped over to his desk, snatched the receiver and yanked it up to his ear.

"Forgive me for interrupting, Comrade Director," his secretary said. "Mr. Casone is on the telephone. He says it is of utmost importance, an emergency. He sounds desperate."

Blyad! Trush was tempted to tell the unhinged Italian to go to the devil, but he thought better of it. He dismissed his staff, told his secretary to put Casone through, and picked up the line. He wished he had chosen a Finnish or a Danish contractor, someone with cooler blood, cooler head. Next time. Right now he had to deal with what he had.

"Alberto?" he barked. "What is it *now*?"

Without any of his customary greeting preambles, in a tone laced with panic, Casone blurted out, "Baran is going to Milano Friday. You *must* stop him."

Trush took a moment to assess the situation. The first thing he had to do was to calm the frantic Italian. He didn't know what Casone might do in his desperation. Whatever action he took, Trush feared, would end in disaster.

"You should relax, Alberto. Have more faith in our way of doing things."

"What?"

"I am happy to hear from you, but important business should be conducted in person. Other means of communications may not be secure. You have been in our country long enough to know that, and I have repeated this warning to you many times."

No response for a beat. Then, "My sincerest apology, Signor Trush, but I fear—"

"Stop, Alfredo. I got the message," Trush growled. He sat down and analyzed his situation.

The last two racks of equipment were being installed. The network should be operational in a day or two. It would be too soon to dispose of Baran just yet. Nikolai and his staff alone could not complete the intensive final network installation and testing phases. They needed the American manufacturer's technicians. Besides, liquidation of Baran would introduce unacceptable delay, as Cellcomm would stop the project, withdraw the technicians, and try to sort things out before committing a new American manager to the venture. Having lost two managers, Cellcomm could decide to withdraw the equipment and pull out of the venture altogether, an unacceptable situation to Trush for two reasons. One, he would be cut off from a source of hard currency. And two, if that were not bad enough he would not meet the minister's deadline of August 12. He would fall into disfavor with his *patron* and would lose his special status, if he were not outright dismissed for mismanaging the venture and failing to carry out the minister's directive.

On the other hand, if Baran discovered his scheme, he was also certain that he would be discharged and, depending on what the prosecutor chose to do, he might find himself behind bars. The State could decide to make an example of him to show foreign investors that the law was enforced and their investments were protected.

All this required that the right balance be struck between doing nothing and taking extreme action, a balance that the flappable Italian would almost certainly fail to find if he attempted any action himself. First, Trush had to attend to his immediate problem.

"Alberto?"

"Si, Signor Trush."

"Do nothing until you hear from me."

"But—"

"And I mean nothing," Trush repeated in a near shout.

"But—"

"Nothing," Trush screamed. "Did you hear me?"

"Si, Signor Trush. Nothing," Casone replied in a low, timid voice.

Trush hung up and considered his options. Only one was viable: disable Baran. But disabling the American would be risky. The inflicted injuries had to be such that he couldn't travel but still be able to continue managing the project to its conclusion. Trush decided that he couldn't trust the southern goons to perform such a delicate operation. He was facing a dilemma. He called in Markova.

When Markova arrived and was seated, Trush said, "Alla, perhaps you could see a solution to an intricate problem."

"What is the difficulty, Comrade?"

"First, the Sovcell network should be completed by the end of the week. That is good. We will be able to meet the minister's deadline. Second, Baran is going to Milan. That is not good. He intends to meet with Corrotto Construction management, and if he succeeds in his plan, well..." Trush knew it was not necessary to finish his sentence.

Fear spread on Markova's face. "He will discover our 'arrangement' with Casone, and then..." She did not finish her sentence.

Trush nodded. "We need to stop Baran. But whatever we do, Baran must remain capable of finishing the final network installation and testing. Otherwise, we will miss the deadline."

Markova looked intently at the portrait of Lenin on the wall behind Trush, as if she expected the god of socialism to provide the answer. A smile spread slowly on her face. "In American movies," she began, appearing eager to lay out her solution, "it always turns out that no matter how strong, independent, or determined the hero may be, he can always be controlled through his heroine. It seems that the American hero cannot bear to see his heroine suffer physical pain. A mere suggestion that his beloved might fall into danger gets the hero's undivided attention." A self-satisfied grin spread on Markova's face. It said she had just found the answer to Trush's dilemma.

Trush gave her a dubious look. "Hero, heroine? What are you talking about?"

"I am talking about our hero, John Baran."

Trush's face brightened. "And do we have a heroine?"

"We most certainly do."

"And who would that be, Alla?"

"It would be the ballet dancer, our own prima ballerina."

"Juliana Kovar?" Trush frowned. He did not like the conversation's drift. In case something went wrong with whatever scheme Markova would suggest, he did not want to incur the possible wrath of the secret police. He had received reports that the ballerina had a highly placed admirer: a KGB general. He gazed at Markova, waited for her recommendation, but was ready to reject any proposal that harmed the ballerina.

Markova adopted a self-assured stance as if to bolster her conviction and flashed a triumphant smile. "It is simple, threaten to harm Kovar and Baran will fall in line."

Trush was puzzled for a few moments, but then smiled. "I am beginning to see the wisdom of this American movie plan. Since it is only a threat to harm her, I shall employ your suggestion. Thank you, Alla." He stood up.

The meeting was over.

Chapter 47

Later that afternoon, John exited the Prospekt Marksa Metro and started toward Hotel Metropol. Situated in the heart of Moscow, the Russian luxury hotel opened in 1901 and was the only hotel in Russia to boast hot water, refrigerators, elevators, and telephones. Remodeled and managed by an international hotel chain, Metropol was the choice of Western businessmen for its central location and Western service standards. Located across Prospekt Marksa from the Bolshoi Theater, Metropol was within brief walks to the Kremlin and Red Square. Sovcell sales personnel made slow progress in convincing Metropol management to set up a rent-a-mobile phone center, and John decided to speed things up by making his own pitch straight to the director of operations.

He descended the steps into the pedestrian underground to cross Prospekt Marksa. In the confines of the passageway, he sensed something. Looking quickly behind him, he took a mental snapshot of the pedestrians in the underground. As he stepped out of the passageway, he took a right and headed toward Lenin's museum, away from the hotel.

At the entrance to the museum, he casually glanced back and took another mental snapshot. Three males, two dressed in shabby Russian clothes and one dressed in a leather jacket and dark pants matched his underground snapshot. Maybe nothing. Turning around, he started toward Metropol and his appointment. Just before entering the hotel, he quickly scanned the area around him. Red hair, athletic built, Leather Jacket followed fifty feet behind, the same man John saw in front of the electrical engineer's apartment building in the Taganskaya district—an unlikely coincidence.

John entered the hotel lobby, turned, and watched through the glass doors. Leather jacket strolled by, looking around like a tourist, and then he disappeared into the pedestrian underground in front of the hotel. Since John was in the hotel already, he decided to make the sales call and worry about the Leather Jacket tail later.

He identified himself at the reception desk and informed the clerk of his appointment. Fifteen minutes later he was shown into the hotel operations director's office. He made his presentation of Sovcell services, and saw that it was well received.

"I like the idea," said the rugged-looking Canadian who might have been running a timber harvesting operation in British Columbia, if he wasn't running Metropol. "We'll promote rent-a mobile as an enhanced service to our customers. God knows it's nearly impossible for them to reach their home countries." He eyed John skeptically. "I'm not from Missouri, but in this environment you have to be. I'll order your service when it's actually working."

John understood. This "show me" attitude was prevalent among foreign businessmen in Moscow. As far as John knew, none of them were from Missouri. "Fair enough. I'll be back with a working mobile telephone next week. You can dial your home office in Vancouver and get an instant connection from right where you're sitting, or from anywhere in Moscow."

The Canadian opened his eyes in wonder. "It'll be a miracle."

"Expect one." John made a follow-up appointment and left the hotel. Outside, he looked for Leather Jacket, but didn't see him. As he walked to the Sverdlov Square Metro, he stopped in front of the entry, and checked the crowd behind him. Fifty yards away, Leather Jacket ambled toward the Metro. John wondered who the Leather Jacket was, but decided that at that instant it didn't matter. It was first things first: *Lose the tail.*

He zigzagged Sverdlov Square, circled two blocks, went through the Central Department Store, and again stood at the entrance to Sverdlov Square Metro. A quick glance behind produced no sign of Leather Jacket. Stepping inside the Metro, John rushed down the escalator, nudging the Russians to clear his way. He boarded a train that had just pulled in—he'd worry about its destination and transfers later.

Who's the tail? he wondered. He thought of four possibilities. The KGB, Trush's operative, Casone's operative, or the Armenian gorilla's accomplice. Because of the red hair, John considered for an instant that his follower might be from the CIA or some other foreign intelligence service. Then he dismissed it: no credible reason. He also didn't think it was the KGB. If it were, why would the KGB agent make his tailing so obvious? They were professionals. He didn't think Casone had the balls to be directly involved in the surveillance of his moves. That left two possibilities: Trush's operative or the gorilla's accomplice. When he thought about it more, he wasn't sure the last two were different interests.

The train slowed and screeched to a halt. John jumped off and caught the train in the opposite direction. He transferred at two different Metro intersections and finally headed northwest on Zamoskvoretskaya, the Green line. In another ten minutes, the train pulled into Aeroport Metro station. He hopped off and hustled to the street level.

As he rounded the corner into Telman Square and started toward his apartment building, he instinctively looked at the Ernst Telman statue. Three men leaned against its base and looked his way. He didn't think it unusual until he recognized two of them. One was the Armenian gorilla, and the other was Leather Jacket. The dark-skinned third man wore a Lenin's cap and looked larger than the Armenian gorilla: another gorilla from one of the "stan" republics? An Uzbekistan gorilla? John's pulse quickened. He picked up his step to a trot. Out of the corners of his eyes he saw the gorilla and the third man leave the statue and race toward him. He tried to sprint, but it was too late. They grabbed his arms, pinned them against his back, and swung him around.

Seeing the commotion, other Russians in the square scattered. Leather Jacket walked up, grinning. He didn't have a Makarov, but in his right hand he held what looked like a lead pipe wrapped inside a newspaper. John stared at the weapon. Had Leather Jacket watched too many gangster movies? John felt a sharp jab into his right kidney. He glanced behind him. The Armenian gorilla pressed a Makarov pistol into the small of John's back. Leather Jacket studied John for a moment and then said something

John didn't understand, but it sounded angry. He didn't recognize the language; it wasn't Slavic or any of the Romance languages. Angry words sounded angry in any language. He spoke again, and they all laughed. John saw no humor in the situation.

Then Leather Jacket said in Russian, "You Americans never learn. You are too inquisitive. If you do not want to see your darling ballerina's legs broken, you will forget about Corrotto and the contract. This is your last warning." He raised the lead pipe over his shoulder, telegraphing his move. John sprang into action. He smashed his right foot into Leather Jacket's chest, knocking him back. The lead pipe swooshed by in front of John's face. Gaining speed and force from the recoil of his kick, he twisted his body clockwise and broke free from his holders' grip. Surprised by John's move, the Armenian gorilla brought the Makarov into position, aiming for John's chest. John lunged toward the gorilla. Sudden, piercing pain shot through his head, white flashes danced in his eyes, and the lights went out.

Chapter 48

John slowly opened his eyes. The eyelids' movements scraped a nerve, thrusting needle stabs into his eyeballs. Pain throbbed in his left arm and his ribs. He smelled a mixture of disinfectant and floor polish, and the first thing he saw was Chris standing at the foot of a bed in which John lay flat on his back. "Where am I?" he asked and shut his eyes. His words pounded his head like artillery shell explosions.

"You're in Botkin Hospital," Chris said. "You've been out for a while."

John surveyed his surroundings. A dozen men with bandaged heads, legs, and arms lay around him in an open ward. Some moaned loudly, aggravating his headache. He turned to Chris and spoke quietly to minimize the pain. "What happened? The last thing I remember, I was slugged on the head with a lead pipe."

"You were slugged in more places than your head. Your left arm is banged up and two of your ribs are broken, but the damage is limited. You're lucky; normally the hoods leave you completely disabled or dead."

John felt the ice packs on his left arm and his chest. "A man in a leather jacket and red hair slugged me. He said that we Americans never learn, that we are too inquisitive. What do you make of it?" Trush?

"Well, yeah. I doubt it was a robbery. There's no cash in your wallet, but I wouldn't expect it to still be there. Anyone could've taken it: the paramedics, the ambulance driver, or even the hospital staff. Your credit cards and ID weren't taken, I checked. So the message must be for you to lay off. In other words, stop snooping around, you're getting too close to something they don't want exposed."

"Now I remember, the man said something else that carried a threat. He said that if I cared about my darling ballerina, I must forget about Corrotto and the contract. This was my last warning. He threatened to break her legs."

"Trush, Casone, or both are behind this. They'd have a reason if, as we suspect, they're in collusion on the kickback scheme. And I probably don't need to remind you about what happened to David when he put the pressure on Trush."

"I can't stop now. I made a promise to David's father that I'd get to the bottom of what happened to David." John eyed the cracks in the walls and the worn linoleum on the floor. "Where is this place?"

"Like I said, you're in Botkin Hospital, though you may find it hard to believe that this *is* a hospital. It's just down Leningratskyi Prospekt from Telman Square, close to Aerostar hotel."

"How'd I get here?"

"Someone must have called an ambulance. The doctor said you were lying unconscious in Telman Square when you were picked up."

"How did *you* know I was here?"

"I got a call an hour ago. The caller said, 'You find friend in Botkin Hospital,' and hung up."

"How'd this caller know your number and who you are?"

"I'd say you were being followed by somebody who knows everything there is to know about you, me, Sovcell, and, I wouldn't be surprised, the gas mileage we used to get on the old Volvo."

"And another thing, before I was slugged in Telman Square, I had just shaken off a tail in the center of Moscow. The red-haired man in the black jacket followed me."

"Trush is feeling the pressure. Applying the screws to Casone is paying off."

John moved his left arm and felt ice pick stabs piercing his chest and his neck. He winced. "It's paying off all right—I can feel it. I need something besides these ice packs to kill the pain."

"The doctor said that since you are a foreigner he had no medicine to give you, and he couldn't attend to you properly unless he received hard currency. I don't know if that's an official policy or an enterprising effort on his part, but I'd say it's the latter. I'll call World Medical and arrange for your repatriation. Your head should be scanned for any brain damage."

"No need for a scan. I know I have brain damage—I came to Moscow. Forget about World Medical and pay the doctor. I'm getting out of here. I want to be in the Sovcell switch room when we turn on the network."

"Are you sure you don't want me to arrange for you to return Stateside? Not getting proper medical attention is already an indication of brain damage."

"Just pay the goddamn doctor, Chris. I'm getting out of here."

"Okay, okay, I'll take care of it right now." Chris left to find the doctor.

John thought about his first meeting with the gorilla. The gorilla probably had a message for him then, but didn't have a chance to deliver it. Today was the second meeting. Leather Jacket had delivered the message: a last warning. Would there be a third, a *final* meeting?

Chapter 49

The next morning John returned to work. His left arm and his ribs ached, but the medication Chris purchased with hard currency had reduced John's pain to a tolerable level.

He reviewed the project's status. All equipment was installed, and most scheduled tests had been performed. The remainder of the tests would be done today. According to the manufacturer's tech reps, the network would be ready to provide service before the day's end. If the test results met expectations, John would recommend to Trush that Sovcell cut the network into limited service at 1 P.M. on Friday, August 9. The real traffic over the weekend would give the technicians a chance to work out the bugs that scheduled testing couldn't uncover. A formal announcement of start of service offering to the public could then be scheduled for next week.

The remaining tests were finished in the afternoon, and the results indicated that the network carried traffic with good transmission quality with the exception of two outlying areas that had insignificant foreign business presence. John saw hope for the venture's success. He placed a call to Trush to deliver the good news. The Russian answered, "Yes, Mr. Baran?"

"I have good news, Mr. Trush. All scheduled tests are finished, and the network is provisionally operational. I recommend we begin limited service—we call it a soft cut—tomorrow at one o'clock."

"Marvelous, marvelous," Trush exclaimed, it seemed, with great joy. "But if the network is operational, why are we waiting until tomorrow afternoon and why limited service?"

John sighed. "Because we need tonight and tomorrow morning to clean up faults in the network that the tests weren't able to discover. I assure you it's necessary to do that. The tests are not perfect."

Silence on the line. John waited.

"Very well, Mr. Baran," Trush said with resignation in his voice. "I must defer to you in this matter. Tomorrow at one o'clock, I shall have the minister, other dignitaries, and the press present. We shall make a joint announcement you and me, and then we will have a reception for our guests."

John groaned. "No, Mr. Trush, formal announcement of Sovcell services must wait until next week; we need the weekend to flush out service faults and errors. We will do it with a limited number of users under our control. If it goes well, then we will announce our service to the general public next week."

Another silence on the line.

"Mr. Baran," Trush finally spoke, "is this 'soft cut' really necessary?"

"It is necessary if we want to avoid a possible public embarrassment in case an undiscovered fault brings the network down and severs all connections. How would the minister explain it to the dignitaries and the press?"

A still longer silence on the line.

"I understand," Trush said. "We shall follow your plan."

…..

At 1 p.m. the following day, John, Chris, Nikolai, and Trush assembled inside the switch room to commence the soft cut of the network. John took two mobile phones and gave one to Trush. He raised his right hand and crossed his fingers. "Here goes, keep your fingers crossed."

Trush gave John a strange look.

Nikolai, seeing Trush's expression, offered an explanation, "It is American superstition, Comrade Trush. It is hoped that bad luck is averted by making sign of cross."

"Very good, Nikolai," John said. "It is *strongly* hoped."

Nikolai flashed a confident smile, while Trush shook his head.

John and Trush took their mobile phones outside the metal-enclosed switch room to place a call over the Sovcell network. John left the building, stood in the parking lot, and was ready to dial Trush's mobile number. He said a quick prayer and crossed his fingers again. He dialed and waited. He hoped and prayed for a quick, clear connection. With an operational network, revenues would begin to flow, and Ober would be pleased. That out of the way, he could focus his time on finding out what really had happened to David.

He heard a ringback tone and then, "Allo?" The call had succeeded. The network was operational. *Thank god,* John let out a silent yell. When he said hello into the receiver, he heard an immediate response.

"Excellent, excellent, excellent," Trush shouted with exuberance.

The transmission quality was superb. Thank god again.

"You are to be congratulated, Mr. Baran, and we will celebrate," Trush commanded.

"You must congratulate Nikolai and his technicians, Mr. Trush. They deserve it more than anyone else." John terminated the call and went back into the building. As he walked down the hall toward the switch room, he saw Trush's face break into a broad smile. The Russian waved his hands, nodded his head, mumbled to himself, and congratulated everyone in sight. It was a rare picture to see: a smiling Russian acting happy.

Trush hurried up to John and shook his hand with gusto accorded heroes of the Soviet Union. "The minister will be pleased, and we must celebrate. I will have food and drink brought in, the workers deserve it."

John needed to quickly squelch the idea. He was as happy as any Russian there and wanted to celebrate with them, but a celebration party would delay the final testing under live traffic conditions. "No celebration, Mr. Trush. We must now place test calls to verify the many different conditions and areas of operation. The celebration can come later when the network officially cuts into service."

Trush's face clouded up, but then, after a moment, he smiled. "You Americans, all business. But you are correct, we will do as you say."

A happy and agreeable Trush wasn't the normal Trush. John's senses tripped an alarm of caution. What did his father say? *A happy communist is a devious and dangerous communist. He's celebrating his victory over you, except you don't know it yet.*

Trush put his hand on John's shoulder and with glee in his voice said, "You must join me tonight at Markova's apartment for a special party to celebrate this glorious achievement."

"Thank you," John said. "We'll be happy to come."

"We?"

"Chris and I."

"The invitation is for you only, John. It is a private party."

It was the first time Trush called John by his first name. Did that mean anything? "I understand," John said, but he didn't understand. He thought it strange that Trush didn't want Chris at the party. Was Trush observing some hierarchical protocol? John debated whether he should refuse an invitation that excluded Chris, an integral member of the Sovcell team. In the end, he decided not to make an issue out it. "I'll come alone."

Trush handed John a folded sheet of paper. "This is the address and directions to Markova's apartment. She already left to make preparations. The party starts at nineteen hours, the dinner is at twenty hours." Trush made his rounds congratulating everyone again, and left the building.

Chapter 50

At four o'clock, John's secretary reminded him that he had a five o'clock meeting with the country manager of an American consumer products company. The meeting was about Sovcell services and the possibility to provide a number of mobile phones for the company's representatives in Moscow. He checked in with Chris. "I have to meet with a potential customer in an hour. I'll see you over the weekend. I'll call." He didn't tell Chris about the party in Markova's apartment, as he didn't want Chris to feel slighted.

"I'll drive and provide support. My winning personality will dazzle our prospective customer."

"Look, Chris, the meeting could last into late evening, and I don't want to tie up your Friday night. I'm sure you have more pleasant things lined up for tonight. I'll take the Metro."

Chris smiled in an apparent acknowledgement of the more pleasant things.

John waved a quick 'so long' and was out the door before Chris could ask any questions.

…..

Later that evening, Chris was still in his office finishing the week's financial reports when he heard a knock on his door. He went to open it. Nikolai stood outside the door, his face registering surprise.

"I saw light under door and wanted to turn off," Nikolai said. "You still here, Mr. Ashley? You should be going."

"Going where?"

Nikolai looked uneasy, as if he'd said something he shouldn't have. He shuffled in place and turned to leave.

"Going where?" Chris repeated the question with insistence.

Nikolai stopped, eyed Chris uncertainly.

"Where, Nicolai? Where am I supposed to go?"

"Party at Markova's apartment," he said after hesitating for a long moment.

"I wasn't invited. What am I missing? What kind of a party is it?"

"I'm sorry you were not invited. It is private celebration of network working."

Suddenly, fear for John's safety gripped Chris. "Was John invited?" he asked, but he knew the answer.

The Russian said nothing.

"Goddam it, Nikolai, was John invited?"

Nikolai gave a barely perceptible nod.

"Is he going to the party?"

The Russian stood silent.

"Answer me! Is John going to the party?

Another barely perceptible nod from Nikolai.

Deep in thought, Chris shuffled back to his desk and dropped into the chair. He sat immobile, silent, staring at the top of his desk.

"Good night, Mr. Ashley." The Russian turned to leave.

Chris jumped to his feet. "Nikolai, get me keys to a car."

The Russian gave Chris a puzzled look, but he left and returned with a set of keys. Chris grabbed the keys and dashed for the door, but then stopped—he'd forgotten something. "I need directions to Markova's apartment, Nikolai."

The Russian looked apprehensive. "Why you need directions to Alla's apartment, you were not invited to party?"

"Give me the goddamn directions *now*. I don't have time to consult a map."

The Russian vacillated, but then drew a sketch of the route and held it out. Chris yanked the piece of paper out of Nikolai's hand and sprinted for the exit. Over his shoulder he yelled, "I'm inviting myself to the party."

He shot out of the building, rushed to the parking lot, jumped into the Zhiguli and drag-raced toward the gate. When he reached it, he saw the gates closed and locked. He looked for the guard, but didn't see him. Shit, had the Russians already picked up the habit of quitting early on Fridays? He jumped out of the car and rushed back into the building.

As he approached Nikolai's office, he heard one side of a conversation: Nikolai was talking to someone on the phone. Chris couldn't understand the hushed words, but they sounded urgent. When Nikolai saw Chris walk through his doorway, he said something hurriedly into the receiver and quickly hung up.

"The key to the gate, Nikolai. And where's the guard?"

"I will open gate, Mr. Ashley." Nikolai fished out a set of keys from his desk. "Guard not working tonight."

Chris ran back to the Zhiguli and waited, gunning the engine. He had a strong foreboding about the party. He had to get to John before the Russians acted. He feared the worst—another paralyzed American.

As Nikolai opened the gate, Chris floored it and hurled the vehicle into the side street. He turned onto Gorky Street and headed southeast toward the Garden Ring Road. Before switching into a faster left lane, he looked in the rear view mirror to see if the lane was clear and saw a black Moskvich very close behind him. As he pulled into the left lane, the Moskvich followed his move and began to tailgate Chris' Zhiguli.

Dumb Russian drivers. Chris pulled over into the right lane, allowing the Moskvich to pass. The traffic signal ahead turned red and both cars stopped at the intersection, their front bumpers even. Before the signal turned green, Chris's door flew open and four strong arms yanked him out of the car. He tried to resist. He felt a blow to his head and collapsed onto the pavement. The two men picked Chris up and heaved him. He sailed through the air, collided with a cement wall, and crashed to the ground. His back smashed into the concrete sidewalk, but he remained conscious. Forcing his eyelids open, he raised his head and looked in the direction of his car. The Zhiguli's rear tires spun and burned rubber. Blue smoke shot from the exhaust. Friction connected the tires with the pavement, the vehicle leaped forward, bolted down Gorky Street, and disappeared into a side street.

Chris' eyelids closed shut. His head fell back on the concrete.

Chapter 51

TrenMos Restaurant, Southwest Moscow

John's meeting with the country manager of an American consumer product company Friday evening turned into a dinner meeting at the TrenMos restaurant. TrenMos, a Soviet-American joint venture with the American partner from Trenton, New Jersey, offered a menu popular among American expats.

After John's presentation of Sovcell services, the manager looked skeptical. "Such a service can't be made to work in Moscow. I've been here nine months and I'm convinced that such a feat is impossible to pull off in this environment."

"I hear what you're saying, but this very afternoon I've made a successful call over our network."

The manager gave John a stop-putting-me-on look.

"Believe it," John said. "I'll bring a couple mobile units to your office to demonstrate the service."

"Can't wait, and if they actually work, I'll order a bunch."

They had dinner and talked about the business climate in Moscow, living conditions for expats, and, too, the Philadelphia Phillies statistics and prospects.

At 7 P.M., John excused himself. He said goodbye, left the restaurant and walked to the nearby Frunzenskaya Metro. He still didn't trust Russian taxi drivers, and the Metro was a convenient and cheap way to get around in Moscow.

According to Trush's information, Markova's apartment was located in one of Stalin's "gothic" buildings just off the Garden Ring Road near the American Embassy. John knew that only the Party elite, the privileged, resided in the building, and he wondered just how elite and how privileged Markova was among the important. The party was to start with drinks at seven, and dinner would be served at eight. The Russians' favorite pastime would take up an hour. John planned to join the party for drinks and would decline dinner.

He stepped off the train at Barrikadnaya Metro, walked to Markova's building, and entered the ugly monument to another communist era. The security guard, a frail senior citizen who looked like he had survived the Great Patriotic War, stopped him with a raised hand and a suspicious stare. "What business do you have in this building?"

John told him.

The veteran made a call, spoke, listened, and hung up. He pointed to the elevators and gave John the floor and apartment number. Walking to the elevator, John could feel the dampness in the building as if somehow water had been trapped in the stone walls and was now slowly seeping out. He tried to picture German prisoners of war working on the Stalinist monstrosity, and concluded that no matter how ugly the Russian design, the construction had to be solid. Stalin's buildings were to symbolize the power of the State, but instead they displayed the tasteless excess and creative bankruptcy of the Soviet architecture. He took an elevator—they all seemed to be working—to the twenty-first floor, found the apartment, and knocked.

Trush opened the door with a smile on his face. "Welcome, John." He thrust his right hand forward; he held a glass of clear liquid in his left hand. John smelled vodka fumes as he shook Trush's hand and wondered again if being called by his first name a second time had any significance. Were they buddies now?

Trush continued to smile in a strange, expectant way, as if John had come bearing gifts. "I am happy to see you join our celebration of Sovcell's glorious achievement. Please come in."

A smiling and happy communist? *Trouble ahead.* He stepped across the threshold and beheld the apartment of his marketing manager. By Soviet standards, the place was huge. Two or three units had to have been converted into one to get that much floor space. Except for those present, there was nothing Soviet about it. The furniture was Western, probably from a Scandinavian country. And the extras: Italian window treatment, rugs from the Caucus republics, and Blaupunkt sound equipment.

He surveyed the guests. In addition to Trush and Markova, another man, John recognized as Trush's boss, the Minister of Communications, leaned on a massive mahogany bar with a glass in his hand. He was a small man, his features almost miniature, but his eyes were alert and he projected an image of being in command. When he saw John walk in, he left the bar, marched over, and introduced himself. He shook John's hand as if he was welcoming a new member into his elite family. Then he marched back to the bar, poured half a glass of Stolichnaya, and offered it to John. John took it. Everyone else had a drink in their hand. The minister raised his glass. "To the glorious Sovcell achievement," he said and looked around as if to make sure everyone had assumed a proper toasting stance. They had. He turned back to John. "You must be congratulated for your accomplishments, Mr. Baran. *Tost,*" the minister commanded and brought the glass to his lips. He emptied its content in one throw and looked around the room, as if to make sure everyone followed the his example. John drained half of his drink.

Markova took center stage and raised her hand to gain everyone's attention. She wore a black pantsuit and a loosely fitted, white blouse that revealed only the proper amount of her endowments. She could've been dressed for church, if she were a churchgoer.

"To celebrate Sovcell's achievement," she announced, "we are having fresh trout, broiled to perfection. Please take your seats at the table."

Fresh trout? Except for an occasional appearance of the slimy sturgeon, John hadn't seen any other fish in the State stores, markets, or Soviet restaurants. Pity, he'd already eaten dinner at TrenMos: chicken and mixed vegetables. He flagged Markova's attention. "I'm sorry Alla, but I already had dinner."

Everyone in the room, including the cook by the dinner table, froze and stared at John as if he had just committed a most hideous crime. In a split second, he realized what he'd done. He spurned his hostess' kindness, an unthinkable transgression in the Slavic culture and violation of Xenia,

Zeus' law of hospitality: a hideous crime indeed, punishable by a thunderbolt strike. He hastened to repair the damage. "I shall be happy to join you at the dinner table."

The stares dissolved into faint smiles, and the celebratory exuberance of the moment slowly returned. Trush refilled everyone's glass, and the guests slowly moved into the dining area, babbling about the glorious achievement, parroting the minister. Trush moved next to John as if he was assigned to escorting John to the table and making sure he took the proper seat. He invited John to sit next to the minister, while he pulled out a chair on the opposite side. Markova took the seat next to Trush.

Markova's cook brought out individual portions of borscht consommé and placed the bowls in front of the guests. John didn't get one. He relaxed. He was pleased that Markova had accepted his decision to decline dinner. He would just nurse his drink. But before the guests could pick up their spoons, Markova stood, went into the kitchen, and returned with another bowl of borscht. She placed the bowl in front of John and said, "You must try my creation." She glanced at Trush, who acknowledged her with a strange smile and an eager nod. John noted the exchange between the two Russians and wondered if he'd missed something.

Chapter 52

The guests picked up their spoons, sampled the borscht, and praised Markova's culinary art. John picked up his spoon and held it over his bowl. The others looked at him, apparently waiting for him to taste the borscht and join in praise of Markova's gastronomy. He lowered the spoon into the bowl, filled it with the red liquid, and raised it. Markova peered at him with curious expectation in her eyes.

John froze.

A cold, thistly feeling crawled down his spine. Chris's words struck him like a lightning bolt. *David's stroke had to be induced. Something he unknowingly ate or drank.* Would Markova dare, like this, in front of the minister? Is the minister in on this? The answers at that moment didn't matter. What mattered was action.

He eased his spoon back into the bowl. "I'm sorry, Alla, I'd better take my medication before I try your special preparation. I need my 300mg of Zantac to control acidity in my stomach. I smell vinegar in the borsht."

Markova's face registered disappointment, but then she smiled and nodded, as if giving John her permission.

"Unfortunately," he said shaking his head, "I don't have it with me. It's in my car," he lied.

The Russian troika looked annoyed. They waited it seemed, for John to get on with it.

He sprang to his feet and quickly moved toward the door. "I'll be right back with the pills and I can't wait to taste your borsht, Alla."

As he reached for the door handle, loud banging from the other side startled him. The troika looked in the direction of the entry door. Markova, appearing surprised, as if she didn't expect anyone, hurried to the door. As soon as she opened it, Colonel Lisov and two other men rushed in. One of the men, older, graying, carried a small stainless case; he looked like a scientist. The other man, younger, tall, dark, methodically scanned the apartment.

Lisov marched straight to the dining area and surveyed the table. He pointed to John's bowl. "Mr. Baran, is this yours?"

As soon as John nodded, the colonel placed his hand over the borsht as if forbidding anyone to touch it. "Did you consume any of it?" he asked.

John shook his head and pointed to his stomach. "Acid problems."

The younger man flashed his identification in front of Markova's face: an opened, red folding-case with the KGB sword and shield emblem on the inside of the case, next to his photograph. He made a get-moving motion with his hand and escorted Markova to her bedroom.

The scientist stood gazing at Lisov, as if he was waiting for instructions. John closed his open mouth and saw that his wasn't the only jaw that had dropped—rush and the minister looked more stupefied than he was. Lisov said something to Trush that John couldn't hear, but it was obvious that Trush didn't like what he heard. He stared at Lisov for a moment and then left the apartment in silence. Then the colonel said something to the minister, and the minister left in silence. Lisov walked over to the scientist and pointed to John's borscht.

The scientist marched to the table, placed the metal case in a space he had cleared, and opened it. John walked over to look. The inside of the case appeared to be an elaborate chemistry set, surrounded by electronic equipment. He pulled out an eyedropper with one hand and lifted a test tube with the other. Uncorking the test tube, he dipped the eyedropper into John's bowl, drew out the red liquid, and squeezed it into the test tube. Then he corked the test tube, opened a compartment in the suitcase that contained four holes, and placed the test tube inside one of them. He closed the compartment and pressed several buttons. A bank of lights on one side of the suitcase began to flash in a complex sequence.

Frozen in place, John watched the lights dance. He focused on a digital timer in the corner of the suitcase. Thirty seconds elapsed; the lights kept dancing. At exactly sixty seconds the lights went out, a small screen at the top of the suitcase lit up, and a Cyrillic message scrolled across the display.

From John's vantage the display was upside down, and before he could read the message, the scientist closed the case. He turned to Lisov and silently nodded. As if that was the signal he was waiting for, the colonel headed straight to Markova's bedroom.

Two minutes later Markova and the young KGB agent emerged. Markova wore a light coat and had an overnight bag with her as if she were taking a weekend trip. She shot John a lethal glance and left the apartment in the escort of the KGB agent. Lisov came out of the bedroom with a small metal box. He gave the box to the scientist and headed straight toward John.

"Mr. Baran, please wait for me in my car downstairs," he said. "It is the white Volga with a driver in it. His name is Vladimir."

"But—"

"I will explain later, please go."

John heeded the colonel's directive and left the apartment. He stepped into an elevator and raised his hand to press the button. His hand shook.

Chapter 53

Outside Markova's apartment building, John spotted Lisov's Volga parked down the street. A man sat behind the wheel smoking, looking bored. John approached the car. "Vladimir?"

The driver nodded. "*Da.*"

John explained Lisov's instruction, and the driver pointed to the back seat. As John climbed into the Volga the smell of Russian cigarette smoke whomped him. He got out and stood next to the car to avoid inhaling noxious gases from the burning Russian weed. He noticed that his hands still had a slight shake, and he began deep breathing exercises to relax. He had a million questions for Lisov.

The entry door to Markova's building opened, and Lisov and the scientist walked out. They spoke for a minute, and then the scientist quickly walked to the Lada behind the Volga, climbed in, and drove off. Lisov started toward John. Seeing the colonel approach, the driver jumped out of the car, put out his cigarette, and opened the rear door. Lisov asked John to get into the back seat and then joined him. He gave the driver directions to John's apartment, and the driver pulled out into street traffic.

Lisov peered at John and shook his head. "You are very lucky, Mr. Baran."

"What was in the borscht?" John shot his first question for Lisov.

"We have been watching Markova for some time," the colonel said. "She is a resourceful and clever woman with many connections. We don't yet know how, but she obtained a most highly classified and dangerous compound. That is what she had put in your borscht."

"What kind of compound?"

"I cannot tell you," Lisov said, but the tone and timbre of his voice lacked the force of finality.

"You can't tell me? Markova put something into my borscht to seriously harm me, maybe kill me, and you can't tell me?"

"It is most highly classified."

John kept pressing Lisov for an answer, but the colonel stonewalled every approach and rejected every argument. If Lisov wouldn't identify the substance, then John wanted to know who was behind the malice. He concluded that Markova was simply carrying out the orders given to her. Given by whom? Trush? The minister? Someone else? He asked these questions, but Lisov provided no answers.

He was out of arguments and ideas of how to get Lisov talking. Then he remembered what Chris had said: *Russians will kill for hard currency.* John wondered if they would simply talk for hard currency. As he contemplated *buying* information from Lisov, a pang of caution jabbed him. The KGB colonel could run him in for attempting to bribe the Soviet secret police. The approach to get Lisov to talk for dollars had to be handled delicately and discreetly.

He reached into his pocket and fished out a hundred-dollar bill. He held it in his left hand on Lisov's side in such a way that the driver could not see it. John casually looked straight ahead as if the money in his hand didn't exist. Out of the corner of his eye, he saw Lisov glance down and then look away as if he didn't see the bill. He didn't speak or in any way acknowledge the presence of Benjamin Franklin.

The driver left the Garden Ring Road and turned onto Gorky Street. The traffic was sparse, and John knew that he had at most fifteen minutes left before they reached Telman Square and his apartment building. He decided to raise his offer for the information. Fishing out two more one hundred-dollar bills, he held the three hundred in his hand. Again, Lisov glanced at the money, said nothing.

The driver passed Dinamo Stadium on the right and then the Aerostar Hotel on the left. John had less than three minutes left to break down the colonel's intransigence. He pulled out all the Benjamins he had left and held in his hand five crisp one-hundred-dollar bills.

Lisov took notice, but again he didn't respond in any way. He tapped the driver on the shoulder and pointed to a spot in front of the Ernst Telman statue.

John had struck out. The hard currency bribe, the most reliable method of acquiring anything in Russia, had not worked. He got out of the car and when he turned to thank Lisov, he saw the colonel climb out of the back seat to join him. John thrust out his hand and said, "I don't know how to thank you, Colonel Lisov, for—"

"Let us take a walk." Lisov broke in and pointed in the direction of the square behind Telman's statue. He led John past the statue into a wooded area and stopped in a spot that was hidden from his driver's view and out of earshot of the people walking in the square. He faced John and began speaking in a slow, deliberate cadence.

"Mr. Baran, now that we are alone, I must tell you that I will require more than five hundred dollars to disclose information."

John perked up. His faith in the mighty hard-currency bribe was restored. Chris was right, and a KGB colonel was not above the money's power.

"You do not realize the risk I would be taking," Lisov continued. "But I want to give my family the things they desire and deserve." He shook his head as if he didn't believe he was saying these things. "The Western clothes and cosmetics my wife has been admiring are expensive. I blame Gorbachev for the condition we are in. His reforms have contaminated our culture, and materialism is corroding our ideology."

"Is that bad?" John asked.

"I do not know. But I do know that my wife cannot make a dress, nor a sandwich, out of ideology." Lisov gave John a serious look. "And I do not even know if I can trust you."

"You can trust me, Colonel Lisov. How much do you require?"

"Three thousand America dollars."

"I don't have three thousand on me."

"I will take the five hundred now and the rest later. You said I could trust you, can I?"

"Yes. Now, what was in the borscht?"

"The substance in your borscht was one of the compounds developed by our Institute of Microbiology of the Ministry of Defense, the IMMD.

We believe Markova obtained the substance through her GRU contacts. IMMD carried out work under the direction of GRU for military applications. I know because I worked for the GRU before I took my current post."

"What do you call this compound? How does it work?"

Lisov said nothing.

"How does it work, Colonel Lisov?" John raised his voice to a level that could have been heard by a passerby.

Lisov looked around the square, and when apparently satisfied that no one was paying any attention to them, said, "The compound is called MBR-5 and is composed of 'smart' biomolecules."

"Smart molecules?"

"They work like your smart bombs in Iraq. They affect the brain only, their programmed target. I do not know the precise action, but the molecules somehow bind to other material in the brain and accumulate until they obstruct the flow of blood to the brain cells. The action causes an ischemic stroke, paralyzing the victim."

John froze. *David Chernov.*

Chapter 54

Wrinkles gathered on Lisov's forehead as if he was searching his memory. After a moment, he nodded and spoke. "When the victim of MBR-5 is exposed to radiation, such as X-rays, the biomolecules are activated and burst. They 'explode,' killing the host. Medically, it looks like a fatal massive hemorrhaging stroke."

"Son of a bitch," John blurted out in English. *Dr. Chu's firecrackers.*

"What?"

"*Sookyn syn*, favorite America expression," John made the translation. "When did you begin to suspect Markova?"

"After Mr. Chernov was paralyzed, the hospital classified his condition as an irregular medical episode and reported it to our Medical Anomalies Center, the MAC. One of the MAC members, a bioweapons expert representing the IMMD, recognized that Chernov's condition could have been caused by MBR-5 and as a routine procedure initiated an inventory check of the compound stored in the IMMD and the Army stockpile. The inventory check revealed three vials missing from the IMMD, and Markova was put under surveillance."

"But how did you know to show up tonight? You had no proof that Markova had the compound in her apartment, or that she was going to use it tonight."

"I had expected Mr. Chernov's autopsy results to confirm my suspicion, but as you said, there was no autopsy. If there had been an autopsy, and my suspicion was confirmed, I would have acted sooner."

"So, you suspected Markova, but you couldn't have been sure. Still, you burst into her apartment. The minister and Trush were there, and they are important people. Wasn't that risky?"

"I reviewed all surveillance data on Chernov, Markova, and, of course, you, and I concluded that Markova had to be the one to use the compound on Chernov."

"But how did you know she was going to use it on me tonight?"

"As soon as my agent reported that you had entered Markova's building, I concluded that you were in trouble."

"Why? Trush invited me for the celebration of our network becoming operational."

"I am sure he did. But I have knowledge of what the minister and Trush were planning for Sovcell future."

"And what's that, a takeover?" Harry's warning flashed in John's memory.

"That, Mr. Baran, I absolutely cannot tell you. My personal survival could be jeopardized."

John saw a determined look on Lisov's face and decided not to press the issue. "So, if an autopsy had been performed on David Chernov, we could have discovered the cause back in July."

Lisov hesitated. "Possibly, if your people knew to look for the biomolecules."

John took a deep breath and exhaled. "Is Trush part of this?"

Lisov was silent.

"There *must* be a connection."

"Mr. Baran, Comrade Trush is a high-ranking official and a personal friend of the minister. Accusing him or even casting suspicion without evidence will be detrimental to the accuser."

"What will happen to Markova?"

"You do not have to worry about Markova anymore. She and her conspirators at the GRU will be nullified."

"Nullified?"

"Yes, for practical purposes she will be put out of commission."

"Back to the IMMD compounds; for what purpose was it developed? Aren't biological weapons prohibited, like since the early 70s?"

"I cannot comment on the policies of Secretary Brezhnev, or the purpose of the compound. I have already told you too much."

"What do I do now? Am I in danger? I'm sure Markova has other accomplices, and they could be anywhere, even inside Sovcell. And by your count, there is still one vial of MBR-5 missing."

Lisov nodded. "You are correct. Markova used one on Chernov and one tonight. We have recovered the third missing vial in her bedroom."

"Is she the only one in this? What about Trush, his accomplices, or even the minister?" John tried again to exact information from Lisov.

"You will be safe. Act as if nothing happened and enjoy your weekend. Now I must go. Goodnight, Mr. Baran." Lisov put out his hand, palm up.

John reached in his pocket and pulled out the five bills, folded them once, and slapped the wad into Lisov's palm. Lisov closed his palm, shoved the money into his pocket, and hurried off toward his car.

John watched the Volga speed away. A cold shiver shook him, and it wasn't the air of the August Moscow night. He walked to the apartment at a brisk pace.

He entered his building, ran up the steps to his apartment, and hoped that the bottle of Stolichnaya in the kitchen cabinet had a good belt left in it. When he put the key into the door, he heard the phone ringing. Rushing in, he picked up the receiver.

"John, are you all right?" Chris screamed.

"Yeah, I'm okay. I'll call you right back, I have to disarm the alarm." He didn't want to see the militia's friendly faces again. He called Chris back on his mobile unit.

"I had a horrible vision," Chris said. "I thought of another Friday night party at Markova's apartment: the night David was invited to Markova's special party. Saturday morning, he was paralyzed."

"Did you know that you are clairvoyant?"

"What?"

"Markova tried again; I'll explain later."

"Son of a bitch," Chris yelled. "I was trying to get to you and warn you, but Russian thugs attacked me and stole the Zhiguli I was driving."

"Screw the Zhiguli! Are you all right?"

Chris told John what had happened.

"Are you hurt?" John asked again.

"Not really, my head is okay: a bump, some swelling."

"Another Moscow carjacking, shit like that happens here."

"I think there was more to it."

"What do you mean, more to it? What else could it be?"

"Nikolai knew where I was going," Chris said.

"So what? Are you telling me he had something to do with it?"

"I think he wanted to stop me before I got to you."

"I don't believe it."

"Well, it's just my 'clairvoyance' talking."

"Enough shit for one night. Let's get some sleep. Thanks for trying to help me." John ended the call and went to look for the bottle of Stolichnaya.

After he downed his first shot, John had questions. With Markova out of the way, what will Trush do now? If the minister was involved, as Lisov seemed to suggest, what action will he be taking?

Chapter 55

KGB Chairman Kryuchkov, Defense Minister Mazov, and Interior Minister Pugo entered Vice President Gennady Yanayev's Kremlin office. They marched straight to the conference table and took seats. Kryuchkov turned to look at the vice president. Yanayev sat at his desk, gazing unsurely at his visitors.

The KGB chief had convened the group and hoped for a productive meeting. They had to decide how to bring about the state of emergency needed to take control of the country. The vice president, the KGB chief reluctantly agreed, would play a role. He glared at Yanayev and waited for the vice president to join them.

Yanayev did not move. He stared at the bottle of Stolichnaya on his desk. Then he lifted the bottle with a shaking hand, dumped two fingers of the vodka into a water glass, and knocked it back. He opened a bottle of carbonated water, filled the glass, and guzzled it as if he was trying to wash down a bad taste. He smoothed the hair on his balding head and lifted the bottle in anyone-for-a-drink gesture.

Kryuchkov grimaced. *Our vice president, the drunken clown.* He had second thoughts about proceeding with the meeting.

Yanayev put the bottle in his desk drawer, slowly rose, shuffled over to the group, and dropped into the seat at the head of his conference table.

Kryuchkov groaned. He didn't really want Yanayev's involvement in their conspiracy, but saw no other way to make the declaration of the state of emergency at least have the appearance of legality. He turned to the vice president. "Good morning, Gennady."

Yanayev surveyed his visitors and mumbled, "Good morning, comrades."

Kryuchkov began. They may have been in the vice president's office, but it was the KGB chief's meeting. "Comrades, our Union is on the precipice of collapse. I do not need to tell you the extent of this danger." He glanced around the table and waited until everyone nodded agreement. They did. "It is our sworn duty to prevent the Soviet Union from disintegrating." He peered at Yanayev. "We have decided that we must declare a state of emergency. This action will not be well received at home or abroad, and some think our citizens could oppose it with force. Unless we convince Mikhail Sergeyevich to make the announcement in his official capacity as president, our people and the world will brand our actions a military coup."

Interior Minister Pugo frowned and shook his head. "If our president is as good a communist as he claims to be, then he should agree to declare the emergency. It is in our country's interest, and it is in his best interest. But he will not do it. His love affair with the West and his addiction to their praise and aid in support of his reforms will not allow him to do it. In the eyes of the West, he is a hero. Just last year they humored him with the Nobel Peace Prize, a meaningless token for the treasonous concessions he made to the West—concessions of land we won with our blood during the Great Patriotic War. Then, in addition to that, he has weakened our Union by his arms reduction treaty. He is a traitor to the Motherland."

Kryuchkov didn't really believe that Gorbachev was a traitor, but he didn't contradict the Interior Minister. The Party was already fragmented. Mikhail Sergeyevich was a good communist, but he was led astray by Western influence. Kryuchkov hoped that their president would wake up, realize his reforms were destroying the Union, and in the end join the KGB chief in saving the Soviet State.

"If he declares a state of emergency and ditches his reforms," Pugo continued, "the West will lose faith in him. That, comrades, would destroy his ego and shatter his image of himself as the great reformer. His Western admirers would turn their backs on him and he would be isolated. He could not bear that. So he denies that his reforms have failed." He looked at

Kryuchkov and nodded as if it were a cue to the KGB chief that he had finished his declamation.

Kryuchkov focused on Yanayev. "So far our president has refused to declare the state of emergency, and we don't expect he will change his mind. It is up to us now. *We* must declare the state of emergency to save our Union. If the Army…" Kryuchkov gestured toward Defense Minister Mazov on his left, "the security troops," Kryuchkov nodded toward Interior Minister Pugo across the table, "or the KGB," Kryuchkov pointed his thumb at himself, "declares an emergency, there will be an outcry by our people and by the world community. And as I said, inside our Union significant resistance and organized opposition may arise. Some say the situation could become grave. A civil war could even break out. But if *our government* itself declares the emergency, resistance, should be manageable."

Vice President Yanayev looked confused. "But Mikhail Sergeyevich is the Soviet government, who else would declare it?"

Kryuchkov, Mazov, and Pugo stared at Yanayev.

Yanayev saw the stares and shook his head. "I am *not* the government as long as Mikhail Sergeyevich is the president."

"Declare him incapacitated," Mazov said. "Take over the government."

Yanayev gazed at Mazov with an expression of confusion and disbelief. He shifted his eyes to Pugo, who nodded his agreement with Mazov's proposal. He looked at Kryuchkov, and Kryuchkov nodded his agreement.

Yanayev slumped in his chair. His eyes were empty, his expression blank. "The government is more than this office," he said in a low voice.

Kryuchkov said, "We will recruit the prime minister, his cabinet, majority of Politburo, and important Party members."

"There will be opposition from the reformers," Yanayev said. "Yeltsin, that radical, will be trouble. And what about Mikhail Sergeyevich, what will we do with him?"

Kryuchkov waved a dismissal. "We will arrest Yeltsin when the time comes and isolate our president in his Foros vacation home."

"And our citizens?" Yanayev asked. "What if they mount significant resistance? I hear the so-called democratic movement is gaining strength. Thousands could protest."

"The Army will contain their resistance," Mazov said.

The vice president shot Mazov a cynical look. "If it is a token resistance, General, then you can contain it. But what if our citizens rise up and start a civil war? Can you contain a civil war? Will your soldiers shoot their own people? What orders will you give, General? And will your officers obey your orders?"

"You are falling into panic, Gennady," Mazov scoffed.

The vice president lowered his head and said nothing. Silence hung over the conference table.

Kryuchkov knew they had a problem. Yanayev maybe be a drunken clown, but he wasn't stupid. He had a point, and Kryuchkov didn't like the direction the meeting was taking. He looked at Mazov and then at Pugo. "Comrades, we need a diversion. A diversion created outside our Union that will appear as a threat to us. If we could recreate the specter of American imperialist aggression, then our citizens will unite behind us against that threat. It has always worked in the past. Chairman Brezhnev did that for eighteen years. So, comrades, how do we create and hype a threat that will return us to the Cold War, the days of Soviet power and glory?"

As if the KGB chief had issued instructions to find the solution to their problem, they all fell silent, seemingly struggling with their assignment.

Chapter 56

Two minutes passed in silence, and then Pugo spoke. "When I was chairman of Latvian KGB, I used a drug to neutralize opposition and nullify troublemakers." He turned to Mazov. "The GRU provided it. What do you call it, Comrade General?"

Mazov hesitated as if he didn't want to divulge a secret and didn't answer. Kryuchkov gave Mazov a sharp look and nodded, indicating to the general that he should answer the question—it was not a secret among them.

"We call it MBR-5," Mazov said, "strategic bioweapon five. We still have stockpiles of it." He gave Pugo a stern look. "Are you suggesting we use MBR-5 on our citizens?"

"Of course not, General," Pugo said with indignation in his voice. "I was going to suggest we use the bioweapons *outside* our country to create a diversion."

"Where?" Kryuchkov asked. He began to see the possibility.

"America." Pugo said.

"You are joking, Comrade Minister," Mazov said and laughed.

"Perhaps, Comrade General," Pugo said, "you should explain how MBR-5 works and allow our comrades here to decide if I am joking."

Mazov looked around the table. Kryuchkov, Yanayev, and Pugo gazed at him with expectation. He focused on Kryuchkov and waited.

Kryuchkov nodded for the Defense Minister to proceed.

Mazov took a deep breath and began. "The MBR-5 compound was developed in the early seventies. It was a brilliant discovery by our molecular biologists at the Institute of Microbiology of the Ministry of Defense in Zagorsk. MBR-5 is a preemptive-strike weapon. A minute amount of MBR-5 taken internally induces complete paralysis within eight hours. If the victim is then exposed to radiation, he dies."

Yanayev's face shouted skepticism. "How many Americans, Comrade General, are we going to convince to swallow the drug?"

Mazov gave Yanayev a disgusting look and continued. "The code name for the preemptive strike was *Udar*. It was designed to work as follows. First, a calculated amount of MBR-5 is released into the enemy's water supply. Within eight hours, consumers of the contaminated water are paralyzed. Second, a high-altitude RPB explosion is detonated and the paralyzed die. The military plan called for activation of *Udar* in case of imminent breakout of hostilities. It was designed to cripple the assailant before he can strike the Motherland."

"What is an RPB explosion, Comrade General?" Yanayev asked.

"A Radiation Pulse Bomb explosion," Mazov said. "It generates a radiation pulse that triggers MBR-5. Once triggered, MBR-5 kills its host. Medically, death appears as a massive stroke."

The vice president's jaw dropped. "America retaliates, and such a diversion will be the end of us all."

Mazov opened a bottle of carbonated water, filled a glass and drank. He plunked down the empty glass on the table and peered at Kryuchkov. "The problem with *Udar* today is that we cannot trigger it, even if we wanted to use it. First," he held out one finger and frowned, "the missiles that were armed with RPB warheads have been deactivated. For that you can thank our traitor president for signing the Arms Reduction Treaty with Reagan four years ago. And second," he held out two fingers, "*Udar* was designed to be used against NATO forces in Europe. We do not have a plan to use it in America." He stopped and stared at the empty glass in front of him.

Kryuchkov considered calling for Yanayev's bottle of Stolichnaya, but dismissed the thought. He needed sober reasoning.

Pugo said, "We do not need an RPB explosion to create a diversion. Mass paralysis in American city will be diversion enough. America will go on alert and threaten to retaliate. We will go on alert, and our people will unite behind us."

"Time is short," Mazov said. "We only have nine days until the signing of the New Union Treaty. Once that is signed, we will not have a Soviet Union to save. The problem is that nine days is not enough time for our military to develop a plan."

"I disagree, Comrade General," Pugo said with forced assertion in his voice.

Mazov sat up in his chair and glowered at Pugo. "And what do you disagree with, Comrade Minister?"

"I disagree with your statement that there is not enough time to develop a plan," Pugo said.

Mazov let out a derisive laugh. "And I suppose you already have a plan?"

"I have an idea, Comrade General."

Kryuchkov peered at Pugo with interest. "What is your idea, Boris?"

The Interior Minister straightened in his seat and pushed his chest out. "We ship MRB-5 by a Greek freighter to an American East Coast port. We can disguise it by transporting it in, say, olive oil containers. Our Greek friends will accommodate us. Our agents in America will pick up the cargo and transport it to the target city and release it into the city's water supply. They have nine days to select the city for most effect and viability of the plan and arrange the required transportation. Our Second Chief Directorate agents can do that in less than nine days. They are not military planners." Pugo looked at Kryuchkov, who nodded quietly. Bolstered by Kryuchkov's approval, Pugo looked at Mazov with an expression of triumph. Mazov's face turned red. The veins in his neck bulged.

"What if America retaliates by attacking us?" Yanayev said. "They will know who is behind this *Udar*. Maybe we should deploy *Udar* in Western Europe. It will be safer for us."

Kryuchkov shook his head. "First, Bush is not the cowboy Reagan was; he will not attack. And second, we need a credible enemy for our people to unite behind us. There is only one credible enemy, and that is America." He turned to Mazov. "MRB-5 has been refined several times so it is highly concentrated now. Is that not correct?"

"Five times as concentrated as the original MBR-1," Mazov said. "But it will still take at least one tank load for a large city like Baltimore or Washington."

"Then we will select a smaller city," Kryuchkov said. "We can choose a port city to minimize transport. I shall have my staff prepare a detailed plan immediately. And yes, General Mazov, it will not take nine days." He glanced around the table, waited. When no one spoke, he went on.

"We will be ready with the MBR-5 plan, a modified *Udar,* but we will not execute the plan unless things go badly for us. We will know on the second day of the state of emergency if we need to proceed with the bioweapons attack on America."

"And who will make that determination?" Mazov asked.

"I will," Kryuchkov said. "And I will give the order. The KGB will execute the entire plan." He paused as if he'd forgotten something. "Of course, I will need the Army's assistance."

Mazov nodded. "Of course."

"Any questions or reservations?" Kryuchkov asked.

Silence.

"We will not discuss the American *Udar* plan with anyone outside the four of us here," the KGB chief said. "I do not want the Prime Minister or Politburo members to panic when they hear about our distraction plan. They would not approve of our daring scheme." He scrutinized Mazov, Pugo, and Yanayev individually as they nodded their consent. He turned to Yanayev. "Gennady, prepare a draft of the announcement of the state of emergency for our discussion." He stood up. "We will meet again, and I will let you know when and where."

The meeting ended.

As Kryuchkov strode to the exit, the daring scheme buzzed a warning in his head. Could their action to save the Union bring an end to all of them, as the drunken clown had proclaimed?

Chapter 57

That Saturday evening, John exited the Kremlin Palace of Congresses concert hall after the Red Army Choir performance, turned left, and crossed the Trinity Bridge. He turned right in Aleksandrov Gardens and headed for the Prospekt Marksa Metro. Though he had listened to the choir many times before, today was the first time John witnessed a live performance of the seventy-member group. His father hated Communism, but he still played the Red Army choir records. The Alexandrov ensemble, as it was known in Russia, had no equal. The crescendos in *Kalinka* made his skin tingle.

As he was about to enter the metro station, a strong hand took hold of his arm and guided him away from the entrance. He tensed and turned to face a possible assailant, ready to defend himself. "Let's walk," Moore said, looking straight ahead.

"You should be careful, Roger, how you approach someone. You could get a fast karate chop, or worse."

"Did you enjoy the concert?" Moore said. "I don't care for the Red Army, but I like their choir."

"I didn't see you in the audience."

Moore ignored John's comment and headed toward Red Square. "Have you seen the sights?"

"What're you talking about?"

"St. Basil's Cathedral is an awesome sight when it's lit up at night. Its multi-colored onion domes are dazzling."

"Something dazzling? *In Moscow?*"

Moore led them past Lenin's Museum, and stopped in the middle of Red Square. It was nearly ten o'clock at night. Few people milled around in the distance, but none within earshot.

John looked at St. Basil's, and he saw that Moore was right. "I wish I had my Kodak Instamatic," John said. "The site looks a bit like Disney's Cinderella Castle on a starry night. It's a shame we won't see any fireworks."

Moore gestured toward the Kremlin. "The fireworks will be coming from there."

John turned to face the Kremlin. The Spassky Gate opened and a black Chaika pulled out. A ZIL limousine and two other Chaikas followed. The convoy turned right and sped down toward Moscow River. Moore eyed the vehicles. "The hard-line communists are working overtime preparing those fireworks you wanted to see."

"You mean—"

"Yes," Moore said. "This morning, the KGB chairman held a meeting in the vice president's office in there." Moore waved his hand toward the Kremlin. "Together with the Defense Minister and the Interior Minister, they decided that they had had enough of Gorbachev and his reforms. They plan to stop him from 'destroying' the Soviet Union."

"Holy shit, the fiber connection worked, and you're serious. When and how?"

"If a 'state of emergency' isn't declared by Gorbachev by August 19, nine days from now, the hardliners will declare it themselves. They'll follow with a military coup d'état. I'm telling you this so you can make plans for yourself and your venture. We are troubled by a dangerous element in their plan, a real threat to the U.S."

John froze. "What kind of threat?"

"If the coup goes badly for them, they plan a bioweapons attack on an American city as a distraction. When the U.S. and the USSR turn hostile to each other, the coup planners feel that Soviet people will support the new regime, minimizing, or eliminating, opposition to their takeover."

John sucked in his breath. "Jesus! What kind of bioweapons?"

Moore related the conversation the CIA had picked up about MBR-5 and the plan for its use.

"Goddamned commies! They've used that same stuff on David Chernov. He was paralyzed and died when he was exposed to X-rays." John paused, calmed down. "What city and when?"

"We don't know. And the coup planners don't know that either. Their agents in the U.S. will select the city."

"We've got to stop them. Anything I or our venture can do?"

Moore shook his head. "We've notified our government. The FBI and border security will be on alert. President Bush will notify Gorbachev and Yeltsin, and we hope Gorbachev can stop the conspirators before they can act. The U.S. doesn't want to see hardliners take over the Soviet government."

"What do your contacts tell you about the attack?"

"Nothing yet. We're waiting for our moles in the KGB and the GRU to find out the details of the planned shipment of the 'olive oil' to the East Coast. We'll stop it before it reaches our coast."

John grimaced. "Western ventures in the Soviet Union will be in deep shit if the hardliners take over." He thought about how Sovcell could help the CIA effort, and an idea struck him. "Roger, our network is now operational, and our partner, the Communications Minister, had distributed twelve mobile phones among important Party officials. I'd think the high military command would've gotten the units. Since we control the network— "

"You can eavesdrop on their conversation," Moore jumped in. Then quickly added, "I doubt they'd use the phones for official business, especially the hard-line bunch planning the takeover."

"Still, it's worth a try, just in case they do. Who'll be calling the shots on the coup?"

"Looks like Kryuchkov, the KGB Chairman, is taking charge, while Mazov, the Defense Minister, will command the armed forces." Moore glanced at the Kremlin towers and turned to leave. "I've got to go, John. If anything more develops, I'll let you know." He waved a goodbye and walked off in the direction of Lenin's Museum, exiting Red Square.

John stood, staring at the Kremlin. He imagined scores of paralyzed innocent Americans. The thought terrified him. He found it hard to believe that the communists would commit such a horrific act in the middle of flourishing détente. But on second thought, he concluded that communists were capable of committing whatever served their purpose.

In the Metro on the way back to his apartment, he grappled with three thoughts that whirled around in his head like a Kansas tornado. First, the potential bioterror attack on an American city disturbed him deeply, and he searched for ideas of how he could help stop it. Though he accepted Moore's assurance that the CIA would thwart any such attack, the fact that it was even a possibility troubled him. He tried to push it to the back of his mind, but he couldn't purge it.

Second, his close call at Markova's party last night told him that he was on the right track in suspecting Trush in David's paralysis and death. He'd have to be extremely careful in his dealings with the Russian, as, no doubt, Trush would try again. John didn't know exactly what he could do about that, but he'd remain vigilant.

And finally, Lisov's silence on the minister's involvement suggested that a conspiracy had been devised to take over Sovcell. He didn't know what he could do about that either, but he was determined to stop it, whatever it took.

Chapter 58

At noon, John stood by the Ernst Telman statue, waiting for Provodnikov. A mixture of excitement and anxiety flooded him as he watched the conductor drive up in his white Volga and stop on Leningratskyi Prospekt in front of the statue. His meeting with the ballerina was on.

Except for the smaller size, the Volga could've been the old '63 Chevy Biscayne that his father used to pick him up after school. And he did feel like a schoolboy about to go on his first date with the prettiest girl in West Scranton High. Butterflies fluttered in his stomach when he thought about meeting the most beautiful Odette to dance on a Moscow stage.

Provodnikov pushed the passenger door open and waved John into the car. "One hour," he said after they got underway. "It is not very far, but Moscow roads do not allow us to travel fast safely. As you know, Moscow drivers ignore that tenet and cause many accidents."

John barely heard what Provodnikov said. He was composing phrases that he'd say when he met Juliana Kovar, but he didn't come up with anything he liked, or anything he thought was appropriate. It all sounded like silly schoolboy babble. What does an American in Moscow say to a beautiful prima ballerina of the Soviet National Ballet? He didn't know. He decided to occupy his mind by following the conductor's route on the map.

Provodnikov headed northwest to Moscow's Outer Ring Road, the Moscow beltway, and eased onto the road heading south. Disabled vehicles with their hoods open—victims of the Moscow heat—dotted the beltway shoulders like dead quail. Drivers and their passengers stood around their cars, smoked, and with bored resignation watched the radiators shoot steam into the sky. Provodnikov looked at the scene and shook his head. "Most Russian-made cars should be in the junkyard, not on the road." He patted the dashboard. "The German idea of regular maintenance is keeping this one in running condition." He continued on the beltway and then turned off heading west.

"What's our destination?" John asked.

"Peredelkino, it is just ahead. It is a complex of dachas, a writers' village."

"Why is your dacha in the writers' village? Don't conductors have their own village?"

"My dacha is not here. We are going to the cottage of my good friend, a great writer."

"I thought you said—"

"It will be safer. It is more secluded, and the writers there enjoy privacy."

Inside the village, eight-foot, wooden-board fences surrounded the dachas. Narrow dirt roads made it difficult for rare opposing traffic to pass. John felt like they were moving through a maze, one of those English high hedge gardens where you couldn't figure out exactly where you were, but Provodnikov drove as if he'd been here many times.

He stopped at an unmarked gate, got out, and unlocked it with a key that must have weighed at least a pound, one of those medieval contrivances. He pushed the heavy gate open and drove into what looked like a Spanish villa courtyard, except it was a Russian dacha courtyard. Lilac bushes concealed the wooden fence around the perimeter of the cottage. Circular and rectangular beds of irises, geraniums, and petunias populated the manicured lawn.

John climbed out of the car. A strong fragrance, laced with scents of different flowers, filled the courtyard like an evening fog would fill a valley. The heat magnified the scents, turning the courtyard into a perfumery. He hadn't seen anything like it anywhere in Moscow.

Two connected brick and wood buildings with large windows, sprawled at the end of the courtyard. The structure could easily have been a summer home of the well to do on Cape Cod. "Your friend must truly be a great writer." John said, surprised by what he saw.

"He is *more* than that," Provodnikov said without further explanation. He closed the gate, locked it, and started toward the front door. John joined him. Provodnikov rang the doorbell and waited. The butterflies in John's stomach picked up tempo.

An elderly woman wearing an apron opened the door and invited them in with a simple greeting. John followed Provodnikov into the house. As he entered, he quickly scanned the interior of the dacha and his eyes froze, as he focused on her. Wearing a pale blue summer dress, she sat on the sofa in what served as a living room at one end of the dacha. As she stood and faced him, their eyes met and locked in a gaze. For the next few moments he didn't hear anything the conductor had said.

"Please be introduced," Provodnikov repeated, stepping closer to John as if to assure himself that John heard him the second time. Still gazing at the ballerina, John nodded. Provodnikov, having performed his social obligation, left them standing and went into the kitchen at the opposite end of the dacha. John stared at the ballerina with his eyes wide open.

"I am Juliana Kovar, and I am pleased to meet you, Mr. Baran," she said, extending her hand.

"I'm very happy to meet you, Miss Kovar." As he took her hand, he felt an explosive current race through him as if an electric circuit had been closed at the instant they touched. He stood dazed, looking at her. Her rich, glowing auburn hair hung in long graceful curls over her shoulders. Her ivory face was a perfect oval with a musk-rose flush on the cheekbones. He sensed a faint floral fragrance of perfume. She offered a small, shy smile, but her eyes were sparkling—they were saying something.

"Please call me Juliana, Mr. Baran." Her smile brightened.

Goosebumps spread across John's skin. "Please call me John, Miss Kovar."

They stood gazing at each other.

Chapter 59

Provodnikov came out of the kitchen and made the announcement: "Lunch is being served." He came up to John with a tray of two half-full glasses of clear liquid and invited John to take one.

John smelled the vodka fumes rising from the tray. He smiled and said, "Ladies first."

"Juliana does not drink vodka," Provodnikov said. "She will be having tea."

"I'll have tea also," John said.

"I recommend you take this," Provodnikov insisted. "It will help you digest Russian food." John smiled and shook his head.

They moved into the dining area next to the kitchen and were seated around a small table covered with a flaxen tablecloth and set with Gzhel plates—like those his mother owned—and sterling flatware. John gazed at Juliana sitting directly opposite from him. She smiled and pointed to the hors d'oeuvres on the table.

"Please," she said.

He looked at the appetizers: pickled herring, smoked sturgeon, sliced beets, tomatoes, and scallions were neatly arranged on a large Gzhel serving plate. Vinegar odor rose from the plate. An opened bottle of Stolichnaya stood next to the appetizers, and John thought that maybe Provodnikov had a point about exploiting vodka's remedial digestive powers. He helped himself to some smoked sturgeon, but decided against the liquid therapy.

The cook came out of the kitchen with a large plate of broiled chicken drumsticks and placed it on the table next to a basket of dark rye bread.

"Bush's legs," Provodnikov said, pointing to the drumsticks. "We are in a sad state of affairs when the Soviet Union cannot feed itself and must accept help from your president. Our Ukraine was the bread basket of Europe, but now we can't even harvest potatoes: they are rotting in the fields." He pointed to the bread on the table. "We used to feed that to our pigs, but now our people cannot find it in our State stores. What is wrong with our system?" He asked the question as if he didn't expect anyone to provide the answer because it was a mystery beyond comprehension.

John glanced at the plate of chicken drumsticks. How many Russians saw Bush's legs as evidence that there *was* something wrong with their system? Provodnikov's question, John hoped, was a hopeful beginning to an awakening.

The cook brought out a plate of still steaming boiled potatoes, placed them on the table, and wished everyone a good appetite. Over lunch they made small talk, mostly about the Russian climate and Russian love of the arts. John kept looking at Juliana so much that he thought she might become embarrassed, but she didn't; she always returned his gaze with a smile.

When lunch ended, Provodnikov said, "We must leave the dacha at three o'clock. Juliana and I have to be at the theater before five o'clock to prepare for the evening's performance. My associate will drive Juliana to the theater, and I will drive you back to Moscow." He stood and strutted off to the writer's study in the adjoining building. The cook cleared the table and disappeared into the kitchen behind closed doors.

John and the ballerina sat alone. He summoned the courage to take her hand and lead her into the living area where they sank into a sofa. He was searching for an opening comment when she broke the silence.

"How do you like our country? I like America," she said, without waiting for an answer to her question.

"Were you in America?" he asked.

"Yes, three years ago. On a cultural exchange program."

"What did you like about America?"

"Your country is bright and cheerful. And, of course, for a woman you have beautiful clothes and jewelry and infinitely more cosmetic products. The people are friendly, pleasant, and seem to be happy. But they appear to be always in a hurry, not enjoying the moment."

John laughed. "Sounds like New York City. It's not the same in Middle America." He looked into her eyes. "Would you like to live in America?"

"That is not possible."

"All things are possible, Juliana."

"You Americans, you are so optimistic."

John took her hand and placed it in his with her palm open. "I can read your future."

"Are you a fortune teller?"

"Only for certain people." He ran his finger across her palm and stopped. "I see from the curve of this line that you will soon go to live in America," he said and looked into her eyes. Her face blushed, her hand began to quiver, and she tried to pull it away. He firmed his grip and pulled her closer. Her body trembled. She closed her eyes slowly, her lips inviting. He kissed her lightly. She pressed her open lips to his. John felt shivers shake his body. She threw her arms around him in a locking embrace. They sat holding each other. Time stood still.

Still in the embrace, she said, "What business are you conducting in Moscow, John?"

He released her and drew back to study her face. She appeared to be serious. *Valid question; an odd moment to ask.* "We provide mobile telephone service to customers in Moscow."

"Those gadgets that you can use to make a call from anywhere?"

"Only in Moscow, so far."

"Could you show me how they work?"

"I'd be happy to, anytime." He was delighted she showed interest in his work, but at the same time wondered about her motivation. Was she interested in using the service herself? Could she afford it? Unlikely. Was she more than just curious?

"Can you do it tomorrow?" she asked with expectation in her voice.

"Of course, but where, when, and how are we going to meet?" He wondered about the she-cannot-be-seen-with-an-American manifesto proclaimed by Nikolai and Provodnikov. Was there substance to their claim?

"I am visiting the Tretyakov Gallery tomorrow afternoon," she said. "We can meet there and since I'm not dancing on Monday, we can spend time together without being rushed."

"But I thought it was unwise for you to be seen with an American in public." John dug for the truth. "Something about it appearing suspicious?"

She smiled, but said nothing.

So, John thought, were Provodnikov's theatrics surrounding their meeting designed to extract hard currency, or was Juliana's interest in mobile services serious enough for her to take the risk of being seen with an American? He concluded that hard currency commanded Provodnikov's performance. He felt a tap on his shoulder and turned to see the conductor standing behind him.

"We must go a little early," Provodnikov said. "We must account for the traffic of Moscovites returning from their dachas."

John and Juliana said a long, drawn-out goodbye. He didn't want to part from her, and he sensed that she felt the same about him. As he started to leave, he saw a curious, deep longing in her eyes. He gave her a quick hug and rushed out.

On the way back to his apartment, he thought that their mutual attraction was genuine enough, but a question of an ulterior motive on her part gnawed at him. Whatever it was, he decided, would soon surface.

Chapter 60

Cellcomm's Venture Partner Facility. Monday, August 12

Trush sat at his desk, preparing to start his Stolichnaya-sturgeon morning routine. He paused and stared at the vodka and the smoked fish in front of him. He had ample time over the weekend to think about the debacle Friday night. He had expected to hear about it from the minister on Saturday, or even Sunday, and he expected nothing good. He considered himself lucky that Lisov had apparently not tied him to Alla's illegally obtained compound and the attempt on Baran's life, and he expected his luck to continue. He was sure Alla Markova would not talk.

His superior was another matter. The minister instructed him to complete the installation of the network and bring it into service by August 12, and he had done that. Following the service cut, the minister had instructed him to do whatever was necessary to convince Cellcomm to abandon their capital adventure in Moscow, and the minister allowed him to decide what method to use. The method he chose failed. It exposed the illegally obtained GRU compound and incriminated his accomplice. He was sure that Lisov's and the KGB's interest was only with the illegal compound; he didn't think the KGB would officially concern itself with or pry into the minister's plan to take control of the venture. They would simply look the other way where interests of important Party members and the State were concerned.

He expected that at any time now, his superior would call and deliver a damaging reprimand for Trush's bungling the job and embarrassing the minister. He needed a convincing plan ready to demonstrate that the minister's objective would be met, and he had such a plan.

As he reached for the Stolichnaya, a red phone shrilled angrily. He picked up the receiver.

"Burian," Thrush's boss called out in an icy tone.

"Yes, Comrade Minister."

"My office. Immediately!"

Before Trush could acknowledge the minister's command, the line went dead.

…..

That Monday morning, John was in his office reviewing the weekend traffic and network performance reports when he sensed someone standing outside his office. He looked up. Fred Stillwell, the American equipment manufacturer's lead technician responsible for cutover and testing of the system stood just outside his open doorway. John motioned for him to come in. The tech entered.

"What can I do for you, Fred?" John asked.

"Nikolai didn't come in this morning so I wanted to give you an update on the system."

"So, how's the network performing?"

"Not bad, overall. The interconnection with Moscow City Telephone Network is also working smoothly. But there are a number of glitches that I need to clean up. As soon as I get the fixes, I'll load the patches and my company will be ready to officially turn the system over to you by the end of the week, I'm hoping."

"Does Nikolai know this?"

"He would have known it this morning, if he showed up. We had a meeting scheduled to review the results."

"Thanks for the update. I'm sure Nikolai will show up anytime now," John said and thought nothing more about it. The technician nodded and left.

John's thoughts turned to his upcoming afternoon meeting with Juliana. He felt excitement and anticipation, but still wondered if her interest in him had more to do with what he did than who he was. Or maybe, this was an attempt by Juliana to enlighten him about Russian arts. Most Russians, communist propaganda notwithstanding, viewed Americans as technologically savvy, but they had a low opinion of

251

Americans' cultural development. Nikolai said so: *High technology, low culture.*

In preparation for the visit to the gallery, John had done homework. Provodnikov's library contained a wealth of material on Moscow museums and theaters. He reviewed the information on Tretyakov Gallery and picked out an oil painting he wanted to see. The canvas, titled *The Appearance of Christ to the People,* measured 25 feet by 18 feet and took Alexander Ivanov twenty years to complete. It took Michelangelo only four years to finish the Sistine Chapel ceiling. Having seen the Sistine ceiling, John wanted to see what twenty years of artwork on a single canvas looked like.

At 1:30 p.m., he took his mobile phone, tested it, put the two-pound "brick" into his computer satchel and headed for the metro. He boarded the train to Tretyakovskaya Metro station, exited to street level, and walked toward the gallery. What he saw when he reached the gallery entrance surprised him. The building's colorful gingerbread façade looked out of place among the dreary Moscow structures. He stared at the surroundings: grounds cleaned, grass cut, flowers placed in front of the statue of Pavel Tretyakov, the nineteenth-century Russian art collector and philanthropist. The entire site looked out of place in Moscow—perhaps in some quaint Bavarian mountain village, but not in Moscow. Too much color. He stood admiring the scene.

At 2 p.m., he saw Juliana approach the gallery from the Metro's direction. She wore a plain linen dress, her hair made up into a bun, exposing her slender neck. She smiled as soon as she saw him, walked up and gave him a quick hug. She pointed to the satchel slung over his shoulder. "You brought the mobile gadget so I can see how it works. Wonderful, thank you, John."

He pulled out the cell phone and displayed it for her. "It's simple, you punch the number you want to call on this pad and press 'Snd', the send button, and your call will be on its way."

"And what do I do when I am finished, how do I hang up?"

"Press this 'End' button under the Snd button."

"May I try?"

John gave her the brick.

She punched in a number, pressed "Snd," and held it to her ear. After ten seconds her face lit up. "Papa?" Then silence. Then, "Yes, yes, I am using Mr. Baran's American gadget to call you." Silence. "Yes, the one I told you about. I am trying it out, but I must go now. Bye, Papa." She studied the phone and giggles with delight. "Miraculous technology."

John returned the phone to his satchel. "It's an expensive miracle. This gadget costs over three thousand America dollars right now, but the cost will drop dramatically as usage increases and technology improves. He turned toward the gallery entrance. "Shall we go in? I want to see Ivanov's big canvas."

She put her hand on his arm to stop him. "Do all connections go through some central machine?"

"The mobile switch in our building." *What prompted that question?*

"Then you can listen in on the conversations, yes?"

Her curiosity seemed to take on a definite purpose, and he wondered about that purpose. "It's possible to do that, but it's against the law. Why do you ask, Juliana?"

Just then they heard loud voices behind them as if some sort of rally had started. They turned to look.

Chapter 61

A throng of Moscovites surrounded a speaker in the square a short distance from the gallery. The speaker stood on a makeshift platform and yelled something out. The throng of about two hundred answered with an incoherent chant. Highly animated, the speaker waved his hands and shook his fists. Curious, John and Juliana moved closer to the crowd around the platform. Juliana took one look at the speaker and disgust spread on her face. "That is Vladimir Marinovksy, the communist extremist. He ran for the president of Russian Federation in our elections held in June. Our first-ever election made possible by Gorbachev's democratization reforms. Yeltsin won, thank God, but Marinovsky came in a surprising third. He is dangerous for our Democratic movement and for all Western interests in our country."

"So what is he campaigning for now?"

They moved into the crowd to better hear what Marinovky was shouting about.

"The capitalist pigs say they come to Russia to help us," Marinovsky cried out. "But do they help us?"

"No!" the crowd roared.

"They come here and take our oil, take our gold, and take our women." Marinovsky screamed. "They rape Mother Russia of its treasures. What will we do?"

"Drive them out. Drive them out," the crowd screamed.

"The West is our enemy and if I were elected, I would have taken Alaska back from the United States, nuked Japan, and flooded Germany with radioactive waste," Marinovsky shouted.

The crowd roared and began chanting: "Marinovsky, Marinovsky, Marinovsky."

A sudden chill shook John. He took Juliana's hand and quietly led her away. When they were back in the gallery's courtyard, he faced her and said, "I'm the American pig he's talking about, except that I strongly disagree with him. But I'm not going to hang around trying to prove it to him. Now, back to my original question: why were you asking if I can listen in on the mobile conversations?"

"People like Marinovsky," she said in a low voice John could barely hear, "and hard-line communists in the government are planning to stop Gorbachev's reforms, maybe overthrow him with a military coup. They will return the country back to communist dictatorship and end any hope for democratic rule."

How does she know this? Not questioning her statement, he said, "What does listening to the mobile conversations has to do with that?"

She drew John away from the gallery crowd to a secluded spot. He thought he saw fear in her eyes. In a near whisper she said, "Americans are friends of Democracy, right? They always side with those fighting for liberty and freedom, do they not?"

John flinched. Where was she headed with those questions? He was slow to answer. "Yes, historically you're correct, but individual cases differ in the amount of support America gives to such causes."

"Does not America support the democratic movement in Russia?"

John nodded. "In principle."

"Do you support it, John?"

He saw where she was headed with these questions, and he didn't like its direction. "I do."

She leaned toward him until her lips were just inches away from his left ear. "Top military commanders and hard-line Politburo members that oppose democratization have those mobile gadgets. When they use them to communicate, we, or *you*, could listen in and find out when they plan to make their move to stop the reforms."

This conversation is dangerous. He planned to do the same thing, but only he and the CIA would know about it. If he brought a Russian national into the scheme, well, he couldn't predict what would happen. He sought to discourage her. "A number of things are wrong with your proposed scheme, Juliana. First, you assume they'll discuss their plans using the wireless connection, but they know that the network is not secure and they won't do it. Second, I ...we don't know whose conversation to monitor. Which one of them will discuss the plan and when? Third, even if you know the exact hour of the expected move, what are you going you do about it? And finally, if this scheme is discovered, well... you know what will happen."

Her expression turned serious and determined. "Okay, your first point. Our communist leaders have grown fat, lazy, and careless. They assume no one will dare eavesdrop on them, and they will talk, use the gadgets. Second, I will give you the name of the official who will ultimately give the order to the troops. Third, if we know when the troops will move out to take their position, our democratic movement will alert its supporters and organize resistance. We will have thousands of people in the streets to stop them."

"You have an organized democratic movement? Who's the leader?"

"We are not 'officially' organized. It is more like a network of democratization supporters. We do not have a declared leader. That would be dangerous. We have a spiritual leader."

"Who?"

"Andrei Sakharov."

"He died over a year ago," John said.

"Yes, he died when he returned to Moscow from his exile, but his civil liberties and human rights ideas did not die with him. We believe, as he did, in the hidden strength of the human spirit to continue its struggle for freedom."

"That's very noble, but what will you use to stop the tanks and armed infantry, maybe even air forces?"

"Bodies. We do not believe our soldiers will shoot their own people."

"Are you sure about that? Soviet history isn't on your side. Even if you are right, you forget my last point. What if the scheme is discovered?"

"It is a risk I and the supporters of democracy are asking you to take for our cause. You are an American, you know what that means. Papa says that you have always fought for freedom, yours and other people's."

John gazed at her. She was much more than the most beautiful Odette to dance on a Moscow stage and her spirit was infectious. His cold reasoning told him to stop now, don't go any further, but his basic instinct pulled in its own direction. Yes, he wanted to help the democratic movement, but mostly he wanted to see her again, be with her. He gave her an anxious look and said, "Give me a day to look into this eavesdropping scheme, and I'll let you know tomorrow if it can even be done," he said in a tone that he hoped threw cold water on the idea.

A warm smile spread on her face. "Papa said Americans are a brave people, and he is right. Thank you, John."

Brave? He was already taking a big risk by helping the CIA eavesdrop on the Kremlin. Were two risks twice as risky? No, more than that—the total risk exceeded its sum, as either one separately or both could occur jointly. But he forced his caution aside. "When can we meet tomorrow?"

"I'm not dancing so I can meet you anytime. Where?"

He didn't have any idea where, so he said, "Telman Square, late evening, say, eight o'clock." The square had worked for him in the past. He stopped short of suggesting his apartment, even though it was the first thing on his mind.

"That's where my conductor has his apartment. I know the place."

"I'm renting your conductor's apartment," John said. "Now that I think about it, it will probably be safer for us to meet in the apartment." He observed her carefully for any reaction.

"Eight o'clock, Provodnikov's apartment," she said, smiled with delight, and took his arm. "Now, let us go see that canvas."

Chapter 62

Sovcell Facility. Tuesday, August 13

John arrived in his office to find Fred Stillwell, the American technician, waiting for him. The tech appeared concerned. They sat down at the conference table.

"What's up, Fred?"

"Your operations manager didn't come in this morning," Fred said and seemed to wait for an explanation from John.

"Nikolai didn't show again?"

"Two days in the row. The Russian techs reporting to him say they don't know anything about his absence. Somebody needs to understand what I'm doing and take over when I leave."

"That's strange about Nikolai, it's unlike him. I'll look into it. Can you work with one of his brighter techs?"

"I guess," the manufacturer's rep said and stood to leave.

"Hold on a minute, Fred. I've got some questions for you."

The tech sat down.

"Our mobile switch has the capability to monitor the connection quality, right?"

The tech nodded. "System transmission quality parameters can be measured at the test access port."

"Can I listen in for a subjective evaluation of the connection?"

The tech looked surprised by the question. "Objective measurements completely describe the quality of the connection. There's no need to listen in."

"Fred," John said and leaned forward so that the tech could hear his low voice. "Can I listen in on the conversations?"

The tech appeared to consider John's question in earnest. With an expression that said he knew exactly what John had in mind, the tech said,

"Yes, with a special command, but I'm not allowed to activate that feature for you."

John ignored the 'not allowed' part. "Can I do it remotely?" Sitting in the switchroom and listening to mobile subscribers' conversations was out of the question for more than one reason.

"That feature is not offered on commercial installations. It takes special software, and I'm not authorized to install it for you. Only our government can purchase that capability. Even then, it has to be approved pretty high up."

"Well, Fred," John began to weave his tale, "we do have a request from the government. Only it's not *our* government."

The tech looked confused. "What do you mean?"

"Our official partner, the Communications Minister, wants to know if your equipment could provide such a capability. I don't know what his motive is behind the request, and I didn't ask. He's the government. All you'd have to do is rig it temporarily so that the feature could be demonstrated."

Fred's facial expression went from confusion to understanding, to worry, to anxiety. "I don't know. I can lose my job if the company finds out about it."

"They won't find out about it from me. Besides, the minister might decide to order this equipment for his own network, generating sales for your company." John pressed the tech, tightening the tale's weave.

Fred's face took on a friendlier expression. He paused and seemed to concentrate. Then he stood. "Okay, I'll get to work on that rigging for you, but it'll only be temporary," he said and left.

John's thoughts turned to his manager of operations. He picked up the phone and called Nikolai's home number. No answer. He tried again. No answer. He walked over to Chris' office and shut the door behind him. "Nikolai hasn't showed up for work again today. I've tried unsuccessfully to reach him, and I'm beginning to worry. It's completely unlike him. Any ideas?"

"Like I said, I have bad vibes about Nikolai," Chris said.

"Ah, you and your vibes." John didn't want to hear it. Bad vibes about Nikolai, if borne out, would put a monkey wrench, no, gorilla wrench into operations. Depending on the reason for his absence, it could mean anything from the need to simply replace him to something more serious, if Nikolai's absence was connected to some plot against the venture. John didn't want to think about it. He changed the subject. "Listen, Chris, we had a successful network cut and we haven't had a chance to celebrate. What say you and I have dinner tonight at the Savoy to mark the occasion? I'm buying."

"Bodacious. But I need to leave dinner early. I've something lined up for tonight."

"Again?" John shook his head and walked out. *When does he sleep?*

…..

Shortly after five, John and Chris left for the celebration dinner. John drove. As he pulled into Gorky Street, he said, "Is this Savoy restaurant any good? Harry Morton seemed to be impressed with it."

"I like the Savoy hotel and the restaurant. It's a Western pearl among the Soviet hospitality swine. The hotel has only 67 rooms and it's expensive— you can pay over four hundred dollars a night—but its luxury matches its price. The dining room you'd swear is right out of Versailles Palace."

"I've never been to Versailles, but it sounds like I'll be leaving the restaurant broke. What do you order in a French palace in Moscow?"

"Salmon Kulebyaka wrapped in Blini, of course."

"Of course, we'll eat like kulaks."

John pulled up to a curb close to Savoy and parked. Inside the restaurant, he surveyed the French palace. Chris was right. Gilded marble columns, gilded ceiling mirrors, and the gilded marble floor resembled the pictures of Versailles Palace he had seen in travel books. After they were seated in what looked like Louis XVI chairs—give or take a Louis—he let Chris order their dinner.

John spied other guests. Behind small tables in the corners of the restaurant, Western businessmen snuggled close to their Russian female companions who were clearly in the same profession as the Hotel Kosmos hussies, but whose services, obviously, commanded a premium. The women giggled, wiggled, and ogled at their foreign companions. Expats were spending their hazardous duty pay with delight. Many of the men looked older and were probably married—their wives patiently waiting for them to conclude their business and return home. At large tables in the middle of the restaurant, Westerners appeared to be in business discussions with their Russian prospects.

Dinner arrived, and they dug in. Salmon Kulebyaka wrapped in Blini had been prepared superbly, but was a bit on the heavy side, both on the stomach and the wallet. Finished, they ordered after-dinner drinks and talked. Chris lifted his brandy. "We're finally operational, so here's to raking in the dough."

John raised his sniffer. "Ober will be pleased. Westerners will get connected to their home offices, and we'll get hefty bonuses."

Chris looked at the couples in the restaurant and, as if he was reminded of something, quickly glanced at his watch. "Sorry, got to go."

"Leaving the palace already?"

Chris smiled, waved a goodbye, and left.

As it was only eight o'clock, John decided to explore the most expensive hotel in Moscow. Having seen the swine, he wanted to check out the pearl. He crossed the lobby and found a small bar with one couple huddled in a corner, an expat and a young local female. He took a seat at one of the tables and ordered a beer. He sipped his drink and peered at the two statues that were supporting the ceiling in the bar's entrance.

A Russian national came through the hotel entry doors into the lobby, walked over to the bar, and looked in. He was sinewy and of dark complexion, probably from one of the southern republics. He examined the small bar as if looking for somebody. His gaze lingered more than a few moments on John. Then, seemingly not seeing anyone he recognized, he walked out. Fifteen minutes later, a different Russian did the same thing. In another fifteen minutes, the first Russian repeated the same procedure and walked out. John's warning light switched on. He didn't know what the two Russians were up to, but his senses told him to get going. He bade farewell to the two demoted Titans supporting the ceiling and quickly walked out.

Chapter 63

John climbed into his Zhiguli, pulled out onto Prospekt Marksa, and headed west toward Gorky Street and his apartment. Consciously aware of his safety, he thought about the two Russians ducking their heads into the bar. Who were they looking for? He checked his rearview mirror. Nothing unusual: one car, a black Lada, followed him as he left the hotel.

As he made a right onto Gorky Street, the Lada trailed behind. No reason to suspect anything, yet. He was on an eight-lane major thoroughfare, and the Lada was probably just part of the traffic. Maybe it was headed for the airport. In that case it'd be going in the same direction all the way to Telman Square.

Wanting to prove his own supposition, he decided to test it. He passed Pushkin Square, turned right into a side street, turned left on the next side street, and was headed toward the Garden Ring Road. He looked into the rearview mirror. The Lada stayed with him. His pulse quickened, but he kept himself from panicking. He made a right on the Garden Ring Road, got off on another side street, made enough turns to complete a U-turn, and headed in the opposite direction on the Garden Ring Road.

He checked his mirrors: The Lada tracked in his traffic lane, four cars behind. He felt panic creeping in. He decided that if he was going to shake off his pursuer, the Garden Ring Road's six lanes of racing traffic was the place, and the time was now. He picked up speed and switched lanes without signaling his turns, barely squeezing in between the cars. Headlights flashed, horns blared. If he were spotted by a GAI, he knew he'd be flagged down. Better to be picked up by a traffic cop, he thought, than by his pursuer.

He accelerated and continued his lane-switching maneuver. He saw the Lada fall behind, but still in pursuit. In a few minutes he would be passing the American Embassy, and he decided that if he couldn't shake off the Lada, he'd pull up to the embassy compound guardhouse and seek entry and safety. He had his passport with him. If there was a problem, he could call Roger Moore for help.

Just before reaching the embassy, he decided on a final maneuver. He pulled over into the left-most lane and then cut across the six lanes of traffic into the right-most lane at an angle as perpendicular as he could make it to the direction of the traffic. Tires screeched, horns blared, and he heard a crash, then another, and another. He accelerated and looked into the rear view mirror. A multiple-car pileup halted the traffic. He saw no Lada behind him—it was entangled in the crash. And there were no GAI's flashing blue lights either. He let out a sigh, but dared not conclude that he was completely in the clear.

He passed the embassy and turned right on Kutuzovskyi Prospekt, drove along the Moscow River, and pulled into the SovinCenter: a complex of shops, restaurants, and a Western-style hotel. He parked and shut off the engine. He sat there for a few minutes until he relaxed. He stepped out of the car, entered the building complex, walked into the Brown Bear Pub, and ordered a bottle of beer.

Who were the pursuers? Was Trush trying to finish the job that Markova had failed to pull off at the celebration party in her apartment? He had to assume the answer was yes. So, was it safe to go to his apartment? Should he check into the Mezhdunarodnaya Hotel in the complex and stay overnight? And then what would he do in the morning? No, he decided to wait an hour and then start driving—he'd have a better chance of reaching his apartment at night, and he would be safer in his apartment than in any public building in Moscow.

At 11 P.M. he left the pub and walked to the parking lot. Darkness had fallen, but the evening did not diminish the sultry mixture of smog that hung in the Moscow air. He pulled out of the SovinCenter and took side streets on the way to his apartment—he wanted to stay off main thoroughfares. He got lost twice. When he reached Telman Square area, he parked two blocks away and walked cautiously toward his apartment building. He looked frequently over his shoulder, but didn't see anything suspicious.

As he entered his building, he saw something unusual: the security attendant, who had always been at her station, wasn't there. He started to look for her and was startled suddenly by a familiar voice from behind the elevator cage. He froze.

"Good evening, Mr. Baran," Nikolai said and stepped forward. "You are very difficult man to subdue. You have more tricks than Harry Houdini." He grinned with self-satisfaction. "Did I use correct simile?"

John focused on Nikolai's right hand: A Makarov pistol pointed back at him. "This is an unpleasant surprise," John said. "I'm disappointed in you, Nikolai. You've become a key player in Sovcell operations, with a bright future for you in our venture. And look at you now, throwing it all away." He advanced toward his operations manager.

"Stay where you are, Mr. Baran, I know your tricks. I have also been trained in them, in GRU. Major Orlov at your service." Nikolai gave John a mock salute with his left hand. "And do not worry about my future, but worry about yours."

"You commies are getting tiresome." John kept moving. His anger trumped his fear.

Nikolai raised his arm and pointed the pistol at John's face.

John stopped.

The Russian waved the weapon toward the exit door. "Start walking. We shall be taking little trip."

John walked out of the building and stopped. Nikolai directed him away from the square and into a wooded area in the back. As they walked, Nikolai maintained a six-foot separation between them, holding the gun hidden in his coat pocket. John thought of trying something, but he decided that the odds of succeeding stunk. He didn't think he could pull off any of the tricks he had in his repertoire. Nikolai knew how to handle his weapon.

"What do you plan to do, Nikolai?"

"I shall answer all your questions in time. Keep moving, Mr. Baran."

They came to a white Lada parked on a side street, and the GRU agent handed John a set of keys. "You drive, Mr. Baran." Then as an afterthought, he added, "Do not cross solid line."

Chapter 64

John climbed in behind the wheel, and the Russian slid into the back seat directly behind him. "Drive the way you would if you were going back to America," Nikolai said and thrust the barrel of the pistol into John's neck.

"The airport?"

"Correct, Mr. Baran. And do not try any funny stuff."

"But I don't have a plane reservation." *Keep talking*, John told himself.

"Cute, Mr. Baran, but where you are going, you will not need reservation." Nikolai gave the pistol a shove. John started the car, left the side street, got onto Leningratskyi Prospekt, and headed northwest toward the airport.

"What do you plan to do?" John repeated his question and hoped to keep Nikolai talking. John needed a plan.

Nikolai laughed, but said nothing.

"Why are you doing this?"

"You see, Mr. Baran, I am in slight predicament."

"What is the problem?"

"You are problem, Mr. Baran. You did not know when to stop snooping." Nikolai seemed to take a minute to reflect. "I know you had figured out what was going on with remodeling contract. But I will tell you anyway, just to set facts straight, for record."

"Please, do set the record straight."

"You see, Mr. Baran, I was architect of kickback scheme. Comrade Trush was pleased with my proposal, and we both, as you would say, made out like bandits. But situation now is past point of no return. So, to protect Comrade Trush and me, you must be taken care of. I do not want to do this, I am sorry. You have become my friend, but friendship is irrelevant when survival is at stake. As you say, business is business, and orders are orders."

"Whose orders, Nikolai?"

"Drive, Mr. Baran. Concentrate on road."

"And who else is part of your gang of bandits?"

Nikolai said nothing.

"Who else is in this?"

"Markova made up our troika," Nikolai said after a moment.

"And the Minister, is he the troika driver?"

"Comrade Minister has his own plan."

"And what's his plan?"

"Control of Sovcell."

"How?"

"You will regret you had started your capitalist adventure in our country. Your company will throw in towel, pull up stakes, split, go home. It is naïve to think you can poison our system with capitalism. This is *our* country, and you are parasites here. Bloodsuckers. To quote our great patriot, you take our oil, our gold, and corrupt our women. I blame *Glasnostic* Gorbachev for importing capitalist contamination into our Union. There is only one way to deal with this disease."

Holy shit! John needed to do something quick. They came to Leningrad Highway, and he turned right, heading for the airport. Later, as he eased into the right lane, ready for the airport turnoff, Nikolai jabbed the pistol barrel into John's neck. "Straight, Mr. Baran."

John obeyed. He drove passed Sheremetyevo 2, the international terminal, and then Sheremetyevo 1, the domestic terminal. Civilization thinned. "What is your plan now?"

"Enough talk, exit there," Nikolai said, pointing to an upcoming road on the right. John made the turn. The road was deserted, and its pavement turned into a dirt road that was elevated with no shoulder. The drop-off on either side of the road looked to be at least three feet. The headlights revealed a dense pine forest on both sides of the road, and the tree line was no more than ten feet away from the pavement. This was it. John saw what was coming. He sprang into action and punched the gas pedal to gain as much speed as possible.

Nikolai tapped the gun barrel on John's head. "Slow down, Mr. Baran, we are going to pick some mushrooms."

At that instant John floored the accelerator and sharply turned the steering wheel to the left. The Lada tipped, made an abrupt left turn on its two right wheels and headed off the pavement into the forest. Nikolai was thrown into the right rear door. John held on to the steering column. The Russian cursed and fired his gun aimlessly. John crouched down, opened his door, jumped out, and landed in the ditch, weeds and shrubs cushioning his impact. The Lada sailed in the air and slammed into the trees. The sound of crumbling metal pierced John's ears. He lifted his head and looked.

Its body compressed, the Lada pinned his would-be executioner in the back seat. Steam rose from the crushed radiator and gasoline poured out of the collapsed tank. Nikolai did not move, and for a split second John thought of helping, pulling him out of the car. But when gasoline vapor reached John, he scrambled away from the crash. When he discovered he wasn't seriously hurt, he ran. He heard a whop, dove to the ground, and covered his head with his hands. When no explosion followed, he turned to look. The Lada was burning like a runaway bonfire, and the Russian had no chance. John stared at the burning heap for a long minute. A fitting end for the Russian—*David* had no chance.

Trush's troika: *Two down. One to go.*

Chapter 65

Leningrad Highway, 35 Kilometers Northwest of Moscow

John took a last look at the burning Lada, ran into the pine forest, and began to make his way back to Leningrad Highway. When he reached the highway, he looked back. Faint light flickered through the trees like from a distant campfire.

He brushed dirt and pine needles off his coat and slacks and crossed the highway. He had to get back to Moscow—he was out of place, and sooner or later he would be discovered and picked up. He tried to flag down a vehicle, but no one stopped. He pulled out a twenty-dollar bill, and stuck the money out toward the road. Then he quickly jerked his hand back—a Russian hitchhiker shouldn't have hard currency. He remembered he had a pack of Marlboros and prayed that the cigarettes would live up to their reputation. He pulled the crushed pack out of his inside coat pocket, squared the box, and held it up in view of the oncoming traffic. It was dark and it would be difficult for fast-moving drivers to see exactly what he held in his hand. He edged further into the pavement and hoped for a slow moving vehicle. Several cars passed, paying no attention to him. Trucks passed. Vehicles sped past him without slowing down, as if he were some pedestrian antic.

"Come on, come on!" The next car seemed to move slower. It passed him, but then its brakes screeched, bringing the vehicle to a stop hundred feet away. He ran up to the car and saw that the front passenger window was open and the interior light on. The driver inside looked a trim young man with a thick crop of dark hair and alert eyes; an athlete, a soccer player, John thought. A lit cigarette hanging from the driver's lips formed a smoke cloud over his head. The stench of cheap, fast-burning tobacco walloped John as he leaned in through the window. He jerked back to get some air and began to explain that his car broke down on a side road in the woods and that he needed a ride to the nearest Metro station. The soccer player looked at John suspiciously, and then he looked at the pack of Marlboros.

"Rechnoy Vokzal is thirty kilometers down the highway," he said. "A pack of Marlboros will not fill my gas tank." The soccer player waited, it seemed, for John to respond with a solution to his fuel supply problem. John hesitated for a moment but then decided to let the dollars do the talking. He was desperate. He pulled out the twenty and tentatively held it out to the driver. The soccer player quickly grabbed the money, shoved it into his pocket, and motioned for John to get into the car.

The drive to the Metro started out quiet. The soccer player tried to make small talk, but John just hmm'ed and nodded. He didn't want to risk revealing that he was a foreigner. The young man continued to recite a litany of complaints about living condition in his country. John offered no comment. The soccer player started to moan about his in-laws. He continued to whine until he pulled off Leningrad Highway into a side street and stopped in front of a Metro station. "We are here," he said and pointed to the building. "Rechnoy Vokzal."

"Thank you," John jumped out of the Lada, and ducked inside the station. He ran to catch a departing train, hopped on, and slumped on the bench seat inside the car. He thought about Nikolai burning inside the Lada wreck. His heart pounded and his pulse knocked in his ears, and he started deep breathing exercises to calm down his heart rate.

A passenger directly across the aisle, an elderly woman with a friendly face, looked at John as if she was seeing a ghost. "Are you not well?" she asked with concern in her voice and, it appeared, was ready to come over to help.

John looked around the car. The few passengers in the car raised their heads from their books and newspapers and stared at him waiting, apparently, to hear his response.

"I will be all right," John said to the woman. "Thank you. Next time I must not run so fast to catch the train." His apparent ghostly look wasn't due to his running—images of Nikolai burning alive had drained some of his color.

The woman nodded and returned to her reading, and he others did the same. John turned and looked at the Metro map above his bench seat. His station would be the fourth stop. He closed his eyes and continued breathing exercises until his heart rate slowed.

Fifteen minutes later he stood on the Aeroport Metro platform, feeling more or less normal. As he walked up the Metro stairs, he wondered if Nikolai had other accomplices stationed around the apartment. That, John convinced himself, was unlikely. It would have been far-reaching to have a Plan C, even for a GRU major. He was fairly sure that Nikolai's attempt to terminate him was already Plan B—Plan A, the Lada pursuer, having failed. Still, he exercised caution.

As he exited the Metro, he made a left turn and walked away from Telman Square. It took time to walk around the large block. When he had completed the circle, he approached his apartment building from the rear. He surveyed the area, but saw nothing suspicious. He entered the building and saw the security attendant on duty. He walked up to her and said, "There was no one here earlier. Was there a problem?"

She gave John a sad look. "I was temporarily removed from my post."

She was following orders, John thought. Would she now attempt to report his presence to Nikolai, as instructed? And when she failed to reach him, what would she do then? The safe assumption was that she would report the information to somebody, if Nikolai had left instructions for her to do so. But if the Trush-Orlov-Markova troika worked alone, as Nikolai had said, then there would be no one for the security attendant to report to except Trush. He doubted that Nikolai would have instructed her to contact Trush directly at his home and at this late hour. Even if he did, or even if the troika had other accomplices, John's apartment would still be the safest place for him in Moscow.

He jogged up to his apartment, shut the door, and armed the security alarm. If anyone broke in, militia would be alerted. He went into the kitchen, poured half a glass of Stolichnaya, drank it, and went to bed.

There was nothing else he could do. Tomorrow would be another day and he needed to be alert and ready to deal with whatever Trush was going to do next.

Chapter 66

The next morning, John got up and found his door intact and the security system armed. Image of burning Nikolai still on his mind, he called Chris.

"We need to find a replacement for Nikolai," John said when Chris answered. "I'll explain when I get in."

"Did you see him? Where is he? What happened?" Chris shot the questions.

"We need a replacement. I'll explain later."

"I had a feeling about Nikolai. Bad vibes."

"Just be careful, Chris." John ended the call.

He made coffee, sat by the kitchen window, and drank it. He looked out onto the courtyard of trees and weeds. *Moscow.* He shook off Nikolai's flashback and thought about Roger Moore and the coup plotters' distraction plan. He shuddered as visions of paralyzed Americans formed in his mind. Had the CIA's Russian moles provided the information necessary to stop the attack? What if they didn't or couldn't? The consequences were too ghastly to contemplate.

If the moles didn't deliver, could John, somehow, get that information? An idea struck him. Since Lisov could be bought, maybe Lisov himself could buy the information from his contacts. He called Moore's embassy number and was told that the Cultural Counselor was unavailable. He identified himself and stressed the importance of his call. In a minute Moore came on the line.

"I only have a few moments, John, we're in a crisis mode here. What's up?"

"It's about the olive oil shipment. If your birds didn't sing, maybe I can help."

Momentary silence.

"How?"

"Not on the phone."

"Of course, come right over. I'll have you escorted to my office." Moore hung up.

John wolfed down the rest of his coffee, dashed out of the apartment, and headed for the Zhiguli, still parked where he left it last night.

…..

Forty minutes later, John presented his passport to the male receptionist at the old embassy building. The man examined the document and asked John to wait. Within three minutes, a Marine sergeant in dress uniform came out of a side door. "Follow me, sir," he said. He led John upstairs, stopped in front of a closed door, and knocked. Receiving permission to enter, he opened the door and stepped aside. John entered, and the sergeant closed the door behind him.

Moore sat behind a desk and held an animated telephone conversation. He saw John come in, terminated his call, and invited John to sit. He sighed. "I just came up from the "bubble," our situation room, and the situation is *not* good. Our birds didn't sing. They can't get any information on the bioweapons attack. They say there's no such plan. God, what if there is such a plan, as they discussed in Yanayev's office, but it's kept a complete secret? If the KGB took control, as Kryuchkov said he would, they probably compartmentalized its execution in a way that our moles can't discover it?" He paused and looked at John, shaking his head as if the situation was hopeless. When John said nothing, he went on. "We've alerted the FBI, Customs, and border security, and I don't know what else to do. If Kryuchkov took charge of the bioweapons operation, I'm not optimistic we're going to get much useful information. The coup plotters are planning to meet again, but even if they discuss their plan again, we can't listen in."

"But I thought—"

"They're meeting in a KGB safehouse outside Moscow, not in the Kremlin. The safe house is secure." He peered at John with a distressed expression. "You said you might be able to help. How?"

John related his experience with bribing Lisov. "The colonel came into his current position from the GRU, so he has contacts there, and he knew about MBR-5. I could try to buy information from him about the attack, and if he doesn't know anything about it, maybe he can buy the information from his contacts."

Moore glanced at the calendar on his desk. "It's August, so your colonel could be spending time at his dacha somewhere outside Moscow. The plotters will have to seize control of the government no later than Monday morning, the nineteenth, to stop the signing of the treaty. I'm surprised they haven't made their move already. I expect them to launch the coup this weekend, at the latest, when the government is out in their dachas." Moore looked weary. He wiped the perspiration off his forehead. "When can you get to the colonel?"

"I don't know his telephone number at his dacha. I'll have to get that first."

"You want us to help?"

"No, you've got enough to worry about. I'll get it."

"Do whatever it takes, John, and don't feel constrained by money."

John stood. "I'll get on it right away, but before I go, a quick question."

Moore gave a nervous nod.

"You know anything about an active Russian democratic movement or a dissident group?"

Moore nodded.

"Of course you do," John said. "That was a stupid question."

Moore shrugged.

"Do you know a Prima Ballerina named Juliana Kovar?"

Moore nodded again.

"Is she part of this democratic movement? Can she be trusted?"

"Yes, and I'd also say yes to the second question."

"Thanks, Roger." John turned and left the room. A new image of Juliana and her democratic movement formed in his mind and he liked that picture.

Chapter 67

Back in his office, John called Provodnikov. When Provodnikov answered, he said, "I'd like to meet with you to discuss a matter that is important to me and could be profitable to you."

"I never pass up profitable matters," the conductor said. "Telman Square at 16 hours."

A few minutes before four, John stood in the living room of his apartment and looked down into the square. He saw Provodnikov park his car on Leningratskyi Prospekt and walk toward the wooded area. John left his apartment to meet the conductor.

Provodnikov looked extremely upset, as if a major catastrophe had befallen him. John had never seen the conductor in such a dreadful emotional state. "Is something wrong?" he asked, but he knew— Provodnikov found out about Nikolai.

Provodnikov shook his head in dismay. Visages of grief and anger flashed on his face, his eyes unfocused. "Nikolai, my nephew…I cannot believe it…he is dead, burned alive."

"Oh, my god!" John put on the act. "What happened?"

"I don't know. Militia called me at my dacha. They found Nikolai's burned body in his car outside Moscow…an accident, they said." Provodnikov's expression went from grief to anger. "The idiots tried to blame it on my nephew's drunken driving." He paused. "I demanded chief investigator be assigned to determine the cause of the crash and possible homicide. Nikolai's body was found in the back seat. Dumb militia. Who was driving?"

Chief investigator? Possible homicide? Possible trouble. John thought about the evidence that might be found. First, no one saw him and Nikolai in the car together last night. Second, any physical evidence of him driving Nikolai's car would've been scorched beyond useable. John thought about possibly damaging circumstantial evidence the investigator might assemble, but dismissed it as unlikely. Besides, he wasn't ready to hop on the plane and exit the country—he had unfinished business.

Provodnikov ambled aimlessly in a small circle, stopped, turned to John. "About your call this morning; you spoke about an important matter involving money."

John waited a few moments to allow for a mood shift. "Important matter to me that could mean money to you. I need information for which I'm willing to pay."

The conductor's expression morphed into one of anticipation. "Depends on information and depends on pay."

"I need information on how to contact Colonel Lisov. He's not in his office."

"Is that all?" Provodnikov said, as if he was disappointed with the triviality of John's request.

"No, that's not all. I need you to arrange a meeting for me with Colonel Lisov. I don't want to attempt the contact myself, you understand."

"Hmm…" Wrinkles gathered around Provodnikov's eyes as if he was weighing the situation and, John was sure, figuring out how much hard currency he could extract the situation. When he seemed to have decided on a course of action, he said, "I will call Colonel Lisov and tell him you have sensitive information for him that cannot wait. He'll come. The KGB will go to any length for 'sensitive information.' Of course, he'll be disappointed when he finds out that you do not, as I assume, have information *for* him, but are seeking information *from* him. You will have to give him a little reward for his effort."

John nodded without showing any surprise to the mention of reward. He was already acclimated to the Soviet socialist culture.

"And I will need a little reward for my effort."

"Of course you will."

"And you want to see him as soon as possible?"

"Of course I do".

"Then I will make the call now." Provodnikov started toward the building. "I will use the telephone in the apartment."

Inside the apartment, Provodnikov consulted a little book he had pulled out of his pocket and dialed a number. He waited a minute and then hung up. "Lisov is not in Moscow." He looked inside his little book again and dialed another number. Within fifteen seconds he straightened, opened his eyes wide and said, "Colonel Lisov?" He listened, nodded, and said, "Yes, this is Taras Provodnikov." He waited a few seconds and then said, "My health is good, thank you, and how is yours?" He looked at John and rolled his eyes. Then he nodded again and said, "Comrade Colonel, an American friend of mine would like to meet with you. He has very sensitive information that can only be delivered in person, and it cannot wait."

Surprise came over Provodnikov's face. He looked at John and said into the telephone, "How did you know Comrade Colonel?" Then he started nodding his head. "Yes...yes...yes...thank you." He hung up and turned to John. "He knows it's you."

"How?"

"He said he knows who my American friends are and who among them is likely to make such a request."

"The meeting?"

"Sunday morning at ten o'clock in front of Bolshoi. Lisov will be strolling among the trees in the small park-like area in front of the theater."

"*Sunday?* Can't he make it earlier? Did you tell him the matter cannot wait?"

"He said he cannot make it any earlier because he has important guests arriving tomorrow and he has to prepare."

The timing troubled John. Sunday was almost certainly too late. If the coup starts on Friday or Saturday, the attack could come on Saturday or Sunday. By then any information Lisov could obtain about the attack would be useless. Still, hoping for a miracle, he decided to go through with the attempt to get the details of the hardliner's plan.

Provodnikov extended his hand, palm up. "Now, before I leave, that little reward for my effort."

John gave him a questioning look.

"One hundred dollars."

John stared at him.

"Well…fifty dollars. That is little by your standards. Is it not?"

John slapped a fifty into Provodnikov's palm. "Thank you."

Provodnikov shoved the bill into his pocket, gave a nod of appreciation, and departed. John saw the conductor stride across the square, get in his car, and drive off. Provodnikov was helpful, but the meeting with Lisov, John feared, would come too late. Even if the hardliners waited until Monday morning, the last moment to start the coup, could he convince Lisov and could Lisov succeed in buying the information from his contacts in time to help stop the attack? The identity and destination of the freighter containing MBR-5 in olive oil containers would have to be known before Tuesday morning, the day the KGB chairman would give the order to proceed with the attack, if the coup went badly for him. Time to acquire the information necessary to stop it looked impossibly short. He reflected on the matter and a perverse thought struck him.

Maybe I should pray for the coup to go well for the hardliners.

Chapter 68

The American tech walked through the open door into John's office with a smile on his face.

John sensed good news was forthcoming. "How'd you make out, Fred?"

"I got it. In fact, I've added a bonus feature for you." The tech pointed to John's mobile phone on the credenza. "Let me have that unit."

John handed the instrument to the tech.

"This bonus is neat," Fred said with glee in his voice. He was obviously proud of his accomplishment. "Whenever you want, it lets *you* enter the subscriber number you want to listen to."

"Excellent! How?"

"It's simple, press the star button followed by 77 and then enter the caller's number and presto, you're bridged onto his conversation, and the caller can't detect it. If he's not using his phone, and this is the neatest part, the system will ring your phone when he makes a call or receives an incoming call. You press this button to answer, and you're in business. If you don't want to listen in, press 'End' to hang up."

"That *is* neat. You're a genius, Fred."

The tech grinned. "I used to work in design." Then he stopped grinning. "I must disable this capability and clear out its software before I leave. You understand."

"I need for it to work through Monday. Will you still be here then?"

"Looks that way. Without Nikolai, things are going slower than I expected." He waved a see-you-later and left.

John called Chris and asked for a print out of the latest list of Sovcell customers, their numbers, and their billing information."

"What do you need it for?" Chris asked with notable curiosity in his question.

John wanted to tell him to just do it, but instead he said, "I'd like to get to know our customers, analyze who's using our services."

"You'll have it this afternoon," Chris said then hung up.

Later in the day, Natasha, Chris' favorite, big-breasted analyst brought a stack of printouts and placed it on John's desk. "Mr. Ashley said to tell you to enjoy your reading, Mr. Baran." She smiled politely, turned, and left. Looking at her fanny as she walked out, John saw the reason for the "preferential treatment."

He dove into the stack, looking for the identity of the twelve users to whom the minister had distributed the mobile units. When he found the group of specific numbers, he let out an expletive. *"Shit!"* All twelve numbers were being billed to the minister with no identification of the individual users. The minister provided no listing of who had what number. He stared at the page. Then an idea struck him and he hoped it'd work. He copied the numbers—he'd find out tonight.

. . . . .

That evening back in his apartment, John sat down at the kitchen table, took out the list of twelve numbers, and began his eavesdropping operation, testing his idea. The first number he tried—nothing, dead silence. Either the phone was not in use, or he'd botched the procedure. He continued and got the same result for the next four numbers. *Damn!* Was he doing it wrong, or was the Soviet brass not using their phones for some reason? He continued. He tapped in the six's number and landed on a conversation in progress.

You're a genius, Fred.

Two senior military officials griped, denouncing Gorbachev's military budget cuts as dangerous to the Union's security. When they addressed each other, they used only their rank, not their names. John didn't know to whom he was listening, important decision-makers or subordinate members of the military elite. He hung up and put the phone down. *Crap. This isn't getting anywhere.* He needed the phone number of the conspirator who would be issuing deployment orders to the military. He checked the time: five minutes before eight. Juliana would be arriving anytime now.

He heard a knock on his door and opened it. As soon as she saw him, she broke into a warm smile. She wore an ivory blouse and a knee-length azure skirt. Her perfectly erect posture tilted her firm breasts upwards. Her slim waist flared into rounded hips. Her nubile curves struck a vibrant chord in him. This wasn't Juliana the ballet dancer; this was Juliana the woman. He wondered if it was a good idea to have her in his apartment; he wasn't sure he could trust himself. She stood, waiting. "Oh, I'm sorry, please come in," he said and stepped aside.

She entered, and he closed the door. He turned and stepped into her outstretched arms. They embraced, their lips met, and their kiss was a smoldering heat that could join metal. He felt arousal and a burning desire to take her. He pushed himself away. "I've good news for you about the listening gadgets." He took her hand and led her to the living room couch. Then he went into his bedroom, came out with a sleep sound machine, put it on top of the piano by the window, turned the select button to white noise, and turned up the volume. He came back, closed the living room door, and sat on the couch next to her.

He glowered at the corner of the living room. "Listening bugs. They listen to us and now we will listen to them," he said, pointing to his mobile unit on the bookshelf.

She seemed to take a moment, then her face lit up. "That is wonderful."

"One problem. Whose conversations do we listen to?"

"General Mazov, our Defense Minister. He will be issuing the order for the Army to take their positions. Listen to him and you will hear when they plan to take control of the country. We must find out the timing of their move."

"I like your enthusiasm, it can be catchy, but a couple of practical matters first. Assuming General Mazov discusses the plan using his mobile unit, I need more than his name. I need his mobile number."

"You do not have that? Your system must know your customers' phone numbers, does it not?"

"Yes it does, except for twelve high officials in the government who have our phones.

She went silent, looked dispirited. John didn't like what he saw. "Do you know anyone or have any connections in the high government circles?" he asked. They must patronize the arts, the artists, the individual performers.

Her expression turned from gloom, to hopeful, to enthusiastic. "General Petrov of the KGB has been admiring my dancing, and he said he has the mobile gadget. If he has one, General Mazov, a higher official, has one for sure."

"You know the general well?"

"Yes, he looks at me as the ballerina he hoped for, but never had. His daughter took ill and died while she was still in ballet school. I think I can wheedle General Mazov's phone number out of him after he has a few drinks.

Chapter 69

John's expression turned serious. "Don't wheedle too much, Juliana, it would make me unhappy."

She laughed. "You are jealous, no?"

"Of course I am jealous."

"That makes me happy."

"Look, Juliana, you must do your wheedling as soon as possible, because I need that number no later than tomorrow for it to do any good."

"Tomorrow I am dancing in *Raymonda,* and General Petrov will be in his usual seat. And, as usual, he will bring red roses to my dressing room. I will drop a hint, and he will be happy to ask me out for late snacks and drinks. We will go to the Moskva Restaurant in the Hotel Moskva, and they will arrange a private table for us."

"You're going to a hotel with him?"

She nodded and then shook her head. "It's not what you are thinking—he is like a father to me. He will order a bottle of vodka and begin to drink. Before the snacks end, he will have consumed half of the bottle, and he'll be ready for me to coax the information out of him. He will be eager to boast about his special privilege of having the mobile gadget, and by the time his driver is ready to take him home, I will have General Mazov's number and maybe all twelve of them."

They looked at each other and started to laugh.

"When can I get them from you?"

"Saturday morning I can meet you in front of the theater and give you the list. I have to rehearse Saturday afternoon for the evening performance."

"We better not wait for Saturday morning. After you get the numbers call me immediately on Friday night with General Mazov's number. And call my mobile number, so at least they'll have a hard time tracing the call to me, as they don't yet know I have the unit. On second thought, forget about any conversation, but as soon as I answer tell me the number in reverse order and hang up. I will set up a listening phone as soon as I get the number. If and when I find out when the Army is going to move, I'll call you immediately. I will state the day and the time in reverse and hang up. So, 'Sunday 0060' will mean Sunday 0600, or six in the morning. It's crude, but it'll serve our purpose."

She looked at him with admiration in her eyes, took his hand, and squeezed it. "You are doing so much for us; how can I repay you?"

"Well, since I'm your *greatest* admirer, how about dancing for *me*."

"Now?" she said with a strange look on her face.

"Yes, now."

She smiled and said, "I would love to, but I have no music."

"Provodnikov has a tape of Tchaikovsky's Nutcracker, and I can put it on. The Sugar Plum Fairy dance is lovely."

Her eyebrows flickered a little, and her eyes lit up with sparks of some indefinable emotion. "I will be very happy to dance for you, John."

He retrieved the tape, inserted it into the player on the bookshelf, and, with some help from her, found the fairy dance. He sat back on the couch with anticipation.

Juliana moved to the center of the living room and began her dance. As she came to an arabesque and attempted to lift her leg straight back, her skirt began to rise above her thigh, came to a halt, and prevented her from fully executing the move. She stopped. "This is silly. I cannot dance ballet in this skirt."

"Take the skirt off," he said before he could catch himself.

His suggestion seemed to startle her. "I cannot do that," she said and stood in front of him with an expression of surprise, bordering on shock, yet her eyes were smiling.

"I'm sorry, Juliana, I don't know what came over me." He hoped she would understand and forgive him.

With a dreamy look in her eyes and a secret smile she said, "I would like *you* to take my skirt off."

He wasn't sure he heard her correctly.

She nodded. "Yes, John."

He walked over to her and unzipped her skirt. As he pulled the skirt down, he put his hands on her hips and moved them slowly downward, skimming either side of her lithe body down to the thighs, admiring their strength and beauty. He stopped abruptly not trusting himself, and started toward the couch.

"The blouse too, John. I need freedom of movement."

He turned, unbuttoned her blouse and took it off. He stood, frozen, gazing at her beautiful, desirable body.

"Thank you," she said, her voice soft, floating. She stepped out of her skirt, kicked it to the side, and continued her dance.

He stepped back and sat on the couch, unconsciously holding her blouse. He stared hungrily at her. His arousal strengthened each second. Within a minute, he dropped the blouse, rushed over to her, swept her up like the groom would his bride on their wedding night, and carried her into the bedroom.

Without the slightest hesitation, she said, "I was hoping you would do that."

.....

On Friday evening, John left his office with two mobile units. He arrived in his apartment with the phones and waited for Juliana's call. A few minutes after midnight, one of the mobiles rang. He answered it and heard Juliana recite General Mazov's number in reverse. He memorized it and hung up. He took the other mobile phone and set it up to listen in on the conversations originating from, or terminating to Mazov's number. If the General made or received calls, John would be able to listen in. Fred assured him that he wouldn't be discovered, but even if he was, well…it was too late to worry about that now.

Chapter 70

KGB Chairman Kryuchkov called a meeting of the coup plotters for Saturday evening at 6 P.M., and assembled the group at a KGB safehouse called Object ABC. In attendance were Vice President Yanayev, Defense Minister Mazov, Prime Minister Pavlov, Politburo member Oleg Zaklanov, chief of the military-industrial complex, and various deputies and aides. Interior Minister Pugo, Kryuchkov informed those present, was returning from vacation in Sochi on the Black Sea.

The KGB chief dismissed the safehouse staff and guards for the evening and had the table set with bottles of vodka and whiskey and assorted *zakooska:* caviar, black bread, smoked sturgeon, and garden vegetables. Copies of the New Union Treaty lay in front of those seated around the table. Kryuchkov poured himself half a glass of whiskey and focused on the purpose of the meeting. The attendees needed to agree on when and how the state of emergency would be declared.

Mazov and Pavlov looked at the KGB chief's glass and poured themselves vodka, while the rest poured whiskey. Kryuchkov drank his whiskey, put the glass down, and pointed to the copy of the treaty in front of him. "Traitors of the Soviet Union wrote this," he said with disgust. In his mind, he now blamed Yeltsin more than Gorbachev for the content of the document. Yeltsin had demanded powers for the republics that, if granted, would leave Soviet government emasculated. To Kryuchkov, Yeltsin's ambitions were obvious: rule Russia without interference from Kremlin bosses.

He scanned those present. Everyone seated around the table were Soviet government, the Kremlin bosses. He picked up the document. "Do I need to read to you our obituary, comrades?"

They all shook their head, picked up their drinks, and downed them. Then one by one they voiced, often in vulgar terms, their disapproval of the treaty and its authors and spoke of the miserable state the country was in.

Defense Minister Mazov listened for a few minutes then said, "It is time we declared a state of emergency and imposed law and order. If the Treaty is signed on Tuesday, the Soviet Union will disintegrate."

Prime Minister Pavlov looked distressed. "The poor harvest we are having will add to our troubles. Hunger will be a real threat this winter, and we will need to seek aid from the West. If the state of emergency is declared, the West will take a hard line and demand that we roll back the measures before helping us. They will want us to restore the freedoms our citizens have gained during Gorbachev's reforms."

Mazov scrutinized the Prime Minister. "What are you saying, Comrade *Premyer,* that we do nothing?"

The Prime Minister gave Mazov a sharp stare. "You know perfectly well, Comrade General, I'm not saying that." He waved his hand around the table. "I'm here for the same reason all of us are here. But we need to be prepared for internal opposition and discontent. Our citizens will demand food, which, as you *must* know, is already scarce. They may even shout 'Give us bread' to remind us of our past. Are you prepared to have your troops fire on them, General? Do you need a lesson in our history?"

Mazov's face turned red. He looked at the others and spoke, his voice layered with impatience and irritation. "Our *Premyer's* panic and his dramatics contribute nothing to this discussion and do not change our objective. We must—"

"Comrades." Kryuchkov tapped the table with his empty glass. He wanted to squash the bickering—this train was going off the track. "I think we should go see Mikhail Sergeyevich and convince him to transfer power to us for a month. When order is restored and controls are implemented, he can take back his presidential powers. He will be grateful to us for restoring order."

Mazov scowled. "Our president must be *told* to either declare a state of emergency or transfer power to the vice president." He waved his hand in Yanayev's direction.

Yanayev reached for the whiskey bottle and, seeing it was empty, raised it above his head. Kryuchkov saw the bottle, called one of his aides, a colonel, and sent him for more spirits.

Zaklanov, chief of the military-industrial complex, peered at his colleagues. "Comrades," he waited until he got Mazov's attention, and spoke directly to him. "I don't believe Mikhail Sergeyevich wants to sign this treaty. Yeltsin and other republic leaders have forced this document on him. I believe that he'll gladly throw out the treaty if we make it look like we forced him to do it. He wants to preserve the Union as much as we do."

Mazov sneered. "Gorbachev says that the treaty will save our Union." He let out a derisive laugh.

Zaklanov shook his head. "It will not save the Union as we know it, maybe a union of independent republics, a commonwealth. We know what that means for all of us at the Center." He raised his voice to stress his point. "Gorbachev knows it, too. And he doesn't like it either."

Mazov threw up his hands. "So, comrades, where does that leave us?"

Kryuchkov grew concerned—the meeting strayed from its objective. He had to set the train back on its tracks else the gathering would degenerate into a squabble, as it usually did when the attendees consumed more and more alcohol. It was time to take charge. If they didn't like his plan, he would listen to their arguments. He tapped his glass on the table again. They all turned and waited for Kryuchkov to speak.

Chapter 71

The KGB chief scanned his colleagues to assure himself he had their attention and then spoke. "Comrades, tomorrow we shall isolate Mikhail Sergeyevich and send a delegation to visit him. They will return with either a signed declaration of the state of emergency, or not signed. If it is not signed, we will reconvene tomorrow night and sign the declaration ourselves. Gennady," he waved toward vice president Yanayev, "will announce the state of emergency on Monday morning." He looked around the table to see if there were any objections.

Mazov peered at Kryuchkov as if the chairman had missed an important element: Mazov's role. "And when do I deploy the military forces to back up our announcement?"

"You'll move your forces at dawn on Monday so that they are in position when Gennady makes the announcement."

The door behind Kryuchkov opened, and his aide came in with three bottles of whiskey and two bottles of vodka. He opened them and put them on the table. Yanayev filled his glass and passed the bottle.

Prime Minister Pavlov raised his hand to get Kryuchkov's attention.

"Comrade *Premyer?* Kryuchkov said. "You disapprove of our plan?"

"No, Comrade Chairman," Pavlov said. "I'm still troubled about the threat of hunger this winter. Can we rely on help from the West, as the Mossad Jew Robert Maxwell promised he would arrange?"

All heads turned in Kryuchkov's direction. He noted the stares and debated with himself whether he should reveal to his colleagues the "deal" he sought to strike with Israel. And why not tell them, he thought. They had all piled into the same boat, and they would float or sink together. He gazed at the Prime Minister and said, "Maxwell himself promised nothing. He arranged for me to meet the former director of Mossad and other high Israel officials. We met on Maxwell's yacht, the Lady Ghislaine, in

Yugoslav waters, and I asked for Israel's help with our attempt to stop our Union from disintegrating."

Yanayev's, Mazov's, and Zaklanov's eyes widened.

Yanayev put down his drink and seemed to sober instantly. "What kind of help, Comrade Chairman?" He peered at Kryuchkov intently.

"I asked for Israel's early recognition of our new government after we announce the state of emergency and take control," Kryuchkov said and looked at Pavlov. "I also asked that Israel use its influence in Washington to convince the Americans that democracy could not work in Russia and that it was better to allow the country to return to a modified form of Communism."

"And what did the Israeli delegation say?" Pavlov asked.

"They listened, but made no commitment. They would discuss the proposition with their Prime Minister."

Mazov shifted in his seat. He seemed edgy. "Proposition? And what commitment did *you* make to the Jews?" he asked Kryuchkov. "The Jews would not jeopardize their standing with America without a very, *very* high price."

"I told them," the KGB chief spoke very slowly, allowing everyone to follow his argument, "that if democratization succeeds, the Soviet Union will no longer be the enemy and a threat to the West. The strategic value of Israel to its greatest ally, the United States, would greatly diminish."

Mazov's face couldn't disguise his cynicism. "What did you *promise*, Comrade Chairman? Your argument has no *value* to them."

Kryuchkov gazed at Mazov for a moment, but then looked back at Pavlov. "We will free hundreds of thousands of Jews and dissidents in our Union and encourage them to emigrate to Israel. Expel them if necessary."

Pavlov jumped in his seat as if he'd been jabbed with a needle. "A catastrophic brain-drain! Our universities, institutions, and critical professions could not withstand it."

Mazov glared at Pavlov. "More of your theatrics and panic, Comrade *Premyer?*" He turned back to Kryuchkov and said, "And what did you promise Maxwell for this little favor?"

"The Soviet Union will forgive Maxwell's debt to us," Kryuchkov said. Then he looked at his colleagues one by one to ascertain their reaction to the deal he had made. No one spoke.

"Have we heard from the Israel government?" Pavlov asked.

Kryuchkov shook his head. "No, but we'll know soon enough if we have an agreement."

The room fell silent.

Yanayev poured himself another drink and passed the bottle. The others joined him. Kryuchkov saw a black cloud descending on his comrades and wondered if they hadn't embarked on a dangerous collision course with "Democracy"—a collision that could bring an end not only to them but to Communism itself.

Chapter 72

Sverdlov Square, Central Moscow. Sunday, August 18

At 9:45 A.M., John stood in front of the Bolshoi Theater, waiting for Colonel Lisov. He brought his listening mobile phone with him, in case Mazov communicated using his mobile unit. John carried it with him always.

He looked up at the effigy of Apollo in the Chariot of the Sun perched on top of the Bolshoi pediment. The Greek god of music and light, among other things, was supposed to drive the chariot across the heavens, carrying the sun. Today, Apollo had forgotten his cargo, and instead spread exhaust fumes across the sky. A smog blanket covered the city already, and the rising temperature would turn it into a pollution-smothered hearth. Moscow needed a massive Iowa summer storm, a downpour to scrub the air of its pollutants and wash the dust and street trash down the storm sewers.

John counted the horses hitched to the Apollo chariot: four. He was pleased to see that the pervasive Soviet *agitprop* hadn't removed one of them to form a troika. As he studied the edifice, he sensed someone behind him and quickly turned.

Lisov stood and looked at the building. He smiled. "Did you know that the Bolshoi Theater is as old as your country?"

John gave Lisov a curt nod; he had heard it many times as the Russians had little else to brag about. "Where can we talk?"

Lisov pointed behind John to a spread of trees surrounding a neglected, dry, circular fountain. "You have information for me?" he said and started walking toward the trees.

John followed. Lisov stopped beneath the crown of a mature tree, out of earshot of the strollers on the Marx Prospekt sidewalk. John saw no one within sixty feet. Sunday morning in Moscow—most were sleeping it off.

294

Lisov's face took on a serious look. "What is this sensitive information? I left my family and guests in the dacha outside Moscow and traveled here to hear this information that cannot wait." His expression said that this better be important.

A jab of panic pierced John. The colonel was expecting something he wasn't going to get. John was troubled by another aspect of this meeting. If he asked about the planned bioterror attack, he'd reveal that he knew such a plan existed. Lisov would want to know the source, and John couldn't tell him without jeopardizing CIA's Kremlin bugging operation. But he had to proceed because the safety of Americans was at stake. He eyed Lisov with caution, uncertain of the colonel's reaction to his next statement. "I have a very large sum of money to buy specific information that you may be able to get."

With a look of displeasure on his face, Lisov shook his head. "I did not think the conductor engaged in disinformation, but I see he did." His tone carried annoyance. He stared at John, his eyes narrowing. "What is the reason for this reprehensible action?" he said and waited for an explanation.

John hesitated for a moment and then decided to lay it on the line. "Thousands of innocent people could be paralyzed and may die if a planned bioterrorist attack is not stopped."

Lisov seemed surprised by the statement. He stared at John for a long moment. Then he shook his head, as if he didn't believe John.

"There *is* such a plan," John emphasized.

Lisov seemed to appraise John's assertion for a moment and then said, "MBR-5?"

John nodded.

"Where? How?" The KGB Colonel was asking the American for information about his own government.

"A coup is planned by the hardliners. They want to stop Gorbachev's reforms and—"

"Yes, yes, I know about the ever coming coup, and you should know that many of us are not in favor of it. What has that to do with MBR-5?"

"If the coup goes badly, the conspirators plan to create a distraction by releasing MBR-5 into the water supply of an American city. They hope Soviet citizens will unite behind them when the U.S. threatens to retaliate."

Lisov drew back, as if what he heard would somehow harm him. "I would not know and cannot know of such a plan."

"But the plan exists."

"And how do *you* know?"

"Our agents obtained the information from their inside contacts that aren't in favor of the coup," he lied.

Lisov raised his eyebrows as if questioning John's statement. Still looking unconvinced, ha said, "Your moles inside our government?"

John remained silent.

"Well then, what is the problem? Your agents can get the plan details from their contacts."

"Their contacts know nothing about the details only that the plan exists."

For a long moment, Lisov seemed to consider this and then nodded as if he was ready to accept the existence of the plan. "It is probably a special operation, and it would be impossible for me to know about it."

"But you were in the GRU and know people there. They control MBR-5."

"So?'

"So you could find out if anything happened to large quantities of MBR-5."

"Any attempt to gain and sell that information is certain death for all involved in this treason."

"But you said you weren't in favor of the coup. Stopping the attack could help derail it."

"I have not been in favor of many things, but I am still alive."

"I have a very, *very* large sum of money to buy this information," John said and prayed that his faith in the power of hard currency would not be crushed now. "Our agents," he continued to press Lisov, "can smuggle you or your contacts out of the country if you're compromised. You could live very well in a safe place. It's been done before, and you know that."

Lisov looked away and seemed to be lost in thought. Then he turned back to John. "What is a very, *very* large sum?"

"You can name it," John said and quickly added, "within reason."

Lisov again appeared to be analyzing the situation. He looked around the park area, at the Bolshoi Theater, at Hotel Metropol, and then at John. "If it can be done at all, I will find out how much will be required to buy the information." He shook his head, as if he didn't believe what he'd just said.

"If you know about the coup timing," John said, "then you know it's urgent that the information be obtained before tomorrow."

Lisov stared at John for a moment, thinking, and then said, "What you ask is impossible. Time is too short."

"You must try."

Lisov shook his head. "Impossible."

"Thousands of people could be paralyzed."

Lisov's expression softened. "Very well, Mr. Baran, I shall try. I will stay in Moscow and contact my GRU sources. I will know by the end of the day if any of my contacts will even consider entering into such a dangerous proposition. Let us meet at 6:30 tonight in say, Gorky Park, but I would not expect anything."

"Where in the park?"

"Along the riverfront are benches. Find an empty one and sit. If you can't sit, stroll the walkway along the river."

"6:30, Gorky Park, riverfront. Thank you."

Lisov turned, strode toward the Bolshoi Theater, and disappeared behind the building.

…..

Back in his apartment, John used his mobile phone to call Roger Moore at his residence.

"I was just leaving for the embassy," Moore said. "What've you got?"

"I found the bird that may be willing to sing, but its price could be very high."

"Spare no expense to hear its song. Even if it becomes necessary to free the bird from its cage."

"I'll know by seven o'clock if we have a willing bird."

"Call me at my direct office number, I'll be waiting." Moore gave John the number and signed off.

Chapter 73

Late Sunday afternoon, Gorbachev was in his vacation retreat in Foros, Crimea, working on the speech he planned to deliver at the signing of the New Union Treaty. The retreat, a three-story mansion, was the zenith of communist opulence. It sparkled with gold and marble, had an indoor swimming pool, and boasted an escalator that led down to the Black Sea— a retreat fit for an imperial czar.

At 4:50 P.M., his aide broke his concentration. "You have visitors, Comrade President," he announced.

Surprised, Gorbachev looked up at his aide. Then he nodded, signaling the aide to show the visitors in.

Politburo member Zaklanov, Deputy Minister of Defense and commander of ground forces General Varennikov, and Gorbachev's own chief of staff, Boldin, walked in. Gorbachev looked annoyed. "What is this? Who sent you?"

"The committee," Varennikov said and explained that it was the State Committee for the State of Emergency. "The GKChP," he spelled out the Russian abbreviation. He named its members and stated their purpose.

Gorbachev stared at Boldin. He appeared not to believe his own chief of staff had joined the conspirators. "You too, Valery?"

Boldin looked away.

"Who appointed such a committee?" Gorbachev demanded. "I did not."

"It does not matter," Varennikov said. "You must support the state of emergency declaration, or you must resign."

Gorbachev's annoyance turned to anger. "You are nothing but adventurists and traitors, and you will pay for this." He looked at Varennikov and shook his head in disgust. "Only those who want to commit suicide can now suggest a totalitarian regime in our country. You are pushing us into a civil war."

"Law and order must be restored," General Varennikov declared.

Gorbachev glowered at the general. "What must be restored is the Union. We will sign the Treaty and law and order will be restored. The *new* Union law and order."

Zaklanov stepped forward. "There will be *no* signing, Mikhail Sergeyevich. You want to preserve the Union, and we want to preserve the Union. Your new Union will destroy our Soviet system, and in the end it will destroy all of us. You do not want that. I know. Why are you capitulating to Yeltsin, his radicals in the White House and the renegade republics?"

Varennikov nodded his agreement with Zaklanov's assessment and put an ultimatum to Gorbachev. "If you do not sign the state of emergency, you must resign. *Now.*"

Angered by Zaklanov's threat, Gorbachev blared, "You will never live that long."

Zaklanov looked at Gorbachev with almost pleading eyes. "Mikhail Sergeyevich, we demand nothing from you. You will stay here, and we will do all the dirty work. In a month all will be back to normal."

Gorbachev glared at his visitors with contempt. "You are all going to meet defeat."

Varennikov sneered at Gorbachev's defiance. "Your refusal to sign the declaration presents no problem to us. We will take care of everything without you." He turned to his comrades. "We are wasting time." He started to leave, then stopped and pointed his finger at Gorbachev. "We will take the necessary action without you, Comrade President. The state of emergency will be declared, and you cannot stop it. Your orders and decrees will mean nothing." He motioned for his comrades to follow him, and they filed out.

Gorbachev stared at the open door. *So, the upheaval has finally begun.* He was not completely surprised by the visit, or the action the GKChP was taking. But it was difficult to accept that his own KGB chief, whom he had promoted to the post, and his own chief of staff had turned on him. Gorbachev's efforts to preserve the Union he loved would now be blocked by Kryuchkov and the hardliners. He did not believe that returning to totalitarian rule would preserve the fragile Union. Only a new treaty with the republics, his treaty, could do that now.

GKChP's action, he was sure, would result in widespread disorder and maybe even a civil war. It was too late to return to totalitarianism. He feared that the coup, once started, would set into motion a transformation, an upheaval that could bring down the Soviet government and in the end Communism itself.

.....

At 5:50 P.M., the chief of the Directorate for Government Communications, Lieutenant General Beda, ordered all of Gorbachev's direct phone lines cut. All communications into Gorbachev dacha at Foros from Moscow and other locations were transferred to a KGB operator who was courteous and, in a mellifluous voice, sang the same song to all callers: "Mikhail Gorbachev is not to be disturbed."

A regiment of the Sevastopol KGB Directorate blockaded all land access to the dacha, and the KGB's Border Guard ships blockaded all access to the dacha from the sea. The President's own guards maintained constant surveillance.

The conspirators had acted.

Chapter 74

At 6 P.M. John arrived at Gorky Park, Moscow's park of culture and leisure. The entrance portal looked like a copy of the Brandenburg Gate in Berlin, minus the Quadriga. Instead of Victoria's chariot and four horses, a communist agitprop-collage with Lenin's face perched atop the gate.

Maxim Gorky, a writer, was himself an ardent communist activist, but was said to have been poisoned during Stalin's 1936 purges, and was denied the honor spot in the park named after him. The honor, instead, went to the god of Socialism, as it always did in the Soviet Union. Lenin, it seemed, received credit for everything under the communist sky.

Parents with children strolled out of the entrance and queued at the bus stop in front of the park, or walked to a nearby Metro. For some, Muscovites' favorite Sunday family excursions were ending. An evening breeze picked up and promised to loosen the scorcher's merciless grip on the city.

The park possessed a history. In 1928, Moscow's mayor had been so fascinated with his visit to Berlin's Lunapark that he determined to build a similar facility for the citizens of Moscow. Was Gorky Park a faithful copy of Lunapark? No way, John thought. The Soviet system couldn't faithfully copy a retractable ball point pen. An ambitious program in the 1980s to copy the American space shuttle amounted to naught. The shuttle, called *Buran* (Russian for blizzard), was built at a painful expense the Soviets economy could ill afford and never carried any cosmonauts into space.

John walked through the entry gate, strolled through the amusement rides area, and headed toward the towering Ferris wheel. Children's shrilling laughter filled the air. At least *they* were having fun in Moscow. When he reached the pond, he turned right and walked toward the river, as instructed by Lisov. He found a vacant bench along the river walk and took a seat, facing the water. Waiting, he studied the Moscow River's murky passage, watching assorted refuse flow by. A man quietly walked up and sat down next to him. John looked up. He saw Lisov frowning and shaking his head.

Alarmed by Lisov's action, John stared at him stupidly; he didn't want to hear the bad news.

Lisov stood and strolled to the natural area of the park, away from the amusement rides and the crowds. John followed and came abreast. Lisov looked dismayed. "My contacts know of no plan you spoke about."

"But there is a plan," John insisted in a loud voice.

Lisov looked around as if to see if anybody could've heard, and seemingly satisfied that they were safe, he turned and replied in a quiet voice, "But I found out that a friend of mine, a colonel, commander of a special unit, was sent on assignment to Sevastopol on August 8. It's a port on the Black Sea."

"What kind of special unit? What kind of assignment?" John was reaching for a straw.

"I do not know what the unit does, and I don't know what mission he is on."

The straw floated away like the refuse in the Moskva River. "Then why did you tell me about it?"

"Because, my contacts say that at the same time a large amount of MBR-5 was removed from the Army's secret storage facility. The two events may be connected, and there may be a plan, as you said."

John saw a slim hope. "Where did the stuff go?"

Lisov shook his head. "Impossible to know. If I begin to inquire now, it will raise suspicion. It is best that I wait until my friend returns and find out directly from him. He is secretly sympathetic to the democratic movement and will help if he believes it will stop the hardliners from seizing power."

"When will you see him?"

"He is expected to be back tomorrow. I don't know exactly what time."

"But tomorrow is Monday, it will be too late," John cried out.

Again Lisov looked around to see if anyone heard them. "I cannot attempt to contact him before his return, because it will raise suspicion. Besides, I do not know where he is right now."

John gripped Lisov's arm, gave him a look of desperation.

Lisov stopped. "I must leave now. I will call you tomorrow if I obtain any information." He marched off toward the park exit.

John stood and watched Lisov disappear among the trees. He thought of the two things Roger Moore had said. The coup would start no later than tomorrow, and the bioterror attack would be ordered the next day if the coup went badly. Strange, but again he found himself hoping that the coup would go well for the hardliners.

He looked at his watch: seven o'clock. He had to deliver the bad news to Moore.

.....

Forty-five minutes later, John met Moore in the U.S. embassy outside the cafeteria. Moore looked defeated, as if he'd just thrown his last log into the fireplace on a frigid night. "Anything?" he asked, his voice hopeful.

John shook his head. "But there's a glimmer of hope," he added quickly.

Moore pointed to the old embassy building. "We'll talk in there."

When they were seated in an office, Moore asked with keen interest, "Tell me about your meeting. I want to hear all the details." An expectant expression spread on Moore's face.

"Not many details to tell. First, he colonel knows nothing about the planned attack, and his contacts in the GRU don't know either. It's a mystery to them. But—"

"Shit." Moore blurted out and slouched in his chair. "I went over the transcript of that conversation in the Kremlin, and there's no doubt about it. They talked about the plan. Pugo suggested it, and Kryuchkov bought it." Moore frowned and shook his head as if they'd just arrived at a dead end on a one-way street. He looked up at John with a spark of expectation. "What about the glimmer of hope you mentioned?"

John told Moore about Lisov's colonel friend, the commander of the special unit, his secret assignment in Sevastopol, and the movement of large quantities of MBR-5.

Moore sat up straight, eyes alert. "When did it happen?"

"Lisov said August 8th."

A light bulb seemed to turn on behind Moore's eyes. "Don't you see, John, they're transporting the MBR-5 by ship. If they loaded it around that time, a fast freighter may be ready right now to pull into a port somewhere on the East Coast."

"Son of bitch, I missed that. What can we do?"

"We, or the U.S., can do a lot. Our agencies can identify all Soviet ships that departed Sevastopol and all Greek freighters that are heading for our East Coast, plot their actual course. We have a very good chance to stop the incursion."

"But not foolproof."

Moore shook his head uneasily. "No."

"Lisov's colonel friend is returning tomorrow," John said. "I may get more information. We may find out the plan's details."

"Maybe," Moore said. "Lisov's colonel would know part of the plan, his part." Moore seemed to consider what he was about to say. "When Lisov contacts you tomorrow, meet his demands—Money, asylum, whatever it takes. We *must* stop the freighter."

"I hope to God in time." John stood. "I'll call you as soon as I get something from Lisov."

"John," Moore said in a cautionary tone. "Once your colonel and his friend agree to sell information, you'd better let us, the CIA, handle the arrangements from that point on. We've done this before."

John wanted to argue, wanted to get in on the action. What he really wanted to do is board the olive-oil-carrying freighter fully armed. He'd stop it in a heartbeat. But reality dictated a different course: let the CIA and the U.S. government do their job and he would do his. "You won't get any arguments from me, Roger, I haven't yet done any such deals."

He said goodbye and left.

Chapter 75

Thirty minutes later, John exited Aeroport Metro, swung a right into Telman Square, and headed to his apartment. *Sunday night. Upheaval will erupt within hours.* As he rounded the corner, a man stepped out of a parked car on Leningratskyi Prospekt and quickly walked toward him. *Lisov.* John slowed to a stroll. *Something happened.*

The colonel caught up. "My friend returned this evening, and he called me at my apartment. We met." Lisov started walking toward the wooded area in the square. John followed and prayed for good news. As soon as they stopped in a secluded spot, John pushed for details. "What'd you find out?"

"Yes, there is a plan, but my friend does not know all of its parts."

"*Christ.*" John shook his head, trying to throw off his horrid MBR-5 headache. "What was he doing in Sevastopol? What does he know?"

"He supervised the loading of MBR-5 into a Russian cargo ship. Then he traveled with the ship to the Aegean Sea where the cargo was transferred to a Greek freighter, and another agent took over from there. My friend delayed his return to Moscow until today for reasons he did not explain, but it had nothing to do with MBR-5."

"What's the name of the freighter, and what's its destination?"

"He does not know the destination port or the ultimate target."

"What?"

"The agent accompanying the freighter to your country knows the destination, but my friend does not. And that agent probably does not know the target. The target would only be known to our agents in your country, who will carry out the final phase of the attack."

"So what information does he have to sell?"

"The name of the Greek freighter, quantity of MBR-5, and method of shipping."

"How much does he want for that information?"

"One hundred thousand American dollars and a safe place if the hardliners succeed."

John considered this. If the Coast Guard or the Navy had the freighter's description, they could stop it, even if it changed its name for cover. According to Moore, they would know all the Greek freighters in route to the East Coast. Would the CIA still want to buy what Lisov's friend offered? John would let the station chief make that decision. "Okay," he said, "from this point on your colonel friend will have to deal with Roger Moore of the American Embassy. He will handle all the arrangements."

"The cultural attaché?" Lisov said and smiled.

"You know him?"

"We know all the agents in your embassy."

"Of course you do." John shot Lisov a cynical look. "I'll call him right away. He will tell me how your colonel friend can contact him tonight, and I'll immediately pass those instructions to you. The rest of the exchange will be between your colonel friend and Roger Moore. I'll get moving on this right now." John turned to go.

Lisov stopped him.

"We need to have a small exchange between us."

"Of course, we do." John shook his head. "How much?"

"Five thousand dollars for setting up the connection."

John grimaced.

"Well," Lisov said, seeing the expression on Baran's face, "Three thousand."

"I'll have to get the money from our cultural attaché."

Lisov nodded. "You know how to contact me," he said and strode to his car.

John hurried to his apartment. Inside, as he was about to call Moore, the listening phone in his satchel rang. He pulled it out, hit the button, and listened.

Ringing at the called number, then answer.

—*Allo?* Someone answered.

—Marshal Saposhnikov? The caller asked.

—Yes?

—This is General Mazov. Why am I not able to reach you through normal communication channels? I should not be using this mobile device. Why are you not returning my calls? Are you evading your Commander?

—Of course not, Comrade Minister. There must be something wrong with normal channels.

—Listen! The GKChP committee has just met and the decision has been made. General Varennikov and his ground forces will move out at dawn tomorrow. Five o'clock. Have your air forces on high alert, ready to support our ground forces. Understood?

—Yes Comrade Minister.

The line went dead.

The Soviet bosses hadn't only grown fat and lazy, as Juliana had said, but also careless. John picked up his normal mobile phone and called Juliana. When she answered, he said, "Tomorrow, 0050," and hung up.

Next, he called Moore at his residence. "We have to meet, I'm coming over."

Chapter 76

The morning of the expected coup, John awakened with a knot in his stomach. The dreadful anticipation of the coming upheaval turned the knot tighter by the minute. He made coffee and sat down at the kitchen table. He thought about dumping a couple of ounces of Stolichnaya into the cup of coffee to loosen the knot, but decided against it. It wouldn't help anything— it never did.

His telephone rang, almost startling him. He got up and picked up the receiver.

"Turn on your TV," Chris shouted. "Look outside, there's a *coup.*"

So, the upheaval had started. "There is what?" He tried to sound shocked.

"Coup, coup," Chris yelled. "Another revolution."

The knot in John's stomach loosened, as anticipation turned into reality. He forced some humor to lighten the situation. "I think you've been in Moscow too long, Chris, you need a vacation, maybe an R&R trip to someplace like Zanzibar."

"This is no goddamn joke, John."

He put the phone down, turned on the television, and went to look out the window. A low rumble began to shake the floor. The windowpanes vibrated. Tanks and armored personnel carriers moved southeast on Leningratskyi Prospekt toward Moscow Center. He went back and looked at the TV. Ballerinas whirled across the screen. He changed the channel— dancing swans. He turned the knob to Channel One and saw a news conference.

Five men, with microphones in front of them, sat behind a table on a raised platform, facing reporters. The one in the middle was making a speech. John went to the phone and picked up the receiver. "Chris, you there?"

"Yeah, I'm in the office. Did you see the conference on Channel One?"

"What in hell's going on?"

"The Russians here tell me that the coup leaders, the ones on TV, don't like Gorbachev's reforms and want to return to the old communist glory of the Soviet Union. They are fed up with Gorbachev's *Perestroika*, *Glasnost*, and the democratization reforms. The reforms threaten their power, and they want to return to complete State control. They'll kill the new Union treaty Gorbachev negotiated, and they'll come down hard on the Soviet republics that began to move toward independence. The Russians here say that if the coup succeeds, the hardliners in the new government will be hostile to the foreign investors."

"Including Sovcell?"

"The State would take control of the venture, nationalize if necessary. They tell me privately that they're afraid the State would run the venture into the ground the way they've done with all of their enterprises. They're afraid for their jobs."

"Holy shit, there'll be another Brezhnev in the Kremlin. It'll be Cold War II, or maybe even World War III."

"What're we going to do?"

"Hold the fort, Chris, I'm on my way."

"Hold the fort?"

"Make sure no one interferes with the operation of the network."

"And how do I hold the fort against tanks?"

"I don't know, talk, threaten with our partner's ministerial authority, but don't let them touch anything."

"What if the minister is part of the coup?"

"Then we're in deep shit." John hung up. He sat down to view the news conference. After a few minutes, he figured it out. Gennady Yanayev, the vice president of the USSR, had assumed command because President

Gorbachev, Yanayev said, "had been taken ill and is therefore incapacitated."

A reporter commented that Gorbachev was vacationing in the Crimean resort of Foros and asked how he could contract an illness so fast. The manner in which he asked the question challenged the veracity of Yanayev's statement. The tribunal ignored the reporter's question, and Yanayev continued his diktat. "A State Committee for a State of Emergency, the GKChP, has been formed to prevent chaos, anarchy, and the disintegration of the Soviet Union." The vice president's voice quivered, his florid face tensed, his bloodshot eyes darted from reporter to reporter.

John looked closer at the coup leaders behind the makeshift tribunal table. The junta didn't look to be decidedly in command. Anxiety, even fear, rather than triumph, governed their facial expressions. The camera zoomed in on Yanayev's hands: they shook.

Yanayev announced the GKChP decree: "A state of emergency is to be in effect for six months, activities of political parties and movements are suspended, and censorship of the press is to be implemented."

"Jesus Christ," John cried out. The bastards must've shut down all communications already. Sovcell's Intelsat link was cut off for sure. If the coup leaders took control of the country, they couldn't allow unimpeded international communications. He called Chris.

"Is Sovcell operational?" he asked. "Are international calls going through?"

"The network is fully operational," Chris said. "International traffic is heavy and increasing. Our pre-subscribed customers must've found out their telephones worked and started using them. A high volume of calls is being placed to Western Europe, UK, and the United States. The coup leaders haven't shut down our satellite link."

"Are they inept? How come we're still operating?"

"Maybe for now, but I don't think it'll last long. As soon as they sober up they'll figure out what to do, and the shit will hit the fan."

"You think they're drunk?"

"You can bet on that. They wouldn't have the guts to do this sober."

"Then let's hope they stay sloshed." John tried for a lighter side of the serious situation they were in. "You think we could take a few of our cases of Stolichnaya over to the Kremlin to keep the coup leaders whacked out?"

Chris laughed. "Hey, I'll take a van full of booze over there if it'll help."

"I'm going to try to call Ober, and then I'll be on my way to the office." John hung up. He checked the time and backed up eight hours: past midnight on the East Coast. He tried to place a call to Ober's home number using his mobile phone, but he was blocked; he got an all-circuits-busy tone. He tried to place an international call on the Moscow phone, but nothing, a stupid waste of time. He dialed the local access number for Sovam Teleport, the Moscow end of San Francisco/Moscow Teleport, and placed the phone receiver into the acoustic coupler connected to his Compaq notebook. To his surprise, he received a response from the email system. He sent a message to Ober's office reporting on what had just happened and then left the apartment to catch the Metro.

Chapter 77

When John walked out into Telman Square, he saw people running among the tanks on Leningratskyi Prospekt, shaking their fists, and shouting at the soldiers. One man was almost run over as a tank aimed for him. John rushed into the Metro station and boarded the next train. The Metro appeared to run normally. The passengers, who usually had their noses in books or newspapers, instead talked to each other in hushed voices. Most looked frightened. But some had an expression of triumph on their faces, as if it was time that someone took action to stop the deterioration of their country.

As he rounded the corner and walked through Sovcell's entry gate, his eyes bulged. A T-72 tank hunkered in the parking lot towering over the cars, its turret pointing its main gun at the Sovcell building. He closed his eyes for a moment and opened them again. The tank was still there. He stared at the behemoth. Two crewmen sat on the turret smoking, chatting, and looking bored. He moved cautiously toward the entry door. The crewmen gave him a casual glance and returned to their conversation. Besides the monstrosity in the parking lot, everything else looked normal. Sovcell's guard at the door greeted John with a nod, but otherwise said nothing and returned his gaze to the tank.

Inside the building, he found Chris and the technicians in the kitchen, huddled around a television set.

"Not good," Chris said when he saw John come in.

"How bad?"

"The Russians tell me that the unholy trinity is part of the coup."

"Meaning?

"The Defense Minister, the KGB chairman, and the Interior Minister. In other words, the military, the secret police, and the security troops—the unholy trinity."

"Who else is taking part?"

"In addition to Yanayev, their proclaimed leader, the heads of the military, security troops and the KGB, there are the Prime Minister and three others. A band of eight, the Russians call them."

"What about our venture partner, the Communications Minister, which side is he on?"

"We don't know."

John groaned and cracked a feeble smile. "Can we call in the Marines from the U.S. Embassy?"

Chris chuckled. "They're probably busy right now holding down their own fort."

"In that case let's circle the wagons and dig in, continue to monitor the network, complete all the calls we can," he shrugged, "and wait and see what happens."

"Sounds like a plan."

John went into the equipment room to scan the system monitor. Heavy-load indicators flashed for trunk groups to the U.S., the UK and Western Europe. Chris joined him. "We're hauling in the dough. Look at those traffic levels."

One of the salespersons ran into the switch room and announced that he had news from the White House, the seat of the Russian Republic government. "Yeltsin, the president of Russian, issued a decree. The decree declared the GKChP unconstitutional body and called on people not to obey it."

"That's incredible," John said. "How could the coup leaders allow anybody to issue any statements condemning them?"

"Yeah," Chris said. "Why isn't Yeltsin in the basement of the Lubyanka, locked up? The coup leaders aren't that stupid. And even if they are drunk, they still know how to deal with the opposition."

"Maybe their chain of command has some loose links," John said.

"Those links are risking certain death, if they disobey," Chris said.

The salesperson frowned. "There will be showdown. The coup leaders will move against the Russian Republic government, and the Army will attack Yeltsin and his supporters at the White House."

A salesperson in the field called in. A technician took the call and relayed the news. "Salesperson is outside Hotel Ukraina. He says tanks advancing on the White House stopped by thousands of protesters assembled to defend it. He says he is going to join the protesters— McDonalds is distributing hamburgers to White House defenders."

The democratic movement had mobilized its supporters, John thought. *Way to go, Juliana.* "How'd they stop the tanks? Were they armed?"

The technician repeated the question to the salesperson, waited, and listened. "Protesters not armed," the technician said. "They built barricades from bricks, concrete blocks, tree trunks, cobblestones, and rusted bathtubs." The technician raised his hand, listened. Everyone went quiet. "Yeltsin climbed on top of a tank and called Vice-President Yanayev bandit. People cheered and formed human shield, and Army did nothing."

"That's astonishing," John said. *Fantastic,* he thought. He imagined Juliana in the front of the crowd shaking her fist and screaming at the tanks and the army troops.

"No reaction from the Army?" Chris said with a surprise on his face. "Maybe so far. I can't believe Yanayev and his gang lost their nerves. They're finished if they don't follow through with force, and they know it. I'm waiting for the massacre."

John gave Chris a stare. "I say you're wrong. I hope you're wrong. I don't believe the soldiers would shoot unarmed fellow Russians. This coup is cracking."

Chris shook his head. "What will be cracking soon are the Army's guns."

Chapter 78

John's secretary burst into the equipment room and rushed up to him. "Comrade General Director is on the telephone for you, Mr. Baran. He wants to speak with you without delay," she said in a directive voice, impressing upon John that it was his superior calling.

Chris raised his eyebrows. John shrugged and followed the secretary to his office. He picked up the phone. "Yes, Mr. Trush?"

"Mr. Baran," the general director said in yet another directive voice, "you are ordered by the Minister to shut down Sovcell network immediately."

Shit! The Minister is part of the coup. John hesitated for a moment as he thought about what to say and then decided to take a stand. "Mr. Trush, Sovcell is an American joint venture, and the Minister cannot shut it down. He can shut down his own network, but he has no right to shut down Sovcell." John took liberty in interpreting the joint venture agreement. In truth, he himself didn't know exactly what rights the Minister had when it came to issuing unilateral directives.

"Mr. Baran!" Enmity oozed out of the telephone handset. "If you don't shut the network down at once, we will shut it for you." The phone clicked and went dead.

John slammed the phone down and looked up to see Chris standing in his doorway, waiting, apparently, to hear what their general director had to say.

"The minister *commands* us to shut down the network. *Immediately.*"

"I'm not surprise," Chris said. "He must be sober. What're going to do?"

"Screw him. He's chosen the wrong side." John said and then briefly thought about Harry's *over my dead body* resolve, but quickly dismissed it. "We're here to provide service and we'll do it as long as we can. Did you see those traffic levels? Customers are generating revenues for us. Let the Minister send an army to stop us. Sovcell will be *our* 'White House'."

'Where are we going to get the bodies to defend it?"

John pointed a finger at Chris and then at himself.

Chris shot John a freakish glare. "This'll be our *Alamo*, not the White House, John," Chris said, his voice agitated.

"Nah, you heard what happened. No hostile action was taken by the army."

.....

Later that morning, the lead technician, Nikolai's "replacement," burst into John's office. He didn't knock. "Mr. Baran, Mr. Baran, soldiers are outside our building. They want to come in."

John flew out of the office and charged toward the entry doors. Within seconds he took a position blocking access to Sovcell. Chris was right with him. Standing on the building's entry door landing, John surveyed the scene in front of him.

Four steps below, the Sovcell guard confronted an army major, apparently trying to prevent the officer and his three men from entering the building. The guard kept his AK-47 shouldered. He had guts, John thought, protecting *private* property, or half private in Sovcell's case. The major's insignia said he was KGB security troops. He saw John and Chris, pushed the guard aside, and walked up to the landing. "Which one of you is Baran?" His mannerism was abrupt.

"I am," John said.

The major glared at John as if he didn't believe the American defied the Minister's order. "I am here to disable your mobile network. My men are communications specialists, they know what to do. Step aside!"

John and Chris stood their ground, blocking the doorway.

The major put his hand on the holster of his side arm. John looked up and stared directly into the barrel of the tank's 125mm gun. The two crewmen on the turret had their side arms drawn and pointed at John and

Chris, one each. The KGB officer started up the steps toward the entry door.

John raised his hand in a stop-there signal. "Sovcell network is the property of the United States of America and you cannot disable it or touch it in any way." He didn't know if the major knew anything about the joint venture law and hoped that the bluff worked. He didn't think that the officer would risk hostile action and set off a major incident of international proportions. He prayed he judged correctly.

The major stood for a minute, gawking. Then he turned, marched to his vehicle, and made a call on his radio. John couldn't hear the conversation, but it ended with the officer nodding several times. The major motioned his men back into the vehicle and they took off. The crewmen holstered their weapons and lit their cigarettes. The Sovcell guard cracked a faint smile.

"Whew," Chris exhaled.

"Whew is right," John said. "But I don't think it's over."

…..

Thirty minutes later, the switchroom lead technician rushed into John's office again. "We lost AC power," he said, alarmed.

"I was waiting for the next shoe to drop," John said under his breath. "How much time do we have?"

"Eight hours on the batteries."

"And the backup generator?"

"Three days on full tanks."

"Well, we've got three days to make money. Keep the network operating."

The tech smiled, nodded, and marched out.

John wondered if a third or a fourth shoe were going to land. If they did, he was sure, they wouldn't be as innocuous as a local power cut. But why didn't the minister order his Intelsat organization to cut Sovcell's satellite link? *Strange.* Either the minister was inept, which was unlikely, or he didn't want to lose half of the hard currency revenues Sovcell was collecting. Or maybe the minister was only going through the motions of shutting down Sovcell, obeying coup plotters' orders, and his real sympathy lay with democratic reforms. The last possibility, John thought, was a long shot.

Chapter 79

As the first day of the coup wore on, there seemed to be little happening. The Army took up their positions in the city and stood in place. No hostilities broke out. Outside the presence of the military, life in Moscow, at least on the surface, seemed to follow its usual routine. Public transportation and communication systems were operating normally. *The calm before the...what?* John wondered how long the eerie normalcy would last.

Late in the afternoon he received an email from Cellcomm. Ober wanted an assessment of the situation. He saw CNN coverage of the coup and was concerned about John and Chris' safety and the security of the venture. John asked the switchman to seize a trunk to the U.S. for his call to Ober, and two minutes later he was connected to Cellcomm and heard Klaudia's excited voice.

"Are you and Chris all right, was anybody hurt, did the military take over Sovcell?" She shot the questions like burst out of a machine gun.

"We're fine, Klaudia and everything is operating normally. This is a weird coup, and maybe all hell will break loose at any moment, but so far the coup looks like a farce." He didn't want to trouble her with the shutdown attempt by the Minister.

"That's not what we're hearing here. The media is portraying it as 'grave.' World peace is threatened."

"If the media didn't hype it, it couldn't sell their product. Is the chief there, Klaudia? I need to give him an update on what's happening."

"Just a moment."

John tried to anticipate Ober's reaction to the upheaval in workers' paradise. Would the boss recall him and Chris back to the States?

"What in hell is going on, John?" Ober bellowed over the telephone. "You guys all right?"

John gave him a rundown on the day's events, including Minister's attempt to shut down Sovcell.

"Damned commies," Ober shouted. "And I see you've got some balls, too. Great job!" A pause. "But if that's the best coup they can stage, they're finished." His tone positive, upbeat. "Keep the network operating, we need the money. This thing will blow over, and I wouldn't be surprised if we're seeing the end of the evil empire."

"I hope you're right about the end, Chief."

"God knows it's time. Any system of government that violates the natural law of justice and human rights cannot last. The Nazis disappeared in twelve years, so why in hell are the commies still around?"

"We invaded Germany, Chief." John reminded his boss.

"Well, what the hell are we waiting for? If we can beat the Nazis' fighting machine, the commies will be a cakewalk for us. But I've digressed." Ober cleared his throat. "The proper thing for me to do now is to put your personal safety ahead of the venture. You and Chris must plan to get out of there on a moment's notice, just in case this thing turns ugly. Perhaps you should even get out now. What do you think? You're there on the ground."

John thought about it. How were they going to get out if things turned to ugly? Make a run for Finland? How far would they get? But he didn't say that to Ober. Instead, he said, "I'll stay and hold the fort, and Chris, I'm sure, will do the same."

"Good, good, just so it's your decision," Ober said. "Keep me informed. Now I have to report to the chairman, and he'll get an earful of what I really think about venturing in that red swamp."

John heard Ober mutter something that didn't sound like pristine English or pristine German.

"Let's talk tomorrow same time." Ober ended the call.

John looked at Chris standing next to him. "The boss offered to repatriate us, but I told him that we'd stay." He watched Chris' reaction.

Chris frowned.

John quickly added, "If I haven't spoken for you, you can leave any time."

Chris paused, then grinned. "Ah, hell, I don't want to miss the excitement."

"We might get more excitement than we can handle."

Chris dismissed John's comment with a short, nervous laugh. "It looks like the hardliners are in a stalemate with the reformers. Let's hope this shit just blows over."

The day continued uneventful, and then news about the coup's progress, or the lack of it, started to trickle in. By evening, some of the Red Army's elite commando divisions had gone over to Yeltsin's side and were now protecting the White House. Yevgeny Saposhnikov, commander-in-chief of the Soviet Air Force, shifted his position and warned the coup leaders that his planes would bomb the Kremlin, if Army tanks advanced on the White House. The stalemate continued with no hostility. As Sovcell continued to operate normally, John asked the switchroom supervisor to beef up the night shift and encouraged everyone else to go home to get some rest. He went into Chris' office and said, "I'm leaving to get some sleep, it's almost eleven o'clock."

Chris closed his notebook computer and began to gather his papers. "Me too."

.....

In his apartment, John turned on the TV and looked for news of the bioterror attack, just in case the hardliners pulled the trigger early. He saw nothing related to it. The first day of the coup limped to an end and the hardliners hadn't acted. According to Moore, if they hadn't seized complete control by the second day, and it looked like they wouldn't, Kryuchkov would order the MBR-5 distraction attack for sure, or else the coup would collapse and the conspirators' fate would be sealed. And if the U.S didn't intercept the Greek olive oil freighter, well...a new ballgame.

Chapter 80

The next morning, the second day of the coup, John arrived at the Sovcell building without trouble. The Metro operated normally. Some of the passengers in John's Metro car looked pleased, apparently happy with what was going on. John leaned closer to an elderly couple and overheard them talking. The man said, "Tanks are still on the streets in Moscow Center and I am waiting for the bloodbath." With a smile of satisfaction, he predicted, "Our Red Army will wipe out Yeltsin's supporters and the Soviet Union will return to our communist glory." John tensed and stepped away.

When he walked through the gates into the parking lot, he saw that the T-72 hadn't moved, but that the main gun had been lowered and turned away from the building. The two crewmen still sat on the turret, still smoked, still chatted.

Seeing John walk in, Chris blurted out, "Yahoo, we're hauling in cash by the bushel. The coup is good for our business. The network's fully loaded, hell, it's overloaded."

John peered at Chris. "Is counting money accountant's heaven?"

"And I've concluded that the coup leaders haven't got the guts to carry this to conclusion. They're just a bunch of drunks. The sun is setting on the old Kremlin."

"So how do you think it'll end?"

"I don't know exactly, but it'll end badly for the communist hardliners."

"Is that your clairvoyant—?" John stopped when he saw the switchroom supervisor burst through the doorway.

"Mr. Baran, Mr. Baran," the supervisor cried, crisis written all over his face. "The generator cable is cut. We are running on batteries only!"

The third shoe? More like a slipper, John thought. He expected more. "When did it happen?"

"Fifteen minutes ago."

John noticed that Russians were always ready to sound the alarm—even enjoyed it—but they were short on proposing a course of action to solve the problem. Instead, they always kicked the problem up the line, fearing of making any decisions themselves.

"Did you see any army personnel outside our building?"

The supervisor shook his head.

"Splice the cable," John told the Russian. "And assign one of your techs to guard the generator."

"Splice the cable?" the supervisor said, looking momentarily uncertain.

"Reconnect the generator," John repeated the command.

"Yes, Mr. Baran, we can do that," the Russian acknowledged.

"Then do it." *Christ.*

John turned to Chris. "Sabotage, kindergarten style."

"Who?" Chris asked.

"Whoever, it's not a serious action, done more for appearance than effect."

.....

In the afternoon, Sovcell salespeople in the field reported further developments. New tank divisions were headed toward the White House. In response to the threat, thirty thousand protesters regrouped to defend it. A hundred thousand Soviet citizens were on the streets in the center of Moscow. In a brief confrontation two people were shot, and a tank crushed one of the protesters. The ensuing outcry and fist-shaking by the White House defenders caused the tanks to retreat, resulting in a temporary standoff followed by a lessening of tensions. The situation appeared to be stable again.

At 9 P.M., John walked into the kitchen to see if there was any further news on the television or, God forbid, a report of bioterrorism attack in the States. As he watched, the dancing swans were interrupted by a news announcement. The GKChP imposed a 10 P.M. curfew on Moscow, but there was nothing about an attack in the United States. A switchman watching the TV sneered. "Look," he said, "in protest people are raising the old Russian flag. Nobody will observe curfew. This is not going well for the GKChP. They say that no one has seen the band of eight since Monday morning." Then he let out a deep belly laugh and added, "They are staying home—they came down with 'coup flu.'" The other technicians on duty joined in the guffaw. John didn't think it was that funny, and thought about quoting Yogi Berra to them. *It ain't over till it's over.* But he feared that the Russians wouldn't know Yogi Berra from Yogi Bear and may take his comment as an affront to the protesters.

The second day of the coup was ending, and it looked bad for the hardliners. Still, he heard no news about any bioweapons attack. Had the freighter carrying MBR-5 been stopped? Had the coup plotters changed their minds? He went to his office and called Roger Moore. When Moore answered, John said, "Looks like the coup isn't turning out the way the hardliners planned it."

"No, it's not." Moore's voice was calm, cheerful.

"I haven't heard anything from the States."

Momentary silence.

"And you won't," Moore said.

"What happened?"

"Right now we're checking the olive oil's virginity."

"I wish I were doing that."

"I know how you feel, but you've done your part. Thanks."

"You must tell me about it sometime."

"I will."

John signed off. Then he called Ober and gave him a quick status report.

"It's extraordinary that you're still operating," Ober bellowed. "The heavy traffic will generate heavy revenues. God knows we need the money to offset what we've spent to get this operation up and running. The hardliners' lack of will to follow through is an indication that things have changed in the Soviet Union. It's not as if the use of force is foreign to them. They must be getting soft. Material comfort imported by capitalism is corrupting their ideology. We're succeeding, John."

"Yes, Chief. They do appear to have lost their taste for ideological blood."

"Commies lost their taste for blood? Hell must be freezing over." Ober blared. He waited a moment and then said, "Going forward, John, I want frequent updates from you and immediate notification if things take a turn for the worse. We must assume that this thing can still turn ugly."

"You'll get it, Chief, if I'm able to do it. It'll depends on how ugly the turn."

Ober grunted and ended the call.

Chapter 81

The evening arrived and the quiet continued. At 9:30 John left for his apartment. He didn't want to violate the ten o'clock curfew in case the Military enforced it. He quickly made his way to the Mayakovskaya Metro. He liked the Moscow subway: quick, efficient, cheap, and dependable, though at times overcrowded. He dropped his token into the slot on the turnstile, walked through, caught the escalator down to the platform, and joined the crowd waiting for the next train heading toward the Aeroport Metro. The station's architecture and artwork gave him a pleasant lift. Compare to the dreary city above ground, the Metro station was an "underground palace."

He looked up at the ceiling to study its artwork and focused on a mosaic of three Soviet aircraft. His study of World War II fighting machines told him they were Petlyakov Pe-8s. The heavy bombers headed, no doubt, west to bomb German positions, or maybe Berlin itself. The Great Patriotic War lived on.

His peripheral vision captured something familiar and pulled his gaze to the escalator. A large, dark-skinned man wearing a Lenin's cap, descended to the platform and joined the crowd behind John. As John searched his memory to place the man, he heard the train in the tunnel thundering toward the station. Suddenly the memory clicked: The Uzbekistan gorilla who, together with the Armenian gorilla and the Leather Jacket, had attacked him in Telman Square and put him in the hospital. He quickly whirled around. Uzbekistan Gorilla charged straight at John like a Pamplona bull, pushing and shoving the waiting passengers aside. John dove to his left. Uzbek's momentum carried him through the empty space where John stood and slammed him into the back of a petite elderly woman who faced the track, waiting for the train that had just entered the station. Propelled by the Uzbek's impact, the woman and her bag of vegetables sailed over the tracks and landed in a bizarre position. Her neck rested on the far rail and her body lay inside the tracks. John watched in horror as the onrushing train's wheels sliced through her neck, severing her head.

Uzbek Gorilla gawked at the scene. When what he'd done registered, he bolted for the escalator. John sprang to his feet and shoving the screaming passengers aside, took off in pursuit. When he got to the street level, he scanned the area, but all he saw of the assailant was his Lenin's cap laying on the Gorky Street sidewalk, thirty feet to his left. He spent a second deciding whether the cap was the gorilla's attempt to misdirect John, or whether it had accidentally flown off his head. He concluded that the southern goon's mentality didn't extend beyond physical violence, and he raced down Gorky Street. He ran past the cap, stopped when he came to a side street, and looked.

The Uzbek careered down the street. John shot after him with his afterburner on and quickly gained on the assailant. In the next block, the Uzbek dashed into a wooded area on the right and seemed to slow down to rest. He turned and gaped in disbelief, as John was about to jump him. The Uzbek reached inside his jacked, pulled out a pistol, and tried to aim it, but he didn't make it. John dove and smashed his right shoulder into the man's chest and struck the pistol-bearing arm with his left hand. The tackle landed the Uzbek flat on his back, and he tried to scream but only managed to wheeze and pant. John ripped the Makarov out of Uzbek's right hand and threw it aside. He walloped the Uzbek's head to subdue him and then applied a rear neck choke, tightening his hold. He yelled into the man's ear. "Who sent you?" He knew the answer, but wanted confirmation.

The Uzbek didn't answer. John increased his pressure. "Who sent you?" The Uzbek grabbed John's arms and tried to pull them off his neck. John squeezed harder. "Who?" The gorilla let out disconnected sounds between his gasps. "Tru...Tru..."

"Trush?" John said.

The Uzbek tried to nod.

John firmed his hold and violently twisted Uzbek's neck to the right, and when he felt the snap, he released his grip. The assailant's listless body slumped to the ground. John did a quick visual 360 of the park-like area. A few Russians in the park and more on side streets stood and stared at him. He picked up the pistol, wiped it clean, and dropped it on top of the dead Uzbek. He didn't wait for the scene to develop and shot down a side street. He turned left on the next street, and when the park was out of view he slowed to a brisk walk. He continued for three blocks, checking if he was followed. He wasn't. He turned left at the next block and walked back to Gorky Street. He saw a group of passengers boarding a stopped tram and dashed for it. He jumped on board and squeezed in like another sardine. The door behind him closed and the tram began to roll.

He got off at the Belaruskaya Metro stop and took the subway to his apartment. He thought about the grisly death of the babushka—a horrid tragedy brought on by another Trush's attempt to dispose of John. It was high time he dealt with the head member of the murderous troika.

Chapter 82

On the third day of the coup, John arrived at Sovcell early and found the Army tank gone from the parking lot. As the day got underway, things began to happen. Yeltsin announced that the coup leaders were trying to flee the country, and by evening the band of eight, with the exception of the Interior Minister Pugo, had been arrested, and lesser officials had been detained. Pugo, the authorities reported, had committed suicide. Skeptics questioned that determination, as the officials didn't explain how Pugo had managed to put three bullets into his own head.

For a fleeting moment, John wondered if the CIA had a hand in it to pay Pugo off for his MBR-5 idea, but he dismissed the thought. The Interior Minister had his own enemies—thousands seeking freedom from the oppression of his security troops.

Later in the day, the White House announced that Yeltsin had sent Russian Republic officials to Foros to bring Gorbachev safely back to Moscow. The hard-line conspirators had been defeated. The coup had collapsed.

The technicians, analysts, and other Russian employees broke out into an impromptu celebration. Out of nowhere, it seemed, bottles of vodka appeared on the kitchen table, and everyone had a glass in hand.

John stepped in. "I'll be happy to join the celebration, but not now, and not during working hours."

A wall of frowning Russians stared at him.

"It's critical," he said, "that we keep the network running. At full load, problems could develop very quickly, and we can't allow any downtime. Our customers are depending on us for their connections, and we're depending on them for our revenues: *money,* to pay yours and my salary. I must ask you to return to your assigned duties."

A few frowns faded. Some began to nod. John watched as they slowly shuffled out of the kitchen and returned to their jobs. As the last one of the Russians filed out, John's secretary walked into the kitchen.

"You have a telephone call, Mr. Baran." She raised her eyebrows, as if she considered the call strange.

"Who is it?

"The woman did not identify herself," she said as if she disapproved of the caller's manners. She turned and went back to her station.

Back in his office, John picked up the phone. "Hello?"

"Mr. Baran? John?"

"Juliana," he said with concern and then relief, "are you all right?"

"Yes, I am fine. Today we won. The communists have been defeated."

"I know. That's great. That's wonderful. You've succeeded. Your movement stopped the coup."

"It is thanks to you. John, please come for dinner on Sunday. Papa wants to meet you. I have told him much about you, and he wants to meet the brave American who helped the democratic movement defeat the coup."

"What time?"

"Seven o'clock." She gave him the address and directions.

.....

The next day, in Sovcell's kitchen, John watched the television coverage of Gorbachev's return from Foros. Russians credited Yeltsin for derailing the coup and enabling the shaken Soviet leader to return to power. Gorbachev walked down the ladder from his plane to take charge of the now frail Soviet Union. Would the reforms he'd started continue? Would the Soviet Union be unaffected by the attempted upheaval? *No,* John was sure, business as usual would not continue for Gorbachev or the USSR. Yeltsin, the President of the Russian Federation, seemed to have achieved political status that was equal—superior in the eyes of many—to that of Gorbachev. Could this misalignment of status exist for long?

Probably not, John thought, but he didn't know how it would play out. The Soviet Union's political equations remained to be solved.

The world's interest in what was happening to the Communist empire generated high demand for international communication services. Sovcell's business was booming. At eight dollars a minute for calls to the U.S., revenues were mounting, and the mobile phones were in constant use. A correspondent for a major U.S. news agency stayed connected on his Sovcell phone for thirty hours, reporting on the coup. Sovcell's mobile services operated without interruptions, and John expected that it would continue that way.

At 4 P.M., he received an email from Klaudia asking him to call Ober. Since the network was still fully loaded, he asked the switchroom supervisor to set up the call for him. When he was connected, he heard Ober's booming voice. "Great job you guys are doing," Ober bellowed, as if John and Chris had single-handedly protected and defended Sovcell's network against the Red Army and had, in addition, brought down the coup. "Thanks for the timely email reports," he said in an upbeat tone.

Something's up.

"I have good news for you, John."

"Yes, Chief?" John said with caution. Good news from Ober could mean many things.

"I've hired your replacement," Ober said. "You can plan to return home as early as next week. Your replacement is in Minsk right now. He was with a mobile communications venture in Belarus. The venture folded, and he'll be in Moscow early next week."

Crap. The news caused John to pause. "That's…great." But he didn't feel or sound great. He had reasons not to leave Moscow. He didn't want to part with Juliana, next week or next year, and he had to settle David's account with Trush.

"Aren't you glad to get out of that shithole?" Ober apparently had sensed John's lack of enthusiasm.

"I was just thinking about something."

"Well, stop thinking and start making plans to get over here," Ober said. "I want to talk to you about a project in Poland. You speak Polish, don't you?"

"Yes, I do. But I don't have operating experience. You said so yourself."

"I've changed my mind."

"But you said *I* could name my next assignment." John had nothing against Poland, but he wasn't ready to leave Moscow.

"Well?" Ober bellowed.

"I want my next assignment here in Moscow, in Sovcell."

"Moscow?" Ober said, as if the city wasn't of any particular interest to him now. "You've done a great job in there, but it's time to move on to another challenge, repeat your miracle in Poland."

"*Moscow*, Chief. You said I could name my next assignment. I'm naming it: *Moscow*."

"But I already hired your replacement."

"Send him to Poland. Warsaw is closer to Minsk than Moscow."

Silence hung on the line.

John pushed. "You promised, Chief."

Ober remained silent.

Half a minute passed.

"Chief?"

"Oh hell, stay there. You do seem to have everything under control." Ober signed off in a somber tone.

Not quite everything is under control. John thought. *Not yet.* He looked up and saw his secretary standing in his doorway.

"A Mr. Storton*ee* from Milan is on the phone," she said, putting a Russian twist into the Italian name. He said he would wait until you were finished with your call."

John picked up the phone and pressed the flashing button, "Baran."

"Hello, Mr. Baran, this is Angelo Stortoni of Corrotto S.A. in Milano."

They exchanged greetings and John said, "What's the reason for your call, Signor Stortoni? How may I help you?"

"I am operations vice president for Corrotto worldwide, and your letter of 12 August was referred to me by our management for action."

"And what action have you taken, Mr. Stortoni?" John scrambled to retrieve a copy of the letter from his file.

"I have made a preliminary investigation regarding your accusation of Signor Casone and found sufficient irregularities to warrant further action," Stortoni said in flawless English. He sounded apologetic.

"What do you plan to do, Mr. Stortoni?"

"After preliminary inquiry I have suspended Signor Casone and Signor Sospettori, pending full investigation."

"And what did your preliminary inquiry reveal?"

"My apology, Mr. Baran, but I should say nothing at this time until the full investigation is completed. But let me assure you that if your accusations are borne out, severe action will be taken to protect Corrotto's name and reputation. Sovcell, of course, will be fully compensated for its loss."

"When do you expect to complete your review, Mr. Stortoni?"

"Since Corrotto cannot afford to be under a cloud of suspicion, we'll proceed quickly and complete it as soon as possible. I shall inform you when I have definite information."

"Thank you, Signor Stortoni."

"In the meantime, Mr. Baran, please feel free to call me on my direct number anytime, or visit us in Milano, if you believe it would be helpful to your inquiry into the matter." Stortoni gave his number and said goodbye.

At that moment, Chris ran into John's office and yelled, "You've got to see this, come on."

Chapter 83

John followed Chris into the kitchen where technicians huddled around the television and watched a news report. Yeltsin was presenting Gorbachev with documents that indicated the stand each minister took during the coup.

"The Communications Minister better be on the coup members' list," John said, "or it's a fake list."

"The Russians tell me he definitely is."

"What does that mean for us?"

"The minister will be dismissed and possibly punished in other ways."

"What about Trush?"

"Since Trush is the minister's fair-haired boy, he'll also be dismissed.

"I hope that SOB doesn't disappear on me."

"He won't be allowed to go farther than his dacha. He might even be detained by Yeltsin's people."

John drew Chris outside the kitchen and said in a low voice, "How can one get hold of an AK-47 here in Moscow, like the one our guard outside the building has?"

"What?" Chris' face contorted into a weird expression.

"Don't yell. You heard me."

"Are you crazy?"

"Do you want me to repeat the question?"

Chris shook his head for a long minute and then seemed to calm down. "The underworld," he said in a flat tone. "You need contacts in the underworld. Try muscle mobsters that sell 'security.' What do you want it for?"

"Did I say I wanted it?" John didn't wait for an answer, turned, and walked back to his office.

.....

The following morning, Chris marched into John's office with a triumphant smile on his face. "Listen to this, the Russians say that the communications minister and Trush were dismissed from their posts, and no replacements have been named. So, my friend, as first deputy general director, you take over for Trush. You're the general director of Sovcell, and Cellcomm has total control of the venture."

"I'll be *acting* general director, Chris. Ober would have to change the venture agreement with our partner for an American general director to be named."

"One other thing, and you won't believe this, Gorbachev resigned as General Secretary and dissolved the Communist Party."

"Thank god. It's about time. Ober said it was long overdue. Speaking of the chief, I've got to call him and report on this development. Communist Party dissolution will brighten his day. I'll talk to you later." Chris left for his office. John asked the switch room to set up his call and picked up the mobile.

He delivered his update to Ober, and the response was immediate and loud: "I'll be goddamned, I would've never believed this. Every Sovietologist in the West missed this one. We have to make hay while the sun shines, John." Ober began to expound his grandiose plans for Sovcell: expansion, new markets, new cities, even other Soviet Republics outside Russia.

"That's a big order, Chief," John said when Ober finally stopped talking.

"Well?" Ober barked.

"Okay, Chief. I'll draw up the business plan."

"Shoot it over when you get it done," Ober said and terminated the call, his tone buoyant.

.....

On Saturday morning John focused on his unfinished business. It was time to settle the account with Trush. The third head of the troika reptile

337

had to be cut off, before it made another attempt on John's life, or somehow managed to slither into obscurity.

But first, he called Mr. Chernov and explained what he'd learned about David's onset of paralysis. He assured David's father that he would personally see to it that justice is administered to those responsible for David's death. He would explain more when he visited the Chernovs in their home the next time he was Stateside.

Next, he searched his briefcase for the business card given to him by Mrs. Gromylov, the Rolls Royce lady with the flat tire on Schuylkill Expressway back in Philadelphia. He looked at the crossed-sword emblem on the card, and decided to collect the favor that she said her husband wouldn't fail to deliver. He picked up his mobile phone and punched in the Philadelphia area number for Maximilian Gromylov of Worldwide Private Security.

.....

On Monday morning, August 25th, John arrived in his office and found a copy of *Izvestia* on his desk. Whoever left it, had opened the paper to an inside page and circled a short article. He picked up the paper and began to read.

> *Burian Trush, a former high official in the Communications Ministry, was shot dead yesterday outside his dacha, southwest of Moscow. Officials suspect a contract execution since a Kalashnikov sub-machine gun, used to fire eleven bullets into Trush, was left in a plastic bag near the body. No suspects have been identified.*

John folded the paper and put it away. He sat down and leaned back in his chair. A barely discernible smile spread across his face.

End of troika. Account settled.

338

About The Author

Thank you for reading this novel by A.K. Celer!

If you enjoyed this book, please leave a review on Amazon here:
http://tinyurl.com/moscowventurereviewsamazon
You can leave a review on Goodreads here:
http://tinyurl.com/moscowventuregoodreads

Made in the USA
Middletown, DE
23 June 2019